CW00641693

# HER HUSBAND'S LIE

AMANDA REYNOLDS

Boldwood

First published in Great Britain in 2024 by Boldwood Books Ltd.

Copyright © Amanda Reynolds, 2024

Cover Design by Head Design Ltd.

Cover Photography: Shutterstock

The moral right of Amanda Reynolds to be identified as the author of this work has been asserted in accordance with the Copyright, Designs and Patents Act 1988.

All rights reserved. No part of this book may be reproduced in any form or by any electronic or mechanical means, including information storage and retrieval systems, without written permission from the author, except for the use of brief quotations in a book review.

This book is a work of fiction and, except in the case of historical fact, any resemblance to actual persons, living or dead, is purely coincidental.

Every effort has been made to obtain the necessary permissions with reference to copyright material, both illustrative and quoted. We apologise for any omissions in this respect and will be pleased to make the appropriate acknowledgements in any future edition.

A CIP catalogue record for this book is available from the British Library.

Paperback ISBN 978-1-78513-711-2

Large Print ISBN 978-1-78513-710-5

Hardback ISBN 978-1-78513-709-9

Ebook ISBN 978-1-78513-713-6

Kindle ISBN 978-1-78513-712-9

Audio CD ISBN 978-1-78513-704-4

MP3 CD ISBN 978-1-78513-705-1

Digital audio download ISBN 978-1-78513-707-5

Boldwood Books Ltd
23 Bowerdean Street
London SW6 3TN
www.boldwoodbooks.com

*For Caroline. I miss you.*

# 1

## FRIDAY 31 MAY 2024

There comes a point in every relationship when one partner calls upon the other to make a sacrifice so profound, and so unreasonable, it will test the fabric of their love. That moment came for the Delaneys exactly one week before eminent gynaecologist, devoted husband and beloved father, Matthew Delaney, vanished without trace.

The request came during a conversation which took place after dinner, on a normal, if unusually warm, Friday evening in late May. The Delaneys were seated in their sumptuous sitting room, a reception of impressive proportions, every detail subject to Nicole Delaney's high standards and keen eye. Nic, as she was known to most, was perched at one end of the forest-green sofa, her husband at the other. The scatter cushions had been carelessly swept aside by Matt to make room for the reams of paperwork he retrieved from his study and then spread out in evidence between them. As her husband talked of *reconfiguring* their assets, and *managing expectations*, Nic's glance strayed to the discarded cushions. Her desire to pick them up was an impulse she then resisted, noticing how her husband's expression had assumed a Shakespearean level of melodrama. The lamps were low, pale-pink silk lined in gold, and casting an ambient light across the most surreal of conversations. It was reassuring to be in such familiar surroundings and yet disconcerting to be dragged so far from her comfort zone by Matt's unexpected news. Nic had somehow managed to remain sober enough to be completely in the moment, but drunk enough to feel semi-detached from reality. A potentially lethal combination.

'Are you going to say anything?' Matt asked, wiping a sheen of dark claret from his top lip as he retrieved the bottle of red from the coffee table.

'I don't understand how it can have got so bad so fast?' Nic told him, running a finger around the edge of her glass. 'Why didn't you say something before?'

'Why am I not surprised at that reaction?' Matt replied, raising the bottle to his glass, then hers.

'What's that supposed to mean?' she asked with a brisk shake of her head as she refused more wine. She was, despite being a petite five-foot-four, more than capable of holding her drink, but she had a feeling she might need a clear head.

Matt filled his glass to the brim, then sipped from the edge, as if he was drinking the one pint of beer he allowed himself post-match at the tennis club. Everything in moderation. Well, most things.

'Oh come on, Nic,' Matt said, a ring of red on the coaster as he placed his glass down. 'You leave the finances to me; always have.'

'That's not fair and you know it.'

'Isn't it? You never want to be involved.'

'Only because you always tell me everything is fine. Talk me through it now, Matt; I need to understand.'

He sighed heavily. 'The bottom line is we've lived beyond our means for far too long, and this recent *situation*... Well, let's just call it the final straw.'

She snatched up the sheaf of official-looking invoices Matt had fanned out between them and pretended to read, the numbers and words blurry without her glasses. She could see it wasn't great, the sums owing eye-wateringly large, but surely a few thousand in legal fees wasn't the end of the world? And yet Matt's tone suggested otherwise; the mere fact he'd brought his concerns to her was deeply troubling. He was the optimist of the two of them, his earlier jibes over supper – moans about her extravagant spending habits – the only warning she'd had before those dreaded words: 'Nic, we need to talk.'

Panic, deep-rooted and primal, had surged through her as she'd cleared the plates. Her deepest fear was that he might be about to break the news he was leaving her. But no, it wasn't that, thank god, although why he hadn't said something before this, she had no idea. From what she could tell, the 'situation', as he called it, was of some weeks' standing.

'This lawyer certainly charges enough by the hour!' Nic replied, placing the invoices back down.

'Maybe we should tell Lily to change her course selection to law,' Matt suggested, his tone sarcastic as he referenced their daughter's ambition to follow him into the medical profession.

Lily was upstairs, revising for her final exams. Their daughter's eighteenth birthday was only a week away and then she would be off to study medicine in the autumn.

Matt caught Nic's expression and relented. 'Look, I'm sorry, I had to hire the best defence there is to fight this spurious complaint, and they don't come cheap.'

'Despite the fact this allegation is, as you said, utter nonsense?'

Those had been Matt's exact words when he'd dropped the

bombshell of a serious complaint and then explained that it was simply an unfortunate case of transference from an overly attached patient whom he'd referred on to a colleague as soon as he recognised a potential issue. It had happened once or twice before in Matt's thirty years working in obstetrics and gynaecology – her handsome husband was way too many women's saviour for a few of them not to develop a crush – but there had never been the need for a lawyer before.

'Yes,' Matt advised, swigging his wine. 'It is *utter* nonsense. I promise you. But unfortunately, it appears I have to fight to prove my innocence against this ridiculous allegation, and at my own expense.'

'*Our* expense!'

'Well, quite.'

'OK fine, we will do what's needed, but Matt, please, if there's something I should know...'

'No, I swear, Nic, trust me. Nothing like that.'

Reassured, at least about her husband's fidelity, she was about to offer up a small contribution by way of some recent purchases she could return – a hideously expensive bedspread for the guest bedroom top of her list – when he added, 'That's why I think it's time to sell Three Gables.'

She sat up, her glass almost slipping from her grasp. 'I thought you meant take out another card, or remortgage?' she said, grasping the glass more firmly. 'Not sell our home!'

'We're already mortgaged up to our eyeballs.'

'You said there was still plenty in the pot when we refinanced a couple of months ago.'

'Well, maybe I was trying to be nice?' he sneered, looking the exact opposite. 'It doesn't just happen, this lifestyle of ours, you know? Top-of the-range fucking everything to keep up with the

Stepford Wives at Lily's school, although why you care what they think—'

'That's not fair! You're the one who wanted me to make friends with the other Brackley mums, and you were the one who pushed for private education for Lily in the first place.'

Matt briefly nodded in recognition of this.

'And you love Three Gables as much as I do,' she added. 'Or I thought you did!'

'Yes, I do.' He rubbed his free hand over his face. 'But this place has sucked us dry.'

'So this is my fault for over-spending on the house?'

'No, I'm not saying that. Like you say, the school fees have been a factor too.'

'Well we've paid the last lot now, so—'

'And you think seeing Lil through med school will come cheap? Downsizing was always going to be on the cards, sooner or later.'

'Was it?' She stared at her husband. Three Gables was their forever home, or so she'd thought.

'Look, we are where we are,' Matt concluded.

'Which is where?'

'Caught in the middle of a stupid misunderstanding from an overwrought patient who hasn't got the outcome she wanted, that's all.'

'*That's all?*'

'You know what I mean. Gynae work is challenging, particularly when fertility is in question. I'm a consultant, not a god, but sometimes that's not enough.'

'OK, so is this transference, or sour grapes?' she asked. 'It can't be both.'

'Well, it kind of is in this case, I'm afraid.'

Having batted the blame back and forth and knowing she

couldn't ask him the details of the complaint – he'd never breach
patient confidentiality – they fell into an uneasy silence. Matt
drank his wine whilst she swirled the remnants of hers, the
deep-ruby liquid mesmerising as it spun, a shiver passing
through her despite the warmth of a day now almost done.

She had spent such a pleasant day too, beneath the shade of
her fruit trees at the end of their expansive garden, and then
reclined by the pool to finish planning Lily's eighteenth birthday
party the following week. The latest of her trademark red notebooks – she always had one on the go – was now stuffed with
ideas for the lavish celebration. She mentally crossed through at
least half of the list as she scaled back her plans for their daughter's pool party. She'd have to somehow temper Lily's expectations too. Clearly, there would be some painful cutbacks to be
made, but selling their home? Surely that was overkill? Three
Gables was much more to her than a prudent investment to one
day liquidate. To admit it was so easily disposed of... As if the
hopes and dreams that had brought them here twenty-five years
before, the house tumbledown and in need of love, amounted to
nothing more than a pot of cash... No, she couldn't face such an
all-encompassing change. There had to be another way.

'My dad?' she suggested, sitting up. 'I know he'd be happy to
tide us over, at least until this complaint is dismissed. That's all
we're talking about, isn't it? A cashflow issue.'

Matt shook his head. 'We couldn't ask Gerald to sell his
house to save ours. It wouldn't be fair.'

'No, that's not what I meant.' Her childhood home – a
windswept, sea-soaked, ramshackle but substantial property a
hundred miles south west of them on the rugged coast of Cornwall – was likely worth a bomb, but she'd meant they might
borrow a few thousand from her father's modest savings, not
cash-in her inheritance. 'How much exactly do we need?'

'You want me to go through it all again?' he asked, grabbing a fistful of the invoices and brandishing them. 'It's not pretty; the fees to defend myself at the tribunal are bad enough, but if it goes to an appeal—'

'An appeal? You said the tribunal was a formality!'

He dropped his gaze to his gold watch, fiddling with the band. It had been a present from her for their twenty-sixth wedding anniversary, the twenty-seventh rolling round in September. She'd thought they'd go away somewhere nice, maybe the Maldives once Lily was settled at university. That trip would clearly have to wait.

'Regardless of what it takes to get through the GMC's ridiculously high-handed approach to a ludicrous allegation.' Matt looked at her and forced a smile. 'We never planned to stay here forever. It's not a viable lifestyle. Not on one salary. Even mine.'

'So this *is* my fault because I haven't been well enough to work?'

'No, that's not what I meant, and you know it.' He took her hand and looked at her tenderly. 'We've been through worse and come out the other side, haven't we? You and me. The Fabulous Delaneys. We can do this.'

She couldn't think straight, not with Matt's face so close to hers. She sat back, chin to chest, arms folded. 'It's a lot to take in.'

'I'll make us some coffee,' he suggested, standing up. 'It'll help to clear our heads.'

'Matt?' she asked as he reached the door. 'Is there anything else I should know?'

'No, I told you, that's everything. Trust me.'

She nodded and he walked out, his shoulders back, head high, whereas her movements felt laboured as she made her way towards the downstairs cloakroom.

The toilet seat was cold. She looked up, head spinning. The

original nursery was directly above: the first room she'd decorated after they'd moved in. Another labour of love, and hope.
As so many of her early efforts were. It all felt like a lifetime
ago. It was a wearying thought, and her head lolled forward.
She covered her mouth, stifling the sob that knotted at the
base of her tongue. They had come here with so many plans.
Was she to simply leave her home and those dreams behind?
To pretend the last twenty-five years at Three Gables, every
ounce of her poured into it and yes, most of their cash, had
meant so little? Matt seemed able to cast the past aside as
easily as the scatter cushions, telling her it had always been the
plan to move on, but for her it was a visceral, anxiety-inducing
prospect. One she could not countenance. No, this was not part
of the deal, and she would not sign up to it. Not without a
fight.

'You OK in there, Nic? Coffee's ready.'

'Just give me a moment.'

She tore off a length of toilet paper and pressed the eco-flush,
her rings glinting beneath the aerated water, her reflection
against the beautiful wallpaper startling her as she looked up.
She saw herself as Matt must have all evening. A woman who,
despite strenuous and continuing efforts, was wearing all of her
fifty-four years like a badge of dishonour: mascara smudged, lips
dry, although to the outside world it probably looked like she
had it all. She certainly tried her best to make it appear so. The
consultant's wife, with her perfect marriage and incredible
home. Their longed-for child, Lily, destined for greatness and a
source of much pride and joy. But it was exhausting, maintaining
perfection, or at least the illusion of it. Nic felt for the fine hairs
at the base of her scalp then up an inch from the nape of her
neck and pulled slowly on a single dark strand, easing it from the
taut skin like a blade of grass from dry earth, a sharp jolt of pain

as it came free. The temptation to pull again was instantaneous, but she resisted.

Matt was back in the sitting room when she emerged, the aroma of coffee filling the room. He'd set a tray on the table in front of the sofa: cafetière, mugs, spoons.

'There must be another way,' she announced, his frown indicating there was not as she sat beside him. 'It seems such a shame to leave Three Gables now, just as we can enjoy this place without Lily and her friends trashing it every five minutes.'

'But that's exactly why it's perfect timing,' Matt said, pushing down on the cafetière's resistant plunger. 'We won't need all this space, and you've always loved those Regency conversions in town.'

An apartment? Was that seriously what he was suggesting? She was about to tell him that aside from anything else, she couldn't leave the trees they'd planted as memorials – something she really shouldn't have to explain to him of all people. They'd lived through each of those three tragedies together, the babies they'd lost commemorated in the beautiful trio of fruit trees Matt had suggested they plant – but he was on his feet again now, prowling the room.

'I thought you'd be a bit more supportive to be honest, Nic. I'm fighting for my career here, my reputation, my medical licence, for fuck's sake.' He ran his hand through his thick curly hair then sat beside her again, taking her hand. 'I know this is hard for you, but I honestly think it will be good to have a fresh start. I worry about you here, on your own all day, miles from the nearest town. Without the routine of the school run and Lily to think of, the isolation could well set back your recovery again, and neither of us want that, do we?'

She pulled away from him and got up, then walked to the window, straining to make out the familiar shapes of the trees at the far end of the long garden. It was too dark to properly see them, but she could just about make out the silhouettes by the retaining wall. The saplings had now grown so tall she could shelter beneath them, and she would do exactly that come morning, as soon as Matt left for the hospital and this horrible conversation was behind them. The trees were a big part of her ongoing 'recovery', as Matt referred to it. He would never fully understand her ongoing grief – she'd reconciled herself to that long ago – but how dare he use her mental health struggles as leverage. She needed to be here, in her home, with her trees as some small comfort for all she'd lost. *They'd* lost. To sell was inconceivable. She simply couldn't do it. Surely he could see that?

'I understand your attachment,' he said, standing behind her and looking out too. 'You've achieved miracles here, the place is unrecognisable... But the track down from the road needs resurfacing, *again*, and the energy bills are crazy! The pool heating alone... Time we cashed in on your hard work, don't you think? It's a never-ending project. Twenty-five years is enough. Let's have some fun! You and me, what do you say?'

They returned to the sofa and Matt poured coffee, handing her a mug.

'I'm sorry, I cannot sell the house,' she said.

'Well, sorry isn't much help!' he snapped, his tone accusing as he spooned sugar into his mug. 'And I am all out of ideas, so if you'd like to suggest an alternative?'

'I'm sure we will think of something; there has to be a better solution.'

He shook his head then drank the hot coffee straight down, slamming the mug on the tray as he jumped to his feet. 'I know! I'll just fake my death, shall I? Let you claim the life insurance.

Last time I checked, it was around two million. That should see you right! What do you say, sound good?'

'Stop it!' she replied, putting her mug on the tray, her coffee barely touched. 'That's a horrible thing to say, and keep your voice down. Lily will hear us.'

'It would solve all our problems, though!' Matt replied, still loud.

'No, it really wouldn't,' she said, losing patience.

'Have to make it look good though,' he said, warming to what was surely a sick joke. One that she'd much rather he move on from, but Matt was in full flow, animated as he paced the room. 'I'll need to think of somewhere to lay low for the first forty-eight hours or so.' His eyes were unfocussed as he looked over. 'That's when most people are found.'

'Matt, please.' She patted the space beside her. 'Let's talk sensibly.'

'Sensibly?' He laughed, the sound hollow, as if it had ricocheted around the room, bouncing between them to land with a dull thud on the cream rug where she noticed a few drips of wine had spilt. She reached into her dress pocket and pulled out a tissue, blotting the stains with limited success.

'Actually, you know where the ideal spot for those crucial first few days would be?' Matt asked, eyes hooded as he sat beside her. 'At your father's...' he whispered, conspiratorial, his breath heavy with coffee and red wine. 'Old boy wouldn't even need to know I was there if I broke into the studio in the garden. Been locked up for years, hasn't it?'

Nic pushed him gently away. She was getting annoyed now. Her absent mother's dilapidated art studio was not up for discussion. 'OK, enough now, Matt. This isn't helpful. Let's talk again in the morning. When we've both slept on it.'

She made a move to get up, but he held her back, a hand

across her lap. 'But your father never goes down there, does he? Not that I've ever known. It would be perfect!'

She shook her head and pushed his hand away. 'I don't like Dad being dragged into this discussion, however theoretical, and as for the studio—'

'What is it with you and that place? It's been over fifty years since your mother left, you should—'

'I should what, Matt? Get over my abandonment as a baby?'

Matt shook his head as he always did when this came up. 'I'm sorry, I wasn't thinking! I'm drunk!'

She carried the tray into the kitchen and he began switching off lights.

Exhaustion cloaked them as they then staggered up the stairs and crept past Lily's closed bedroom door, all quiet.

It felt to Nic as though nothing had been resolved as they undressed in their master suite, but they would sleep on it, and in the morning it would be a more rational and sober exchange. She'd make cut-backs, and Matt would find a way to raise some extra cash as he always did. More hours put in at the hospital most likely. His private sector work at The Trust two days a week was more lucrative than the days he gave to the NHS; maybe he could adjust the balance in their favour? Once the complaint was dismissed, of course. Give it a few months and everything would be on track. The tribunal was only a formality. The Fabulous Delaneys would bounce back. They always did.

'It will be fine,' Matt told her, mirroring her thoughts as they stood side by side at the sink in the ensuite. His pragmatism and ebullience were returning, along with his usual sobriety. He squeezed toothpaste on his brush and ran the tap. 'I'll talk to the patient concerned, make them see sense before the tribunal. It's just blown-up because... Well, I obviously can't discuss the specifics, but I'm certain I can convince them to retract the accusation.'

She turned to him, a tub of moisturiser in her hand. It had cost more than she would ever admit to Matt, especially now, so she'd have to make it last. 'Surely speaking to the complainant is inadvisable in the extreme?'

'Yes, you're right,' he said, tongue thick with toothpaste. He spat, then rinsed. 'Don't worry, I'll figure it out. We won't have to sell this place; that was just me panicking. Trust me, Nic. I'll fix this.'

**ONE WEEK LATER**

## 2

FRIDAY 7 JUNE 2024 – 8 A.M.

'Matt!' Nic prodded her sleeping husband awake, the gentle creases around his green eyes deepening against the bright sunlight creeping in. She was still as physically attracted to Matt as the day they'd met over thirty years before. Their shared traumas and triumphs had deepened her love, and if anything, had made it stronger than that first flush of lust, but the chemical reaction when she looked at him was still there. 'Matt! I need you to wake up.'

Lily had stayed at her boyfriend's the night before. The house was blissfully quiet. And they'd made the most of it, a couple again. But the reassurance of the resumption of their sex life after a long hiatus was already wearing off, for her at least. She needed more from her husband. It had been an incredibly difficult week, kicked off by that surprise conversation about selling the house. Matt had assured her that wouldn't be necessary, but she craved his confidence and the surety all would be fine again. And she wanted him, in her arms, offering physical comfort too.

'Sorry, I have to get to work,' he said, rolling away to retrieve his phone.

'I've decided to cancel Lily's party,' she said, getting up and plucking her robe from the floor. She hadn't made a final decision about anything, and wouldn't until he'd agreed. 'I know it's late in the day and we've talked about it before, but—'

'We can't,' he said, hunched over his phone so she couldn't see his expression, or what was so absorbing on screen. He was holding it in his left hand, the right palm still covered with a dressing. 'Not on the day of her birthday.'

'You should put a fresh plaster on that,' she said, cinching her robe. 'It looks dirty.'

'Yeah, sure,' he said, looking up. 'You agree it wouldn't be fair on Lily?'

'I understand that she will be disappointed,' she told him, fastening a bow at her waist. 'But a party is the absolute last thing on my mind. The *last* thing, Matt.'

He looked at her properly then, his expression a reminder of the way he'd looked at her three days before when he'd come home from work wearing that same haunted look, hungry for her and yet wary. As if she was the last person he wanted to see, but also the only one who'd understand. He had days like that at the hospital, when the horrors he encountered clung to him: a patient who'd bled out, or cells he couldn't cut away, a woman's dreams of a child of her own smashed apart, but this wasn't the same and she knew it. A jolt of fear passed through her, the neediness she always made an effort to hide welling up and goose-bumping across her bare skin beneath the silk robe.

'The party goes ahead as planned,' he told her, taking his phone into the ensuite and noisily emptying his bladder before the shower ran.

She slumped back onto the bed, defeated by Matt's intransigence. The party would take up every minute of her day, although that wasn't necessarily a bad thing. It would be a good distraction. And she had the hour she spent with her therapist, Connie, to occupy her too.

She'd been seeing Connie for almost a year now, referred to her after a hysterectomy the previous summer had left her with more than the four small keyhole scars across her waist. And lots of progress had been made, but she'd slipped back of late, the ladder greased by old anxieties, and more recent ones too, so she now felt she was hanging on by the thinnest of threads. It would be good to see her therapist this morning, even if she couldn't talk about everything she needed to. A recalibration was most definitely in order.

She lay on her side, fingers worrying at the widening bald spot on the back of her head as she waited for Matt to finish in the bathroom. A thumb's width of pink skin had been cleared this past week, so prominent she'd been concerned Matt might have found it when his hand had plunged into her hair in the throes of passion the previous night, but he'd made no comment.

The buzz of Matt's toothbrush began. She got up, tired of waiting, her reflection then surprising her in the mirrored dressing room. She looked calm, in control, affluent, as her beautiful robe swished. The wrappings of wealth covered a multitude of sins.

Downstairs, Three Gables was early morning quiet. Rooms were hushed, waiting to be woken. The kitchen was already flooded with sunlight from the patio doors she'd had lovingly restored, despite the cost compared to UPVC replacements. She unloaded the dishwasher and placed her favourite cup, the one painted with lush green palms and pink flamingos, on the pod machine. The Nespresso pods always her preference when she was just making one cup, neat and efficient, whilst the cafetière left such messy grounds. Her fingers fluttered temptingly at her hairline as she waited for her cup to fill. The urge to pull another strand was strong, but it would dissipate soon. She would not end up like those images she'd found online. It was just a difficult time, but like all things, this too would pass.

The weather was hesitant and non-committal as she took her coffee outside, the patio stones cold under her bare feet despite the bright sun, the lawn shivering in a faint breeze, the surface of the pool rippling back and forth. The forecast was good for the party later. Their daughter would be indulged by the weather gods as well as the piles of presents already wrapped and hidden away, although not the car Lily might be expecting. Hardly a necessity, especially as she would be away half the time for her studies, but of course all of Lily's friends had one. Nic had persuaded Matt into the alternative of insuring Lily on her car instead, if that were possible. He said he'd look into it, but he hadn't as yet. Still, it wasn't good to give Lily everything the second she demanded it. Life would teach their daughter that, even if Matt was reluctant to.

She walked towards her fruit trees. The quality of the light as it fluttered through their leaves took her breath away, as it often did. It was hard to imagine that anything bad could happen when she was out here, the trees anchoring her, ropes of roots winding a soothing embrace which chased away, albeit momentarily, the intrusive thoughts. She simply couldn't leave them. *Ever*. They were a memorial and they deserved respect, hers *and* Matt's.

\* \* \*

She was back in the kitchen, seated at the breakfast bar, her feet dangling from the high stool, when Matt finally came down.

'Nice toes!' he remarked, looking at the shiny red polish.

'Thanks,' she replied. 'Lily's chosen blue!'

She'd offered to cancel the salon appointments the day before, part of her cost-cutting plan, but Matt had insisted that wasn't needed. *Go ahead as normal, Nic. Everything as planned.*

He grimaced at Lily's colour choice, but he was pulling the damp dressing from his palm so it could have been that which made him wince.

'You need a hand?' she asked.

'It's OK, I'm a doctor!' he quipped, although he wasn't smiling. He lifted the first aid kit down from the kitchen cupboard and with his left hand redressed the cut across his right palm. 'It's healing nicely now. Don't worry.'

'That's good,' she said, catching his eye and then adding more dressings to her shopping list. 'Will you be OK to operate today?'

'Yes, of course!' he told her, pressing down the edges of the dressing. 'Starting a new one already?' he asked, tipping his head to her latest red notebook, open before her on the breakfast bar.

Keeping a notebook had been her therapist's idea and over the last year she must have bought and filled a dozen of them, maybe more. And amongst the banal to-do lists she'd penned longer passages: recounts of bad days and dark thoughts. Not only current, but historic, some recollections many years past. Connie had said recording her thoughts would help, and sometimes it did, but there were things she could never write down, let alone discuss with anyone, not even Matt.

'Well,' she replied, closing the page. 'If we are to still have this party tonight, someone has to keep track of those all-important last-minute details!'

Matt let the comment pass without reply. He seemed introspective, no doubt already at the hospital in his head. He was dressed in his usual dark-blue suit and a pure white double-cuff shirt, printed tie rolled around his left hand, his dark curls damp above the scowl-riven eyebrows which were forked to the bridge of his nose. She couldn't have loved him more, despite everything, or maybe because of it. The fear of losing him had been an all-pervading and a constant concern ever since they'd met, deepening her desire as it always did. He was so much better than her: clever, gorgeous... He literally saved lives. She couldn't imagine life without Matt. And if it came to it, she would choose him over the house, every time. But he'd told her that such drastic measures wouldn't be needed. He'd fix things without selling their home. And despite everything, she still believed him. They were a team, and now more than ever, they would rely on one another. That's where their strength lay: *together*.

'I'm off now,' he said, disappearing into the hallway.

'Matt, wait!' She jumped down from the stool, the silk robe billowing at her back as she pursued him across the hallway.

'I need to get going,' he said, opening the front door. 'We can talk later, although I'm not sure there's much left unsaid.'

'No, it's not that. You remember you're picking up the cake on your way home? *Patisserie Rouge*,' she prompted when there was no recognition of their previous agreement reflected in her husband's blank expression. 'We talked about this! They close at five-thirty, but don't leave it that late. Your sister is due then, and—'

'It's probably best if you could get the...' He paused as she raised her thumb and forefinger to his eye-level, a sliver of air between her red pointed nails.

'Don't test me, Matt! I'm this close to losing it! I have a list as long as my arm today and this is the one thing, the one thing—'

'I know, but I've got an incredibly busy day. Patients to see at The Trust and—'

'I get it, you're a doctor, I'm the wife, I can't compete, but I've got my regular appointment with Connie at ten, then I have to dash back here and—'

'You're seeing your therapist today?' he asked, a flicker of concern passing across his handsome face as he looked down at her.

'Yes, of course, every Friday at ten. You know that.'

'You think that's wise?'

'I'll be fine, honestly. I just need you to promise you'll be home, with the cake, at five thirty latest.'

'OK, I'll try.'

'I need a Nicole promise, not a Matt one.'

He surprised her then, smiling and pulling her into such a tight hold she could barely breathe. 'I do love you,' he whispered, his chin resting on the top of her head. 'You know that, don't you? Whatever happens. I always have and always will. You've been there for me and you make me happy.'

She wanted to tell him how much she loved him too, but her throat constricted as the fear returned. 'Why are you saying that now?' she asked, looking up at him. 'What do you mean?'

'Nothing, I just wanted you to know.' Then he was across the drive, keys pointed to his navy BMW.

'Oh, and wish Lily a happy birthday from me when she gets home,' he said, glancing back. 'And say I'm sorry, but I'll make it up to her!'

'What? I don't understand. Make up for what?'

A gust caught her hair and she moved her hand to cover the bald patch, retreating behind the door. By the time she looked again, he was in his car and driving away.

**3**
---

Matt's sister climbed out of the furnace-hot car and smoothed her linen tunic. The conspicuous absence of her brother's car was a bitter disappointment to Grace, but sadly no surprise. Matt was reliably unreliable, at least as far as getting home on time. He'd always been the same. Married to the job, as well as the oh-so-perfect Nicole, and in that order.

Grace pushed her size eight feet fully into her Birkenstocks and noted how the skin puffed unattractively between the straps of her sandals as she walked across the gravel drive. It wasn't as if she'd swap places with her ridiculously petite sister-in-law, but the familiar inner scuff of envy caught hold and wrung its twisted way through her almost six-foot frame. It always did when she came to Three Gables. It was all so bloody perfect. Even the front door knocker was super shiny, although no one came to answer her loud knocks.

'I'm going round the side,' she called over her shoulder.

Her husband, Ed, was still trying to coax their daughter from the back seat. Elan was almost eighteen, like her cousin, Lily, but she was behaving like a child, refusing to get out. 'There's no answer at the front,' she added, leaving Ed to it.

She unlatched the side gate and walked the narrow gravel path, pushing past the bins to the second gate which scraped on the patio stones the other side to reveal the vast back garden. It was bedecked with fairy lights, and lanterns hung along the bushes by the path down to the pool, the glistening water across the lawn already frothing with at least a dozen excited teens. And there, on the far side of the patio, gazing towards the view – the imposing Cotswold hills a pencil line on the horizon – was her brother's wife. The oh-so-perfect Nicole Delaney.

'Nic?' Grace called over. 'We're here!'

The simple black silk shift plunged at the back to showcase Nic's razor-sharp shoulder blades, like angel wings. Nic turned slowly. Every inch of her was polished and yet... had there been a tiny patch of bare skin exposed on her scalp as the breeze parted her glossy shoulder-length dark hair? Maybe Grace had imagined it, but the technical term for hair-pulling popped into her head: *trichotillomania*. Or TTM. An obsessive, often involuntary compulsion to pull one's hair out. She'd never had a client present with it in her decade as a trauma therapist, but she recalled a case study during her training, the photos shocking. It was probably only a mild case, or maybe alopecia? Sudden hair loss sometimes went with menopause, particularly after a hysterectomy. It was about time Nic started to show some signs of ageing, but she mustn't be uncharitable. Everyone has their own issues, and Nic had suffered terribly with poor mental health.

'Grace!' Nic walked towards her. 'I thought you'd knock the front door like everyone else?'

'I did,' she replied, gritting her teeth. Nic was one of the reasons Grace had developed bruxism, or at least that was her belief. She had to wear a splint at night which made her gag, so she often didn't, but her jaw ached. 'So where is that brother of mine; running late as always?'

'He'll be here soon,' Nic replied, checking the beautiful watch that hung from her slim wrist. Grace knew how much it had cost; she'd looked it up after Nic showed it off, an anniversary present from Matt the previous September.

'There's no way Matt would miss Lily's eighteenth,' Nic added.

'Of course not,' she replied. 'I wasn't saying that.'

A clatter by the side gate distracted them. Ed had come through and then pretty much thrown the large Tupperware she'd entrusted to him onto the slabs.

'Ed!' she called over, venting her frustration. 'Is the cake ruined?'

'No,' he said, retrieving it and holding it up. 'Lid stayed on.'

Nic rushed to his aid, inspecting the Tupperware and nodding as if the chocolate cake Grace had spent all afternoon baking and then piping might have survived being dropped. She could already see through the plastic sides that it was smashed to smithereens.

'Yup, it's ruined,' Grace said, taking the cake box from Nic and peering inside.

'Oh don't worry about that,' Nic said. 'I've ordered a gorgeous one that Matt's picking up on his way home.'

'Come through, Elan!' Grace told her only child, again through gritted teeth. Elan's continuing reticence as she peered around the gate was adding to the general frustration about the start of an evening Grace had looked forward to all week.

Elan had been such a pretty girl, and she'd seemed relatively happy too. Until the last year or so, when she'd changed, both in appearance and personality. She'd never been particularly outgoing, but she'd been chatty at home, and her recent multiple piercings and tattoos were a 'lifestyle choice' that Grace only pretended to embrace, when the blood-oozing skulls and crawling insects actually turned her stomach.

'No need to go in the pool, sweetheart,' Ed reassured their daughter as Elan tiptoed down the festooned path. 'Only if you want to.'

'Oh, shame,' Nic observed with a tilt of her small head. 'Everyone else is having such fun. Can't we tempt you, Elan?'

'It's your choice, sweetie,' Grace added, more forceful than her husband. 'No pressure. You do you!'

Elan, dressed in shorts and a misshapen tee with some god-awful band on the front, continued slowly down to the pool. Lily, dripping wet in a white bikini, noticed her cousin and began waving gamely.

'Elan's still not talking, I take it?' Nic asked.

'No, not much,' Ed replied, an answer which surprised Grace as Elan had spoken to her precisely zero times in the last few months.

'Gosh, that's what, almost a year now?' Nic asked, gifting Grace a maddening look of pity.

'Yes, almost a year, for me at least,' Grace said, looking at Ed, who appeared not to hear. His attention was on his phone, where he was no doubt checking the latest cricket scores.

'I'll try Matt again now,' Nic suggested. 'Make sure he hasn't forgotten about the cake. Do get stuck into the champagne, Grace,' she said, gesturing to the bottle in the ice bucket on the patio table. 'I know how much you like it, such a treat.'

Grace forced a smile. It was going to be a long night, but it would be easier once Matt arrived.

She grabbed the bottle and ripped off the foil, the cork popping so loudly, even Ed noticed. Then she poured a very large glass and sipped it as she waited for Nic's return, hopefully with news of Matt. But she soon tired of drinking on her own. Ed barely looked up from the live cricket commentary, even when she told him she was going inside to look for Nic.

Grace slipped as she stepped inside the kitchen, her foot sliding away from her. She grabbed the door handle and saved herself from a fall. The floor was slick with spills from the cocktail pitcher that Lily had taken down to the pool, the splashes of liquid bright blue. Grace scoured round for a tea towel to mop up. The counters were littered with emptied snack packets, but she found a cloth and wiped the floor. It was most unlike her fastidious sister-in-law to leave a mess uncleared. Nic usually bordered on OCD levels of tidiness, but then again, she was nowhere to be seen.

Grace poked her head into the hallway. Nic was by the front door, looking out through the glass panel, mobile phone to her ear.

'Everything OK?' Nic asked, turning round.

'Yes, sorry, I just came to see if you'd got hold of Matt?'

Nic shook her head and ended the call. 'Tried him a few times, goes straight to voicemail. He's probably forgotten to switch his phone back on after leaving the hospital.'

'That's a bit odd,' Grace remarked as they went back into the kitchen. 'I mean, even if he was driving you'd think—'

'You'd think what?' Nic asked as she waved a hand over the bin. It opened and Nic dropped in the empty packets as she collected them up.

'Sorry, no, I'm sure you're right.' Grace fanned her face with her hand.

'You sure you're OK?' Nic repeated.

'Just a bad week at work,' she said. Although it wasn't work which preoccupied her, but her brother. 'And I'm worried about where Matt is.'

'Oh, don't be!' Nic said, heading out through the patio doors. 'He promised he'd be here and he will. He made a Nicole promise too, not a Matt one.'

Nic glanced back and smiled, but it wasn't convincing. In fact, she looked as worried as Grace was, maybe more.

* * *

It was almost eight o clock. Two and half hours after the cake shop closed. They'd all tried Matt's mobile, many times, even Ed who barely used his, other than to check the damn cricket score. Lily had come over to the patio table with increasing regularity, phone in hand, asking if her dad had been in touch and whether he'd be long. Everyone was unsettled by Matt's unexplained absence and lack of contact. Well, everyone who was family. The guests frolicked in the pool without a care in the world, music blaring and fuelled by cocktails and god knew what else. All of them except Elan, who sat on the edge, feet in the water.

'Was that a car?' Ed asked, looking up from his phone.

'I don't think so,' Nic replied, although they were all straining to listen against the thud-thud of the music by the pool.

'Shall I go?' Grace offered, already on her feet.

'No,' Nic told her, getting up too. 'But could you two get the barbeque going? The kids must be starving.'

'I'll need your help, Gracie,' Ed said, looking at her as Nic rushed towards the house. 'Not my forte, the coals.'

'Oh for goodness' sake!' She sighed at her husband's ineptitude. She had no interest in food, and Nic was only asking to distract them whilst she got to see Matt first and monopolise him, no doubt.

Grace followed her husband across the patio towards the barbeque area. Ed lifted the lid on the cold grill and peered in whilst she remained fixated on the house. In fairness to Ed, the grill, like every bit of kit at Three Gables, was state-of-the-art and overly complicated for it. He started twiddling nobs and asking for help, but she was distracted then by a sound across the other side of the patio. The side gate was opening, the familiar scrape of wood across the stones alerting her to that.

A warning note struck deep into Grace's heart at the sight of the arrivals, two of them. Ed had noticed too, barbeque tongs raised in an incongruous salute as the first visitor, a young man wearing a luminous hi-vis jacket and a startled look, removed his hat. Something primordial had been triggered in Ed by the police uniform, and her thoughts were rapidly spiralling too, even before the woman in a well-cut trouser suit and fancy trainers noticed Nic, who'd returned from her checks at the front door.

'You're Mrs Delaney, wife of Dr Matthew Delaney?' the young woman asked Nic as she came out the patio door.

Grace opened her mouth to introduce herself and correct the woman's sloppy error about Matt. He was a doctor, true, but as a consultant surgeon her brother's title was *Mr* Delaney, not Dr. But it hardly mattered. Not in comparison to what she feared would be said next. For why else had the police turned up unannounced, if not to impart bad news?

Grace took a deep breath and reached for Ed's hand, which took hers and held it tight. Then she closed her eyes against that awful hi-vis jacket below the fresh-faced police officer's tense jaw, and the clatter of wet feet running up from the pool, and the young woman's solemn voice.

All Grace could think about was Matt on her doorstep two

days before. Her brother, usually so assured, so in control, nothing short of a desperate man.

# 4

Nic couldn't hear her own thoughts, let alone absorb what she'd just been told by the young woman in a cheap trouser suit who'd claimed she was a detective, but barely looked old enough to even be a police officer.

*Missing.* That was the word that stood out. Matt had gone missing: vanished, without trace. But why? And where to? Surely he couldn't have acted on his ridiculous proposal to—

'How can Matt be missing?' Grace asked as they went into the kitchen.

The detective had guided them away from the noise and clamour, but Nic hadn't noticed Grace had come inside with them too, and she really didn't want her there.

'If you've found his car,' Grace persisted as the detective closed the patio door, 'then surely Matt must be with it, or nearby?'

'You're his sister, is that right?' the detective asked by way of reply.

Nic looked at the detective more closely. She had a halo of

dark corkscrew curls framing an immaculately made-up face. Her trouser suit, although polyester, fitted her well and the blouse was pretty, but the outfit looked more suited to office than police work.

'Yes,' Grace replied, 'I am and I'd like a proper answer, please.'

Nic funnelled out a long breath and closed her eyes, swallowing the panic that had surged at this news. Nothing was known as yet. It could simply be a misunderstanding. One that would see Matt back in an hour or two, no doubt full of excuses, but home. She would feel foolish to have even considered he might have acted on his half-baked plan to fake his own death. It had been his dark humour and the wine talking, nothing more than that. But there was something else. Something she daren't even *think* in such official company, lest it write itself across her face, or worse, accidentally leave her lips.

'I'm his younger sister,' Grace advised when the detective still didn't engage.

The curly haired young woman was now rooting through her bag for something.

'Only by a year,' Grace said, brushing away a tear that Nic immediately resented as much as her sister-in-law's presence. 'Sorry, I... I don't mean to doubt your methods,' Grace went on. 'It's just Matt is very precious to me.' Grace looked at Nic. 'To all of us, I mean.'

'No, don't apologise,' the detective replied, finding a pen in her bag and then tapping it on the glass door and beckoning to the young officer outside who was trying to handle the mob of teens. 'Ryan will explain everything to you whilst I chat with Mrs Delaney, OK?'

Grace looked affronted and she tried not to feel smug. Now was not the time to score points. There was far too much at stake.

'I thought I'd stay here, with Nic?'

'I'll take care of Mrs Delaney,' the detective assured Grace, who was then handed over to the other officer, the patio doors opening then quickly closing again.

'Somewhere more private we might talk, Mrs Delaney?' the detective asked, biting the end of her pen. 'Away from any further distractions?'

She led the way into the hall and then turned left into the sitting room, her legs giving way as she fell into her usual place on the sofa. The detective took the spot beside her. The same spot where a week before Matt had drunkenly proposed a method to get them out of the 'situation' they were in. Events, however, seemed to have overtaken them. She fought for air, the sensation of not being able to breathe making her gasp.

'Mrs Delaney?'

'Sorry, I'm OK.'

'I understand, you've had a shock. Maybe some tea?'

She shook her head. Surely Matt couldn't have thought this would in any way, shape or form be what she'd want him to do? They'd talked everything through. Made a plan, of sorts. One that involved them pulling together, as a team. She couldn't do this on her own. No, he wouldn't have been so stupid.

'OK, I'm going to go over everything again,' the detective told her, long lashes cast down as she lifted her bag onto her knees and unthreaded the fastened buckles. It was a school satchel design, adding to the detective's childlike appearance. 'OK if I call you Nicole?'

'Yes, of course.'

'OK, I'm Detective Constable Amy Pemberton, and I am here in connection with your husband's BMW which was reported as abandoned about a mile down the road from here, in a densely wooded area. You know the spot I mean, nasty blind bend?'

She swallowed hard. It was a bend she knew well. One she'd feared might catch her out one day too. But Matt was an excellent driver. Not an insurance claim or speeding ticket to his name. He said it wasn't worth the risk, his job dependant on him keeping a clean licence and a blameless record. Like most things, he played it safe.

'Was my husband, I mean, do you think he might have been hurt?'

'I'm afraid we don't know. The car was inverted and the driver door was open. So, he either climbed out himself, or—'

'Inverted?'

'As I say, we don't yet know what happened, but our press office are organising an appeal for witnesses via local radio, social media, that kind of thing. We are taking this a stage at a time, but also very seriously. You said outside that you hadn't seen him since this morning and were expecting him home by five-thirty?'

'Yes, he promised to pick up a birthday cake on his way.'

'What time did your husband leave home this morning?'

'Around eight, maybe a little after. You think he might have been missing all day?'

'It's possible.'

'No, that can't be right... I drove in and out this morning, and all the guests tonight... No one saw his car.'

'It was barely noticeable from the road.'

'But you said someone reported it; how did they see it?'

'I believe it was an anonymous call, about an hour ago. Said they'd been walking their dog that way.'

'That's odd,' Nic observed, wishing she hadn't. The last thing she wanted to do was arouse any suspicion about the nature of Matt's disappearance, but no one ever walked the woods; it was miles from anywhere.

'Indeed,' the detective agreed, her curls tumbling forwards as she leaned over her bag and rummaged for something. 'We were lucky to get the call, but they wouldn't leave a name. The public can be wary of getting involved, sadly. Let's get on with a few questions now, focus the search.'

Pemberton took out a small black notebook and began firing questions about Matt's movements, but they were soon interrupted by a soft knock on the sitting-room door, the younger officer poking his head around to ask, 'OK if we let the party guests go home now, boss?'

'Take names and contact numbers first,' the detective advised. 'But yes, get them out of here.'

'Your brother-in-law has already started to make calls to parents, Mrs Delaney,' he advised Nic, flashing very white teeth. 'He's suggested marshalling everyone via the side gate so it shouldn't cause too much disturbance to you and your family.'

She nodded, close to tears now. Ridiculous it was Ed's kindness that had undone her, but maybe it was the shock finally hitting her. Although she still felt detached, as if she were inside a smoke-filled bubble, looking out. Fighting for air, for answers. But the mist was slowly clearing, allowing her to examine the little information she had. Matt's car was found upside down. The driver door open, no sign of him. So he'd got out. She had to believe that, and that he was therefore OK. Maybe he'd made the anonymous call too, so as she wouldn't worry with no news? But of course she was worried. Where had he gone, and why hadn't he been in touch all day? She reached forward to take a tissue from the box, recalling the tray of coffee Matt had made a week before. *I'll just fake my death, shall I? Let you claim the life insurance.*

'Seems a nice lad,' the detective told her.

'Sorry?' she asked, blowing her nose.

'My colleague; he's new, only eighteen. I'm mentoring him, for my sins.'

'Same age as my daughter,' she replied, only then remembering she'd abandoned Lily.

She got up and walked to the window. There was a huddle of people on the patio, voices lower, calmer, but still agitated. Ed and Elan were with Lily. Grace was beside PC Gilchrist. She looked over and Nic drew back.

'I will keep this as brief as possible, Mrs Delaney,' the detective said.

'Yes, of course, sorry.' Nic sat back down. 'What do you need to know?'

'Just a few details and the sooner the better. Your husband is categorised as a high-risk missing person, which means these first hours are vital to the search's success.'

'High risk? Why?'

'He left the scene of a serious RTA,' the detective replied, looking up from an official-looking form she'd pulled from her bag and begun smoothing on her lap, the notebook tucked away. 'So I suggest we get on with finding him.'

'Yes, of course. So what happens now?'

The detective held up the form.

'I thought everything would be online?'

'It will be, but I'm old school, find it makes me thorough. So, your husband is Matthew Delaney, of this address, and he works as a consultant surgeon at The Trust?' the detective asked, clicking her pen and then abandoning it to the sofa when it didn't work.

'Yes, it's the private hospital across town. He works there Tuesdays and Fridays, The General the rest of the week.'

'I see,' DC Pemberton replied, finding another biro in her

stuffed bag. 'Private hospital, very nice. Buys a decent lifestyle too by the looks of things.'

Was DC Pemberton insinuating something? Paranoia had already begun to creep in, making her guarded, which wasn't a good thing. She had to look as if she knew nothing, which in many ways, she didn't.

'So, who might be able to help us at The Trust?' Pemberton asked.

'Um, Matt's secretary, I guess. Victoria Oliver, but she will have left by now.'

'Victoria Oliver, thanks,' DC Pemberton replied as she wrote on the form. 'Anyone else, if she's not there?'

'You could try main reception, but Plum would be the one who'd know Matt's diary best.'

The detective glanced up. '*Plum?*'

'Her name is Victoria, like the variety of plum?'

'Oh, I get it! *Victoria*. That's funny!' The detective stuck the second pen in her mouth and began removing a blob of mascara with a fingertip hooked into her left eye. She then inspected her finger and wiped it in a tissue from her trouser pocket and retrieved the pen from between her teeth. 'What was your husband wearing when he left this morning?'

'He always wears the same thing to work: navy Paul Smith suit, white double-cuff shirt, a silk tie, pink today; he tends to go a bit jaunty on Fridays…' She attempted a smile, picking up the discarded and leaky biro from the sofa and handing it back to the detective.

'Thanks.' Pemberton tossed the forgotten biro in her bag. She had black ink on her tongue and lips from the replacement. 'Do you have a recent photo of Matt we can circulate?'

Nic searched her phone and scrolled through until Matt's face filled her screen.

They'd been out by the pool when she'd taken the photo, ten days before. They'd been having a drink together after he'd got in from work. Another warm evening, his collar loosened, tie removed, cuffs rolled back. Just the two of them. Lily was in her room, and Nic had been happy, although she hadn't known it. Not truly. No inkling of the trouble to come. The usual stuff to concern her, but nothing as cataclysmic as what was to come.

Matt looked so handsome in the photo, but maybe preoccupied? He often was after a day at the hospital, spent at The Trust if memory served, but it had been so wonderful to have him home at a decent hour that she'd ignored any warning signs. Only three days later he would drop the bombshell about the tribunal and their precarious financial situation.

'Will this one do?' she asked, handing over her phone.

'Yes, that's great, thanks,' Pemberton replied. 'OK if I ping this image to my phone so we can circulate it?'

'Yes, of course.'

DC Pemberton began tapping on both phones with a dexterity which reminded her of Lily. The detective was possibly only a decade or so older than her daughter. It felt too young for this level of responsibility. Her future happiness may be dependent on this woman's capabilities, or lack of them.

'I'll put my contact details in here for you while I'm at it,' she said, typing on Nic's phone. 'We can keep in touch that way, and I'll try and prioritise your calls, but if I don't answer, leave a message.'

'Yes, of course.'

'Any other places I should contact, check if your husband's there?'

'How do you mean?'

'Friends he'd visit, bars he drinks at?'

'I suppose you could try the tennis club. Matt's a member, but he wouldn't be there tonight. It's our daughter's eighteenth birthday party. And Matt's not a drinker. He's a surgeon. He has to be careful of all stimulants, and he is.'

'Yes, of course. Is this the tennis club contact?' the detective asked, holding up Nic's phone.

She squinted then nodded, a hand creeping into her hair, but she resisted the urge to pull, instead pitter-pattering her fingers on the spreading bald patch. Maybe Matt's 'disappearance' was all about the impending tribunal at The Trust? A time-out. A breathing space for him to see sense and calm down, although it was a very unwise move if so. She should have said something to him before. She'd known it was preying on his mind, a ticking time-bomb about to explode with the hearing set for the following Tuesday, but he wouldn't discuss it other than to reiterate that it would be fine. Wouldn't discuss anything, in fact. What if it *wasn't* fine? What if none of this was ever going to be—

'Does your husband have access to any other vehicles?' Pemberton asked, breaking into her thoughts.

'Sorry?' she asked, taking back her phone as the detective held it out.

'Any other vehicles Matt could have driven away after the BMW left the road?'

'No, not that I know of,' she said, considering the possibility which felt oddly hopeful and also terrifying. He could be miles away by now. 'Just my car, and I've been using it today. The white Evoque parked outside.'

'I assumed that brown Volvo wasn't yours.' The detective smiled. 'Lily's?'

'No, that's Grace and Ed's car.'

'Your daughter hasn't passed her test as yet?'

'Yes, but we haven't bought her a car. Touchy subject, actually.'

'Oh, why's that?' Pemberton asked, looking up from the form filling.

'It's a thing at Lily's school, to buy a car as an eighteenth present, but I felt it was too extravagant.'

'All I got for my eighteenth was a card with a tenner inside.' Pemberton laughed, her face looking even younger for it. She was definitely no more than in her late twenties, early thirties at most. 'I'll need to check the garage before I go, Nicole.' Pemberton stuffed the half-finished form back in her bag and stood up.

'That's it?' she asked, getting up too.

'For now, but we'll have a look around the house together first, if that's OK?'

'What for?' she asked, mentally scouring her home, room by numerous room.

'Any missing items, such as a passport, clothes, money?'

'You think he's left the country?' The unwelcome thought hadn't occurred to her. She'd imagined him driving away, and not far, just far enough.

'It's all routine, Nicole. Another box to tick. So, passport first?'

Nic led the detective into the hallway and then down the corridor that led to Matt's study, a steadying hand to the wall as her legs threatened to give way. It was such an odd feeling, a bit like vertigo, except she was currently firmly on the ground.

The smell of Matt greeted her as they went in. Cigars and cologne and dust. He didn't like her tidying in here, but his desk was clear, and the hanging files in the drawer where he stored official papers were neatly labelled. 'I think he usually keeps it in here.'

She sat in Matt's leather desk chair and searched through the one marked *Documents*, tucking away the legal letters and invoices from the waiting detective's keen stare, but there was no sign of his passport.

'I suppose it could be in his consulting room at The Trust?' Nic suggested. 'He occasionally travels to medical conferences in America.'

'Any imminent travel plans you know of?' Pemberton asked, leaning against the door to write in the black notebook she'd taken from her bag. 'Work, or social?'

'No, he'd have told me. His passport could be upstairs, I suppose? I honestly don't know where he keeps it. He always packs for himself and this study is his domain: off limits.'

'Off limits?' The detective frowned.

'He likes to come in here and smoke a cigar and decompress after work; he has a very taxing job and I hate the smell of smoke.'

'OK, let's try upstairs, but can you check for any other missing items in here before we move on: his laptop, phone?'

'The laptop is gone,' she told the detective, heart thumping as she held up the jack of the charger which was still plugged in, the end trailing across the empty desk.

'Is that a surprise to you?' Pemberton asked.

'Not really. I mean, I'd expect it to be here, but he could have taken it to work. His phone would be with him, of course.' Although she noted that the charging cable for that was also gone.

They went upstairs, the detective watching as she checked Matt's bedside drawers for the passport. No sign of it there either. Just balled socks and folded pants, and the lubricant they'd used the night before. Nic coloured but the detective spared her blushes by moving on.

'Where's does he hang his clothes?' the detective asked, looking round the large and tidy bedroom.

'In the dressing room, back the way we came,' Nic explained, retracing their steps to the mirrored doors that ran between the bedroom and ensuite.

Nic looked through Matt's small section of the wardrobes on the left-hand side.

'Anything missing?' Pemberton asked.

'Not sure,' she said, pushing hangers across, the identical suits and shirts lined up. 'He keeps a spare suit and clean shirt with him in his car, but I think the rest are all accounted for.'

'Why keep a spare?'

'He's a gynae consultant and surgeon. He rolls his sleeves up, shall we say.'

Pemberton winced in a knowing manner. 'OK, let's check the garage next.'

'We don't keep our cars in there,' Nic said as she led the way back down the stairs.

'Who does?' Pemberton replied, following close behind.

The hallway was quiet, the kitchen door closed, although Grace's voice carried from behind it. Nic grabbed her keys from her bag on the console table by the front door, pushing her latest notebook deeper inside. The bright-red cover was eye-catching, but Pemberton was distracted by her phone.

A car was leaving and another pulling into the drive as they went out the front. The arriving sports car's tyres were loud on the gravel, George Michael blaring from the open roof. Amber Leatherby, chair of the PTA and mother to Will, Lily's boyfriend, was driving too fast, as usual. The woman was a terrible gossip. And she had the worst possible timing as the detective led the way to the garage door, right by where Amber had just reversed her car and parked.

'Parents over here, please!' Ed called to Amber from the side gate. 'Quick as you can. This way!' But Amber stayed put.

'Let me help,' Pemberton said, picking up the keys from the gravel after they fell from Nic's trembling grasp. 'Which one?'

Nic pointed to a square-topped key as Amber stared at them from the car, not a flicker of kindness in the redhead's hard features, or a word of sympathy offered. They'd never seen eye to eye, warring over the PTA fundraisers – Amber was PTA chair – and then they'd both been less than delighted when their offspring had recently started dating.

The detective opened the garage door, the light coming on automatically as the door went up, narrowly avoiding the back of Amber's car. Inside, the swept floor was largely empty, just the usual collection of garden machinery and tools, and a stack of cardboard packaging from some recent purchases which she'd asked Matt to squash into the recycling bin. In fact, he'd offered, but typical Matt, he had clearly forgotten.

'Sorry to have to ask, Nicole,' Pemberton said, pressing her ink-stained lips with a forefinger. 'Were there any reasons you can think of why your husband might have *chosen* to go missing?'

'You mean deliberately leave?' she asked, glancing to the open-top car. The cabriolet was so close, Amber must have been able to hear every word, even though her head was turned away.

'Arguments? Affairs? Financial concerns? Issues at work?' Pemberton prompted, her voice painfully loud. 'Sorry, I have to ask.'

Nic looked round again and caught Amber looking over her shoulder, staring straight at her. She was there to collect her shit of a son, but also waiting for Nic's reply. Word had clearly spread. The Brackley Mums' WhatsApp group no doubt already lit up with conjecture about the reason the police had arrived at Lily's party. But the detective was waiting for an answer too.

This was her opportunity to share what she knew about the impending tribunal and, as the detective phrased it, their 'financial concerns', but to air those in front of the worst gossip of the lot of them was unbearable. And anyway, what did she know of Matt's 'situation'? Not much, not really.

'No, nothing like that,' she replied. 'Our life together is perfect.'

## 5

'Will's mother has finally picked him up,' Ed announced as he came back into the kitchen through the patio doors. 'That was the last one. And I think the police have just left too.'

'The detective's gone?' Grace asked, getting up from the kitchen table.

She had been waiting there with the girls, as Ed had instructed, quite forcefully for him. He wasn't naturally take-charge, but he had done so, and well. Lily and Elan were on the bench seat by the wall, both lolling as if the news had exhausted them, and poignantly, they were also holding hands, but it hadn't taken much to uncoil Grace's springs. 'I wanted to speak with that detective again before she left!'

'What about?' Ed asked, grabbing a tea towel from the sink and slinging it over his shoulder, the washing up his concern now that the guests were despatched.

'Nothing,' she replied too fast as she sat back down in the chair. 'I just wanted to find out what their next move is, and Nic clearly is in no rush to update me. Where is she?'

'Calling her father,' Ed replied, running the tap. 'She wanted to tell your grandfather herself,' he explained, addressing Lily, who'd cuddled into Elan's side. 'Before he heard it from... well, anyone else, I guess? You up to helping me, girls?'

Lily shook her head but Elan got up and caught the tea towel on the fly that Ed tossed to her.

'You know that detective couldn't wait to get rid of me?' Grace told Ed. 'Sent me back outside.'

'Yes, I know,' Ed replied, passing Elan a plate to dry as she joined him by the kitchen sink. 'I'm sure it wasn't personal. They have a job to do.'

Maybe he was right, but it had certainly felt that way, as if she was nothing. And she'd barely had chance to tell that child of a police officer half of what she knew before he was thanking her and moving on to take the contact details for the departing party guests. As if they were equally as important to the police investigation as Matt's only sibling! A bunch of teens who barely knew him and certainly couldn't have thrown light on the tattered state of the Delaneys' outwardly idyllic marriage. Grace knew plenty about that, and other related matters. Deep concerns that had brought Matt to her door only three days before, begging for her help. Which of course she gave, the thought of that sitting with her guiltily as her husband, entirely innocent of her secret, smiled encouragingly.

Ed had no idea what she'd done to help Matt out of what her brother had described as 'a tight hole', but what choice did she have? It was totally out of character for Matt to admit to any kind of problem, let alone ask for help, and that scared her. Especially now.

'Gracie?' Ed's voice jolted her out of her thoughts. 'Can you close the patio door, please?' He held up his sopping hands as evidence that he was otherwise engaged. 'The wind is getting up.'

Nic's precious fruit trees were swaying in the distance, the light fading fast as she closed the glass door. A drift of blossom had swirled onto the patio in the gathering breeze, pale fruits swelling on the boughs, no doubt, although in the encroaching darkness, it was impossible to see that far.

The memorial trees had been Grace's idea, must be twenty years ago now. She'd floated it out via Matt first, knowing her sister-in-law would reject it out of hand if it came from her. She was surprised Matt had gone along with it, but he had been at his wits' end by then. Six years of failed fertility treatment had given them nothing but two miscarriages followed by a truly horrific still birth.

Nic had found great comfort in the trees over the years. If anything, she had grown a little too reliant on them. 'She's out here every day, Gracie,' Matt had told her last Christmas when she'd asked how Nic was getting on, suspecting the answer would be less than positive. Nic was clearly struggling. 'I get home and it's freezing cold, and she's been out here for hours, or so Lily's told me,' her brother had said, looking helpless and frustrated.

She had tried and failed to explain to Matt that Nic was still grieving. That kind of trauma was something she may never fully get over. But Matt seemed to expect a moratorium on grief, twenty years being long enough. And the fact Nic had been through a hysterectomy only six months before that tense Christmas Day was no excuse for her 'relapse', as he'd called it. Her brother tried his best, but sometimes that wasn't nearly enough.

She turned from the view of the garden as Nic came back into the kitchen.

'Did you get through to your father?' Ed asked.

'Nope, it just rang and rang,' Nic replied, squeezing past Ed and Elan to get to the fridge and pull out a bottle of white wine.

'What did the detective say?' Grace blurted out. 'Are they searching for Matt, actively looking, I mean?'

'They're following all leads,' Nic said, the screw top resisting her efforts, so she passed it to Ed, then remarked to him, 'Dad must be asleep, or ignoring the phone as it's getting late.'

'My old dad was the same,' Ed replied, passing the opened wine and then a glass from the drainer. 'Ignored any calls after nine, didn't he, Gracie?'

'So that's it?' Grace asked, pacing. 'The police have left and we just wait whilst Matt is out there, disorientated, or badly hurt? It'll be dark soon!' Lily looked over and she relented, shaking her head. 'I'm sure he's fine, Lil, but even so.'

'No,' Nic said, taking a large swig of the chilled white and grimacing at Elan, whose eyes had widened. 'I mean, they haven't stopped searching. They are making calls and will put out an appeal.'

'Get on the phone now, Ed!' Grace said. 'The tennis club, Plum, anyone else you can think of... Nic, any other ideas?'

'It's fine,' Nic told Ed, laying a hand on his exposed hairy arm where he'd rolled back his sleeves. 'They have those details already and we have to trust them to...' Nic paused, looking at Lily who was walking towards the hallway, somewhat unsteadily. 'Are you drunk?' Nic asked, putting her wine down then following her and grabbing her daughter's arm. 'Lily? Answer me!'

Grace had smelt the alcohol on Lily's breath and noted her enlarged pupils, the cocktails no doubt laced with illicit vodka, but Nic's challenge was misjudged given the present circumstances. Lily needed her mother's support, not admonishment. She was about to intervene as Lily gave Nic a long hard stare, then Nic's mobile rang loudly on the counter by her wine, startling everyone.

'Hello?' Nic answered, grabbing it. 'Yes, it is. Hold on, please.'

Nic left the room to take the call and Lily went back to sit by Elan, the room silent as they waited and listened.

'Shush!' Grace said as Ed went to speak. 'Who is it, do you think?'

Ed shrugged and Nic came back in then, the call over.

'That was the detective,' Nic reported. 'The search of the woods has been suspended until morning.' Grace sighed and threw her hands up. 'It's impossible in the dark,' Nic told her. 'But I'm certain he will be home soon,' she added, reaching out to Lily who'd got up.

Side-stepping Nic's offer of a hug, Lily then headed up the stairs. Heavy thuds soon followed by a door slam that made them all jump.

'But we must do something,' Grace said, looking at Nic who'd retrieved her wine. 'He was due at five thirty; that's almost four hours ago now. They can't just abandon him overnight. What if he's lying in the woods, bleeding out?'

Grace regretted her choice of phrase immediately, Elan's eyes widening even further as she circled a plate with the tea towel. Ed pulled their daughter into a swift but tight hug, whispering inaudibly to her and she to him. Why would Elan talk to him and not her? But that wasn't really the point right now.

'They actually think he might have been missing all day,' Nic commented, barely looking up from her glass as she slid onto a stool at the breakfast bar and downed her wine.

Grace's hand flew to her mouth. 'No!'

'Are they checking with hospitals?' Ed asked, letting go of Elan and sending Grace a look that she interpreted as a warning to calm down, which was ridiculous.

'Yes,' Nic replied, her tone weary. 'They are.'

'Yes, of course. Sorry,' Ed replied, although he had no need to apologise. 'Maybe we should leave now?'

'We can't go home!' Grace told him, utterly appalled at his suggestion.

'Yes, you should get some rest,' Nic said. 'And I promise if I hear a word, you will be the first to know.'

'Of course we will,' Ed said as he took Grace by the hand, beckoning to Elan to follow. 'Call us if you need anything, Nic. Anytime of the night, naturally.'

'I don't appreciate...' Grace told Ed as he pulled her by the hand across the gravel drive, '...being manhandled out of my brother's home, especially when we still have no idea where he is.'

'Gracie, please,' Ed pleaded, dropping his admittedly light hold. 'I am trying to do what's best for everyone in very difficult circumstances.' He looked past her, back at the house. 'Elan, are you coming?'

Their daughter's halting progress had triggered the porch light, again, Elan's silver-grey hair, another questionable choice, shining mercury-bright beneath it.

'Hurry up, for goodness' sake, Elan!' Grace snapped, turning to Ed, who was now the other side of their rusting Volvo and trying to unlock the dodgy driver door. All the doors were dodgy, in fact. The whole car was. 'Matt's finally had enough and left her, hasn't he?' she said, only half whispering. 'I bet that's what it is!'

'Shush!' Ed replied, eyes turned to Elan, who was bent over on the gravel, hooking a stone out of her sandal. 'We don't know that; all we know is he crashed his car... And Nic's right, the police are doing all they can. Elan, *do hurry up!*'

'Oh, you don't know the half of it!' she told him.

'Don't I?' Ed asked, finally managing to open his door, the keys then tossed over the rusty roof to her.

'I promised Matt I wouldn't breathe a word, but trust me,' she said, catching them and unlocking her door. 'I know what it's been like, and who could blame him if—'

'Oh, heaven forbid you should share a sibling secret!' Ed snapped. 'I'm only your husband, after all!'

Tempers were frayed, understandably, but it was most unlike him to be snippy. 'I don't much care for your tone, Ed.'

'Sorry,' he said as they both climbed in and she twisted round and lifted the button for Elan's door, handing Ed the keys as she turned back.

'If it's important,' he said, starting the noisy but thankfully reliable engine, 'then at least tell the police, even if you can't tell me. For Matt's sake.'

'I intend to,' she replied, buckling up. 'Don't you worry about that. If he's not home by morning, which he will be, then I'll be right on it.'

'Good,' Ed replied. 'Now, where's Elan?'

The rear door opened with a heavy creak, but their daughter only placed one sandal in the footwell, the rest of her still outside. It was hard to see what Elan was looking up at, Grace's seatbelt locking as she twisted round again. She gave up and wound down the window instead, spotting Nic at the master suite bedroom window which was wide open. She ran cold at the thought of what Nic might have overheard, but in a sense, she didn't care. Her only priority was finding Matt, and there was much she could and would tell the detective. If her brother wasn't found by morning. Which she prayed he would be. For his sake mostly, but also for her own.

# 6

FRIDAY 7 JUNE 2024 – 9.30 P.M.

The Jiggins family had finally departed, the taillights of their shit-brown Volvo disappearing down the track in a cloud of exhaust fumes. Nic breathed a familiar sigh of relief, but then Grace's words repeated in her head: *Matt's finally had enough and left her, hasn't he?*

She closed the bedroom window and sat on the bed, trying Matt's mobile number again. And again. His recorded voicemail cut in each time and Matt's empty greeting promising to call back 'as soon as' grated on her already-shredded nerves. She gave up and paced the room, her skin prickling with cold sweat. The silk shift dress she'd felt so good in earlier was now sticking to her. She went into the ensuite, letting the dress fall to her feet and splashing her face with cold water, making a mess of her mascara, and her scalp itched. She found the bald spot and pulled, just three hairs, and only providing temporary respite from the panic that filled her up as soon as she was done. She filled the clawfoot bath, pouring in her favourite scented oil, steam filling the room as the tap gushed and she removed her lace underwear. She was about to climb in when she caught sight of the misted mirror and almost fell, blinking hard to focus on what she'd seen. Or thought she'd seen.

It had been a trick Matt and his fellow medics played on one another in the terrible rented house near the hospital all those years ago. The house she always thought of with nostalgia, for it was where her love of Matt had begun, although the yard was rat infested and the air was blue with cold and lewd lad jokes. But it was the crude drawings on the bathroom mirror she was reminded of now.

'Ethanol,' Matt had explained when she'd first been privy to an anatomical drawing of a cock and balls, revealed in full glory after her shower. 'You dip your finger in the alcohol and it shows up when the mirror clouds,' he'd explained. 'Puerile, I know, but it amuses us guys.'

When she and Matt bought their first home two years later, a boxy house on the older estate next to the recent development where Grace now lived, Matt had taken to leaving romantic missives on the mirror there instead. Usually a heart, or a simple *I love you x*.

Then occasionally at Three Gables, after they'd moved there, he'd do the same, although not in many years. And this wasn't a love token. In fact, she wasn't sure what the message meant.

She stared at the mirror. The words were already fading.

*Trust me x*

She ran more hot water, letting some out as the bath level rose, steam again filling the ensuite. Then she waited, breath held, until the words reappeared.

*Trust me x*

A sound on the landing startled her. Lily was going downstairs. Without thinking, she wiped her hand across the mirror, just in case. Then she rested on the side of the roll-top bath and ran her thoughts back and forth over the swiped message. Matt must have left it there this morning, after his shower, knowing at some point she would be the one to find it. She looked under the sink and saw his cologne and her nail varnish remover; he could have used either. But what did it mean?

The message was short, and to the point, a directive, but also vague, and therefore open to many interpretations. But it did mean that Matt had planned to leave and wanted to let her know... didn't it? And if so, was he asking her to be complicit in his escape? That's what it had inferred, on first glance. She should tell the police. She cast round for her phone. The detective's number was in there. She went to tap it, then paused.

She had already been less than open with the detective about their money worries and the upcoming tribunal; this would be yet another omission if she didn't report it. But the message had asked her to trust him. Whatever that meant. Wait it out long enough to defraud the insurance company? That was total lunacy. But he hadn't been himself for weeks. Even before their drunken late-night conversation a week before. And it had been a hell of a week. Stress did odd things to people, even Matt. But if he'd deserted her deliberately, why trust in him to be doing the right thing by her now?

'Where the fuck are you, Matt?' she asked the smeared mirror. 'Tell me!'

She pulled on her robe and pocketed her phone, then she left the ensuite to check Matt's clothes in the dressing room again. She'd had a quick look earlier, but it was much easier to think without a detective hanging over her shoulder. She counted the suits and estimated there was one, possibly two unaccounted for. He'd been wearing one when he'd left for work that morning, and the other, as she'd told the detective, was kept in his car for emergencies. But as she'd suspected when she'd told DC Pemberton that nothing else was amiss, his khaki rucksack was definitely gone – the one he took on work trips for any carry-on items – and maybe a pair of joggers and a hoodie too, possibly a t-shirt? It was hard to tell. She didn't usually keep track and Matt had a fondness for neutral colours and stuck to the same brands, but she was fairly sure his favourite pair of trainers were also gone.

Her heart flew into her throat as she realised what this meant. Matt had planned his exit, which meant her hope of him walking back in with a tale to tell and a few scratches was looking less and less likely.

Bath oil swirled on the mottled cooling water as she went back into the ensuite. The words he'd written with his finger on the mirror were no longer visible, just a smeared mess. She slid in the bath, hoping it might calm her thoughts, but of all the things that could be running through her mind, it was Elan's white-moon face that submerged with her.

It had been dark by the time the Jigginses were leaving, and Elan had been halfway across the drive, but her niece's stare had felt particularly alarming in that moment when their eyes met. The way Elan gazed up at the bedroom window had felt more of a challenge than a reassurance.

She held her breath under the water, waiting until her lungs were ready to explode before she broke the surface. Her body was still filled with fear as she stood up and looked again at the mirror, her reflection distorted by the swiped handprint.

How could she trust Matt when it was looking increasingly likely he'd deliberately abandoned her? And what did he mean by those two words? *Trust me x.* To hold on, keep quiet, give him time to fix the damage? Surely the fact he'd suggested faking his death only a week before was too much of a coincidence to dismiss now he actually *had* vanished? He'd passed it off as a joke at the time, but this wasn't funny. It was terrifying.

\* \* \*

She dressed quickly in joggers and t-shirt, her intention to go downstairs and find her latest red notebook to jot down some thoughts, but she paused at Lily's closed bedroom door. Lily's music was loud, as always, but behind the thudding base, Lily was talking to someone, the words indecipherable but the tone urgent enough to keep Nic outside the door. The other voice was coming through Lily's phone, or maybe her laptop: male, young, imperious. Lily's boyfriend, Will Leatherby. His impossibly posh accent and pseudo matey tone were instantly recognisable. Everything was 'Lil' and 'babe'. He was not someone Nic had warmed to on the few occasions she'd met him. The word that came to mind, although old fashioned, was 'shifty'.

She knocked loudly and entered without waiting, switching on the main light.

Lily sat up on her bed and snapped the laptop shut. 'Mum!'

'OK if you switch the music off too?' she asked, perching on the end of Lily's messy bed. 'Can't hear myself think, sweetheart.'

Lily's eyes remained cast down to the closed laptop, Will now silenced. Lily then grabbed her phone, and the Bluetooth speaker on her desk was also muted.

'I'm so sorry for asking if you were drunk before,' Nic began. 'I wasn't thinking. It's been such a shock, hasn't it? The police here, your party spoiled.'

'I don't care about the party,' Lily replied, dropping her phone on the bed and rubbing her cheeks with the heels of her hands. She looked so young, like a small child who hadn't grown into her long-limbed body. The shortie pyjamas she'd changed into added to that infantile quality. 'I just want Dad to come home.'

'Yes, of course, that's what we all want,' she replied, placing a hand on her daughter's bare foot and rubbing her smooth ankle, the blue painted toes curling as Lily pulled away. 'Do you know where your father is?'

'Of course not!' Lily replied, green eyes flashing. 'Do you?'

'No, I don't, but I'm sure there'll be a perfectly logical explanation.' She patted Lily's thigh as a parting gesture, her daughter stiffening. 'Get some rest. I'm going to sit up and wait for news.'

'I won't sleep!' Lily called after her.

'Try, if you can.'

Nic switched off the light and closed the door, walking down the landing before she turned and crept back. The voices had returned, a blue glow sliding under Lily's door and along the dark landing. She couldn't make out what they were saying, the music playing again, and even louder, but then the track ended abruptly and before the next one began, her daughter's scathing tone fired words like bullets through the door.

'No, of course I didn't say anything, Will! I told you, Dad made me promise. Anyway, she's the one who's driven him away. Everyone thinks it, even Aunt Grace. Promise you won't say anything about this! It's important, Will. I mean it! Dad is taking care of stuff, that's all, then he'll be back for me.'

She waited, breath held, heart thumping, until the music returned, the whispers obscured again. She held the door handle and turned it a quarter, then she let go and ran down the stairs, tears already rolling down her face as she headed back to the smoky interior of Matt's study.

She closed the door and sat at Matt's desk, wiping her damp

cheeks with pressed fingers. Things were complicated between her and Lily, she already knew that, but she'd never heard Lily talk about her that way. Maybe it was just bravado for the benefit of her vile boyfriend.

The shock of the police arriving when all her friends were there, plus the fact Matt was missing, was bound to have upset Lily, but to say it was her fault Matt had gone missing... And what had Lily meant by that other comment? *Dad is taking care of stuff, that's all, then he'll be back for me.* Did Lily know something, or was it her daughter's indefatigable faith in her father talking? Lily most likely knew nothing, but the unease remained.

She took out her phone and tapped on the contact details for her elderly father's landline, forcing herself to face the call she'd been dreading. There was no way he'd answer this late, she'd already tried once with no reply, but she'd give it one last go. She could do with hearing a friendly voice, even though she was the bearer of bad news.

The landline was in her father's sitting room, on a table by the window on the first floor, his chair positioned to afford him the best view of the sea. He'd often sit there and admire the panoramic vista of the bay and the coastal path that ran along-side. It was certainly a stunning spot, although it was dark now so the view would be obscured and she could never think of it that fondly, anyway. It held so many memories, many too painful to revisit, others melancholic in the extreme. Her mother had left when she was a baby, her father more precious to her than she could – or sadly did – often say. She should visit more. The years were passing too fast. He wouldn't be around forever and at almost ninety, his increasing frailty in the three-storey upside-down house worried her. But the bad memories kept her away. What had happened in her mother's studio was not in the least her father's fault, but nevertheless, it was the reason she kept her distance. The phone continued to ring. She counted the rings, willing him to pick up. His hearing was pretty good for his age, but if he was in bed, or the kitchen, both downstairs, there was no way he'd hear the *bring-bring* through the stone walls.

The lack of a reliable means of connection had been a concern for a while. She'd suggested he keep the mobile phone she'd bought him about his person. But of course he never did. He saw no benefit in modern technology. It probably wasn't even charged.

'Nicole? Is that you?' Her father's voice surprised her. And he sounded concerned, although his baritone had weakened, an unsteady quality to it, as if he needed to clear his throat.

'Dad! Sorry to call so late. Did you not hear the phone when I called before?'

'No, sorry. When was that?'

'Doesn't matter. Listen, Matt's been involved in a car crash, Dad. They don't know where he is or what happened; they've just found the car so far.' She waited for a slew of questions, but there was no response. 'Dad? Did you hear me?'

'A car crash did you say?'

'Yes, and the police are searching for him. He's vanished, Dad!'

Gerald's questions came then, still faltering, but she answered them as best she could, skimming over the details and trying to make as light of it as was possible.

'I'm sure there's nothing to worry about, but obviously we're concerned.'

'Missing?' Gerald repeated. 'That's so very odd. Do you have idea where he might be?'

'No, not really, but I was wondering if you could check around, maybe look in the studio?'

'The studio?' her father repeated. 'Why do you want me to look in there?'

Her mother's abandoned art studio was at the end of the long windswept garden. A mausoleum to lost love, and the woman who had walked out on them both with barely a backwards glance, but also the only clue as to Matt's whereabouts. But coming out of the blue, it was a big ask. It had been locked up for almost four decades.

'I know it must sound ridiculous, but something Matt said, only as a joke I'm sure, but it's bugging me... Would you mind?' She drew in a deep breath and closed her eyes. No one ever went in her mother's studio, the door locked and the key, for all she knew, thrown away decades ago.

The studio had been the scene of such a terrible trauma when she'd been fifteen that she and her father had rarely spoken about it since. A loving pact between them as they'd jointly buried the night just a few months before her sixteenth birthday in a history that had no place in her life after she'd met Matt and finally begun a new chapter. And now here she was, asking her dad to go in there again. Looking for Matt. It was crazy. She was about to withdraw the request, but then Gerald asked, 'Is he in some kind of trouble?'

'No! Of course not. Why would you ask me that?'

'Because why else would you think he'd be hiding a hundred miles from home?'

'I know, it's ridiculous, but Matt and I had this weird conversation a few nights ago. It doesn't matter about what, but Matt mentioned the studio, just in passing, and I'm all out of ideas, so could you at least look, just for my peace of mind?'

There was a beat then he replied, 'Yes, of course, but it might take me a while to find the key, and I'll need to find a torch too, and my wellingtons. Shall I call you back?'

'No, I'll hold.'

The line crackled as Gerald placed the phone down. Sounds of him moving around conjured images of her stooped father feeling his way down from the first floor sitting room, his liver-spotted hand grasping the thick length of twisted rope threaded through brass rings, the only means to break a fall, then searching the cluttered kitchen for a lost key and the needed torch. She could almost smell the pungency of salty air as he stepped into the garden, the wind whipping in off the sea, and somewhere at the end, behind the encroaching tendrils of winding ivy, a ramshackle single-storey building with green mould on the window and the stale air of that terrible night thirty-nine years ago, still trapped inside.

She shivered. The seconds ticked by into minutes. Her head was rested on Matt's desk when she next heard her father's voice.

'Nicole? Are you there?'

She reached for the phone, a pile of pulled hairs swept to the floor in her haste to answer. 'Yes, I'm here. How did you get on?'

'The torch under the sink is dead as the proverbial. I think I've got one in the cellar. I can call you back. If you really think it's that important?'

She wanted to tell him yes, it was, but the cellar was dark and the steps treacherous. 'No, best wait until it's light, but can you please check first thing? And look through the window if the key *is* lost? And Dad, don't tell anyone I asked.'

'Who am I going to tell?'

'Right, yes, sorry. I'll call you in the morning. Or sooner if I hear anything. You do the same, OK?'

She hung up, unsure if she should have said anything at all. She'd probably worried her father unnecessarily. Whatever was going on, she and Matt would untangle their problems together, as they always did. And Grace was wrong. Matt might have panicked, done something stupid, but he wouldn't leave her. Not without a word, and those two words on the mirror didn't count. No, he'd soon see sense and it was her job to provide a clear route for him to return. She needed a strategy, and the best way to plan was to write everything down.

She fetched her latest red notebook and her best pen from her handbag on the table in the hall and took them both back to the study. She'd only just started this one, the previous notebook filled and stowed away with all the others. Turning to a clean page, she began a new list, but there were only two words that came to mind. *Trust me.* That's what Matt had asked her to do, and for now, she would. What choice did she have? She'd already lied to the police by omission. She was complicit, for sure, but in exactly what remained to be seen.

As she closed the page, the house felt suddenly silent, the darkness outside complete. What terrified her the most was the unknown. Because Matt had taken matters into his own hands. That much was clear. She just wasn't sure where that left her.

# 7

### SATURDAY 8 JUNE 2024 – 8 A.M.

Grace was not impressed as she rounded the bend early the following morning. The site of the crash, less than a mile from Three Gables as the crow flew, was a scene of conspicuous inactivity. A cordon of tape was the only indication that anyone was still searching the wood for her brother, almost exactly twenty-four hours from when he was last seen.

She pulled in at the side of the country lane and walked back to the tape, ducking under and looking over to where she could see Matt's car, wedged against a trunk in the dense crop of trees. She shouldn't go any closer, though. The last thing she wanted was to jeopardise any vital evidence by trampling all over it in her size eights. At least that's what she told herself as she ducked back. The sight of Matt's inverted car, the front crumpled, side window smashed, was the real reason. The trouble was, no one seemed to be doing much at all.

She walked back to her car and then drove to Three Gables, the long track to Matt's home the next turning on the left and only a few hundred yards from that bend.

It was early still, but she was dismayed to see the blinds were all drawn. And no answer at the front door when she knocked, twice. How could Nic and Lily be asleep when Matt was missing, and possibly injured too? Although Lily was most likely plugged into her earbuds, much like Elan often was. And Ed had slept like a baby whilst she'd lain next to him, eyes wide open, and seen every hour on her phone as she'd checked for news. She could not fathom how they were all carrying on regardless, whilst she was looking for answers, because Matt was not the type to run away from his problems. And she was not the type to sit around and do nothing.

She knocked one last time and then used her front door key, but the security chain was on. She doubled-back and slipped through the side gate instead, retracing her steps from the night before.

The garden bore the scars of the abandoned party: lanterns lining the path, bottles and paper cups littering the pool area. The patio table was still laid and the empty bottle of champagne which was now inverted in a bucket of water instead of ice. She tried the kitchen door. It was unlocked, as was often the case – they had no neighbours round here and took a cavalier attitude to security – but there was no sign of Nic inside the kitchen, or any answer when she called out a hello. It was as Grace went back into the garden that she spotted her.

Nic glanced up as she approached, surprised to see her by the look on her face and the fact she jumped to her bare feet. She had been sitting beneath the trio of fruit trees at the far end of the lawn.

'Grace, I didn't hear you arrive, sorry.'

'Anyone could have walked in,' she said, fanning herself; it was already so hot.

Nic was dressed in joggers and a grubby t-shirt, one of her

ubiquitous red notebooks falling from her hand to the dry grass. 'But it was only you, Grace.'

'Indeed. Is there any news?' she asked as Nic picked up the notebook. It had landed open, a long list on the page that she'd tried and failed to read before Nic snatched it up.

'I would have rung straight away,' Nic snapped. 'As I said I would.'

'Yes, of course, it's just... I stopped at the site of the crash. Matt's car is still there, upside down, but not a soul in sight, let alone a police presence.'

Nic looked at her naked wrist. 'It's still early though.'

'Yes, but...' She drew in a long breath. 'I've no idea how the car got so deep into the woods; you'd have thought he'd have collided with one of the trees way before that, if he'd lost control?'

'What are you saying?' Nic asked, looking her in the eye for the first time since she'd made her presence known. 'That Matt meant to crash?'

'No, of course not. I'm just trying to fathom what's happened. He's never had so much as a dent, and then his car is smashed up and he's missing. Do you think he lost control of the car because he was ill, or—'

'Or what?'

She shook her head. 'I don't know. I'm trying to help.'

'I'll call the detective again now,' Nic said, heading towards the house, notebook in hand. 'Find out the current state of play.'

'Good luck with that!' she called after her as the breeze parted Nic's hair, the patch of bald pink skin most definitely there. 'I can't get beyond that woman's annoying voicemail,' Grace added, then to herself, 'She sounds about twelve.'

Nic disappeared into the kitchen, Grace following more slowly. She'd wanted to give Nic some space in light of their perennial prickliness with one another, but by the time she was back in the kitchen, Nic had disappeared, her light footsteps echoing down the corridor that led to Matt's study.

'Where's Mum going?'

Grace spun round, startled. Lily was stood at the top of the stairs in her pyjamas and ear buds in, as she'd suspected.

'She's calling the detective heading up the search, see if she can get an update. How are you, sweetheart, did you sleep at all?'

'Not much,' Lily replied, coming down. Her blonde hair was tousled. She looked beautiful, in a tragic way.

Grace followed Lily into the kitchen and then took a seat at the breakfast bar. Her messy-haired niece had picked up the bread knife from a crumb-filled board and proceeded to hack at the remaining half of a loaf someone had already massacred.

'So, how are you coping?' Grace asked, cursing herself for sounding very like she was opening up a therapy session.

'Bad night, but Will kept me company.' Lily caught her eye. 'Only online, but we are both eighteen.'

'Yes, right, of course.' She wasn't a massive fan of Lily's boyfriend, one thing she and Nic did have in common. Will was an entitled little shit she wouldn't trust with the time of day, but he was archetypally handsome with his mop of blond hair and designer clothes. She had even noticed Elan's gaze occasionally travel his way.

'I don't suppose your father said anything to you before he left for work yesterday morning?' she asked, framing the question casually, although Lily's shoulders had raised, a tension in them that made her think she had been right to ask. 'Any mention of his plans?'

'I stayed at Will's Thursday night, so I wasn't here when Dad left yesterday morning.'

'Yes, right, I see. And before that... You and your father are so close... Any clue as to his state of mind?'

Lily swung round, serrated knife in hand. 'What does that mean?'

'Nothing. It's just you two are so close. If you are keeping anything back, thinking it's helpful to him, then now would be a good time to share that with a trusted adult.'

Lily eyed her, wary, the bread knife held up. 'You think if I knew where he is I'd keep that secret?'

'No,' she replied, suspicions raised. She'd been working on a hunch, nothing more, but now she had a feeling she was onto something.

'Lily, don't wave that sharp knife around,' Nic told her daughter as she joined them. 'Have I interrupted something?'

'No!' Lily replied to her mother with what felt a disproportionate amount of volume. 'Just Aunt Grace quizzing me.'

'About what?' Nic asked.

'I simply asked if Lily had any ideas where her father might be, that's all,' she replied, fiddling with a pile of junk mail on the breakfast bar. 'Did you manage to speak with the detective?'

'Yes, I did,' Nic said, picking up the flyers and brochures and dropping them in the bin. 'The search of the crash site has resumed in the last few minutes,' she explained whilst disarming her daughter of the bread knife and handing Lily a plate for the wedge of bread. 'They'll let us know if they find anything.'

'That's good,' she replied. 'Some activity at least, but we need to do more.'

'And there was apparently a good response after the social media appeal went out last night,' Nic explained. 'But DC Pemberton says not to pin too many hopes on that; they always get calls from well-meaning and not so well-meaning members of the public.'

'So the detective is there now, just down the road?' she asked, sliding from the stool. 'Back at the scene?'

'I believe so,' Nic replied. 'Why?'

'No reason, but that's good, isn't it? I mean, that they're doing something.' She shouldered her bag and readied herself to leave, but there was one more thing to say first. 'Oh, and on that note of being proactive... Ed and I wondered about missing person posters, with a reward?' She hoped that by making Ed a part of her plan, it might help convince Nic, but her sister-in-law was looking very doubtful. 'I don't think we can waste a moment now, do you? We will cover the reward, of course.'

'No!' Lily said, her mouth smeared with chocolate spread, the hunk of bread thick with it as she waved it at them. Lily looked more like eight than eighteen in her babyish pyjamas and with a messy face, but she had taken Grace by surprise.

'You don't think we should at least try?' she asked.

'I just think we have to trust Dad to come back when he's ready.'

'*Trust him?*' Nic asked. 'What does that mean?'

The landline rang on the counter and both Nic and Lily made a grab for it. Lily got there first. 'Oh, hi Grandpa, yes, I'm OK thanks. I'll put her on.'

She passed the phone to her mother, then Lily stalked out the kitchen and thudded up the stairs, a door slamming overhead.

Nic held the phone to her chest. 'Sorry, Grace, I need to take this; my father is understandably very concerned. Can we catch up later?'

'But I thought we'd both talk to Lily, find out what she knows.'

'I don't think she *knows* anything. She's upset, defensive of her father, as always. Sorry, I really need to...' Nic brandished the phone. 'Can we talk later?'

'Yes, I guess so.'

'Oh, and about the posters,' Nic called after her.

'Yes?'

'Maybe hold fire for now? As Lily says, we need to trust in Matt, and he does have a reputation to maintain in the local community. Let's not rush into anything.'

The crash site was looking busy as Grace slowed for the bend, a uniformed officer turning to see who'd arrived as the Volvo chugged to a halt behind a marked police car. This was it: time to come clean. She owed it to her brother.

# 8

The anticipation for the call Nic had allowed to build in those agonising moments as she'd waited for Grace to leave leaked like a puddle onto the hard-tile floor of the kitchen. A cold wash ran through her. The evacuation of hope was complete and exhausting as her father informed her that yes, he'd checked thoroughly around the house and garden, and yes, he'd looked in the studio window too. There was definitely no sign of Matt, or any evidence he'd been there last night.

She listened as she walked back to Matt's study and sank into his leather chair, closing her eyes against bitter disappointment. The studio had been her sole clue as to Matt's whereabouts. But it seemed it was just a stupid, drunken idea of his, and nothing more. Unless...

'Matt could have been spooked when he saw you, maybe concealed himself somewhere out of sight? Is it worth checking again, Dad? You said the garden's got very overgrown, and without a key, maybe he was trying to break into the studio but—'

'Nicole, I know you're upset, but you need to think clearly. For Lily's sake, if nothing else. How are you coping?'

It was a question her father had asked her many times over the years, the inference, as far as she was concerned, always crystal clear: that she wasn't coping well at all. She'd tried to keep the extent of her mental health struggles from him, but Gerald was a retired doctor, and an astute man. He'd known more than either of them had ever acknowledged, including when her depression came back. The question wasn't a direct reference to that, but still loaded.

'I'm fine. Except for the fact my husband is missing.'

'Yes, sorry, love. Of course. Stupid question. And how is Lily?'

'Lily is fine. We're *both* fine.'

But she was not fine, not at all. Her face fell into her open palms as soon as she ended the call. Because if Matt wasn't in the studio, then where was he?

'You thought Dad was at Grandpa's house?'

Lily's voice came as a shock. Nic hadn't heard the study door open. She closed her notebook and spun round. 'No, I... I was being silly. Clutching at straws. Lily, wait!'

Nic caught up with her in the hall, Lily's long strides outstripping her much shorter ones, even at a jog, but Lily had stopped, hands on hips to ask, 'Why get Grandpa to check, then? No one ever goes in the studio; you shouted at me when I even looked in the window. What's with that place?'

'I told you, it was my mother's. She abandoned me.'

Lily shrugged, as if to say, *So what?*

This was not new information, of course, but still, it was hurtful how dismissive she was.

Lily folded her arms across her bare midriff. 'Anyway, I told you, Dad will come back, when he's ready.'

'I agree with you, of course, but is there a reason you're so certain?' she asked. 'Did he say something to you, anything, however insignificant?'

Lily looked down at her hands. The nails were still painted in a pearlescent blue, but looked bitten. She curled them towards her palms as she replied, 'I just know he wouldn't leave me.'

'No, of course not,' she replied, swallowing more hurt at Lily's tactless remark. 'But if you know something, anything that might help, I'm begging you to share it with me.'

Lily looked up. 'I know he's in trouble.'

'What kind of trouble?'

'I heard you and Dad arguing last week when I was revising. About the patient complaint and the GMC tribunal and the fees for his lawyer. You wouldn't help him!'

'That's not true, of course I would!'

'Really?'

'Yes, but he promised me it would be fine; the complaint was all lies.'

Lily nodded. 'She's obviously just some psycho bitch patient who's lost the plot.'

'Yes, exactly,' she replied, hoping that would be the end of it.

Lily stalked back upstairs, her faith in her father's ability to solve everything as unshakable as always. She had always taken Matt's side in every disagreement. From a young age his constant ally, and he hers. Nic had always felt left out. It was a particular kind of loneliness to be an outsider in your own home. The fact Matt had agreed not to buy Lily a car was notable only because it was such an exception to the pervading rule. He always indulged Lily with everything her heart desired. But he had left Lily just as much as her, despite Lily's claims he never would.

\* \* \*

Nic went back to Matt's study and resumed the list she'd been trying to write in the garden before Grace had interrupted her. So much hope had been lost in that time. Hope that Matt might be in the studio, or would just walk back through the door. But he still wasn't found.

Sunlight was filtering in through the slatted blind, painting tiger stripes across the desk and her open notebook. She moved her hand to warm it in the reflected rays, the wedding photo on Matt's desk then catching her eye. They had been married for twenty-six years. Twenty-five of those spent here, at Three Gables. Years in which her loyalty to Matt had been tested before, but never to this extent.

So many secrets, some she now knew, others, she suspected, still waiting like landmines for her to step on. *Trust me x.*

She had to find him, and before the police did. She needed a chance to talk with him and fathom a way out of the mess he was pushing them further into. He was her rock and she felt unmoored and set adrift by his absence. She could float out to sea all too easily, the waves of panic threatening to take her down. She blinked and squeezed her eyes closed then snapped them open. She had to focus or she would drown in fear. She couldn't allow a return to the darkness of the previous summer when she could barely function. The days, weeks, months following her diagnosis had passed in a blur. Matt hadn't under-stood why the need for a hysterectomy had hit her so hard. She was way beyond child-bearing age and the op had been a complete success. *Why did it matter if she lost her womb and ovaries? The cancer was caught in time!* She hadn't understood it either. They had Lily, and she had a clean bill of health; wasn't that enough? It certainly was for Matt.

She lifted her face to the sun. She couldn't sink into another depression, not if she were to salvage anything from this desperate situation. She had to be the strong one. She had to take control, because for now at least, she was on her own.

## 9

Grace had rushed to get to DC Pemberton at the scene of Matt's car crash and was therefore relieved to see she hadn't missed her. But when she tried to attract the curly haired detective's attention, she was told by an officer in uniform to stand back and then directed to wait in her car; the detective would get to her when she had a moment.

Grace was sweating by the time Pemberton was walking towards the brown Volvo. Even with the windows open, it was unbearably hot inside with no aircon.

'Shall we talk in my car instead?' Pemberton suggested, leading the way to a dark-grey saloon parked further down the country road.

Grace tried not to look for Matt's car amongst the trees as she followed the detective's trainers, concentrating on them and the road, which was quiet until the arrival of a large tow truck which then began reversing into the woods, the *beep-beep* intrusive in the remote spot.

'So?' the detective asked, a large bunch of keys dropped into her lap as they sat in her chilled car. 'What's this all about, Grace?'

Pemberton was fortunate to have an elegant bone structure and high cheekbones, her profile impressive, as was her take-charge attitude. Grace was readjusting her opinion by the minute and feeling less than adequate by comparison, or up to the task she had set herself of sharing what she knew.

'Can I call you Grace?' Pemberton added as an afterthought, her right hand tapping out a beat on the steering wheel. She wore numerous silver rings, including one on her thumb.

'Grace is fine, thank you.'

'You told my colleague you had some important information concerning your brother?' Pemberton prompted.

Between them, a recyclable coffee cup sat in a holder, beside it a healthy snack bar. The detective's breakfast, maybe.

'Yes, well the thing is, and I'm not sure if this is relevant, but '

'Don't worry about that,' Pemberton told her, clicking a pen she'd removed from her trouser pocket with some difficulty in the confines of the driver seat.

'Right, yes, it's just I feel I should tell you...' She couldn't help herself; the tears started to fall with alarming speed. 'I'm sorry,' she said, wiping a finger under her nose. 'We're so close, you see, me and Matt, always have been. You don't think he might have...?'

'Might have what?' Pemberton asked, offering a packet of tissues she'd taken from the door well. 'Are you suggesting he might have tried to harm himself deliberately?'

'No!' she said, waving the tissues and the assertion away. 'Matt's not... I mean, no. He wouldn't. But I *am* worried.'

'Naturally,' Pemberton replied, clicking her pen again as she opened a notebook that she'd taken from the inside pocket of her suit jacket. 'So what is it that's troubling you, specifically?'

This was it, time to decide, but if she shared what she knew, there'd be no going back. Although she'd promised herself, and Ed, that if Matt wasn't home by morning...

'Grace, I'm sorry, but I do have a search to oversee and I'd like to get back to it.' Pemberton glanced over her shoulder and she did the same. The tow truck had reversed amongst the trees, a red post van it had held up then whizzing past.

'Yes, of course, sorry.' She drew in a juddering breath and spoke on the exhale before she could change her mind. 'Matt came to see me last Tuesday.'

'Three days before he went missing?' Pemberton asked, making notes as she nodded. 'What time?'

'Ed had just left for work, so must have been just before nine?'

'And your daughter, she was in school?'

'No, she'd already finished at Brackley, but she sleeps in, which was good as I had my first client at ten.'

Pemberton looked up from her notetaking. 'Client?'

'I'm a trauma and grief counsellor. Went back to my studies later in life, when Elan started school, and now I have a private practice which I run from home. We live out on the Meadow-fields estate?'

The detective nodded. The massive development just out of town was well known locally. The houses had been opposed by residents of the nearest village, but to no avail. The developers were still extending the rabbit warrens of roads five years on from when they'd bought their detached house. One of the first families to move in.

'I thought my ten o'clock had got mixed up about his appointment time and come an hour early. He's done it before, poor guy, has other things on his mind... Anyway, it wasn't him at the door; it was Matt.' She drew in another much-needed breath. 'I couldn't believe my brother was there, on my doorstep.'

'I thought you said you're close?'

'We are, but I don't see him as much as I'd like and he's usually at the hospital at that time. He works at The Trust on a Tuesday and Friday, NHS the other three days.'

'And yet there he was, last Tuesday,' Pemberton prompted. 'Nine a.m.'

'Yes, he was.'

Grace had grown hot, despite the aircon, her inner thighs and underarms now sweaty. She adjusted her position to benefit more from the cool air funnelling through the vents. 'The thing you have to understand about my brother is he's a very proud man. He doesn't admit to any failings.'

'What kind of failings?' Pemberton asked as Matt's crumpled BMW rumbled past them on the back of the tow truck. The front and the roof were caved in, passenger window smashed.

'It looks very damaged,' Grace observed, wiping away more tears. 'Do you think he was badly hurt?'

'We don't know, but the car will be examined.'

'Examined for what?' she asked.

'Any clue as to what happened. So, your brother called round last Tuesday morning because...'

'I assume if you've talked to anyone at The Trust, you're aware a complaint has been made by one of his patients?'

Pemberton nodded, which was a relief. At least she wasn't the one to break that news, and it was also a reassurance that the detective was doing her job.

'The allegation was a complete fabrication, of course,' she continued. 'Matt would never have risked his job by...' She trailed off, not wishing to go into details, and wondering at the veracity of what she'd been about to say. 'That sort of thing can ruin a man,' she continued, back on firmer ground. 'Reputation is everything. Women have to trust their gynae implicitly, and rightly so. But Matt stood to lose everything, his brilliant career gone. He had to hire the best defence lawyer for the upcoming tribunal, and all his money is tied up in that damn house, which Nic outright refused to sell.'

'He asked Nicole to sell and she refused?'

'I haven't discussed it with her. I promised Matt I wouldn't say a word. But yes, that's the gist.'

'Sorry, I don't understand,' Pemberton said, looking up from her notetaking. 'Why would he make you promise not to say anything to Nicole when he'd already told her what was going on?'

'Matt tiptoes around her. She's not that robust, mentally. Has suffered with depression for years and she had a health scare last summer. All fine now, but he may well have played the severity of his situation down.'

'So he asked her to sell the house, she refused, and then he came to you for a loan instead, I'm presuming?'

'Yes, that's right, and whilst we are not exactly rolling in savings, I gladly gave him everything we have.'

'How much are we talking about, Grace?'

'Thirty-five thousand.'

The detective's eyes stretched and for a second, she thought Pemberton might whistle; thankfully, she didn't. 'That's a significant sum.'

'Indeed, and as I say, not money we can easily spare, but Matt promised he would pay me back as soon as the tribunal found in his favour, which it would have, I'm sure of it. But now that he's missing and...' She blew her nose. 'You won't tell my husband, will you?'

Pemberton glanced over. 'He doesn't know all your savings are with your brother?'

'No, and I'm afraid that's not the full extent of my concerns.'

'Yes?' the detective asked, long lashes closing briefly then fanning open.

This was the part Grace had been most dreading. Her cheeks flamed hot, the sweat running down her back. She swallowed. 'I should probably share with you what I know about the relationship between the patient who made the complaint and my brother.'

'Relationship?' Pemberton asked. 'What kind of relationship?'

## 10

SATURDAY 8 JUNE 2024 – 10.30 A.M.

'Of course, if you need me to, I will,' Nic replied, the phone held to her ear as she made a note in her red notebook of the address and postcode for the police headquarters where DC Pemberton had asked her to come in later 'to answer a few questions'. 'But I thought you were just down the road?'

'I'm on my way back to my desk now, so shall we say one o'clock?'

'Yes, that's fine. Was there something in particular you wanted to discuss? News of Matt, I mean?'

'No, nothing as yet. The car has been taken away and the search of the area concluded.'

'Right, OK, then what exactly—?'

'I've got another call coming in. I'll see you in reception at one. Don't be late!'

The front door was knocked as the call ended, but it took her a second to register the sound as she tried to work out the significance of DC Pemberton summoning her to police HQ. All the detective had said was that Grace had shared something she would like to discuss with her in person. Grace must have left

Three Gables and driven straight to the site of the crash to find Pemberton, but what had she told the detective?

The door was knocked again. Nic glanced up the stairs on her way from the study to answer it. All was quiet so maybe Lily had gone back to sleep after their argument.

'Good morning, Mrs Delaney!' A heavy boot stepped forwards, the postman's skinny calves hairless beneath the hems of his cargo shorts. 'Sorry to hear the news; the car looked pretty bashed up when I just drove past.'

'I thought it wasn't visible from the road?'

'The police were getting it onto a tow truck. Shocking business, just shocking. It looked like a nasty crash! But that bend is an accident waiting to happen. Every time I come out here I think, someone is going to be driving a bit too fast one day and—'

'Can I take those?' she asked, extending a hand for the pile of mail in his hands.

'Oh yes, sure! Some are addressed to Mr Delaney, of course,' he told her, flicking through the pile. A red elastic band was keeping the half dozen or so envelopes and flyers together. 'But I still have to deliver them. Not that he won't be coming b—' He grinned, revealing tobacco-stained teeth. 'I'm sure he'll be home soon. You're such a lovely couple. Gotta keep the faith, eh? You think he's... you know... done a runner because of the trouble they say he's in at work?'

It was inevitable word would spread after the police appeal, but the media coverage, although necessary, felt horribly exposing, conjecture about Matt's 'troubles' building fast on social media whenever she dared to look. No one online knew the full extent of it, of course, but it didn't stop the negative rumours spreading. Which probably explained why there had been no messages of support from her so-called friends at Brackley. Matt was right, the mums were fair-weather acquaintances, nothing more.

'Can I take that?' she asked again, losing patience now. There was no way she was fuelling the rumour mill.

'Oh, yes, sure,' he said, handing it over at last. 'And there's one in there from your father,' the postman said. He'd clearly looked at everything in advance. 'I recognised the postmark; that's his neck of the woods, isn't it? Cornwall.'

She closed the door. She didn't have time to be polite.

She dumped the junk mail on the breakfast bar, a mix of medical stuff for Matt and homeware stuff for her; all rubbish. But the A5-sized envelope with a Cornish postmark was intriguing. She felt through the envelope to something smaller and thicker inside and checked the familiar postmark again, confirming it was the local post office to her father. But why was her dad sending her letters? It wasn't his writing on the envelope. In fact, it looked like her name and address had been cut from another piece of post, like the junk mail she'd just received. She ripped along the top edge of the envelope, as carefully as her shaky fingers and urgent need would allow.

Inside was a picture postcard. The kind that people sent from the seaside before social media replaced that need. She'd never sent postcards herself. They never went on holiday when she was a child, her father always needed at the surgery, but she'd seen ones like this in the village store down in the bay, and this view was always the most popular. The same view she'd woken up to every day as a child. The bay was beautiful, but rarely painted in the gawdy palette depicted on the shiny side of the postcard: blue sky, biscuit-crumb sand, glittering sea. She turned the postcard over, her hands shaking even more as she saw the writing on the reverse.

'What's that?' Lily asked, coming into the kitchen.

'Junk,' she replied, startled. She quickly grabbed the junk mail from the breakfast bar and concealed the postcard amongst it. She'd been so absorbed she hadn't even heard Lily come back down the stairs. 'You been asleep, sweetheart?'

Lily shrugged and headed for the fridge. Nic was about to offer to make her something to eat when she changed her mind and left her daughter to it.

Nic closed the door to Matt's study behind her and sat down at his desk again. She pushed her notebook aside, then laid the envelope on the desk, the postcard beside it, before opening the desk drawer. There was a stack of envelopes of all sizes inside, one or two an exact match when she tried them for size against the one that had just been delivered. The name and address on the posted envelope had been snipped from a piece of junk mail, she was sure of it now, and it was stuck down with clear tape. She ran a shaky thumb over the Sellotape, noting the postmark was dated the day before. She placed the envelope down and picked up the postcard next, studying the familiar view of the bay again before she turned the card over, pulse pounding so hard in her wrist, the vein was visible. The illegible scrawl – a joke she and Matt had shared many a time over the years; such a cliché, a doctor with terrible handwriting – was unambiguously her husband's. But this wasn't a loving greetings card or a scribbled Post-it note. Or in any way a 'Wish You Were Here'. His words stabbed at her heart as she read them for a second time, making sure she hadn't misread.

*Don't come after me, or talk to the police! I'm fine, and so will you be if you let me go. Matt x*

She sat back, the postcard still in her hand, thumb and fingers trembling but clamped tight. Other than the vanishing words on the mirror, this was the only clue to Matt's disappearance. And it meant he was alive. He'd made it out of that terrible crash.

The relief was instantaneous. But then the questions started up.

Maybe Matt had managed to avoid her father's searches of the studio and garden and was still there? Her instinct was to drive straight down to Cornwall to see for herself. The postcard depicted the exact same view you could see from her father's first-floor sitting room.

She got up from the desk, notebook and postcard in one hand, her other hand reaching for the door handle, but then she stopped. Matt's message clearly told her he didn't want her to follow him.

*Don't come after me, or talk to the police! I'm fine, and so will you be if you let me go. Matt x*

She paced the small study, still undecided before sitting down to read it again. There was a warning in there as well as a reassurance. To let Matt go, or there would be consequences, for them both.

'Lily?' Nic called ahead as she left the study.

No answer, but Nic could hear Lily still moving around in the kitchen. She crossed to the hallway table, by the front door, and trapped the postcard and envelope inside her red notebook then pushed it deep into her handbag.

Lily was drinking orange juice straight from the carton when Nic joined her in the kitchen.

'We're going to see your aunt,' she told her daughter, closing the fridge door. 'I promised to call round.'

She hadn't promised Grace any such thing, but Lily didn't

know that, and it would be much easier to wrap her head around things if Lily was out of her way. Her daughter was astute, it would be hard to keep things from her, and she was still suspicious that Lily knew more than she was letting on about Matt's situation. Her propensity to eavesdropping was also unnerving. She would drop Lily at Grace's and then get on with a few things from her list.

'I'll stay here,' Lily said, returning the juice carton to her lips.

'I don't think so!' she replied, handing her a glass from the drainer. 'DC Pemberton just called; she's told me to expect reporters at the door.' It was probably the case, and the detective had warned her earlier not to speak to the press.

'Is there any news of Dad?' Lily asked, pouring the remaining juice into the glass and opening a packet of biscuits.

'No, not yet, but I want to get out of here in case we're doorstepped, so can you get dressed now?'

'Can you drop me Will's instead?' Lily asked, walking towards the stairs.

'No, definitely not! We keep this in the family.'

'*Family?*' Lily turned back and gave her a withering look. 'Is that what you think this is, a happy family unit? Bit of a stretch?'

'What do you mean by that?'

Lily shrugged, stuffing a chocolate biscuit in her mouth.

'I'm your mother and right now, I need some respect! I heard you talking to Will last night too; what have you told him? What do you know?'

It could have gone either way, a challenge on either side, but Lily shrugged. 'I told him what I told you,' she replied, swallowing the biscuit.

'Which is?'

'That I trust Dad to come back, when he's ready.'

Nic sighed. 'Can you get dressed now? I have to drop you asap.'

'I thought you wanted to see Grace too?'

'Yes, I do, but then I have to go to see that detective at one.'

Lily's eyes reflected her own concern. 'Why, what for?'

'Nothing, she just wants to go over everything again,' Nic replied, hoping very much that was the case.

# 11

'OK if I crash here for a while, Aunt Grace?' Lily asked, planting a kiss on Grace's overly warm cheek.

'Yes, of course, come in,' she replied as her equally tall niece stepped inside. The Delaneys were making a habit of turning up unannounced.

'Mum wants me to be "with family",' Lily explained, her statement accompanied by extravagant air quotes as she directed her sarcasm to Nic, who was now walking up the front path behind her. 'Apparently, there will be reporters doorstepping us.'

'Is that true?' she asked, alarmed.

'Yes,' Nic replied. 'I don't lie.'

'I didn't suggest you... Sorry, of course. Welcome, both of you.'

Nic was wearing a printed cotton dress and full make-up. Her high heels clipped the step as she came in. The old Nic was back, and looking defiant as ever but also somewhat defeated, if that combination were possible. Her glossy hair was pulled into a severe ponytail, her expression equally taut.

'I have an appointment with the detective who has some new

information to discuss with me, *apparently*,' Nic said, looking pointedly at Grace as she closed the door.

'What new information?' Lily asked. 'You said it was routine.'

'Yes, it is routine,' Nic added, glancing at Lily and offering a tight smile as if she'd only just remembered her daughter was there. 'But apparently, Grace saw her too, at the crash site, is that right?'

'Why don't you go on up?' Grace told Lily, who was scowling at her mother. 'Elan is in her room; she'll be pleased to see you, I'm sure.'

Lily nodded, although they both knew that was unlikely. Elan was never pleased about anything, and frankly, she was surprised Lily was being so amenable, but clearly she was keen to get away.

'Do you have time for a quick chat before I head off?' Nic asked as Lily ran up the stairs.

'Yes, of course,' she replied, wishing she'd thought of an excuse quickly enough. This was clearly going to be an awkward conversation.

They went through to the kitchen, a room about half the size of Three Gables' open plan kitchen-diner, and there was no swimming pool in their garden of course, just a few concrete slabs outside the patio doors where Grace grew herbs and cour-gettes in a raised bed, and the patch of grass that Ed mowed every Sunday. The scent of lavender wafted through, calming her a little until Nic dragged a chair from beneath the table, scraping it across the tiled floor. 'Where's Ed?'

'He's gone into the office.'

'On a Saturday?' Nic asked, twisting round to watch as she filled the kettle.

'He asked his boss if he can print out a hundred copies,' she replied, although Nic seemed not to hear. Her sister-in-law was staring out the open patio door. 'Our printer has given up. Typical, eh? Cup of tea?'

'A spot of milk and no sugar,' Nic replied, turning back. 'I don't have that long. What are you printing? Not the posters! I thought I made my feelings clear on that.'

'Yes, you did. Right, tea,' she said as she grabbed a tea towel and mopped her brow. She switched the kettle on, avoiding Nic's stare as she attempted to change the subject. 'They were towing away Matt's car after I left you.'

'So the postman told me,' Nic said, fiddling with the condiments Grace kept on the kitchen table. She had inherited the cruet set from her mother – a portly chef and his plump wife. They were ugly, but one of the few mementoes she had. Not necessarily happy memories, but she'd rather Nic didn't throw them at her. Her sister-in-law was clearly not happy.

'I stopped off there briefly,' Grace said, making the tea in mugs which she placed on the table. 'Saw the detective,' she explained, hoping that a pre-emptive declaration would count in her favour. 'As you now know.'

'Can I ask what you discussed with her?' Nic asked, her tone stern.

She sat down and wiped her face with the corner of her apron whilst also trying and failing to avoid Nic's sour expression across the table. Grace was a trained counsellor, and in control most of the time, professionally at least, but with Nic – and Matt, come to think of it – her composure seemed to desert her. 'I'm only trying to help the search in any way I can, and I stand by my decision to be transparent.'

'*Transparent?*' Nic asked, voice raised. 'Since when have you ever been that, at least where I'm concerned?'

'That's hardly—'

'I'm his wife! A fact you seem to continually discount!' Nic adjusted her bag, arranging the strap so it bisected her chest, her slim waist cinched with a wide belt.

'That's not true, Nic. It's *you* that excludes me.'

Nic shook her head as if that was ridiculous. 'I'd like you to tell me exactly what you told the detective,' she replied. 'I'd rather not walk in completely clueless, if that's OK with you?'

There was little to be gained in holding back. The detective already knew pretty much everything and Nic was on her way to talk with her. It would be better if she heard it from Grace first, but how to say it best?

'Matt came here, last Tuesday morning. I opened the door, and there he was.'

Nic's mouth fell open. 'What time?'

She shook her head, taken-aback by the specific question 'Um, about nine, I think.'

'Nine?' Nic asked. 'I thought he was at work?'

*Nic didn't know?* She paused. One thing at a time. 'No, he came to ask for my help.'

'Help with what?' Nic asked, as if there could be no way his own sister might be of assistance.

'Matt said things were difficult, financially, and he needed a loan.'

'He asked you for money?'

'Yes, and I gave it to him, willingly.'

'How much?'

Grace got up and closed the door, although the girls were hoofing it around in Elan's room like a couple of baby elephants, music thudding, and Ed was at work, hopefully printing the posters. 'Thirty-five thousand,' she said, returning to the table.

Nic's neat eyebrows flew up. 'I didn't know you had that kind of cash?'

'We don't, at least, not to spare. Ed is going to go mad when he finds out. It was supposed to be Elan's university fund, not that she's... We will need it back.'

'You gave Matt thirty-five thousand three days before he disappeared and you've said nothing to me until now?'

'I wanted to, but he asked me not to worry you. He was trying to protect you from the worst of it.'

'Did he say what it was for?' Nic asked, pushing her tea away.

'For his defence lawyer, to fight the... You *do* know about the tribunal?'

'Of course I do!' Nic got up and walked to the closed kitchen door, hand on the chrome handle, then she turned back. 'Anything else I should know?'

Grace dropped her eyes to the lino floor.

'Just tell me!' Nic had raised her voice again, competing with the loud music; Lily's choice by the sound of it, a deep, thudding base bouncing off the thin walls.

'I'm sorry, Nic, there's no easy way to say this.' Grace drew in a deep nasal breath, dreading what she must divulge; surely the worst thing to tell anyone about their spouse? 'Matt told me that he'd had an affair with the patient who brought the complaint; she's called Deena Jensen.' She caught a flicker of recognition cross Nic's face. 'I felt I should inform DC Pemberton, but Matt promised me it was over so I emphasised that too when I—'

Nic held up her left hand to silence her, then turned to the door and placed it flat against the wood to steady herself, her large engagement ring catching the sunlight, the eternity ring next to it sparkling too. When she spoke, it was so quietly Grace had to strain to hear. 'He told you this, *when* exactly?'

'I'm not sure exactly when he—'

Nic leant her back to the door as she looked at her. 'Tell me when he told you about the affair!'

She swallowed, cheeks aflame. 'It was... Well, it was on Christmas Day that he first said, but he promised he'd—'

'*Christmas?* It's June! You've known for over five months that Matt was having an affair, and you said nothing to me, his wife!' Nic's hands flew up in disbelief.

'I know, but you were in such a poor state, six months after the hysterectomy and still not well. Understandably!' she added, noting Nic's mouth had fallen open again. 'Matt said he felt isolated, alone, distanced from you.'

Nic closed her eyes and slowly shook her head.

'I know that's no excuse, and I asked Matt to tell you what he'd done as soon as he told me, but he explained how you were struggling again as you often seem to at—'

'You're excusing him on the basis I was too ill to be a good wife?'

'No, of course not, there's no excuse for it, I told him that, but you weren't well, Nic, everyone could see that, despite all your efforts to make it a perfect Christmas, which we all really appreciated, by the way!'

'And DC Pemberton knows all this? The affair with a patient, the loan, everything?'

She nodded and Nic swore under her breath before she yanked open the kitchen door and then slammed it behind her.

Nic was at the front door, flinging that open too as Grace caught her up.

'I'm sorry, Nic. I meant well.'

'*Meant well?*' Nic asked, rounding on her from the doorstep. 'In what possible way does this help?'

'To find him, that's all I want. Nothing else.'

'And then what? Even if he walks through the door right now, there's no way back from an admission of a sexual relationship with a patient. We'll lose everything. Not just his job, but the house, any security for the future... *Everything*. You understand what you've done? He will lose his medical licence, no question. He's nothing without his vocation. You know that! Matt's career *defines* him. What would he come back for now?'

'For me!' she shouted after her. 'And Lily!'

There was a beat, Nic pausing on the path to turn and look straight at her before she thought to add, 'And you. Of course, Nic. I'm sorry, I thought I was doing the right... Nic, wait!'

Grace ran down the path after her, bare feet burning as she gave chase, but Nic didn't stop, or look back, pointing her keys at the car and then climbing in.

The driver door was slammed before Grace reached it. She banged on the window, jumping back as the engine started, Nic revving it loudly before the car roared away from the quiet residential close.

Grace had forgotten about the girls until she turned back to the house and saw them waiting, side by side at the open door. Lily asked why her mother had left in such a hurry, but she didn't answer, instead pushing between them and then turning left into her office where she closed the door on Lily's questions. 'What's happened. Aunt Grace? What's wrong with Mum?'

She opened the door and smiled. 'Sorry, Lily, we're all very stressed. Can you give me a minute? There's nothing to report. I just need to catch my breath, then I'll bring up some snacks, OK?'

She closed the door again and sat at her desk then opened her laptop. Matt's handsome, smiling face was looking straight at her. The stupid poster she'd designed in the dead of night, sick with worry about her missing brother and trying to make herself useful, was still on the screen. He looked so in control, so... normal. Had she, as Nic said, just made everything so much worse by telling the detective of her brother's failings?

Nic's response to the affair was also concerning and not what she would have expected of a confused, bereft, betrayed spouse. It spoke of prior knowledge and acceptance of the unacceptable. The affair had not been a surprise to Nic. No, she had known about Deena Jensen and had therefore also known her husband was in deep trouble, Grace was sure of it. The question was, how much else did Nic know and why was she covering for Matt by keeping so much back from the police? Or at least trying to. Yes, Nic knew that name: Deena Jensen. She knew it well.

Grace looked deep into her brother's eyes. The photo she'd used for the poster was taken a year before, at one of the Delaneys' many summer barbeques. Matt was brandishing the same tongs as Ed had been holding when the police arrived, but the days of family barbeques were gone. Of that much, she was now certain. Like Nic had said, there was no easy way back from this.

\* \* \*

Ed came back ten minutes later, calling to her from the hall that he was home.

He had a grin on his face when she came out to see him, a sheaf of printed posters in his hands. 'Come on then,' he said. 'Let's do this!'

And despite, or perhaps because of, Nic's objections, she smiled back and replied, 'Yes, let's!'

## 12

SATURDAY 8 JUNE 2024 – 11.45 A.M.

Nic could have spat on the Jigginses' postage-stamp sized front lawn. She kind of wished she had. Maybe it would have made her feel better. Grace's self-satisfied sibling superiority was still making her blood boil as she exited the horrible estate with its cardboard box houses.

The drive across town proved a helpful distraction as she settled into it, although she remained furious. Mainly with her cheating, garrulous husband, but also his colluding sister. Grace's decision to tell the detective about their current money worries because of the tribunal, and more worryingly, his affair with the patient concerned, was such a public dissimilation of their lives. Everything she'd built up over the last thirty years with Matt, now torn down and in a matter of days. The humiliation of Matt's betrayal burned through her again, almost as painful as when she'd first suspected the affair with Deena Jensen, three weeks before Christmas. Matt had denied everything of course, but it wasn't as if it was the first time.

Nic beat her hand against the steering wheel as she waited at a red light.

*Fuck you, Matt! Fuck you!*

Bad enough Matt had been cheating on her, and with a patient, but to confide all this to his sister months ago was too much to bear. And at Christmas!

Nic recalled Grace and Matt sneaking out between turkey and pudding, Matt polluting her memorial trees with his cigar smoke as the siblings sheltered beneath the bare boughs, whilst she'd cleared a mountain of dishes. It was a time of year she always struggled with, as Grace had said. And Matt knew that too. And yet he'd chosen to leave her with Ed and the dishes in order to share the details of his sordid affair with Grace. An affair she had already convinced herself wasn't happening. Because Matt had promised her nothing was going on, and that he wouldn't do that to her. Not again. She should have listened to her gut when she'd first suspected something was amiss.

It was at a drinks event held at The Trust in early December. The first time she had been out in weeks. She'd made a special effort for the opening of The Delaney Family Room; Matt's pet project for almost a year, the necessary funds raised through donations from his grateful and affluent private patients. The intention was to provide a space for families to relax whilst their loved ones were receiving treatment: squashy sofas and a pool table, a widescreen television and games console, stacks of games beside it. She had cradled her warm white wine and watched her husband with pride as he gave his speech. Then she'd noticed a stunning young woman across the other side of the crowded room who was also watching Matt adoringly. The attraction between Deena and Matt was obvious that night, although she'd told herself she was being paranoid. And so had Matt when she'd challenged him in the taxi home.

*Fuck you, Matt! Fuck you!*

The lights changed and she hit her accelerator hard.

* * *

Ten minutes later, she was circling The Trust's vast car park for a space. She backed into the closest one to the entrance and took a deep restorative breath. Her meeting with DC Pemberton was at one and it was a fifteen-minute drive from here, give or take. There was time for this pit stop on the way.

The breeze when she opened the car door lifted her ponytail, which was only just covering the exposed patch at the back. The baldness was spreading and soon would be difficult to cover, hairs falling from her shoulders as she walked towards the stone steps that led up to the familiar glass doors.

She left her name at reception and waited in a pale-blue chair, only half-watching the silent screen advertising different treatments. Hospital waiting rooms always made her anxious, and they also reminded her of her father. Not that Dr Gerald Wood had ever worked in the private sector. He was now a reluctantly retired GP, but still a vehement supporter of the NHS, and would *not* have approved of The Trust's luxurious foyer. The vast glass atrium was more like a hotel lobby with its coffee machine and spotless carpet. Gerald had never criticised Matt for his choice to split his time between the private and public sector, but Nic knew it grated on her principled, Labour-voting father that his son-in-law had 'cashed in', even part-time.

Matt had also been a dedicated and evangelical advocate of free health for all when she first met him. Something else the two men in her life had in common, besides her. But when Lily arrived, Matt took up a post at The Trust for two days a week. She hadn't really thought about it at the time. She'd been so consumed by her role as mother to a fractious newborn and relieved that at least their money worries had been eased – the renovation and upkeep of Three Gables took every penny Matt could earn – but it must have been a difficult choice for Matt to make. 'I sold my soul to the devil for you, little lady,' he'd once quipped, taking Lily and bouncing her high in the air, the baby's gripes instantly turning to giggles. Paying patients came with high standards and constant demands, and it had never sat well with Matt that they jumped a queue that he saw growing day by day in the NHS hospital the other side of town. But they had a baby to support and private school fees on the horizon.

She should have checked in on him more over the years, made sure he was dealing with the pressures of work and home, but it had been so tough after Lily arrived, so many huge adjustments thrust upon her. That was eighteen years ago, of course, so no excuse now, but she had continued to struggle with poor mental health over the years, most notably last summer when that health scare had, as Matt phrased it, set back her 'recovery' yet again. The reminders of that were all around her now as she sat in the same waiting room where she'd been so often the year before, waiting for results that everyone, including Matt, had assured her would be fine.

* * *

She'd known something was badly wrong for a long time before the diagnosis finally came. The lethargy that consumed her, the heavy bleeding, loss of libido, all clearly more than the usual symptoms of menopause. When the cells the scan had detected were analysed, the results then explained to her, Matt at her side, it was presented as if she were lucky. No need for HRT post-op as she was largely through the menopause, and it wasn't as if she were of child-bearing age. She was fifty-three. They could whip out her useless womb and redundant ovaries and all would be well.

Matt had spoken with the same detachment on the drive home. Exhibiting that barrier of professionalism which she understood but struggled with. And he was right, she *was* lucky; a swiftly arranged operation and she was soon pronounced cancer-free. No further treatment required.

'It's been months,' her frustrated husband told her when he came home from work mid-November to find her crying, again. 'This needs to stop. Is that new counsellor doing anything at all?'

Christmas was looming by then, the shops filling up with mince pies and the days shortening, and his affair with a patient, as she now knew from Grace, would be soon, if not already, underway. She'd dragged herself to the drinks reception in Matt's honour in early December and that's where she'd briefly met Deena Jensen.

She and Matt had argued in the taxi on the way home when she'd accused him of flirting. He'd slept down the hall that night too, as he often did back then.

It became a little easier by spring when the warmer weather meant she'd been able to sit under her trees for longer and bury her suspicions about Deena Jensen, along with so much else. No day passed easily, too many losses to mourn, but time helped. And denial. Lots of that. About Matt, Deena, and herself. For she wasn't blameless, she knew that.

The door to the corridor swung open and Matt's trusty secretary, Plum, came barrelling through, security pass bouncing on her matronly chest, grey hair pulled back in an unflattering chignon.

'Nic, I'm so sorry to have kept you. Is there any news of Matt?'

'No, and I'm sorry to turn up unannounced,' she replied, getting up. 'I didn't even know if you'd be here on a Saturday.'

'Oh you know me, married to The Trust,' Plum replied. The truth of the comment meant the joke didn't land as it should and she didn't know how to respond.

'I heard the appeal on the radio on my way in,' Plum said, fiddling with the crocodile clip that held her hair in place. 'This is all so out of character, but of course he has been under immense stress.'

'Yes. I was hoping we might discuss that?'

There was a split second of hesitation, then Plum said, 'Of course.'

Plum led the way down a long corridor, passing a small engraved brass plaque outside The Delaney Family Room. Nic glanced inside to the comfy sofas and pool table, all pushed aside the night of the drinks reception to make way for his colleagues and some ultra-wealthy patrons, Scott and Deena Jensen the most generous of all, according to Matt. She saw again how Deena's glossy dark hair had shone under the Christmas tree lights. A flashback also came of her dark eyes, and the stain of her bright-red lips on her doll-like face curving even more when Matt had smiled back.

'Nic?' Plum had stopped just ahead in the corridor, plump fingers turning a handle to a door on the right. 'You coming?'

Plum's office was tiny, a desk and two chairs, a filing cabinet and a slatted blind.

'I wanted to ask,' Nic began, clearing her throat as they took their seats facing one another across the tidy desk. 'Seeing as you know Matt almost as well as I do... What is it, seventeen years you've been his right-hand woman? His work wife.'

'Almost eighteen, but I'd hardly claim to know him as well as you do,' Plum demurred.

Plum was far too coy for a woman in her fifties, but they'd always got on OK. A bond formed as Matt's long-suffering home and work 'wives'. Plum had interrupted Matt in surgery for Nic once, when she had started bleeding at twenty-eight weeks pregnant. Then Plum had dropped round a frozen lasagne and left it on the doorstep when she didn't answer the door.

'Matt is facing a patient complaint,' Nic began. 'Pretty serious. I assume you know?'

'The tribunal is not something I can discuss other than in very general terms, but can I just say one thing?' Plum puffed up her chest and straightened her back. 'Regardless of anything, I was shocked when the police contacted me to say he's missing. It's so out of character.'

'Yes, you said, but in that regard—'

The desk phone rang, distracting them both, although Plum ignored the call. 'Maybe we could schedule a meeting?' Plum said when the rings stopped. Then she stood up, balled hands on her desk. 'I don't know exactly what I'm allowed to—'

'Plum, please.' Nic stood too. 'I'm out of my mind here, trying to make sense of Matt's disappearance. Do you think it was because the tribunal date was set for next week? He said it was a misunderstanding, but his sister has just told the police about... Well, let's just say I'm more worried now than ever. I need to understand what I'm dealing with. I know about Deena Jensen and Matt. I know there was something there, wasn't there?'

Plum stared at the phone, as if it might provide the answers, a red light now flashing. 'As I said, I can't discuss it. It's a hospital matter, and a police investigation too. I took this meeting out of respect for your situation, but on reflection—'

'But you know Matt! Better than I do, in some ways. Was he

behaving oddly at work? Did he say anything out of character in the last few days?'

Plum looked at her with surprise and then, as she titled her head, what looked like pity. 'Surely you knew he was suspended pending the tribunal?'

'Suspended?' Nic felt her knees give way, a hand to the desk to steady herself as she sat back down. 'That can't be right. He went to work every day. Including yesterday. Suit, tie...' She looked up at Plum. 'He was here every day as usual, wasn't he?'

But he hadn't been, he'd been at Grace's, and as Nic thought back to that conversation, she realised Grace knew about the suspension too.

'No, he wasn't. A GMC rep came down a week last Tuesday and suspended him.'

'Two weeks ago?'

'Yes, and escorted him from the building. I'm sorry, but whatever Matt might or might not have told you, he hasn't been here in almost, well, yes, almost two weeks.'

'No, that's not possible!' She stood and met Plum's steady gaze. 'He told me yesterday that you'd cleared his diary so he could leave at five and pick up Lily's cake. Why are you lying?'

'Let's talk again soon,' Plum said, walking round her desk and towards the door which she then opened. 'You're upset.'

'Damn right I am!' she replied, following Plum to the door but stopping short of leaving. 'It was you, wasn't it, who reported him to the GMC? What did you tell them, you jealous cow? You've always had a thing for Matt! He used to laugh about it!'

Plum looked as if she might react, but instead, she fiddled with her lanyard again. 'No, that's not the case, on either count, but I *was* questioned as a witness to the incident that took place here.'

'*Incident?* What incident?'

'I'm going to have to ask you to leave now,' Plum said, stepping back into her office so Nic was now closest to the open door. 'I'm finding your behaviour—'

'My behaviour? What about yours?'

'I have been exceptionally loyal to Matt over the years, more so perhaps than I should have been, but I find your attitude—'

'Loyal to him? What does that mean?'

'That, to my regret, I have allowed my professional regard for Matt to blinker me to the truth, allowing him to persuade me I was wrong and delay my reporting of a concern by some weeks, but I know what I saw that day in April when I walked into his consulting room, and...' Plum closed her eyes and shivered, then opened them again. 'I stick by my testimony.'

'Do you? Do you *really*, Plum? And what was it you think you saw exactly?'

Plum looked up at a passing nurse in the corridor, waiting for her to move on before she replied. 'I believe the term for the act I observed Deena Jensen performing on your husband is...' Plum's face turned beetroot. 'I believe the term is fellatio.'

# 13

SATURDAY 8 JUNE 2024 – 12.45 P.M.

Grace came in from the hot car and threw the remaining stack of printed posters on the kitchen table where they fanned out, Matt's grin taunting her, over and over. 'Well that was a monumental waste of an hour!' she told a beleaguered-looking Ed as he joined her.

'You asked me to get a hundred printed. Not my fault we've got all these left.'

'That's not what I meant!'

No one had seen Matt. They were just being polite taking a poster: the shopkeepers, the passers-by, the receptionist at the tennis club. Grace picked one up from the floor and scrunched it into a ball, tossing it in the bin.

'Well, I stapled one to every tree down the High Street,' Ed replied, neatening the pile and then filling the kettle. 'So you never know.'

They were both hot and fractious having covered a lot of ground in that hour. As well as the High Street, they'd targeted the out-of-town retail park too. She had wanted to do something – and quickly, so as not to leave the girls too long – but now it felt as if the posters were pointless and she'd acted as much in defiance of Nic's wishes as anything.

'Thanks for helping,' she said, sinking into a chair at the kitchen table. 'I do appreciate your support.'

'I'm here for you, Gracie,' Ed replied, dropping teabags into the two mugs he'd placed by the kettle. 'And they might jog someone's memory, especially with a reward on offer. Just have to take that out of savings, but worth it, eh?'

She looked at her husband and swallowed. 'Yes, I guess so.'

'You think the girls will want a cuppa too?' Ed asked, oblivious to her panic about the emptied savings account; she still hadn't told him. 'Not sure they heard us come in? That music is a bit loud!'

'Yes, I'll take it up to them, see how they're doing,' she replied, glad of the excuse to get away from Ed's chirpiness and her guilt about the loan to Matt.

It might also be the perfect opportunity to quiz her niece further on why, like Nic, Lily had seemed less than keen on her proactive approach to finding Matt. Lily had been verging on hostile when she'd knocked Elan's door to say they were popping out to circulate the posters. Matt and Lily had a special bond, but trusting an eighteen-year-old to make the right choices with any confidences he may or may not have shared with her was not an option. Not when her brother's future was at stake.

Grace added a family bag of prawn cocktail crisps to the tray after Ed had made the mugs of tea. The crisps were Lily's favourite and might smooth troubled waters.

She gingerly carried the load up the stairs. Ed had filled the mugs way too high and they sloshed their contents, but her mood was lightened a little by the sound of the girls' laughter as she approached Elan's closed bedroom door.

The cousins had never got on that well before. They were

very different, Lily popular at school, whilst Elan was a loner. And Lily could be thoughtless and selfish, much like her father, but charming with it. Yes, Matt and Lily were peas in a pod and she loved them both dearly, but it wasn't always easy to be around such confidence. She too would have struggled in Nic's place when Matt and Lily teamed up. And to make matters worse, the mother–daughter dynamic had always been problematic. Kids sensed when something wasn't right. And although Lily was undoubtedly much wanted by both her parents, who were open with Lily from a very early age about the fact she was adopted, Grace had always suspected it was Matt who'd pushed to adopt, whilst Nic would have preferred to give IVF or surrogacy a go.

Nic hadn't ever found motherhood easy. Maybe because of the terrible journey to get there, and also, Grace suspected, the compromise that had made. She had tried to be there for her sister-in-law over the years, reaching out after the two miscarriages, and then the terrible tragedy of a stillbirth. The grief had been unbelievably painful for them all, as a family, and she'd dreaded telling Nic when she'd found out she was pregnant with Elan. Especially as it had been an unwanted pregnancy. She and Ed had never planned to have kids, but the great hope had been that the unexpected arrival of Lily at the same time would make everything right. But no child can be expected to do that. Or indeed, become the best of friends with their cousin just because everyone else would like it. And Nic had never let Grace in, or Lily for that matter.

Grace balanced the tray on one arm. As always when Lily was there, incomprehensible and explicit lyrics were blaring, but maybe the girls were finally bonding. Which would be nice.

Grace turned the handle and shouldered the door wide open. 'Hi, you two, I've brought tea and crisps, if you're hungry?'

It was a rhetorical question, and phrased accordingly. Grace placed the heavy tray on her daughter's cluttered desk and turned back in time to catch Lily throwing the corner of the duvet over something bright red. The girls were both sitting on Elan's single bed, side by side, and had been looking at something between them. Grace hadn't had more than a split second to see what, but it was a book of some sort. A red book.

Grace tugged back the cover to reveal what was unmistakably one of Nic's ubiquitous notebooks.

'Is that one of your mother's?' Grace asked. Another rhetorical question as the brand and colour were well known to her. Nic always had one on the go. 'Where did you get that?'

'It's one of Mum's,' Lily replied. 'She left it lying around. Almost as if she wanted me to find it.'

She looked down at her niece's defiant expression, meeting it with her own. 'But still private, don't you think?'

'I thought it was a blank one,' Lily explained. 'I chucked it in my bag without thinking.'

'I'll take it now, thank you!' Grace said, hand held out for the private notebook. This was a bridge too far; it crossed not only a professional boundary for Grace, but a personal one too.

'Getting thoughts and feelings onto paper' was something she also recommended to her clients. It was a highly effective technique, but intensely personal and for no one's eyes but the author's. Although Nic always claimed the notebooks were filled with to-do lists when anyone asked. Grace never had, hoping that the scribblings were of help.

Lily handed up the notebook reluctantly, and she took it.

'Sorry, my bad, Aunt Grace,' Lily said. 'But it's just filled with rubbish lists. And we didn't read it anyway, of course!' she added, glancing at Elan.

'So why take it?' Grace asked, brandishing the closed notebook.

Lily looked at Elan who was looking non-plussed. 'Mum was rushing me out and I thought—'

'You thought to grab one of her private notebooks?'

'No, like I said, I thought it was a new one. Mum has loads of them, she buys in bulk... You know she does?'

Grace nodded, knowing that much to be true at least. Matt had told her how much the leather-bound notebooks cost and how obsessive Nic was about keeping in a supply, ordering them from an exclusive shop in London. 'So you took what you thought was a blank notebook for what purpose?' she asked, Elan remaining silent throughout the exchange.

'I suppose I was thinking how Elan struggles to talk to you, and I just thought...' Lily looked at Elan, then Grace. 'You've all been so kind, accommodating me here today, and I thought Elan could... Well, if she's not feeling like talking, then she could write stuff down for you, in a nice notebook. Like Mum does.'

The story was clearly a complete fabrication, made up on the spot, and she didn't much care for the inference that it was only her that Elan struggled to speak to, although it was possibly true, but there didn't seem to be much else she could say to challenge Lily about the theft without making a bigger deal of it.

She wanted Lily and Elan to get on, now more than ever, and lord knew Elan was a hard nut to crack, friendship-wise. She looked at the closed notebook in her hand. As long as it was, as Lily claimed, filled with inconsequential rubbish, then no harm done. Nic wouldn't have left it lying around if not. Although why Lily had taken it remained a mystery. But the girl was a magpie; she'd seen her bedroom. Maybe it was so Nic would miss it and panic what was in there. An act of teenage rebellion and spite at being dragged here in a rush.

'Well, regardless, clearly we should return it to your mother.'

'I can do that!' Lily said, holding out her hand. 'She won't even know it was missing. She keeps them all in her dressing room once they're full; I can put it back there.'

'Does she indeed?' she replied, tucking it in her tunic pocket. 'No, I'll give it to her myself, I think. And please, don't take any more of these, Lily; we all deserve our own private thoughts.'

Lily looked doubtful then shrugged again and broke into the packet of crisps, offering the open end to her with a winning smile.

She took a crisp then left them to it, crunching as she walked downstairs. She'd gone upstairs with the intention to dig deeper into Lily's knowledge, if any, of her father's disappearance, but now she was left with more questions and deeper concerns.

But she did have the notebook.

She ducked into her office and sat at her desk. A quick flick through to check Lily's story wouldn't be a violation of privacy, would it?

She looked at the cover, a deep-red leather. No, she mustn't.

She was about to put it in her bag to return, unread, determined to live by the standards she set herself and had just set the girls, when curiosity got the better of her and she opened it.

Page by page, she read shopping lists and reminders of appointments with Nic's therapist, Connie. A therapist she had recommended to Matt after Nic's hysterectomy. Connie was the best there was for long-term trauma and grief, aside from herself, of course. Then she reached a page about a third of the way in that looked different. Four or five lines were crammed with tight scrawl below the crossed out grocery lists and nail appointments. The next page was the same, feverish lines of deeply personal thoughts, providing a comprehensive and unfiltered account of the background to the adoption. Shocking confirmation of something Grace had long suspected, but hadn't known for sure. That not only did her brother pull strings to orchestrate the adoption, but that he also had a very personal and compelling reason for welcoming Lily into his and Nic's lives. Surely Nic hadn't left this lying around for Lily to read?

Grace's phone buzzed in her pocket and she dropped the notebook in her panic. Cheeks burning red, heart beating fast, she picked up her phone and squinted at the screen. The call was from a withheld number. 'Hello?'

'The poster says there's a reward,' a woman's voice stated. 'Five hundred for information leading—'

'Who is this, please?'

'I saw him. Your brother.'

'Where? Where did you see him?' Grace asked, heart thrashing.

'In a vision. He was falling. You'll want my bank details, I can—'

Grace hung up, her hands shaking as she put the phone down on her desk. But it wasn't just the call that had rattled her.

She opened the dropped notebook again and looked for more of Nic's recount of the time of Lily's adoption, but the rest was lists. Only those few scant lines standing out as she found them again. Truths revealed which would more than explain Lily's increased animosity towards her adoptive mother, but which in many ways were directed at the wrong person.

'How could you be so stupid, Matt?' Grace whispered as she closed the notebook. 'How could you imagine this would be the answer to all your prayers? How could you ever think Nic would be able to live with this?'

# 14

'I'll let DC Pemberton know you're here, Mrs Delaney,' the receptionist told Nic, handing her a clip-on pass with her name sandwiched between two layers of clear plastic. 'Café to your left, toilets to the right.'

'Oh, I don't think I'll have time for coffee,' Nic replied, contemplating the ugly name badge she was supposed to attach to her beautiful dress. 'I'm running a bit late myself.'

'Believe me, you will have plenty of time,' the receptionist advised. 'That is one busy lady!'

Nic dropped the pass into her bag and walked across the wide foyer to an open-plan cafeteria. DC Pemberton's place of work was not what she'd expected at all. Modern and located on an industrial estate on the outskirts of town, the divisional police headquarters could have been any type of contemporary office building. Aside from the bright-blue exterior with its prominent signage, and the double set of security doors – one closing as the other had opened – the home of the regional police force was really rather swish.

She queued for a coffee then moved to a wobbly table which

afforded the best view of the comings and goings between reception and the lifts. There were posters on the wall beside her,
warnings of this and that potential downfall in life, which
temporarily drew her attention, but mainly she looked at the
people who passed by, trying to work out if those in plain clothes
were detectives, or like her, under suspicion.

Ten minutes later and with no sign of DC Pemberton, she
took out her latest red notebook and attempted to order her
thoughts on the page. Grace had put her in an exceptionally
difficult position by sharing so much. It would be best to be
prepared for all eventualities.

'Nicole?'

She looked up to the corkscrew curls and winged eyeliner of
DC Pemberton.

'Sorry, I was miles away,' she said, quickly tucking the notebook back in her bag. 'Is there any news?'

'No, and I'm sorry to have kept you. Lily not with you?'

'No, she's with my sister-in-law. I thought it best.'

'Kids are such a worry, aren't they?' the detective said. 'Got
three myself, not that I'd know about teenagers; that treat is
still ahead of me, although it's just around the corner for my
eldest.'

Pemberton was definitely older than she looked if she had
three kids, one of them almost a teen. 'Lily is technically an adult
now,' she told her, getting up.

'Your only child?' the detective enquired as Nic zipped up
her bag.

'Yes, we adopted Lily as a baby after many years of trying
ourselves,' she said.

'You were lucky... To get a baby, I mean. That's rare.'

'Yes, I guess so.'

The detective pointed at the half-drunk coffee on the wobbly table, sloshes of it everywhere. 'Bring that with you, if you'd like?'

'No, I'm done,' she said. It was undrinkable.

Pemberton set a fast pace, leading the way back past reception in her thick-soled trainers, the tailored trousers and tucked-in blouse showing off a toned physique, and the satchel bag slung over her shoulder. Nic followed, high heels clipping. They went into a glass-sided meeting room by the lifts, the room dominated by a large light wood table, the sign on the door declaring it to be 'reserved for interview'.

'Take a seat,' Pemberton instructed, removing a laptop from her bag and placing it on the table.

She sat beside the detective, as directed.

'Do I need a solicitor?' she quipped, only half joking.

'If you want one, but this isn't an official interview; you came here voluntarily.'

'Yes, I did.'

'Good.' Pemberton opened the laptop and tapped the trackpad with a long nail, the screen angled so it was facing Nic more than her. 'Can you take a look at this?'

The screen was black although it looked as if a video was about to play, a counter in the top left-hand corner.

'Sorry, what am I looking at?' she asked.

'It should start in a sec,' Pemberton said, a grainy, poor-quality, monochrome image then flickering on screen.

The recording was of a country road, with rolling hills just visible on the edges of the shot, a lone car passing by. Then a man appeared from the right-hand side of the screen. The motion-sensitive CCTV camera had obviously picked up movement and zoomed in as he walked towards it, his stance stooped so his face wasn't visible, only the top of his head, and even that a fleeting glimpse. The final part of the recording was of the empty hilltop road again and then it spooled on until Pemberton clicked on the trackpad, returning the clip to the start, the timer reset.

'It's private CCTV capture from outside gates,' Pemberton commented. 'Not great quality, but clear enough I'd say and motion sensitive so it closes in on anyone approaching the property. Can you take another look?'

She nodded, not trusting herself to speak.

The recording began again from the start: the empty road, a lone car passing, then the close up of the man's bent head as he approached the camera. He was wearing a light shirt, his curly hair dark in comparison. The footage ended again as Pemberton tapped the trackpad. 'OK? One more time?'

Nic nodded and the recording looped back to the start.

This time, she noticed the man's dark suit trousers and shiny lace-ups as he entered from the road and walked towards what Pemberton explained were a very high set of wooden gates. His thick curls and a chunky watch were what stood out next, but mostly the long strides with straight stiff arms scissoring, an achingly familiar gait.

'What do you think?' the detective asked, tapping the trackpad to pause the CCTV recording on the close up of him.

The hum from the activity in the atrium behind the glass wall receded as the detective leaned in close enough for the sweat on Nic's palms to feel conspicuous. She placed them on her thighs, the cotton dress absorbing her perspiration. Her heart was thudding so hard, she was afraid it might be audible in the quiet meeting room.

'All I want to know is...' Pemberton said, pointing a pen at the man's bowed head. 'Who is this? Do you recognise him?'

Pemberton stroked the trackpad so the man appeared to stagger backwards, then she stopped the clip at the point he was most clearly facing the camera, his features obscured in shadow as he looked down, back and shoulders stooped, which was not at all Matt's usual stance. He always stood tall, shoulders back, but there was no doubt in her mind that it *was* him.

'Dark curly hair,' Pemberton commented, pointing her pen. 'Tall. Well-dressed. No sign of his car, but he most likely left it down the hill and walked up; I'm going to check that out when I have a minute. There's a well-known beauty spot close to the top. People park in the layby to take photos and start rambles, apparently. There's a path down for walkers. And there's no room for cars to park in front of these gates, I've looked it up on Google maps, plus an unwanted visitor would want to avoid the security camera capturing a number plate.'

'Unwanted visitor?'

'Can you take another look please?' Pemberton asked, chewing on the broken end of the cheap-looking biro.

There was no need. But she did so anyway. Anything other than meeting the detective's appraising stare. It felt as if Amy Pemberton could read her every thought.

'It's a very impressive property called The Glasshouse,' the detective explained as if Nic should know. 'It belongs to a Mr and Mrs Jensen.' The detective paused. 'Scott and Deena Jensen.' Another pause. 'Ring any bells?'

'I've met them both, very briefly,' she replied, mouth dry. 'Well, not exactly *met* them,' she corrected herself. 'We were in the same room once. There was a drinks reception at The Trust. A few weeks before Christmas. The Jensens were both there. They made the largest contribution to the cause, as I recall.'

'The cause?' Pemberton asked.

'The Delaney Family Room. A space for relatives and loved ones that my husband raised funds to provide.'

'Why were the Jensens invited?'

Pemberton already knew the answer, but she cleared her throat and then replied, 'Deena Jensen was at one time, very briefly in fact, a patient of Matt's, as I think you know from Grace.'

'Indeed.' Pemberton raised one bushy but neat eyebrow. 'This footage was taken last Tuesday at eleven in the morning, when you said your husband was working at The Trust.'

'Yes, that's what he told me.'

'And you believed him?'

She tried not to react, but it was another comment clearly designed to provoke. Why Matt had felt the need to keep his suspension a secret still eluded her. Was his trust in her so poor he'd had to deal with his problems alone? Was Lily right when she'd claimed she'd refused to help him? Or maybe he was afraid she was too emotionally unstable to handle it? Or perhaps, more likely, he was simply covering up the terrible consequences of an affair with a patient. Not the first time, either. A swell of fury burst inside her, so visceral, she was afraid the detective would feel the vibrations coursing through her, but Pemberton had already moved on.

'So I spoke to a few people at The Trust after I spoke with Grace, including his secretary, Plum, and let me tell you,' the detective continued, 'asking a woman my mum's age to describe a blowjob... Well, let's just say it wasn't a career highlight!' Pemberton smiled, stopping just shy of cruelty. 'You know what I'm referring to, don't you? An inappropriate sexual relationship with Deena Jensen. I believe the details have recently been explained to you by the witness herself.'

She could only imagine Plum's glee when she'd picked up the phone to the detective the second Nic left her office. 'Yes, Plum said, but we only have her word for what she saw.'

'I have a pet theory about Plum,' Pemberton told her.

'Oh yes?' she asked, sitting back and folding her arms.

'A girlish crush on her handsome boss?'

'No, that isn't the case.'

'Really? It would explain why she failed to immediately report the incident she'd witnessed, wouldn't it? A misplaced sense of loyalty too?'

'I wouldn't know.'

'But you *did* know about the affair between Deena and your husband which had been going on for many months according to his own sister, who told me he'd confessed it to her at Christmas.'

Nic tried hard to compose herself and chose her words carefully. 'I do know now, yes, but Grace hadn't said a word to me until today.'

'No suspicions at all, about the affair, I mean?' Pemberton asked.

'Matt is handsome, and many women's saviour. He often attracts admirers.'

'Indeed, so there have been others, over the years?'

'Others who've been attracted to him, yes, of course.'

'Deena's husband said he'd suspected there may have been something between them when I met with him this morning,' Pemberton said, pausing for effect, or so it felt to Nic as she again tried hard not to react. 'But he didn't know for sure, not until his wife decided just a couple of weeks ago now, in the throes of what sounds like a monumental row just before he left on a two-week-long business trip, to confess she's been sleeping with her gynae consultant for months.'

Pemberton paused for a reaction which Nic tried her best to withhold.

'Matt wasn't her consultant; he'd referred her on.'

'Well, she was,' Pemberton replied. 'He saw her first, so

regardless of any referral, she was a patient of his. Anyway, Scott Jensen, multi-millionaire, then throws his not inconsiderable influence and wealth into ensuring his team of lawyers gets your husband suspended for misconduct on the first day Matt's next due in at The Trust, Tuesday twenty-eighth of May, almost two weeks ago now. And you claim you didn't know about any of this and your husband was at work as normal every day?'

'He said he was, and he had NHS patients too, so he was probably—'

'No, he was suspended from all his patients. Two weeks ago! So where was he, Nicole? Other than visiting his lover by the looks of things.' Pemberton leant back in her chair, hands behind her head, pits damp, a waft of deodorant mixed with perspiration heading Nic's way. 'You're seriously telling me you had no idea of the affair?'

'I'd noticed the way Deena looked at him at that drinks reception, but Matt told me I was being paranoid. And I knew about the tribunal, but he kept the suspension from me. Like I said, he left for work every day, as usual.'

'Why would he make that pretence?'

'I suppose not to worry me unduly.'

'Deena is a very attractive-looking woman from what I've seen.'

Nic looked up from her sweaty palms. 'I wouldn't know.'

'Oh, I thought you said you'd met her? And her husband, Scott, has limitless funds at his disposal to bring down your husband, whereas Matt...' Pemberton paused. 'You do know the extent of your financial situation, or rather lack of it? You're not going to pretend again that you're that clueless?'

All she could do was shake her head at the ignominy of it all. She was hurt, betrayed, but more than anything, humiliated. Matt had fed her half a story in the late-night conversation just over a week ago, where he'd partially come clean then backed away from the scale of it, promising he'd fix it, and now she was having to face up to the full horror of his actions in front of a woman almost half her age who was also a detective. A bloody good one too by the sounds of it.

'He's certainly not a man I'd mess with,' Pemberton continued. 'Scott Jensen, I mean. I don't know about your husband, of course, but these consultants... Demi-gods in my experience. But no one is above the law, or the General Medical Council. What *did* Matt tell you about the complaint? And I'd like the full story this time, not the "everything is perfect" version you gave me, because we both know that's not true.'

'Matt couldn't share the details – patient confidentiality – but he said that it was all lies, or rather a misunderstanding, and he was adamant he would be proved blameless.'

'Why are you still defending him? He was sleeping with Deena Jensen for months, and you knew that, didn't you?'

'No! I asked him after that drinks thing and he told me I was being paranoid.'

'Come on, Nicole, what's going on here? Do you know where he is?'

'No! I only wish I did! I'd drag him back here rather than face all this alone.'

'Well, I'm afraid I'm about to add to that burden. Scott Jensen has now reported his wife missing.'

Nic looked up from her wedding band which she'd begun twisting round. '*Missing?*'

'Scott is convinced they're together, your husband and his wife. Run off into the sunset after that faked car crash.'

'Faked? Is that what you think?'

'I'm more interested in what *you* think. Could they be

together? Was that Matt's plan, do you think, to cover his tracks and run off with his mistress?'

She swallowed. 'I suppose it crossed my mind, after speaking to Plum, that maybe Matt had chosen to run away because of the upcoming tribunal. I never thought he might be with *her*... No, I hadn't considered that as a possibility, but I suppose it is one theory.'

'Isn't it what every wife would assume? If their husband, who'd been having an affair for months, had left without explanation?'

'I didn't know about the affair, I told you that! And we've been happily married for twenty-six years. I trusted him. *Trust* him. We have a daughter. A life. A home.'

'Yes, but sadly that's not enough always, is it? Certainly didn't stop my ex. So, do you still trust him? Even after the blow job from a patient in his consulting room?'

Nic looked down at her hands again, one worrying the other, her murky reflection blurred in the wide gold band on her left hand. 'I don't know what to think any more.'

'According to Scott Jensen, his wife was obsessed with your husband, and had been ever since they had that one appointment with Dr Delaney at The Trust back-end of last year. They went to discuss the fact they weren't conceiving. Deena thought your husband was going to be her saviour, apparently, but Dr Delaney referred Deena to a colleague after an initial consultation, which I think we can take as an attempt to cover himself should the burgeoning affair ever come to light, but of course, it's not as simple as referring her on. She was his patient. He crossed a line.'

'Yes, I see that, but like I said, Matt kept the complaint details confidential and he assured me that it would be dismissed as lies.'

'I'm afraid I do not share that view, and neither does Scott. He is clearly not a happy man, which is understandable, given the fact the doctor they'd trusted with their most intimate concerns was, as Scott puts it...' Pemberton grabbed her notebook then quoted from it: '"Fucking the brains out of my wife on a regular basis, and according to Deena, a regular visitor to my home when I was away, fucking a-hole".'

Nic closed her eyes on the shame. Matt's shame, but also hers. Because she was the foolish wife who'd been ignorant of all this, for months on end, wrapped up in her own problems, ignoring the signs and thereby allowing Matt to dismiss her very real worries as paranoia. Scott was right, he was a fucking a-hole.

'Matt's let himself down, Nicole, and he's left you here to deal with the mess, hasn't he?'

She felt sick to her stomach. She coughed and Pemberton rooted in her bag then pushed a bottle of water towards her. It was half-drunk, red lipstick round the rim, but she gulped it down anyway, barely able to breathe.

'Shall I tell you my current thinking, Nicole?'

She nodded, the water bottle still pressed to her mouth.

'This man' – the detective pointed at the laptop screen – 'captured outside the gates to the Jensens' property last Tuesday morning, June fourth, at eleven... is very clearly your husband, Matthew Delaney. He smashed the security camera, entered the property, or maybe Deena let him in, and then... Well, that remains to be seen.'

Water dribbled down Nic's chin, but the detective ignored her reaction, continuing to expound her theory.

'Scott returned home this morning after a two-week absence and finds his wife's Porsche in the underground parking space, but no sign of Deena. Scott tries everyone and everywhere she might be, but no luck, and he was already concerned having had no contact with her for the last four days. Last time they spoke was early Tuesday morning, around nine, which places Deena at The Glasshouse that morning. He's worried, and I am too because, if she has run off with your husband, I'm going to be pretty relieved.'

She wiped her chin. 'How do you mean?'

'I'm concerned for Deena's well-being. *Very* concerned. I would go so far as to say that a GMC suspension might be the least of your husband's problems. Or yours.'

'*Mine?*'

'You've been covering for him. Which could have very serious consequences.'

'What consequences?' she asked, swallowing saliva.

'Let's take another look, shall we?' Pemberton tapped the trackpad until Matt was once again walking right up to the camera.

His stupidity was unreal, and yet there he was, her husband, in broad daylight, at the home of the patient whose complaint had seen him suspended from the job he often told her was his whole world. He'd risked his career for an affair with Deena Jensen and with it their marriage, their home, maybe even their freedom. *Was it worth it, Matt? Was she worth all this? How good could a blow job really be?*

'Yes,' she whispered, looking at the detective. 'That's definitely my husband.'

Pemberton sat forwards in her chair. 'To confirm, you are identifying this man as Dr Matthew Delaney? Do you want to look again?'

She nodded and the video played until there were empty seconds at the gate, Matt gone. 'Does he come back, after this?' she asked. 'I mean, is there more?'

The detective shook her head. 'The film stops a minute later;

no one else comes or goes. I think he was inside by then. So it's definitely him?'

'I said so, didn't I? And it's *Mr*, not Doctor. He's a consultant. *Was* a consultant.'

Pemberton snapped the laptop shut. 'I'll need to take a statement and prints.'

'*My* fingerprints?'

'For elimination purposes, we're searching the Jensens' home now, as well as your husband's car.'

'Searching for what?' she asked, alarmed by the sudden turn of events.

'For any signs of Deena absconding with your husband,' Pemberton said, getting up and heading to the door. 'Or Mrs Jensen having come to harm.'

'Harm?' Nic grabbed the door as it swung towards her, holding on tight.

'Let's organise those prints, shall we?' the detective said. 'One step at a time.'

It was over an hour later when she met up with Pemberton again in one of the many labyrinthine corridors on the third floor and they headed to the lifts together. She had been handed from Pemberton to various police officers and visited multiple rooms, her hands now ink-stained, her heart heavy. A formal statement confirming Matt was the man in the CCTV images had been taken and then she'd signed it, in duplicate. There was no turning back now. No way for him to come home without facing the consequences. Whatever they might be.

'Am I free to go?' she asked Pemberton as the lift travelled down.

'Of course, but can I issue you with a word of warning?' The lift door opened and they walked towards the reception area together. 'We believe your husband to be a potentially dangerous man, so I'd like to suggest that—'

'You think he killed her?' Nic asked as they joined a long queue to hand back passes, all eyes turning to her.

'Now is not the time to continue to protect or shield him from this enquiry,' Pemberton said, lowering her voice and glaring at the rubberneckers. 'I can arrange for a family liaison offer to—'

'No! That won't be necessary. Matt would never hurt me, or Lily. *Never!*'

They shuffled forward.

'I hope you're right, Nicole, because in my line of work, I'm afraid I've heard that too many times, with some disastrous consequences. Have a think about it. I'll leave you here, but we'll talk soon.'

Nic ran rather than walked to her car after the pass was finally returned and she was able to leave. She locked the car doors as soon as she was inside and then drove away from the hideous blue building, fast, as if she could outrun what had been implied by the detective: that her husband was not only a treacherous philanderer who'd fucked his career when he fucked Deena, but that Matt was also a murderer.

## 15

SATURDAY 8 JUNE 2024 – 9 P.M.

It was thinking about getting dark as Grace pulled into the long track that led down to Three Gables, the Volvo's ancient suspension grumbling and grinding on the parched rutted single-track lane as the setting sun dazzled her, twilight falling. It had been more than thirty-six hours since Matt was last seen. By the morning, it would be forty-eight. The window of opportunity to find him was rapidly closing, and she felt increasingly desperate to do something.

'Thanks for dropping me home,' Lily said as Grace parked by Nic's white car. 'Dinner was so nice. I know it's really awful circumstances, but it's good to be with you all, a proper family. I hate being here...' Lily looked at Three Gables. 'With *her*.'

'Your mum needs you,' she replied. 'But we've loved having you.'

Grace reached out and squeezed her niece's hand, and although she knew she shouldn't, she couldn't resist adding, 'You know you can talk to me about anything? I am always here for you. He is my brother as well as your dad. We both love him so much; we will always put him first.'

Lily nodded, then gulped. 'There's nothing to say, not until we know more, but thanks for the offer; it's nice to know I've got somewhere to go if things kick off with *her* again.'

'No, that's not what…'

The front door had opened and Nic stepped out, watching them.

'It's fine, Aunt Grace. Honestly.'

She smiled, hoping against hope Lily hadn't read as much of Nic's private thoughts as she had. Maybe Lily still didn't know the background to her adoption, the compromise she represented, but as Lily looked over at Nic with pure hatred in her eyes, Grace knew she must.

'You should go in, Lil. I'll return the notebook, say it was my mistake, not yours. I'll tell your mother I picked it up by accident.'

'Thanks, Aunt Grace. I can't face another row with her.'

Lily got out the car and then walked towards the house, almost shoulder-barging her way in. Grace got out too, Nic's expression less than welcoming, but that wouldn't do anyone any good and she had the notebook to return, the red leather pad tucked in her bag which she grabbed from the back seat.

'Thanks for having her,' Nic said as Grace approached. 'You won't mind if I don't ask you in? I'm completely exhausted after that interview with DC Pemberton.'

Grace hadn't dared ask how it had gone, keeping her messages to requests for any updates on Matt and the arrangements for Lily. 'Yes, of course, but I was hoping I might have a quick word about another matter?'

They were framed under the porch light, although it wasn't completely dark as yet, but the overhead bulb illuminated Nic's bald patch, clearly visible as she turned to the front door and pulled it just closed before whispering, 'You haven't told Lily about Matt's affair with Deena Jensen, have you?'

'Of course I haven't! But it might be better to hear it from you than somewhere else. And I'm afraid there's something else I have to explain...' She lifted her bag from her shoulder, the notebook tucked inside. 'I suspect it's why Lily is rather upset with you at the moment.'

'Right, well I'm afraid we have bigger problems than teenage tantrums,' Nic said.

'What's happened?' Grace asked, ignoring the misconception and leaving the notebook in her bag, for now.

'The police showed me images of Matt from a CCTV camera,' Nic explained, the encroaching shadows casting her in a ghostly half-light as she checked behind her again, although there was no sign of Lily and the door was pulled to.

'They've spotted him? Where?' Grace asked, hope bubbling despite Nic's negative tone.

Nic shook her head. 'This was last Tuesday morning, at Deena Jensen's house. Did you know Matt was going there after he left yours?'

'No, of course not!' Grace said. 'He didn't say where he was going... Oh, except to the bank to get some cash against the loan.'

Nic shook her head and sighed. 'So you knew he wasn't going to work? I thought so!'

'Oh god! I'm so sorry, Nic, this must be truly awful for you, but I promise I am not the enemy. I want the same thing as you. Matt asked me not to worry you about the suspension.'

'Well I am now!'

The air stilled, the only sound the creak of the front door as the wind rocked it free of the loosely fastened latch. Nic pulled it shut again.

'The problem is, Grace, the police and Deena's husband both

think she's gone off with Matt. In fact, DC Pemberton said if they don't find her soon, they'll start searching for a body instead.'

'A body?' Her hand flew to her face. 'No, she can't be... dead? You don't think... Oh my god, this is a nightmare.'

'Yes, it is!' Nic replied, reaching out a hand to the porch wall to steady herself.

Grace stepped forward and steadied Nic, who looked on the brink of collapse. 'We should go inside and try and deal with what we *do* know. Together.'

Nic shook free of her. 'Like we always do? I still can't believe you knew about it all those months ago and said nothing. I really can't get past that. Christmas to June is a very long time to lie about something that bad.'

'I know it doesn't reflect well on me, but to put that aside for now, I also need to discuss—' She felt in her bag for the notebook, still tucked away.

'He thought you were too much, Grace; did he tell you that?' Nic said, looking her straight in the eye. It was like a light had been switched on, Nic's fury discharging from every pore, spittle forming, eyes blazing. 'He used to sigh when you rang or turned up on some pretext to see him.'

'That's not true,' she replied, leaving the notebook again.

'Isn't it? It wasn't my fault you never saw him. I encouraged him to pick up the phone, or call round your house, but he said you were boring and needy, always had been, even as a child.'

'I know you're angry, but lashing out at me is—'

Nic turned and shoved the front door hard. Lily was standing the other side, in the brightly lit hall. Nic paused, then went inside, slamming the door behind her.

'I just want to find my brother!' Grace shouted, banging on the door, then she bent down and opened the letter box, looking inside the now empty hallway. 'Do you know anything else about his movements? Does Lily? We need to help one another! I need to talk to you!'

\* \* \*

Grace climbed back in her hot car and waited, hoping that once Nic had calmed down, she would come out, maybe apologise, or not, and despite Nic's cruel words, either way she would forgive her, because she was at fault too, she knew that.

The notebook she'd planned to return was in her bag on her lap, but that wasn't her main concern now. And Nic hadn't given her the chance to return it.

Grace waited but the front door didn't open, and the longer it didn't, the less she wanted it to. Nic was lying about Matt not wanting to see her. They'd always been close. He wouldn't be that cruel. That was Nic's take, not his. Born of jealousy. And spite. There was a lot of that coming from Nic right now.

A withheld number flashed up on her phone. There had been many of those in response to the posters. Already a dozen that day, and mostly she was greeted with silence at the other end. Ed had told her not to answer any more, but she couldn't help herself.

'Hello?'

A cold pit of fear settled in her stomach as silence greeted her, then laughter burst out to fill the void, and a volley of foul language.

*Kids.* Stupid, cruel kids with nothing better to do than... She hung up and started the car then turned it around and drove away. The evening sun had been replaced by darkness, almost completely as she negotiated the rutted track and turned left onto the country road.

The bend where Matt's car had left the road came out of

nowhere as tears blinkered her view. The fine line between life and death was never so faint as when driving home alone along unlit country roads. She slowed down and drove on more carefully, concentrating on the road. She needed to be sensible if she was to help her brother. Matt might have made some monumentally stupid decisions, but he deserved a fair hearing and she would do everything in her power to allow him that, with or without her sister-in-law's help.

## 16

SUNDAY 9 JUNE 2024 – 8 A.M.

Nic lay in bed early the next morning after a second sleepless night. It was Sunday, and therefore two days since Matt had last been here, beside her.

She needed to get up, face the day, but she couldn't seem to drag herself from the bed. Although doing nothing was clearly no longer an option. Especially after the awful experience she'd had at the police station the day before, the ink still on her fingertips despite scrubbing them with a nail brush as she'd soaked in the bath last night. It was an attempt to soothe her nerves after the argument with Grace, but it hadn't worked.

She listened for sounds of Lily moving around the house, or any sounds at all, but Three Gables was eerily silent, although the birds were still singing outside the window, in spite of everything.

It would be good to have a decent conversation with Lily today. Her daughter had screamed at her to leave her alone last night when she'd come in from the argument with Grace, but maybe Lil would be calmer today. She was clearly upset about her father's disappearance, but her anger was directed, as always, at her. Grace had alluded to some issue with Lily she'd wanted to discuss, but she had been too preoccupied to listen to Lily's problems on top of her own. Maybe that was a mistake? Maybe Lily *did* know something.

She got up and headed down the landing but heavy knocks on the front door startled her just as she was about to tap on Lily's bedroom door. She'd planned her opening gambit too, an olive branch extended so they could get to the bottom of it all, together, but the knocks were loud and impatient. Maybe the journalists were here? Doorstepping her as she'd pretended to Lily they might.

She ran down and flung open the front door, hoping against hope it would be Matt, not some sleazy hack after a quote, but it wasn't either. Although the solemn expression of the man who greeted her did little to ease her concern.

'Hello, can I help you?'

The man introduced himself as detective something, she missed his surname, and then he thrust an official-looking document towards her. He was wearing plastic gloves, and a grey suit. He advised her to read the document, not allowing her enough time to do so before he began talking again, loudly announcing that they were there for an authorised search and it would be conducted as quickly and unobtrusively as possible, but she would be required to comply with all their requests. Behind him, two vehicles she didn't recognise were parked on the drive. One a marked police car, the other a large white van.

She stood back, allowing him in, and then a number of other gloved officers followed on after they'd climbed out of the car and van.

'Can I at least ask what you're looking for?' Nic said, her words falling on the deaf ears of the nearest officer who was now in her kitchen, pulling open drawers. 'My daughter is asleep upstairs,' she told the silent woman. 'Should I wake her?'

Pemberton was conspicuous by her absence as Nic asked again what they were looking for, but still no one would say.

She ran up and woke a belligerent Lily before someone else did. 'You need to get up; they're everywhere,' Nic told her sleeping daughter.

'Who?' Lily asked as someone came in and grabbed her laptop.

\* \* \*

Matt's study, the ensuite, and every corner of the house were combed by the gloved officers. Lily joined Nic in the kitchen part way through the search, her daughter loudly proclaiming that they'd trashed her room, which was hard to imagine made much difference given its usual state, but even more shocking to Lily, apparently, was the fact they were 'stealing' her precious laptop.

'What the fuck?' Lily asked, as if that covered it. 'You could have warned me!'

'I had no idea,' she said, stirring the coffees she had offered to make, not knowing what else to do. 'Sorry about your laptop.'

Lily turned on her heel and went back upstairs as Nic asked the women beside her if she took milk and sugar. It was all so bizarre and disturbing, Nic wondered if she was still asleep and it was a nightmare.

The search took under an hour, the team leaving with bagged items Nic tried to mentally log, but it was hard to keep up: Lily's laptop, of course, and Matt's toothbrush and hairbrush, maybe some of the files from the desk drawer that she'd been asked to unlock? They hadn't seemed bothered with her things, which was something.

Nic closed the door on them, and the van and car drove away.

* * *

She could hear Lily was on her phone when she passed her closed bedroom door, but she didn't bother to listen in, instead continuing on to the master suite. She'd given up on Lily sharing anything with her, her daughter's anger so deep there was no way to swim through it. And she had other things to think about now. The investigation into Matt's disappearance had clearly stepped up a notch, which meant she had to do the same. Time was running out to save herself from the worst of it, but she had to at least try.

# 17

Clouds of dust rose up as Nic drove down the track and then turned onto the empty country lane. She'd told Lily she was popping to the supermarket for supplies, although that was a lie and Lily couldn't have cared less that she was leaving the house. She was probably pleased.

She drove into the bend where Matt's car had left the road at thirty miles an hour. Her foot hovered over the brake, but the trees, for a split-second, called to her. She loosened her grip on the steering wheel, the car's front tyres bouncing as they hit the verge of hardened mud and left the road. The woods were straight ahead now, and there amongst them, a flicker of movement drew her eye. Someone was in there, eyes piercing, dazzling her as the sunlight peeked between thick trunks and blinded her. She blinked hard and swung the tyres hard right, back onto the road, then she braked, slowing the car, the road ahead clear. She negotiated the next bend at a steadier speed and checked her mirror, but there was no one in the woods now although her heart beat out of her chest. Matt's car had been towed away the day before. Anything else was a figment of her imagination, fuelled by lack of sleep and ghosts of the past. She could outrun them, and anything else life had to throw her. She must be strong and look after herself now. That much was decided. It had been Matt's choice to deliberately disappear, she was sure of it, but why he had abandoned her, she still had no firm idea. All she knew was he'd left her with a mess to clear up, as always, and like that mountain of washing up at Christmas, she would tackle it bit by bit until order was restored, starting with a house call. One she dreaded, but which she could no longer see any way to avoid. For it was where the trail had begun, with Matt outside those gates to Deena's home. Her careless, selfish husband caught on CCTV. And now she would have to try and limit the damage he had caused.

She drove on, past endless rolling fields and then across town and out the other side, back into countryside. The Cotswold hills surrounded her as she guided her heavy car up the steepest one, the anticipation of what she was about to do building as the gradient increased.

As DC Pemberton had advised, there was a layby near the top: not only a convenient place to park to enjoy the incredible view of the valley below, but also for visitors to the nearby houses, with their high gates and inaccessible drives, to safely leave their cars.

Nic switched off the engine and grabbed her bag, pulling out her current red notebook, which was rapidly filling up with much less palatable lists than party plans. She ran through the bullet points she'd made yesterday, and her thoughts this morning whilst the police search of Three Gables had delayed her.

The idea was to explain to Deena's husband, if he were home, that she had felt compelled to come and see him, to have a conversation neither of them would have wanted to have, but which was clearly now needed, in the circumstances. Truths had to be faced and shared if they were to find their missing partners.

She was about to get out of her car when a bright-blue van backed in right beside her. The layby was empty other than her car. It was ridiculous to park so close. Absolutely no need. The stupid driver then opened their rusting van door into the narrow gap, slamming metal into metal as the wind at the exposed spot grabbed the door and took it.

'Hey!' She rapped a knuckle hard on the inside of her window. 'Hey!' The wind whipped her ponytail across her eyes as she got out of her car, the idiot driver still completely oblivious. 'You hit my car with your door!'

'Sorry!' the culprit called back, raising her voice above what sounded like a pack of baying wolves inside the van. 'The wind must have caught it. Any damage?'

Nic inspected the side of her car, taking her time. There was a dent, quite a bad one in fact, and a lump of blue paint deposited. The woman was a menace, clearly. But she didn't have the time for this.

'No, it's fine,' she said, deciding to let it go. She had far greater concerns, and no desire to get pulled into an exchange of details.

'Well, if you're sure?' the scruffy-looking woman replied. 'We could let the insurance take care of it. Totally my fault, I hold my hands up. I'm the worst at parking.'

'No, it's nothing,' she told her, passing the strap of her bag over her head and turning to walk up the hill.

'It's this way down to the public right of way!' the woman called after her, but Nic ignored her. She had her own path to take.

The road was narrow and steep, with no footpath. The gates of large hillside properties were the only refuge as passing motorists, surprised no doubt by the presence of a lone pedestrian, swung towards her. On the final bend, there was nowhere to jump except into the long grass, her high heels sinking into the verge, her heart sinking too when she saw the soft beige suede of her favourite pair of Jimmy Choos was now stained green and brown. But she was almost there.

She struck out for the last few hundred yards, ignoring the sweat that now stuck her cotton dress to her back. The houses were increasingly impressive, but she knew to expect more from The Glasshouse, situated at the very top of the hill.

It was a property that had attracted a lot of interest when it was built only five years before. Scott Jensen's wealth and his much younger second wife lent a certain local notoriety to the couple that courted publicity with high-profile appearances at charity events where they donated generously. Deena's Instagram followers also ran to over seventy-five thousand; Nic was one of them. Selfies of Deena on the jutting terrace of their multi-million-pound hilltop home were a regular occurrence, the long list of hashtags encompassing every top-end label and garnering thousands of comments and likes. Deena's severely bobbed jet-black hair and smoky eye make-up were her trademark and she always dressed immaculately, if somewhat scantily, the expensive dresses she chose often billowing in the breeze up on the hill to reveal her enviable figure. But nothing since last Tuesday.

Nic shivered. She had no sympathy for Deena, for obvious reasons, but there was undoubtedly a sadness to those posts. Her claims of an idyllic life with her much older 'soulmate' husband had always felt a little too heartfelt. Deena had long been a fascination. One she'd tortured herself with.

The road rose even more steeply for the final few yards, making the last hundred steps or so the toughest. The buttery beige heels and toes of her beautiful shoes were ruined with road grime as well as the grass and mud stains by the time she was at the tall gates, but she'd made it in one piece.

Taking a moment to catch her breath, she noted the hanging wires and broken casing of the CCTV camera that had captured Matt's visit five days earlier. What an absolute—

'Who's there?' a male voice asked, the tone impatient.

Surprised, she took a second to locate the source of the voice: a small metal grille in the stone wall. 'Yes, hi, my name is Nicole Delaney,' she said, stepping closer to speak directly into the intercom. 'I was hoping to talk to Scott Jensen, if he's home?'

There was a long pause. So long that she wondered if that was it, no entry would be granted, then the seven-foot-high wooden gates slowly opened inwards.

## 18

SUNDAY 9 JUNE 2024 – 11 A.M.

Nic stood for at least five seconds after the gates had fully opened, staring up at The Glasshouse. Both startling in its size, and staggeringly beautiful in its simplistic yet epic form, the Jensens' home rose way above her, clinging impossibly to the side of the hill. The scale of it was literally breath-taking. The audacity of such brutal modernism in the tranquil and traditional setting was only to be admired, if not by the neighbours, perhaps, who'd tried and failed to block its construction within an area of outstanding beauty. The Glasshouse was undoubtedly beautiful, although being here felt anything but.

Two enormous glass boxes were stacked one on the other, then raised on stilts, so she had to crane her neck to see the top of the highest one, and above it, clear blue sky was revealed, as if the house were taller than the sheer rock behind.

'Mrs Delaney?' Scott Jensen was leaning over the balustrade of the terrace, a good thirty feet above her, and he was waving. He wore sunglasses, his bald head reflecting the bright light. 'Come on up! Stairs to your right, but watch your step; they're a death-trap.'

His warning was not an understatement. The staircase had no handrails, and no protection from the plunge that fell away to her left as she placed one spiky heel, then another, on the smooth-as-ice granite steps. Each tread was so sleek, they might have been designed with disaster in mind, the gradient dizzying.

She had never been afraid of heights until an incident when she was fifteen had forever linked a walk home along the cliff path near her childhood home with trauma, fear, and then vertigo. She shuddered and kept her eyes firmly down, although tempting glimpses were afforded of the interior of the house when she dared to look: oversized sculptural lights hanging from smooth ceilings, and expanses of white rendered walls cut into the hillside and covered in bold canvases. She stupidly then chanced a quick look back down. The woods near Three Gables were just visible in the distance, but then they became lost amongst the patchwork of fields as the collage began to blur, her head spinning. She forced herself to look only at her shoes, but the steps were rolling beneath her feet, her legs unsteady and lungs painful as she gasped for air, her palms damp as she reached for the non-existent rail. One step at a time. That was all she had to do. Get to the top. Nothing else mattered. Not the sound of the front door opening above her, not the way the small square tips of each stained high heel skated on the granite as she tried to move. Just get to the top. That was it. But she couldn't. She closed her eyes, but that only made it worse.

'Mrs Delaney, are you alright?' Scott Jensen was bare-footed a few steps above her as she opened her eyes. He came down, his hands resting on her shoulders. 'My god, you're white as a sheet! Take my hands.'

Scott went up backwards, her palms gripping his, nails digging into his tanned wrists, but there was no way she was letting go. Not until she was certain she wouldn't fall to her death.

'There,' Scott said, guiding her across the threshold and then closing the glass and chrome door behind him. 'Back on solid ground!'

'I'm so sorry,' she said, immensely relieved to be in the hallway, her pleasure at being 'on solid ground', as he'd said, outweighing any other qualms for now. 'I didn't realise I'd be as bad as that. I generally try to avoid heights.'

'No, it's those steps,' Scott replied. 'I told my wife we should have a barrier installed. They still scare me and I'm used to them.'

So, there *she* was: *Deena Jensen.* If not in person, then in the conversation. *His wife.* Matt's patient. And by all recent reports, her husband's lover of many months.

Nic fought for breath, panic rising again. 'Sorry... Do you think I might have a glass of water? I feel a bit...'

'Yes, of course, but it's a no-shoes house if you don't mind?'

She kicked off her heels by the door, wobbling again as she did so. The floor was mineral-cold on her bare feet, like skimming stones across a glistening sea as she stepped in and out of the pools of sunlight along the long hallway, leaving damp sweaty footprints she hoped Scott wouldn't notice as she followed him. To be inside The Glasshouse was infinitely better than being on the staircase outside, but it was rapidly becoming problematic in a different way. She felt nauseous going deeper into Deena's home. The place Matt had visited, many times, apparently. She was covered in sweat and fighting the urge to leave, even after Scott's surprisingly warm welcome.

Scott Jensen was different than she recalled from the crowded drinks reception at The Trust. Although she hadn't been watching him that night, her attention on his wife. He was maybe five-nine or ten, in his fifties but toned in that gym-bunny, triangular-framed way, thinning hair close-shaven, thick neck tanned above the collar of his branded t-shirt. His physique could be described as squat, but he was lean and his upper arms bulged. He looked like he could handle himself in a fist fight if he needed to, short sleeves rolled back to showcase those biceps, and his nose had been broken, she noticed when he glanced back. He was the kind of man you'd want to keep onside.

'Do you want a beer?' Scott asked as they reached a large open-plan living space. 'I was about to have a cold one, and it's definitely five o'clock somewhere, even if I still have no concept of which time-zone I'm in, or what day it is.'

'Sunday, a little after eleven, and yes, a beer would be great.'

His hospitality was more than she'd expected, given the circumstances, but there was an element of performance in his easy manner. She imagined he could be difficult if crossed, possibly violent too, and he also seemed nervous. It was an odd dynamic, no denying that. In different circumstances, their paths would never have crossed, and she wished they hadn't needed to. All this could have so easily been avoided.

Scott went over to the kitchen and opened a door in the middle of the sweep of smooth units, popping the metal beer caps by hand before he walked back and handed her one, then suggesting they sit down. The seating area was sunken and vast, white sofas arranged around a log burner. They sat either end of the sofa facing a portrait above the unlit fire. To their right was the view, framed by a wall of glass. The terrace beyond was wide and jutting into the blue sky, although she tried not to look out, or think about the drop.

'I guess you must be wondering why I've come,' she said, a draught of cool air whirling across the room from the sliding door to the terrace, which was cracked open, just a little. The room smelt fresh, as if it had been recently cleaned, the cool air as welcome as the cold beer. She took another swig and was about to dive into an explanation of her visit when Scott got there first.

'Shall we save the small talk? Your husband... My wife... Both missing.'

'Yes, exactly. That's why I thought—'

'Sorry, have we met before?' Scott cut in again, looking sideways at her.

'Yes, well, sort of. I was at the opening of The Delaney Family Room, just before Christmas, at The Trust.'

Scott frowned, then realisation dawned. 'Of course, I remember seeing you there now.' He raised his beer bottle to the memory. 'You were wearing a red dress, and your hair was...' He waggled fat fingers from his cauliflowered ear down to his heavy-set neck, indicating the waves she'd had that night.

'Yes, that's right!'

Matt hadn't said a word about her appearance, but of course, his attention had been elsewhere too.

'That was an odd night,' Scott continued as he took another swig of his beer, his wedding band catching the light, a large diamond in it. It was tacky, like the painting above the fire which she'd been trying very hard not to look at. It was of Deena, naked.

'Dee sprang that outing on me,' Scott explained in what sounded like an East London accent. 'She said it might help our cause if we threw some money The Trust's way. As if the consultant fees weren't enough already.'

'Your cause?' she asked, distracted by the painting: Deena's dark nipples, the triangle of pubic hair, those eyes following her. She got up and started to walk around the room on the pretext of admiring the furnishings, her free hand skimming the backs of the sofas whilst she drank her beer.

'We were trying to get pregnant,' Scott replied, watching her from where he was sitting, beer in hand too, his other hand along the back of the sofa. 'I told her it didn't work like that; didn't work at all as it happened.'

'Oh right, sorry,' she said, smoothing the metallic fur of a copper hare on a side table. 'You and your wife were very much in demand that night, as I recall. And Matt said you gave very generously.' She picked up a photo next to the hare, placing her beer down. It was of Scott and Deena's wedding. The dress Deena wore was more suited to a prostitute than a bride, it was so low cut, but she smiled at Scott before placing it back where she'd found it and retrieving her beer.

'Dee always attracts attention when we're out; she's so beautiful. You know... it's weird...'

'What's weird?' she asked, glancing back at Scott as she edged towards the view.

'It's not that you look like Dee, exactly, but there's something...' He was looking at the painting now. 'Do you see it, the similarity?'

She forced herself to look at the painting again. They shared dark hair, of a similar length, and a slim waist, but Deena was curvaceous, with large breasts and pronounced features, dark eyes, long lashes, full lips. Plus, Scott's wife was almost twenty years her junior. 'No, I'm sorry, I don't.'

'I mean, not physically alike,' he added, appraising the portrait of his missing wife. 'Just... similar vibe. Not sure where I'm going with this.'

'No,' she replied, the comparison uncomfortable, to say the least. 'Neither am I.'

'Sorry, Nicole. It's OK to call you Nicole?'

She drank some more beer. 'Nic... that's what everyone calls me.'

'Nic? I like it. I'm Scott, or *Boss*, but never Scotty.'

She laughed, emboldened by his affected ease, or perhaps the beer, and confident enough to then approach the gap in the glass doors to the terrace.

'You like the view?' he asked, getting up and drawing close enough for her to catch his cologne and musky scent. 'Your husband apparently enjoyed it a lot.'

The taste of beer soured in her mouth. She swallowed and tried not to gag as she turned to face him. 'That's not fair.'

'Isn't it? I assume by now you know they were fucking?' Scott asked. 'Deena told me just before I left for my business trip, couple weeks ago. Fabulous timing, as always.' He gave an apologetic smile. 'Sorry, that was crass of me; this must be a nightmare for you too. Any news on your bastard husband?'

'I haven't heard from Matt since Friday morning,' she replied, stepping sideways to move away from Scott and the view. The drop from the terrace was even more terrifying close up, and with only a clear waist-high balustrade, it looked wide open. Scott was a man DC Pemberton had admitted she wouldn't mess with. This was madness.

She retreated to the safety of the sofa, setting her beer down on the chrome table beside her, next to a lamp that had the legs of a flamingo. The Jensens' taste in décor was frankly hideous. But money couldn't buy class.

'I haven't spoken to Dee in days,' Scott told her, still standing. He looked too agitated to sit, circling now as she had. 'She hasn't been to the gym either, or to get her hair done, or nails, or that waxing shit she's always having, not any of her usual appointments. The cleaning company came on Thursday, never saw her. The police say they're turning every stone, but I've got my guy on it too.' Scott shrugged, as if that was a normal thing to do. 'I hope they're found, for both our sakes, but then I'll happily kill your husband with my bare hands.' Scott had stopped a couple of paces from where she sat. He was regarding his beer bottle in his hand as if he might crush it. 'Sorry, but he's been fucking my wife for months. I can't let that go unpunished, can I?'

'Can you stop using that word?'

'*Fucking?*' he asked, unrepentant. 'Makes it ten times worse that she was his patient, doesn't it?'

'My husband's not here to defend himself, so—'

'Is there any defence to that? It happened, Nic, get over it.'

'Matt was preparing his defence for a tribunal. It's only her word, and... I'm keeping an open mind.'

Scott gave her a look, the same one she'd spotted on Pemberton's face when she'd left Police Headquarters the day before. A mix of pity and contempt, and in Scott's case, a dash of menace too.

'My team of lawyers are shit-hot,' he said, tipping the beer to his lips then dropping the empty bottle into a huge potted palm back by the glass sliding door. 'Oh, and you know his secretary walked in on Dee giving him a fucking blow job?'

She recoiled, running her hand along the back of her neck as she got up. She was way out of her depth with Scott, and so was Matt. She needed to get out of here, once she'd done what she came here to do.

'The old biddy, Plum or whatever her stupid-arse name is, covered for him for months.' Scott gave her another pitying look across the room. 'I mean, sure, I tolerate a lot from Dee, she's worth it, let's face it...' He glanced over at the painting. 'But that's taking the piss, ain't it? And as far as the good doctor is concerned... he can go fuck himself!'

She walked in the direction of the hallway, unsteadily,

explaining she should probably leave, but Scott halted her halfway across the room, his hand catching her arm.

'Nic, I'm sorry. I'm being an arse and you don't deserve it. This isn't your fault, but in *my* defence, I just got back from a rough two-week trip and I'm worried sick where the fuck my wife is, OK?'

She reciprocated Scott's sympathetic smile as he dropped his grip on her and backed off, hand to his bald head. He looked so lost.

'Yes, and I'm worried too, about Matt.'

'Course you are. He's your husband, I get that. You married long?'

'Twenty-six years.'

Scott whistled in admiration, or maybe he was patronising her. 'Good marriage?'

'I really should go. Our daughter might need me.'

'You can't leave without seeing the view,' he said, grinning now. 'Come on, Nic, house rules. You made it this far. Come, take my hand!'

A scent of pine and heat flooded her senses as she took a tentative step onto the terrace, Scott's broad hand gripping hers. Even the thought of that drop was enough to trigger her vertigo, his apologies when he saw her expression coming with an insistence she should at least try. He was a bully, no doubt about that. But maybe a charming one.

'Been travelling for a couple weeks in Asia, Africa, US,' he told her, dropping her hand to cross the wide decking before leaning back against the clear barrier. His hands gripped the edge of the Perspex although it looked like he was grasping thin air. Her breaths came short and sharp; she was close to a panic attack.

'I was due to travel home on Friday,' he explained, oblivious to her distress. 'But I was delayed by a day. I tried to get in touch with Dee, been trying for a few days, in fact. I thought she was sulking about me not being around for any last-minute legal stuff that came up before the tribunal next week. She was worried she'd have to give evidence in person. I told her I'd be back before then. Then she stopped answering my calls. Now I blame myself; if I'd been home Friday as planned, she might have still been here.'

She nodded, not trusting herself to speak without throwing up all over the decking. That drop was so close, and it was such a fall, and Matt had gone missing on Friday. Scott must be making that connection too.

'Dee is...' Scott continued. 'Well, let's just say she had a tough time when she was younger. Really tough. It's made her very insecure. I think that's why she told me about her and Matt fuc— Sorry, about the affair.' He grimaced. 'It was to provoke me into cancelling my trip, but I had stuff to take care of, and she won't travel with me. Scared of flying. Like I said to her, it's only couple of weeks. She can be moody, blanks me, that's nothing new, but she's always here when I get home. Whatever's gone down. It's kind of a deal we have.'

'Deal?' she asked, breathless as he beckoned to her and she slowly edged closer to the edge. It had to be done. She just needed to get to the barrier, and she was within touching distance now.

'I allow her a certain... *flexibility*, shall we call it? You're really scared of heights, aren't you?' he remarked, finally clocking her terror. 'What's the issue, something happen when you were a kid?'

'Yes,' she replied, startled by his perceptiveness, although she didn't want to explain the real reason now. 'I lived near a cliff edge as a child. My father drilled a fear of falling into me from a young age.'

'I think he succeeded!' Scott said, then he swept his hand out to encompass the view as she gripped tight to the Perspex, as if her life depended on it. 'So, what do you think?' he asked. 'Worth it?'

She lifted her eyes, and instantly it was as if she was soaring, gliding out into the endless blue, but the view was blighted by the past, images of Matt and Deena, and that cliff-top walk home that ended her innocence at only fifteen years of age. She couldn't breathe. She turned and ran back, Scott dashing after her as she wrenched the sliding glass door wide open. The wind followed them in and lifted a pile of papers on the coffee table and scattered them around the sitting room.

'Can you close the door?' Scott asked, running after the paperwork. 'Bloody snail mail! I told 'em, email it! Save the fuckin' planet!'

She slid the door shut, fingertips all it took, the act cathartic as the glass solidified, a barrier she pressed her palm flat against. A satisfying print was left behind, then she helped Scott gather the scattered papers. They looked like official documents and invoices. Very like the ones Matt had shown her.

'Dee blamed me for the infertility stuff, you see,' Scott said, securing the papers under his laptop on the coffee table. 'But I've already got two grown-up kids, so I don't think I'm the one with the problem, right?'

'I'm not sure it works like that,' she replied, but he was distracted then, searching for something on the large coffee table. He located a phone under the collected papers and stared at the screen whilst she looked at Deena's portrait again, tormenting herself this time with images of Deena pressing that nakedness to Matt. Although she'd found no tangible trace of Matt's presence in her time here. Not a stray hair or a discarded cigar. *Nothing.* And she'd been looking since the moment she arrived. Scouring the place for evidence of Matt's last visit.

'The truth is, I didn't really want another child,' Scott said, making her jump as he spoke. She turned around and he was close behind her, looking up at the painting too.

'No?'

'Not really, but I agreed to try, as Dee's much younger than me and she really wanted a family. That was the compromise. Have to make those in relationships, don't you?' He didn't look at her for a response, scrolling his phone then with a stubby thumb. 'When it didn't happen, she persuaded me to see some-one, said it must be my age. I'm fifty-two, but turns out, even if we went IVF route, there was no way she could conceive; she's got a faulty womb, I think they call it hostile or something like that?'

She nodded, the all too familiar words striking through her as they had when she'd heard a version of them herself. She'd thought she'd misheard at the time, convinced for many years she had. Doctors didn't know everything, after all. And 'unlikely' didn't mean impossible. It's the hope that kills you in the end; that's what infertility taught her, if nothing else.

'Dee wouldn't accept it,' Scott continued. 'Said *Mr Delaney* would find a way. He was the best there was, her only hope. She was clearly taken with him, but it wasn't until that argument just before my latest trip that I knew for sure, or I'd have...' He paused, typing furiously before he looked up again. 'You know your husband will be struck off for this? Soon as he's found. If I don't get hold of him first!' Scott laughed, a deep, throaty sound.

She tried to join in but couldn't, a smile the most she could muster.

Scott glanced at his phone again. 'Sorry, work stuff has blown up. Excuse me a minute.'

'I was about to leave, actually.'

'Sure, give me a sec and I'll help you down.'

She nodded and Scott left the room, his voice travelling down a corridor on the far side by the kitchen. 'Fuck's sake, Gary. You should have been watching her whilst I wasn't around! Yes, every day! We've talked about this. I pay you for exactly this and you've lost her. Actually, you're fired! Yeah? Well fuck you too, bro!'

She went back to the glass door as Scott's voice faded. She hesitated, then slid the door open again and took a few tentative steps into the bright sun, her bare feet treading carefully as she ran her trembling hand over the chrome surface of a gaudy outside drinks bar situated to her left, against the back wall of the house. It was stocked with champagne, and spirits were lined up behind, slender flutes inverted above.

Scott was right: Matt's career wouldn't have survived the tribunal. Her reckless, cheating husband stood no chance in the face of this thug's money and desire for revenge. Matt would be destroyed by the loss of his medical licence. As untenable a situation for him as losing Three Gables had been for her. No way back.

'Never employ family members!' Scott said, donning his sunglasses as he joined her on the terrace. 'You feeling braver, then?' he asked, grinning.

She *was* feeling braver, but not *that* brave.

'I really should go, but can I ask you something first?'

'Sure.'

'Did your wife ever talk about leaving you?'

'Empty threats,' Scott said, confirming her suspicion the

Jensens' marriage was volatile. He ran his fingers over his stubbled chin. 'That was Dee's style, always the drama, but I'll admit, I was angry when she told me about this latest ding-dong, said a few things I regret, but...' He spun a forefinger at the side of his bald head. 'She does my head in, but I love her to death. Know what I mean? You must do. I mean, they've both cheated on us and we still want them back. Fucking idiots, the pair of us!'

He laughed, but she still couldn't. She wasn't sure she did want Matt back.

'Thanks for the drink, Mr Jensen.'

She walked towards the hallway, eyes averted from the painting as she left the room.

'Wait, Nic, I'll help you down!'

Scott caught up with her and then ran ahead towards the front door, talking as she slipped on her shoes.

'Can we keep in touch, Nic? Or is that fucking weird?' He grinned, then the smile faded. 'I mean, you and I, we're in this fucking unique situation, so may as well knock our heads together until something falls out. Right?'

She considered his request before taking out her phone so they could exchange numbers, which they did, the moment awkward, as if they were setting up a date rather than contemplating bad news.

'Let me know if you hear anything,' he said. 'I'll do the same. And I'm sorry.'

'What for?' she asked, staring down the steps as she tried to face the climb back down.

'Fuck knows,' he said, rubbing his palm over his shaven head. 'We haven't done anything wrong, have we?'

'No,' she replied, removing her shoes again and tucking them under an elbow before tentatively edging herself towards the top step. Her foot found air, her body lurching back, reaching for and finding Scott's outstretched hand as she screamed.

'Woah, steady!' he said, pulling her back towards the house. 'I said I'd help you.'

'I'll manage,' she told him, prickles on her scalp and arms, her shoes still wedged under her left elbow as she tried again, facing the drop before swooning then righting herself.

'OK, let's just take those…' Scott prised her shoes away from her and took her hands, his grasp firm as he led her out. They went side by side, step by careful step, arms locked together as if they were doing the most surreal country dancing she had ever experienced. She couldn't look ahead, or too far down, her focus firmly on her bare toes as they curled round each glassy step, her grip on Scott even tighter than on the way up, his right hip bone pressed to her left. An intimacy she found both necessary and comforting, as was his solidity and strength.

'You should get a handrail,' she said as Scott handed over her shoes at the bottom.

'You reckon?' he asked, tone sarcastic as he flexed his square hands which she'd squeezed so tight, it must have hurt. 'Dee said it would spoil the look, but hardly worth risking a fall for.'

'No,' she replied, raising her eyes to the terrace and then quickly back down. 'Sorry, are your hands OK?'

He laughed, shaking them out again. 'They've seen worse than that!'

'Well, thank you, you've been very kind, considering.'

'Take care of yourself,' he said, sunglasses on as he sprinted back up, pausing halfway up to brandish his phone. 'We'll keep in touch, OK?'

She waved, balancing on one foot then the other as she brushed the soles of her feet before pushing her toes into the points of her ruined shoes. Then she smoothed her ponytail and put on her sunglasses. She'd done what she came to do and the gates were opening to let her out. Time to go.

Just before the gates fully closed behind her, she looked back, taking a final glimpse through the gap. Scott was leaning over the side of the terrace again, looking down, not a trace of a smile on his face, his expression grim. A man not to be messed with.

## 19

SUNDAY 9 JUNE 2024 – 12.30 P.M.

Grace wiped the sweat from her brow as she basted the crisping leg of lamb. Lord alone knew why she was cooking a roast lunch. It was almost thirty degrees, but Ed liked a proper Sunday dinner, as he called it. His slight figure moved up and down the back garden as he mowed their small patch of lawn. Both of them were clinging to scraps of normality in an ocean of worry and panic, the sweet smell of cut grass wafting in.

The trouble was she couldn't stop going over the conversations that had taken place between her and Matt about Deena. Had she totally misread the situation? Had it been more than an affair between doctor and patient? Had he loved Deena Jensen and decided to run away with her? Had she, however well-intentioned, relied on her brother to make a choice that he had resisted until it was too late?

* * *

'She's not really my patient...' Matt had told her when he'd first confessed to an affair, exhaling cigar smoke into the bare branches of Nic's memorial trees on Christmas day. The Christmas lights inside Three Gables were looking sadly unfestive through the drizzle. Like a melancholic watercolour painting. 'I only saw her for an initial consultation, sis, then I quickly referred her.'

'Oh for goodness' sake, Matt! I thought after last time you'd have learnt your lesson.'

'Thanks for dragging up ancient history,' he'd replied. 'Two lapses in decades of faultless professional practice is hardly—'

'Two is two too many, Matt,' she had told him, feeling bolder for the surfeit of champagne she'd used to wash down the dry turkey. 'You have to end it with this woman, you know that, don't you?'

'Yeah, I will. Soon.'

'When?' she'd asked, refusing a puff on his cigar and stamping her feet to keep warm. She'd felt nauseous, maybe due to the champagne, or perhaps her complicity in another of her brother's dirty secrets. It had been a strained Christmas.

With her professional hat on, she would have loved to sit Matt and Nic down and begin an honest conversation about Nic's ongoing mental health issues, but family didn't work like that. At least, not theirs. Nic was so obviously struggling, it was impossible to enjoy the 'perfect' Christmas Day her sister-in-law had worked her socks off to provide. A frozen turkey at home with Ed and Elan and a few crackers would have been more fun, maybe, but she had so looked forward to seeing her perennially busy brother. He'd been elusive for most of December, and now she knew why.

'I know I should never have gone there – Deena, I mean,' Matt had said, cold air exhaled between puffs. 'That's her name. Deena Jensen. But it's been a shit time, Gracie. You must have noticed? And frankly, I'm sick of coming home to find my wife crying. She's barely functioning. We aren't even... I needed something for me; is that so hard to understand?'

'You're seriously blaming this affair with a patient on your wife's struggles with poor mental health?' she'd countered, voice raised, then lowered as Nic had waved from the patio door. 'Nic is ill.'

'The cancer is gone!' Matt had said, angry then, or maybe just frustrated. 'She's bloody lucky.'

'Yes, I know that... But the hard stuff, the hidden away stuff, that's clearly still there. She needs you. She's been through hell. All those dreams of motherhood...' She'd looked up at each tree, Matt's eyes remaining firmly on the frozen ground. 'I don't think she ever processed the fact she wouldn't have a child of her own, and the hysterectomy just dredged it all up again.'

'I'm sorry, I don't see the issue; she was way beyond childbearing age.'

'I'm sure you don't, but this isn't about how old Nic was, or if she still needed her womb. A hysterectomy is a turning point for any woman. No going back... Jeez, you're the gynaecologist; maybe try and show some empathy? And end things with this Deena, now! Apart from anything, you could lose your job!'

'Yes, of course,' he'd said, trampling the cigar butt into the muddy lawn as they walked back to the house. 'As soon as Christmas is over.'

\* \* \*

But he hadn't ended the affair with Deena. Not in January, nor February, or the intervening months, instead fobbing her off whenever she asked, and then it was June and he was at her door last Tuesday asking for money because he'd left it too late, and with disastrous consequences.

'Deena wouldn't take no for an answer. I tried, I swear. I stopped taking her calls, ignored her messages. That's why she's lashed out, and he's got a whole team of lawyers.'

'Who has?'

'The husband, Scott, and he's loaded and an absolute fucking head case.'

Matt had been pacing her kitchen, as she did now, the fatty basting spoon still in her hand as she went over that last conversation with her brother again, tormented by her part in it all.

'He threatened me,' Matt had told her.

'Who did, the husband?'

'Yeah, Scott Jensen. He turned up at The Trust, couple of months ago. He said if I went near his wife again, he'd kill me. Then this guy called Gary – he works for Scott – started following me in his beat-up old Merc, and he threatened me too.'

'Oh my god, Matt! And yet you still kept seeing her?'

'Deena swore she'd told Scott he'd got the wrong end of the stick, nothing was going on, Gary was just making sure, and if we were careful...'

She hadn't known whether to kill Matt or wrap her arms around him. 'Are you in danger? Is this Gary outside now?' She'd run to the sink and looked over her potted herbs to the quiet cul-de-sac. Just an ordinary Tuesday morning in late May. No sign of a thug in a Mercedes, or anyone else as she recalled.

'No, it's fine, or it will be. I'm going to speak to Gary, give him something to leave me alone.'

'No!' she'd told him, turning back. 'He could be violent; you mustn't.'

Matt had shaken his head, as if she were being ridiculous. 'I can deal with him, but I need this complaint to go away. And to do that, I need your help.'

'OK,' she'd said, sitting him down again at the kitchen table and taking his hands in hers. 'But I need the truth, all of it. What are we dealing with here, complaint-wise, because if it's just your word against Scott's, then surely...?'

Matt had pulled away and run his hands through his curly hair, and that's when she'd noticed his steady surgeon's hands were trembling.

'Matt?'

'Plum, mad old bat, thinks she saw something between me and Deena, and she's going to testify to that.'

'You were in your consulting room with Deena? You absolute idiot!'

Matt had ignored her shock and carried on. 'I thought I'd convinced Plum she'd got it all wrong, but Scott's lawyers must have got to her. It wasn't what she thought.'

'What did Plum witness?' she'd asked, her hands trembling too, but mainly because she was angry.

'Oh god, this is mortifying,' Matt had replied, avoiding eye contact. But then he'd looked up and asked her, 'You really want me to say it, Gracie?'

The timer pinged and returned her to the Sunday dinner preparations. Ed had finished the lawn now and was trimming the edges with the shears. He raised a hand when he noticed her and she smiled back. Then she prodded the lamb with a fork and concluded it needed another few minutes. She didn't care for bloody meat.

A cloud of steam dampened her already sweaty face and stung her eyes as she opened the oven door and slid the tray back in. The nature of the allegation against Matt was indeed mortifying, but it wasn't her humiliation to bear; it was her brother's. She'd made him accept that much, grudgingly, although he'd still maintained it was mainly a misunderstanding on Plum's part. Either way, she'd transferred hers and Ed's life savings to her brother and that was the last she'd seen or heard of him, or the money.

Her mobile phone rang. The number was displayed this time, which made a change. The pranking kids and the parade of weirdos usually withheld theirs.

'Hello?' she asked tentatively as Ed came in through the patio doors.

'Yeah, hi,' the male caller said. 'The poster said there's a reward for information about the doc?'

'Who is this?' she asked, avoiding Ed's mimed pleas for her to hang up after he'd removed his gardening gloves and tucked them under his elbow.

'My name's Gary. I work for... Never mind. Look, I know the doc and I think I know where he's hiding out.'

'Give me that!' Ed grabbed the phone and ended the call.

'But I need to talk to them!' she said, reaching out. 'I think they might be genuine.'

'The police said not to engage and you promised me.'

'This one sounded different, though. He gave me his name, said he'd seen—'

'Listen,' Ed said, handing the phone back. 'The police know what they're doing. They can filter calls. Decide what's genuine. We shouldn't have got involved. Those posters, your number everywhere, it was a mistake. I'm going to collect them all up, put a stop to this. It's clearly pointless and it's upsetting you.'

Tears sprouted so fast, she had to put the phone down and press the oven gloves to her eyes to stem them.

'Hey, hey,' Ed said, patting her shoulder. 'This is just as much my fault. I'll go out after lunch and take the posters down. That should stop any more crank calls, OK?'

She nodded. 'Thanks, Ed.'

'Good, now I'll just go over that patch beside the fence again, if I've time before lunch?'

'Yes, perfect.'

Ed returned to the back garden, the whirr of the mower assuring her she wouldn't be overheard as she retrieved her phone from the counter and pressed redial. She needed to speak with this man, Gary, because she recognised that name.

There was no answer, and just a generic message. She'd try again later, but if it was the same Gary that Matt had said was following him, at Scott's behest, then maybe the caller really had met 'the doc'. And maybe he knew where Matt was hiding out. Hope at last! Although her heart sunk as she then wondered if any good could come of finding this man Gary.

## 20

SUNDAY 9 JUNE 2024 – 4 P.M.

Nic was jolted awake from a deep sleep by loud knocks at the front door. She was on the sofa and it was almost four when she checked the clock on the sitting room wall. Two hours since she'd got back from The Glasshouse to the silent treatment from Lily and with a thudding head. She'd taken two codeine, which always knocked her out. The knocks came again, jolting her to her feet.

'OK, OK! I'm coming!' she said as she crossed the hallway, glancing up to see if the thuds had also roused Lily, but there was no sign of her.

She opened the stiff front door and raised a hand to shield her eyes from the late-afternoon sun. 'Oh, hi, it's you.'

DC Pemberton was leaning against the wooden post that held up the porch, a casual pose. 'Yes, sorry to disappoint you, and just to state up front, no news of Matt's whereabouts.'

'You could have called to tell me that!'

'Yes, I did, twice.'

'Oh right, yes, sorry, I must have missed that,' she said, taking her phone from her bag and seeing the missed calls from the detective stacked up on her screen. 'I had a migraine so I took some codeine. They always wipe me out.'

On reflection, it had been stupid to detach, even temporarily, but it wasn't just her headache. The loneliness had been crushing, worse than if she'd actually been alone in the house. Lily had only said one thing to her when she'd got home, an impolite request to leave her alone, so she had, leaving her phone in her bag as she'd collapsed on the sofa and closed her eyes, just for a moment.

'Few things I'd like to discuss, if you're up to it?' the detective said.

'Yes, of course, come in. I'll make some coffee.'

'Lily home?' the detective asked, following her through to the kitchen and pulling out a chair from the table then sitting down.

'Yes, she's in her room. Shall I get her?'

'No need,' Pemberton replied, searching her satchel bag. 'Just checking she's OK. Tough time, for you both.'

'Yes, very. Lily isn't talking to me, in fact.'

'Oh, why's that?'

'Not sure. Someone to blame, I guess?' she replied, wondering if that were true.

Pemberton looked up from the notebook she'd retrieved and was consulting. 'Why would she blame you?'

'I'm her mother,' she replied. 'Everything's my fault. Milk, sugar?'

'I don't suppose you have any oat milk? Or soy?'

Nic opened a cupboard, then the fridge, and stared blankly inside. They were usually bursting with supplies, organic produce from the farm shop, waxed paper bundles of meat from the butchers in town, but there wasn't much there at all, despite a stop off at the supermarket after The Glasshouse to justify her excuse to Lily for leaving the house. She hadn't even put the shopping away and could barely remember what she'd shoved in her basket. And Lily hadn't left her room.

'Sorry,' she said, rinsing a couple of mugs. 'Lily flirted with veganism, but you know, just a fad at that age.'

'Not a fad for me, I'm afraid. I'll have it black.'

'Yes, sorry, course.' She filled the cafetière but plunged too soon, two grainy but weak black coffees placed on the table between them as she sat down. Standards were slipping, and as she had always suspected, it was a very greasy slope. The terrible coffee scalded her tongue as she took a sip. 'How's the search going – any leads?'

'I might ask you the same.' Pemberton's thumb was clicking a pen on and off. On and... off. The detective then lifted her notepad and cracked the spine, closing it with a snap of her pressed palms.

Nic blanched, the coffee she'd just swallowed regurgitated into the back of her throat. The police pocketbook was a powerful threat, especially to a fifteen-year-old girl caught drunk on the beach by the village police officer. She wasn't quite so impressionable these days, of course, but she wished she could refer to her notebook too. The latest one was still tucked away in her bag, on the table in the hall, with her phone. She wiped her mouth with the back of her hand. 'Sorry, I don't understand your meaning?'

'I think our paths may be crossing,' Pemberton replied, picking up her mug. 'I was up at The Glasshouse earlier, just missed you, I believe.'

Nic put down her mug. The spider's web was criss-crossing. She needed to be careful she didn't end up the fly, caught in its threads.

'Why did you visit Scott Jensen, Nic?'

'I wanted to... to liaise, I suppose.'

'Liaise?'

'Yes, to find out what he thought, and if he knew anything, about... I mean, we both have a missing spouse, so I wanted to pool our thinking.'

DC Pemberton lifted her chin then rested it on her free hand. 'That was a bad idea. You need to leave the investigation to us.'

'I can see it might look like I'm meddling,' she replied, pressing her hand to her lips and rubbing at non-existent lipstick. 'But I wasn't trying to compete with your investigation; I simply wanted to hear his thoughts.'

'I already told you, he thinks his wife has run off with your husband. Is that what you think too?'

She had no idea how to reply. Should she say yes, it had always been her fear Matt might leave her, or was it time to share their late-night discussion when he'd suggested he fake his own death to defraud the insurance company? Or that maybe he was running away from an imminent tribunal which would almost certainly strip him of his medical licence, which by his own admission was his *raison d'être*? None of those theories would help his cause, or possibly hers, but what *would* help now? She coughed, then found she couldn't stop.

'Are you OK?' Pemberton asked, putting her mug down.

'Sorry, I...' She ran to the tap, not bothering with a glass, the flow tepid as she scooped it up and gulped it down.

Pemberton got up too, watching with concern from the other side of the kitchen. 'Did you choke on something?'

She shook her head, unable to speak. She'd found a glass amongst the filled sink and began filling it, but the coffee grounds from the dirty water were in the bottom and made her cough again, spluttering as she said, 'I'm alright, just...'

Pemberton went back to her seat at the table and waited until she joined her, checking then that she was OK to proceed before she said, 'It's clearly very distressing for you to consider your husband might have left you to be with Mrs Jensen, but as I said to you yesterday, that may be a preferable outcome to the alternative.'

She remained silent, still not trusting herself to speak, although the urge to cough had passed, at last.

'OK, let's move on for now,' Pemberton said, picking up her notepad. 'I've been doing a bit of digging into your husband's financial situation.'

'That's my financial situation too!' she replied, finding her voice. 'Sorry, but are you allowed to do that?'

'Yes, we are. The search this morning found a number of outstanding bills, and your sister-in-law told me she has recently leant Matt thirty-five thousand pounds.'

'Yes, she told me that too.'

'And yet you didn't tell me?'

'I assumed you already knew; you seem to have a hotline to her.'

Pemberton sighed. 'Grace has been most helpful. She also said Matt suggested selling the house, but you outright refused to even consider it.'

She took a breath to calm herself; the extent of Grace's meddling was hard to swallow. 'Matt said things were a bit tight, but he also said it would be fine, no need to sell.' She tried not to, but she couldn't help but then glance to her trees. 'I would have agreed to it though, if needed, but he assured me it wasn't.'

'I asked you on Friday evening if there were any financial concerns,' Pemberton said. 'You mentioned none of this.'

'I'm sorry, Lily's boyfriend's mother was within earshot. Amber is the worst gossip. I was embarrassed.'

'You've had ample opportunity since then. Isn't finding Matt more important to you than saving face?'

'Yes, and I should have said, but I suppose in the back of my mind, if I'm honest, I was also trying to make sure that when he does come back, his reputation has remained largely intact, for all our sakes.'

'I doubt that's going to be possible, and having taken a deep dive into your husband's bank accounts and credit cards, I have to say, it puts a whole new slant on things.'

'Well yes, there are some issues, and financial concerns due to the extortionate legal fees, but it's not such a big deal that we needed to sell.'

'This a very big deal! Are you not aware of the level of debt?'

'Matt takes care of the finances but he assured me it was manageable.'

'Well I'm sorry to tell you that's not the case.' Pemberton flicked through her notepad, finding a page. 'Right, yes, so over the last three months, Mr Delaney has burned through over three hundred thousand pounds.'

'No, that can't be right! We don't spend anywhere near that!' She couldn't compute the scale of it. It couldn't be right? Could it? Matt had told her they were in trouble, but a few thousand in legal fees was the extent of it, as far as she knew.

'Yup, his credit cards are up to their limits, a recent remortgage... An overdraft...' Pemberton continued. 'He was in debt up to his neck. I'm surprised your cards are still working.' Pemberton looked at the supermarket bags on the kitchen counter. 'Separate accounts?'

'Um, yes, separate accounts, separate cards too. Matt transferred funds over when I needed them, but nowhere near that figure.'

'Yes, I've seen the regular bills and relatively small sums paid to you,' Pemberton conceded, consulting her notes again. 'But the bulk of the funds were transferred to an account in the name of Miss D L Jones.' The detective paused. 'Deena Jensen's maiden name? Deena Jones.'

She shook her head, stunned by it all. 'I swear to you, I had no idea about any of this. Why would he pay her all that money?'

'An initial transfer of seventy-five thousand in early April,' Pemberton read, as if she'd asked for a breakdown of the payment schedule rather than a justification for transferring every spare penny they'd had to a multimillionaire's wife. 'Which is when the alleged incident between them at The Trust took place. Followed by forty in mid-April, then three transfers of thirty-five through May, then a final amount of thirty thousand last Tuesday. A quarter of a million, exactly,' the detective concluded, looking up from her notes. 'The only amount your husband retained himself was five thousand of the thirty-five thousand loan from your sister-in-law, which was withdrawn as cash last Tuesday. I'm thinking maybe for travelling expenses?' Nic shook her head. 'Five thousand can buy you a ticket pretty much anywhere, I guess. Maybe not first class, not that I've ever... You haven't located his passport as yet, I suppose?'

'No, it's not here.'

A lump lodged in Nic's throat, so painful she thought she might pass out if she couldn't swallow it. Matt had given all their money to Deena Jensen. Risking their home. The home she'd told him she couldn't leave. Then *he'd* left anyway, and without a word, other than a couple of cryptic messages that now felt more like threats, and with debts that were so huge, she'd quite possibly have no choice but to sell up. Even that might not be enough to dig her out of such a deep hole. She had no idea.

She got up and unlocked the patio doors, ignoring the detective's query about where she was going. She needed to see her trees. Even if she couldn't go down to them, just to see them might help. Three trees for three lost chances, gently swaying at the end of the garden in the late afternoon sun. Three babies she'd loved more than life itself, but never held, never even had a funeral for. Matt had been the one who'd suggested they plant the memorial fruit trees. A rare moment of tenderness and empathy from her logical and sometimes emotionally remote husband. She knew he'd suffered too, but since Lily's arrival, it felt as if she grieved alone. Matt knew what the trees meant to her, and how hard it would be to leave them, but surely he'd also known he was more important to her than any house or trees or even babies?

'I found the frequent transfers quite perplexing,' Pemberton said as she stepped onto the patio too. Nic glanced across. The detective's curls were buffeted by the wind as she stared straight ahead. 'I mean, it makes sense, paying Deena to try and keep the affair hush-hush,' Pemberton continued, undeterred by her lack of response. 'But there are some aspects of this case I just don't get. Like the fact your husband transferred further sums, post-complaint, right up until three days before he vanished. The cat was out the bag by then, but OK, maybe Deena promised she could still get Scott to call off the dogs – just to mix up my cat and dog metaphors!' Pemberton smiled at her own joke, holding back a particularly disobedient lock of corkscrewed dark hair as Nic caught her eye. 'But why Deena wanted the money in the first place, that's a head-scratcher. Scott Jensen is worth literally millions, so why would his wife demand money from Matt which she could easily get from her own husband? Scott never refused her anything: clothes, car, jewellery. Unless she wanted to leave him, of course? That kind of makes sense if she needed the funds to start over? I'd imagine he's the kind of man who'd make it hard to make the break if it wasn't what he wanted, don't you think?'

She shrugged, although she knew exactly what the detective meant.

'Or perhaps Deena wanted to take away everything you have? If she couldn't have Matt then she was out to spite you?' Pemberton returned her gaze until she looked away. 'Anyhow, it's good old-fashioned extortion whichever way you stand it up, wouldn't you say?'

'Yes, I would,' she responded icily. 'No other word for it.'

They went back inside and she made better coffee from the Nespresso machine. She'd have preferred to pour wine but didn't feel it was appropriate, and the strong brew helped some as she drank it straight down.

'Right!' Pemberton said, flicking through her notepad again as if they were resuming a business meeting across the kitchen table. 'So the tribunal was due to go ahead this coming Tuesday?' Pemberton asked, pausing to glance up at the ceiling. There was no sign of Lily, but her music had returned, reliably loud.

'Yes, so I believe.'

'Yes, it was. I double-checked with the General Medical Council rep who advised me of your husband's suspension,' Pemberton replied, reading her notes again. 'So if the money passed to Deena was a continuing effort to suppress the complaint, it clearly hadn't worked.'

'No...Clearly not.'

'But you knew about the debts?'

'No, I've told you! I had no idea of the extent of it at all; Matt played it down to me.'

'I'm sorry, I still find that hard to believe. I've seen your signature on the remortgage document. You knew you were in trouble back in March when you signed up for the extra funds, almost fifty thousand.'

'Matt told me refinancing was prudent, to release equity and pay off the credit card debt I'd amassed over Christmas.'

'Your husband allowed you to feel solely responsible for your financial hardship when he was soon passing the money straight across to a patient of his with whom, according to his own sister, he'd been conducting a consensual and passionate love affair since Christmas?' Pemberton's tone was scathing. 'Wow!'

'No, you're twisting what happened. I know I wasn't solely at fault, but Matt was right. I do spend too much.'

Pemberton pushed back the same curl from her face. 'This isn't your fault, Nicole. And Matt saying it was sounds like gaslighting to me.'

'No, Matt was never like that.'

Pemberton folded her arms. 'That's what's known as coercive behaviour. Pure and simple.'

'I wasn't there for him. I should have been more understanding, more aware. A better wife.'

Pemberton shook her head. 'Anyway, the money hasn't been touched.'

'The money he paid to Deena, you mean?'

'Yup. It's all still in her sole account. Every penny. The whole quarter mill.'

'Then why take it? Why break us?'

'I guess because she could?' Pemberton said, shrugging before she closed her notebook. 'I should get going.'

Nic led the way to the door, opening it to allow the detective to leave. Pemberton stepped out into the warmth, then paused beneath the porch. 'Oh, there was one thing I did want to share with you, about your husband's BMW.'

Her pulse quickened. 'Yes?'

'I've requested a more detailed report,' Pemberton explained. 'But traces of blood have been found in the boot.'

Fear lodged hard in the cavity of her chest, her stomach constricting so she could barely form the words as she asked, 'Whose blood?'

'I'll get back to you as soon as I have more information. We need to see if the samples we've captured throw up a match with DNA we're cross referencing.'

'You mean the DNA you took here, Matt's toothbrush and hairbrush?'

'Yes, that's part of it; I'll get back to you once I know more.'

'You think Matt was hurt in the crash, don't you?' she asked, holding on to the open door for support. 'That's the only logical explanation, isn't it?'

From the corner of her eye, she detected movement, turning back to see that Lily was sitting on the bottom stair, knees to chest. Her daughter was out of sight of the detective, but must have heard every word they'd exchanged.

'Too early to say,' Pemberton replied. 'But I'll keep you updated on our findings. Oh, and I finally got the chance to go to the cake shop.'

'Sorry?'

'The patisserie. Your daughter's birthday cake was never picked up. They offered it to your sister-in-law yesterday when she called in with one of her posters, but Grace refused the cake and it was about to go out-of-date, so I took it for my kids. Hope that was the right call? I don't eat dairy, but they will hoover it up, all that refined sugar.'

'Yes, absolutely. No point wasting it.'

Pemberton smiled then turned and walked to her grey car.

Nic closed the door and leant her throbbing head throbbing

against it. When she opened her eyes, Lily was still sitting on the stairs, now sobbing into her hands.

Nic ran to her, attempting a hug, but Lily pushed her away, covering her eyes with her forearm, inconsolable.

'It's OK, Lil, I'm sure your dad is fine. That blood, we don't even know it's his.'

Lily looked up, an expression of abject misery on her face, tears flooding her beautiful eyes as she shouted, 'You don't understand. I've totally fucked up! I've fucked up!'

## 21

Lily wiped a hand under her nose. 'I know I should have said something straight away and now they've found blood in Dad's car and... I should have told the police on Friday night, shouldn't I?'

'Told them what?' Nic asked, just about holding off the urge to shake it out of Lily if she didn't explain soon.

'I saw Dad, in there,' Lily said, glancing to her right, the door to the downstairs cloakroom closed. 'He was washing blood from his hands.'

'What?' Nic asked, taking too long to process this new information. 'When?'

Lily's chest heaved again, another sob before she continued. 'Last Tuesday lunchtime when I got back from my final exam at Brackley. You weren't here, still at your PTA meeting, so Will ran me home, remember?'

'Oh my god. Did Will see your father here too?'

'No,' Lily sniffed. 'He didn't.'

'Good, that's good, but why didn't you tell me before?'

'Dad told me not to,' Lily said, the simplicity of her logic maddening.

'So that's it, he asks you to cover for him and you comply, whatever?'

'He said you'd kill him for buying me a car, but if I kept quiet until my birthday, you'd have to—'

'What are you talking about? We didn't buy you a car.'

'You didn't, Dad did!' Lily shouted, then she sniffed again. 'And then he went missing and I was scared to say anything. I didn't want to make it worse.'

'All the more reason to tell me!'

'OK! I said I'd fucked up. But I'm not the only one, am I?'

'What's that supposed to mean?'

Lily shrugged, crying again.

'OK, let's just calm down and work this out.'

Nic crouched down, a hand on her daughter's jumping knee to try and still the rhythmic bounce which had gained pace. Lily was officially now an adult but in many ways still a stupid little girl who did anything her father asked. There was a lot to unpack here, but the most urgent thing was to find out what Matt had been up to when Lily saw him, apparently washing blood from his hands. But that was most likely from the cut which Nic already knew about, the one in his right palm.

'Take a breath,' she said, cupping both of her daughter's elbows to try and still her. 'Talk me through it. So Will dropped you home at what time?'

Lily's expression turned from defiance to something more akin to guilt. 'Will actually came in, just for half an hour or so, but he'd gone by the time Dad arrived.'

'Got what he wanted and buggered off, did he?' Nic couldn't resist, although she was relieved that Will hadn't been there to see Matt; that would only complicate matters. 'And have you told Will about your father and the blood?'

'No, of course not. I'm not an idiot!'

'OK, good. So Will left and then your dad came home?'

'Yes, but I didn't hear him at first. I'd jumped in the shower after Will left.' Lily had the good grace to look somewhat embarrassed at the obvious connection between the two events. 'I thought I heard something as I got dressed, so I came down, and Dad was in there.' Lily again looked to the cloakroom door. 'Washing off blood and dirt from his hands.'

Nic stood up, trying to work it out. Then she remembered something. 'He'd cut it at work, you know that!'

'That's what we'd agreed to tell you, that it was a nick from a scalpel, but he'd actually cut it in the garage, clearing the floor of broken glass and muck and dust before my car was delivered.'

'Lily, there is no car,' she repeated, frustration creeping in now the dread had diminished, a little. 'I've been out there, with the detective.'

'I saw it!' Lily stood up too and headed to the front door. 'It came on a tow truck whilst I was in the shower and Dad had even arranged for a big bow on top! Come on, I'll prove it to you!'

The gravel dug into the soft arches of Nic's bare feet as they crossed the drive to the double garage. Lily's feet were bare too, but it didn't stop her running ahead with the keys. Lily unlocked then lifted the up-and-over door with relative ease on account of her height. The light came on as they walked in, Lily spinning round as if she might have missed the car she'd was so certain would be in there.

'It was right here!' Lily said, pointing to the swept floor. 'I promise you. A brand new black Golf!' Lily paced the empty spot where the car had supposedly been, as if it might reappear, then she started searching behind the stacked cardboard boxes and eventually produced a crumpled pink bow which she held up. 'This was on top!' Lily told her, triumphant. 'I told you it was here!'

'So where is the car now?' she replied.

'Stolen, I guess,' Lily said, still looking at the bow. '*Shit!* I can't believe that on top of everything else, my car has been stolen by some low life!' Lily threw the bow back behind the boxes then looked over to her. 'What?'

'Nothing... Do you recall the number plate?'

'I didn't notice, but it was brand new!'

'OK, we need to tell the police.' Nic set off back towards the house.

'But I'll be in trouble!' Lily called after her, running out of the garage.

'Is that all you care about?' she asked, the gravel digging in again as she rushed across the drive, Lily at her heels now. 'I only hope we're not too late!'

'Too late for what?' Lily asked, overtaking her. 'You think it was Dad who took it, don't you? But he wouldn't do that. Not to me.'

'Wouldn't he?' she asked as they went into the hallway. 'I think your unfailing faith in your father may be unfounded.'

There was a beat, then Lily replied, ice-cool, 'At least he's my real father.'

Nic had grabbed her phone and was scrolling for the detective's number, but she stopped and looked up. 'What are you talking about?'

'Dad told me,' Lily said, chin jutting.

'Told you what?'

'That he's my biological father.'

'What?'

'You heard!' Lily spat, then she headed for the stairs.

'Don't you dare disappear to your room!'

'So you're not denying it?' Lily asked, running up anyway.

Nic followed, but her legs gave way halfway up. It felt as if there was no blood left in her head, her body empty, her heart missing a beat as she fought for breath. A shadow crossed her; it was Lily leaning over her crumpled body.

'How long have you known?' Nic asked, looking up to her daughter's expression of sheer disdain. She couldn't believe Matt had told her, after everything he'd promised, and after all these years.

'Since he called me Friday morning to wish me a happy birthday.'

'Friday?' she asked, forcing herself to get up from the carpeted stairs and look directly at her daughter. Friday was the day Matt disappeared! 'What time?'

'Is that important?' Lily asked, her face a sneer.

'Yes it's important!' she shouted up. 'It's the last time anyone saw him, you stupid girl!'

Lily's face crumpled.

'I'm sorry, I didn't mean that, Lily, wait!'

* * *

Lily was pulling clothes from hangers and shoving them in the holdall she used for school trips when Nic went into her bedroom two minutes later. She'd heard her on the phone to Will and wanted to give her time to calm down. But not time to pack and then leave.

'Please stop that! We need to talk!'

'Will's picking me up in five minutes,' Lily replied. 'And don't try to stop me!'

'We need to talk about this. Why didn't you tell me?'

'I wanted to speak to you straight away,' Lily said, scrunching a glittery top in her fist then pushing it into her bag. 'I wanted to give you a chance to tell me the whole story from your perspective.' Lily looked up from her frenzied packing. 'I felt sorry for you. Assumed Dad must have cheated on you and you'd done the decent thing, taking me in, and that it was Dad's idea not to tell me he was my real dad, to save you the heartache and humiliation as you're so fucking emotionally weak. But you weren't here, or answering your phone when I got home. Unavailable as always.'

'I was with my therapist,' she replied, her voice small as she leant against the bedroom wall. 'You know I always go to see Connie on Fridays at ten.'

'Ah yes,' Lily said as she went into her ensuite, emerging soon after with her toothbrush and make-up bag. 'The amazing Connie who tells you to write everything down, all your stupid prosaic little musings about *poor* you. How you hate me, how you wish you'd never agreed to raise your husband's love child!'

'What? What are you talking about?' She looked behind her, down the dark landing to the door to the master suite, behind which her filled notebooks were stacked on a high shelf in her section of the dressing room, away from prying eyes, or so she'd thought. 'How dare you go through my things! What have you read?'

'How dare I?' Lily demanded, the green flecks in her eyes flashing anger. 'Aren't you listening? You weren't here! You think I don't deserve some answers too?'

'What have you read?' Nic repeated, panic bubbling through her limbs so fast she could barely stay upright.

'Don't worry, I'm not interested in your self-indulgent crap and endless to-do lists. I flicked through one about your therapist and how much you love her, then I struck lucky, found the motherlode in the second one I looked at!' Lily was taunting her now, and enjoying it, as cruel as her father could be. 'Can you imagine how I felt when I read how you forced my birth mother to give me up?'

'No, that's not true, I never wrote that!'

'How you made Dad promise he'd never tell, the only way he could keep me. How do you think I felt to read all that on the morning of my eighteenth fucking birthday and then have to pretend I wanted a fucking party when all I wanted was my dad, my *real* dad, to come home so I would never have to talk to you again, you fucking psycho bitch!'

Nic sunk to the floor after Lily barged past, packed bag in hand, the sound of her daughter's heavy footfall clattering down the stairs then forcing her into action.

She almost fell as she ran down the stairs, desperate to catch Lily before she left, and to explain to her that whatever she had read was an uncensored account of an imperfect arrangement that had felt like the best solution at the time, given Matt had presented her with an affair and an eight-month pregnancy. The arrangement that led to Lily's adoption was chronicled in the bluntest of terms, and she had never meant for anyone to read it, especially Lily, who'd clearly twisted those words even further. The notebooks were a safe space to vent her feelings; that's what Connie had told her. But how on earth could she expect Lily to understand that she'd loved her nonetheless? She really had!

Lily was at the front door as Nic reached the bottom of the stairs, the stuffed but unzipped bag thrown down so Lily could open the door.

'Lily, please don't leave! We need to talk about this. What I wrote, about your adoption, it wasn't ever meant for—'

Lily headed out, bag in her hand as a sports car approached at speed. Will's car was just like his mother's, the roof down, rap music blaring into the late-afternoon sunshine and blue skies instead of George Michael.

'What do we have to talk about?' Lily demanded, rounding on her as Nic followed her out onto the drive. 'About why Dad finally left you? I think that's pretty clear. No wonder he had affairs. It must have been a nightmare living with you; it has been for me!'

'Please, just listen for a second. You said you wanted to hear my side of the story? Let's do that much. We can go through what I wrote together; let me explain.'

'Yeah, sure... Like maybe explain why you made Dad keep this a secret my whole life!'

'Because I knew it would make me lesser in your eyes, and I already felt like that! Can you imagine how hard it was, to always be the odd one out? You might not be mine biologically, but I've always loved you as if you were, please know that much.'

'*As if!*' Lily roared, her open bag falling into a heap on the gravel as she threw it down, clothes and a toothbrush tumbling out. 'That isn't the same thing, is it?' Lily crouched down, collecting up her belongings. 'Not the same at all!'

'No, I didn't mean it like that. I'm sorry. I'm so sorry—'

'Leave it!' Lily screamed when she tried to help her collect up clothes and underwear to put them back in the bag.

Will had got out of his car and was looking over from where he'd parked, by the open garage. He was wearing board shorts and no top. His lip curled as Nic glared at him. If he dared to say a word, she wouldn't be responsible for her actions.

'I tried so hard with you, Mum,' Lily said, the last word striking through Nic's heart so the tears she'd resisted began to fall.

'I know this must be so hard for you, Lil, and I'm sorry if I've—'

'I really wanted to love you,' Lily said, stepping back as Nic reached out. 'Or even *like* you, but it was never reciprocated, always this barrier between us. And I thought it was because of the babies you'd lost before you adopted me, and I felt sorry for you... I really did.' Lily wiped the back of her hand under her streaming nose and stood up to her full height, holding a hand up to halt Will when he walked over. 'But it all makes sense now. Total sense! Dad said he knew it was selfish of him to call out of the blue on my birthday and tell me the truth, but it might be his last chance and he had to let me know.'

'Last chance?' she whispered, her voice thick with emotion as Will retreated to his car. 'What did he mean by that?'

'I don't know,' Lily said, looking less than certain for the first time since the argument began. 'But he asked me to trust him to come back for me when he's ready.'

'He said that?'

Lily nodded and took a deep juddering breath, fixing her with a green-eyed stare.

'Just for you?' Nic asked in barely more than a whisper.

'Yup, just me,' Lily said, chin jutting again. 'And who can blame him for leaving you? He must have been so sick of your neediness dragging him down. All the lies you made him tell about me and my birth mother. He's probably relieved to be out of this hideous situation of living with a total psycho! I know I will be. Let's go, Will!' she said, heading to his car.

'That's not fair!' she shouted after Lily as her daughter threw her bag in the tiny boot then climbed in next to Will. 'Lily, please, don't go,' she said, reaching the car and holding on to the door. 'Where is my notebook now? Do you still have it? Promise me you won't show it to anyone else!'

'I'll make you one promise,' Lily said, turning to her. 'I'll find her. My *real* mum.'

'*I'm* your mum,' she said, lip trembling.

'*You?*' Lily regarded her with utter contempt. 'You're nothing to me. A haggard shell with your bald patches and emotional breakdowns and the parties where you pretend everything is so fucking wonderful but no one except you enjoys them! You've never been there for me and now I know why; you never wanted me in the first place. I was just a way to trap Dad.' Lily turned to Will and said, 'Let's get the fuck out of here.'

Will didn't need asking twice. The stones on the drive, then the dust on the track, kicked up as they sped away. Nic turned to the house, utterly bereft, but as the sound of car tyres spinning too fast receded, another sound crept in. She stopped and listened for it again. What had she heard? The crunch of a boot on gravel? It might have been her own steps, but then again, she was barefoot. Heart quickening, she ran inside and locked the front door.

## 22

Grace looked past her niece to a very fancy-looking sports car executing a noisy three-point turn in the quiet cul-de-sac. Ed was watching too, stood behind her in the hallway, and she noticed a neighbour who was watering the flower beds, also staring.

'OK if I stay a while, Aunt Grace?' Lily asked, wiping her nose with the back of her hand, the other hand clutching an overly stuffed holdall. 'I've left home.'

'Oh my goodness, what on earth?' Grace asked. 'Yes, come in, of course!'

Ed cupped his niece's shoulder, then wordlessly carried her bag upstairs. They had a spare room, but it was filled with Ed's train set. The girls would just have to share. They could drag the old camp bed out the garage if needs be, but hopefully it wouldn't be for long.

'Right, let's go in my study, shall we?' she told Lily, guiding her niece towards her consulting room. 'I think you and I need a chat.'

Grace muted her phone and then sat Lily in the client chair and took the one facing her. The desk was beside them, by the shuttered window that overlooked the front garden and her nosey neighbour. The chairs had come from Ikea and were comfy and informal, and a low table between them was set with a napkin-covered carafe of fresh water and a glass, ready for clients, and of course, a box of tissues.

'Can you talk to me about what's happened?' Grace asked. She had tried not to fall into her usual pattern of speech when opening a session with a client, but it still sounded like one of her stock openings.

Lily looked up. 'She's not my mum. You and Dad and Elan are my blood, not her.'

Grace paused, choosing her words carefully again. There was clearly no point pretending they hadn't both read Nic's account of the painful set of circumstances that led to Lily's adoption. The offending red notebook was still in Grace's bag, right beside her, but she could barely believe that it was out in the open at last, and that she would be the one to help Lily work out her feelings about a family secret that had been buried for the last eighteen years. That Matt was Lily's biological father.

'I understand that what you read must have been very hurtful to you, but we can't know for sure the full story, or your mother's true feelings, not from those few lines written last summer when, let's face it, she was very unwell.'

'That wasn't how I found out. Dad told me himself, then I went looking for proof and read it in her own words.'

'Matt told you?' Grace asked, leaning forward in her chair. 'When?'

'He called me, Friday morning, then I went home to talk to Mum and when she wasn't there I—'

'He told you the day he went missing!' she said, fingers pressed to her lips.

Lily nodded and pulled on a tissue, wiping her nose. 'I was at

Will's. Dad called first thing to wish me happy birthday, then he just blurted it out.'

'How did he sound?'

'I guess he sounded *normal*? I'm sorry, I should have said something sooner, I know that, but I've been so scared to tell anyone, even you. Mum went ballistic at me when I tried to talk to her; that's why I came here.' Lily plucked another tissue from the box and sniffed. 'She hates me, and I hate her. She's the real reason he's left us, not the tribunal. Dad would have cleared his name. It's her that's driven him away.'

Grace opened her mouth to refute that claim, then closed it again. She wasn't sure how she felt about Nic's culpability in Matt's situation, not yet.

'Elan is going to help me find my real mother,' Lily told her, blowing her nose. 'We know her name from the notebook. She's called Katie Creel. She went back to New Zealand after *Mum* made her give me up.'

'OK, that's enough now!' she said, drawing the line she perhaps should have drawn sooner. 'You need to try and see things from your mother's point of view. Nic's, I mean.'

'Are you joking?' Lily asked, a flash of Matt's temper in her niece's eyes.

Matt wouldn't lose his cool that often, but when he did, it was sudden and fierce, like Lily's now.

'I understand your anger,' she replied, using her reflective counselling skills. 'But I don't believe any of this is why your father is missing, and I don't think you do either, not really.' Lily opened her mouth, but she spoke first. 'What we must do now is call the police and tell them about his call to you on Friday morning. Can you check exactly what time it was?'

Lily took out her phone. 'It was eight fifty-two, and Dad was driving. I could hear the car engine.'

'OK, good,' she replied, looking through her contacts list on her phone for DC Pemberton's number. 'If he was driving, then that means it was before the crash...' She looked up, sensing there was more. 'Lily, what is it?'

Lily had dropped her gaze to her hands, balled tissues in scrunched fists. 'You need to tell them about my car too, I think it's been stolen, maybe by Dad.'

* * *

After Lily had explained about the missing black Golf that Matt may or may not have stolen so soon after its purchase, Grace suggested Lily should go upstairs and see Elan. She would pass all this new, and potentially crucial, information to the police. It was hard to keep the annoyance out of her voice that this was only now coming to light, but she managed to keep calm as she showed Lily out of her study.

She closed the door and immediately called DC Pemberton, but frustratingly, if not a total surprise, the busy detective didn't pick up, her recorded greeting all the response she got. She quickly typed a message asking Pemberton to call her asap as she had new information to share, and then she went upstairs to tell Ed everything that Lily had just told her.

The girls were ensconced in Elan's room, music blaring, door closed. She paused, then walked on towards the spare room where Ed was playing with his trains. She expected his usual benign, comforting acceptance, but when he looked up from the circling locomotives, his expression was furious.

'Ed, what's the matter?'

'Shush!' he said, leading the way into their bedroom. 'You and I need to talk.'

'What's wrong?' she asked the second their bedroom door

was closed. Her immediate thought was that Ed must have checked their joint savings account and found it was empty.

'You knew all along, didn't you?' he said, walking to the window and briefly glancing out. It was a still June evening, the warmth cloying in their over-insulated home.

'Knew what?' she asked, opening the window and buying time to think as Ed sat on the bed.

'About the adoption! It was only because Elan filled me in whilst you were talking to Lily that I know now.'

'Oh that!' she said, sinking onto their bed beside him.

'Yes, what else?' Ed asked, side-eyeing her.

'No, nothing,' she replied, her relief then stolen by another thought. 'So Elan chats to you as well as Lily?'

Ed frowned. 'Yes, sometimes, when it's just the two of us. Is it true that Matt is Lily's biological father?'

'Yes, apparently. Why am I the only one Elan never—'

'When would you have told me?'

'That's what I was coming to talk to you about now!' she replied, still reeling from the fact Elan seemed to talk to everyone in this house but her. Her daughter had said nothing to her, literally nothing, in months. She had assumed that was a unilateral policy, but it seemed not.

'OK, good that you were finally including me,' Ed said, his voice more even. 'But you do cut me out. You know you do. Elan said you confiscated a notebook of Nic's from Lily yesterday, and yet you said nothing about that either!'

'I'm sorry, I was still deciding what to do for the best. Can I please tell you the other thing Lily has just told me?'

'Yes, of course, sorry,' Ed said, taking her hand. 'But blimey, Matt's her real father! Do we know who this Katie Creel woman is?'

'I think she might have been a patient,' she said, and Ed's

eyes widened. 'But listen, Matt bought Lily a car, for her birth-day. It's possible he's stolen it and that's how he drove away from the crash. If we can trace it, we might find him too!'

'What?' Ed shook his head and stood up. 'You need to call the police, give them the number plate of this other car.'

'Lily doesn't remember it, she only saw it briefly, but I've called the detective and left a message.' She held up her phone then fanned her face. 'Should I call Nic, see how she is? Sounds like she and Lily had a terrible falling out.'

'Do you still have her notebook?' Ed asked.

'Bloody hot flushes, back with a vengeance,' she told him as she got up and went to the open window.

'Gracie?'

'Yes, I do still have it, but I was going to return it, I promise,' she said, fanning herself. 'I told you, she literally closed the front door on me. Do you want to read it?'

'No, I do not!' Ed held up his hands. 'I want you to return it to Nic and apologise for this egregious violation of her privacy. I'm surprised I have to say that to you, of all people.'

'Yes, yes, you're right. I shall try again, first opportunity.'

'Damn right! I'd have thought better of you, to be honest, in your profession.' He went to the bedroom door but didn't leave, turning back to tell her, 'When this is behind us, and god willing that brother of yours is found safe and well, we will talk about where I rank in your priorities, because I am your husband and you need to remember that.'

'Yes, of course, and I'm so sorry.'

'Right, good,' he said, offering a tight smile. 'Anything else you want to get off your chest before we declare a truce?'

She opened her mouth to tell Ed about the huge sum of money she'd leant Matt, but it was such a betrayal of trust and on top of the others he'd already called her out on, she just couldn't do it.

'No, nothing.'

'Good!' He grinned. 'Tea?'

'Yeah sure, thanks, I'll be down in a sec; just try the detective again.'

She waited until Ed had gone downstairs, whistling as he went, then she sent a detailed voice note to the busy detective with the few details of Lily's 'stolen' car that she knew – black, brand new, Golf – and telling her that Lily was staying with them now, due to a fallout with her mother. What this all meant for Matt was hard to know, but she had to try and speed up the search.

Grace had always idolised her big brother, but it was getting harder with each new revelation to defend his actions. When they'd been younger, he'd often scared her with his sudden schemes and impossible plans. That was part of the excitement with Matt; you never knew what to expect. He was full of surprises, and not always the good kind. He'd lured her up trees and into bars, palmed her off on friends, then rescued her when things got messy. Her saviour, and her downfall. Her big brother. She loved him so much, it was impossible to ever say no to him.

She could see him now, stood in their hallway the previous Tuesday, his profuse thanks for the loan only just expressed when he'd made another request.

'Can you keep an eye on Lily for me, sis? I'd rest easier knowing you were there for her.'

She hadn't asked why, flattered by Matt's faith in her and assuming he'd asked because Nic wasn't as good a mother as she was, but now it felt like a prescient request. As if he'd known he wouldn't be there himself.

She neatened the bed and then checked her phone. Still no

response from the detective, but she'd missed a call from someone else whilst she'd been lost in her thoughts. Her phone was still on silent after she'd muted it for her chat with Lily.

The number belonged to the man called Gary who'd called at lunchtime in response to the posters. Ed had taken her phone and ended that call, telling her it was just another chancer, but she was convinced this Gary was the same Gary Matt had told her was following him. Scott's henchman.

She pressed redial and cleared her throat as she prayed for Gary to pick up this time. When he did, it took her a moment to find her voice, which she kept low, just in case Ed's whistling in the kitchen stopped. 'Yes, hi, sorry, my name's Grace, Matthew Delaney's sister. You called me earlier, I think you knew my brother. Is that right?'

'You're his sister? I thought you was the wife.'

'You know Nicole?'

'Nah, but I met your bruv.'

She had a million questions, but she didn't want to scare Gary off, so she waited, hoping he would talk, her pulse pounding in her ear against the phone. 'When did you meet Matt?' she asked when he didn't volunteer the information.

'We had an arrangement, but...'

'Gary, you still there?' She held her breath as the silence spun out.

'Look, I changed my mind. I don't need this, it's too complicated; forget I called.'

'Please, don't hang up! I can pay you, more than the poster reward.' She had no idea how she'd raise the funds, but that didn't matter right now. She had to reel him in.

'Nah, I ain't getting involved, not even for five hundred. Not even for five thou, to be fair. I done my best, but if he's done a runner then—'

'Please, Gary, I love my brother.'

There was another long pause. Then he added, 'Nah, listen, this ain't my business, and it's got trouble written all over it. I'm out.'

'Wait! Please, are they together, Matt and Deena, is he at least—?'

But Gary had gone and he ignored her persistent calls, every one unanswered. Then Ed was calling up that the tea was ready, and when she didn't answer, couldn't answer, her voice too full of emotion, he came running up the stairs and into their room.

'Gracie, what is it?' he asked, looking at the phone in her hand.

'I had a call, from someone who'd seen the poster. No, listen, I think he's genuine, Ed, I really do.'

'OK, tell the police. That's all you can do, OK?'

She nodded, keeping the rest secret from her concerned husband. Ed would only try and convince her Gary was lying, when she knew in her heart he wasn't.

This man had met Matt and was somehow mixed up in what was increasingly sounding like a planned escape. But Ed was right; she'd have to trust the police to find Gary. She wouldn't know where to start.

## 23

MONDAY 10 JUNE 2024 – 8 A.M.

Nic woke with a start and immediately gasped. How could it be Monday morning already? The third day since she'd last seen her husband. It was unthinkable and yet true.

In the few fitful snatches of sleep she'd managed, she had suffered the most vivid and terrible nightmares. Tumbling rocks in her brain as she tossed and turned, images already intense, embellished with unbearable ferocity, each flash of chaos and violence crashing in on the next. The presiding one was of blood on Matt's hands. More and more of it, however much he washed it away. Rivers of it cascading from the sink to the cloakroom floor, the lilac birds on the handprinted wallpaper taking flight and swooping around the hallway. Then she recalled the other nightmare, one that had made its unwanted presence known to her many times over the last eighteen years. In this one, Lily's mother was knocking loudly at the front door of Three Gables which then began opening by itself so Katie Creel could snatch baby Lily from her arms; then Katie was running away with Lily into the woods and Nic was running after her but the ground began moving beneath her feet, earth flowing with bones and blood, and there were eyes, watchful between the trees, until eventually the wood swallowed Nic up.

She sat up, exhaustion fogging her brain whilst adrenalin pumped through her body. She grabbed her phone from the bedside chest where it was charging and checked for any messages from Lily. There was nothing from her daughter, but there were a couple from Grace saying 'Lil' was fine and not to worry, she was welcome to stay as long as she needed, and then expressing concern about the stolen car. She ignored Grace and tried DC Pemberton again, but the busy detective's voicemail was still the only response. How on earth did she run an investigation when she was never available? But like the NHS, the police service was a stretched public resource; she probably had multiple cases she was pulled between. Matt wasn't the detective's only priority.

She lay back and scrolled the local news app and social media. There was nothing new about Matt, public interest already waning, and no mention of Deena. She paused, then tapped her therapist's number. Connie was invariably busy, like DC Pemberton, but to Nic's surprise, she answered straight away.

'Nicole, how are you? I was so sorry to hear about Matt. Any news?'

'No, not really... Connie, I know it's not our usual day, and short notice, but can I see you?'

'I've actually just had a cancellation. How soon can you get here?'

## 24

MONDAY 10 JUNE 2024 – 10 A.M.

Connie's small office was located in a three-storey grey building at the end of a spur road running alongside a retail park.

The supermarket where Nic had mindlessly shoved items in her basket on her way back from The Glasshouse the day before was situated there, and as the car park for the offices was usually rammed, she parked by the shops and walked over.

Connie didn't have a receptionist. There was a buzzer to press outside the entrance with Connie's name on, and then she would appear to let her in. Connie smiled as she approached the glass door and they walked together to her consulting room.

The room always reminded her of Grace's study. Maybe it was coincidence, but she had a feeling Connie and Grace might know one another. It was an uncomfortable thought and one she pushed away whenever it occurred. Matt had supplied Connie's name, saying he'd heard she was the best. She was definitely the best so far. But as Connie often pointed out herself, it was an ongoing process, and recovery was a journey, not a destination.

Connie sat in the comfy chair facing her and poured her a glass of water. 'I thought of reaching out, when I heard about

Matt, but that's not always appropriate, so I'm pleased I was able to fit you in.'

Connie was dressed in her usual floral dress and beads. Nic swore it was always the same outfit. Which she kind of liked, as if each session were suspended in a bubble of time. No end, no beginning, always the same.

'Would you like to discuss what's happened since we last met?' Connie asked.

'Oh god, where to start?' she said, sipping her water. 'It's all such a mess.'

'Take your time. We can discuss anything you like.'

'Yes, thanks, maybe if I look over my notes?' She put the glass down and took out her red notebook. She'd have to start another one soon. It was filling up fast.

Connie smiled encouragingly, taking a pad and pen from the desk beside her.

'I don't recall exactly what I wrote after we discussed Lily's adoption,' she explained. 'The notebook is missing. Well, not missing exactly... I've made some notes again, for today.'

'You find it helpful?' Connie asked, going with the change in direction without question, another reason she found her style preferable to others she'd tried. The men didn't seem to enjoy her scattergun approach.

'Yes, it has been helpful, but unfortunately, Lily has read my previous account.'

Connie looked up from her own notetaking, the foolscap pad resting on her floral-covered lap. 'Are you saying your daughter deliberately took your private notebook?'

She nodded.

'Right, I see,' Connie replied. 'That must have been very difficult for you both?'

She nodded again. 'Yes, it was.'

She had told Connie that Lily was adopted right at the start. It was no secret after all, but she hadn't explained the specific set of circumstances that led up to it. That was not something she could share easily. That Matt was Lily's 'real' father.

'She has no idea what I sacrificed to keep her!' she blurted out. 'I gave up every shred of pride, every pretence at... I've lived a lie for eighteen years!'

'I want you to take a breath,' Connie said, pushing a lock of grey hair from in front of her silver-rimmed spectacles. It was curly like the detective's, although the women were likely thirty years apart in age. She had never managed to accurately age Connie, but she had to be sixty plus. 'In through the nose and out through the mouth,' Connie coached her. 'Good. And another. Breathe deeply and mindfully. Nice and slowly.'

'I feel like I'm being punished for Matt's mistakes,' she replied, fed up with the slow breathing. 'And now he's told Lily, and he's not even here to deal with the fallout!'

'Punished?' Connie asked, sitting back, her pen tapping her top lip.

The gesture reminded her of Pemberton again; something she could have done without as she tried to order her thoughts and decide what she might share now, and what still very much needed to remain buried in the past. It was a fine line, and one she dared not cross, even though it undoubtedly limited the success of these expensive sessions.

'OK,' Connie said after an extended silence. 'How about you take me back to the time of the adoption and tell me what you feel able to; might that help?'

She nodded, although it was hard to go back to the day Matt had first told her about his relationship with Katie Creel.

* * *

The irony was, she'd just begun to pick herself up after the losses of three babies in six years, although the terrible but pointless longing for a child would not let her be. It had undoubtedly affected their marriage, but she had decided to take back some control by that spring in 2006, channelling her grief into extreme gym sessions to wrestle her post-pregnancy, post-youth, post-caring body back into shape. She had also been seeing a therapist called Colin Masterson. Colin wasn't a natural fit. He wore cardigans with leather patches on the elbows and said 'uh-huh' a lot and talked about her mother's abandonment of her as a baby, as if that was the key to everything. But she was determined to get mind and body back on track and somehow, rather miraculously, by early May 2006, those dark days had finally started to dwindle and she began to emerge, stronger, hopeful; dare she say, more resilient. They would be fine, she and Matt, she'd decided, because she loved him and he loved her. It was time to reconcile herself to the fact she had a lot to be thankful for, Matt at the very top of that list. Then came the bombshell. Matt had been dealing with his grief by having an affair. Well, not really an affair, but more than a one-night stand. And as if that wasn't enough, Katie Creel, who was shockingly only eighteen years old at the time, was his patient.

'Oh my god, Matt!' she'd told him, completely appalled. 'A patient? Are you mad?'

'I'm not proud of it,' he'd admitted. 'But I never treated her myself, not invasively.'

'Are those the kinds of distinctions you're making these days?'

'It's a grey area.'

'It's really not!' she'd screamed at him, pulling so many tufts from the beige velour sofa they'd owned at the time, she'd had to replace it soon after.

'She was working at the tennis club,' Matt told her. 'We got talking. She was travelling on a gap year and she asked me about a gynae matter so I offered some advice... and a consultation. I'm so ashamed.'

He'd looked so wretched, she'd almost reached out to him, then the hurt and anger had surged again, so she'd said nothing.

'It was such a stupid thing to do, I can't believe I... But she was there, and you were—'

'I was what, Matt? Grieving for another lost baby? Our third in six years? Or is the word you're looking for... *frigid*? Have you ever thought about how I felt being opened up, my cervix dilated, a dead child scooped out?'

'I do understand the procedure!' Matt's lack of empathy was shocking, but then it got so much worse. 'And god, how do I say this?'

'Say what?' She couldn't imagine it could get any worse, unless he was in love with this Katie and about to leave her.

'She's pregnant.'

She could still feel the pain of those two words, the way her world had split into two.

'She'll get rid of it?' she'd asked, so stunned it had felt as if someone else was speaking, not her.

'The thing is,' he'd said, 'she's due in a month.'

Even now, she still couldn't compute the betrayals that had spanned those eight months before Matt had been forced to come clean about his imminently due lovechild. The pain of the affair was nothing compared to the fact he would finally be a father, but not with her.

'But don't you see?' Matt had said, falling onto his knees and reaching for her hands. 'This could be the answer to all our prayers.'

'Are you fucking kidding me?' she'd asked, the words still so clear in her memory. And she'd snatched her hands from his.

But it was no joke. Matt was deadly serious in his plan to adopt the child Katie had at first claimed she'd wanted to keep, outright refusing to even consider a termination, only to change her mind as the birth loomed and reality finally dawned. She wanted to go back to New Zealand and resume her studies, as if none of it had ever happened. And in many ways, it *was* the perfect solution all round. Katie was so young; of course she didn't want the baby. Whilst Nic ached for one.

A week later, a heavily pregnant teenager looked out at the swimming pool in Three Gables back garden and observed, in her Antipodean twang, 'Didn't think people had pools in England; doesn't it always rain?'

'How do we know for sure the baby is my husband's child?' Nic had asked. 'You seem to have a fairly relaxed approach to sleeping with married men.'

Katie threw a conspiratorial glance to Matt and then produced a letter of paternity. Matt had covered the cost of the test, along with Katie's living and healthcare expenses so she could stay in the UK until the baby was born. He'd wanted his child all along. The breadth of the arrangements in place had literally taken her breath away. Such treachery. It wasn't fair. None of it was. Not least that a selfish bitch like Katie Creel could fall pregnant so easily and deliver such a perfect little girl just a few weeks later.

In the eighteen years since, there had been many happy days. Times when she had looked at Matt with Lily and felt truly blessed. But there had been many more times when she'd known from the stab in the pit of her stomach that she wasn't a part of that happiness, and that one day – despite his promises to never tell, a stringent condition of her agreement – Lily would find out.

\* \* \*

'Lily is my husband's child, by another woman,' she said, condensing all the hurt into that one short, factual sentence as she explained it to Connie.

'Must have been a very hard decision to adopt her in that case?' Connie responded, seemingly taking the revelation in her stride.

'Yes, but I still wanted Matt, despite everything. In fact, I needed him. I was unwell, have been for years, as you know.'

'Yes, of course, you needed the stability of your marriage, your home.'

'Yes, exactly, and to have a baby too, that was... too tempting. But I did have my conditions.'

Nic leaned forward and poured from the tall jug to top up her glass, her hands trembling as she took another sip. 'My first stipulation was the baby would be called Lily, after my mother; it was her middle name. And the second was, no one must ever know that Matt is her biological father. Lily included. I have my pride. But Matt has gone and told her now, the day he disappeared, in fact.'

'I see, and I assume that has changed Lily's feelings towards you somewhat?'

'Yes, you could say that.'

'And how about your feelings towards Matt?'

That, of course, was the big question, and a brave one considering the circumstances, but Connie always did get to the root of it all, or close as she could with the information Nic provided. Connie was fearless, and insightful, but she didn't know the half of it.

\* \* \*

Nic couldn't recall the drive home after seeing Connie. One minute she was walking to her car, the next she was almost there. It was often like that. The mental exhaustion of those deeply reflective fifty minutes would hit her like a truck the moment she left that grey building. All she wanted was her bed. She was exhausted.

The Evoque rounded the final bend, the track that led to Three gables the next turning on the right, when something caught her eye. She thought she'd spotted movement in the distant crop of trees. Then it was gone. She checked her mirror, scanning the trees that shimmered behind her now. She could have sworn someone was watching her from deep within, but all she could see and then hear was a squawking crow as it rose up, startling her.

She swung the car into the track, still with that feeling someone had been there, in the woods, keeping an eye on her, but the drive was empty as she parked.

She ran from the car and fell into the house, then she slammed the front door and drew the chain across, shutting out the rest of the world. She didn't even notice the post at first, checking her phone before she spotted an envelope, face down on the mat. She picked it up and walked to the bottom of the stairs, about to call up to Lily, when she remembered her daughter wasn't living with her at the moment and maybe wouldn't ever again.

She took the envelope into the kitchen and climbed onto a stool at the breakfast bar, noting that her name was printed on the front of the plain white envelope, but no address, and no postmark. Just 'Nic Delaney' in Calibri. She ripped it open.

A single sheet of paper was inside, folded in three. She opened it up to read the printed message written inside.

Don't pretend you don't know why I left. This is all your fault.
Matt x

She dropped the note on the counter, then her feet to the floor, rushing to the sink just in time before she retched over the piled dishes several times before she was done and could rinse her mouth out and dry her hands on her dress.

The note had been hand delivered whilst she was out, which meant Matt was close by, watching the house. Maybe in the woods? She'd sensed a presence as she'd rounded that final bend, and she was right. The postcard had only been sent as a decoy, to buy him some time by throwing her off the scent and make it look like he'd gone to Cornwall. But this was more calculated, printed and therefore planned, presumably before he left on Friday; but why wait to deliver it now?

She went back to the breakfast bar and sat down to read the note again, looking for meaning and reassurance, but she found only anger and threats.

Don't pretend you don't know why I left. This is all your fault.
Matt x

His words scared her. They scared her so much, she had to hold on to the edge of the breakfast bar to stop herself from falling. Whatever happened next, clearly she and Matt were no longer a team; quite the opposite, in fact.

She picked up her phone and tried the detective. And this time, she answered.

'Nicole, hi, sorry I missed your calls, very busy here. Everything OK?'

'No, not really. I think you were right; I think am in danger.'

## 25

MONDAY 10 JUNE 2024 – 4 P.M.

DC Amy Pemberton had promised she'd get to Three Gables as soon as she could, but it was almost four hours now since Nic had called her to explain about the hand-delivered note and her worry that Matt was close by, watching her.

The detective was busy, she always was, and in fairness, she had offered to send someone else over straight away, but Nic had refused. She didn't want to explain to a complete stranger that whilst she loved her husband, he did have a temper, and yes, she was frightened of him, and yes, she did believe the note was from him, and yes, he could be that calculated as to plan a warning three days into his disappearance.

She called again and DC Pemberton answered, thankfully, but she sounded even more harried than before. Nic got the impression she'd interrupted something important, but she again offered a colleague to come over, and Nic again refused, explaining she'd rather wait for Pemberton herself, and confirming that yes, she had locked all the doors.

She couldn't even sit under her trees, afraid to open the patio doors she'd bolted and double-checked. Matt must have been waiting for her to leave the house and hand-delivered that note whilst she was with Connie. She'd made it easy for him, by falling for that postcard. And now he was threatening her, the note had left no room for doubt.

Don't pretend you don't know why I left. This is all your fault.
Matt x

The fields and trees encircling Three Gables' grounds provided her husband with endless cover should he want to bide his time, as well as numerous points of entry through hedges and over low walls when he was ready to break in. They'd never worried about security much, being in the middle of nowhere, but the lack of neighbours to run to and the empty track meant she now felt exposed and alone. Crazy to think of Matt and feel afraid, but she did. There was no point denying it any longer. Her husband scared her. She had no idea what he was capable of.

The vibrations of an incoming call penetrated her thoughts. She was surprised to see Scott's name on screen, but they'd swapped numbers and agreed to keep in touch.

'Scott?'

'Yes, sorry to bother you, Nic.' Scott's London accent sounded even stronger down the line than in person, which was saying something. 'You're the only person I could think of who might... Who would... Sorry, I shouldn't have called.'

'No, it's fine; we said we'd liaise. What's going on? Are you OK?'

'Not really. The police are here. They've been here all day, in fact.' He sounded worried. 'They've been searching the house and now they're bringing in dogs to comb the hill! They won't tell me why. It's doing my head in. Are they at yours too? Hang on!'

She listened and heard a door slide back, the terrace's sliding glass door she guessed, and voices, then a single loud bark, then more excited dogs, setting one another off. She imagined police officers crawling over every inch of the Jensens' pristine home, the dogs scrabbling up the hill behind. That's where Pemberton must have been all day, answering her calls as she supervised the search up at The Glasshouse. Sweat prickled on her palms as she held her mobile to her ear and paced the kitchen. She had checked for any signs of Matt when she'd been at The Glasshouse the day before and seen none, but she wasn't a detective, or a forensics expert, and she didn't have a dog who sniffed out evidence unseen by the naked eye.

'Nic?'

'Yes, I'm still here, Scott. What are they searching for, do you know?'

'They won't tell me, just keep asking me to check again if anything of Dee's is gone.' It sounded like he was outside now, the wind whistling round him. 'I asked them, how am I supposed to know if any of her shoes are missing? She has dozens of pairs, and I've told them over and over that Dee doesn't own a passport, she hated flying, said it scared the shit out of her. Feel like I'm a broken record, broken-hearted more like.'

The sound of a car on the drive distracted her. She ran to the front door and opened it on the security chain. The Jigginses' ancient beige Volvo had parked facing the house and Grace was climbing out, Lily too. 'Sorry, Scott. I need to go. Maybe talk later, if there's news? And thanks for letting me know. I hope... Well, I hope it turns out OK.'

'Yeah, you and me both. Bye, Nic. Good luck!'

Grace was striding towards the house as Nic unhooked the security chain and opened the door fully. And Lily was with her. A bite of jealousy took root in Nic's belly as she noted a look pass between them that spoke of a shared mission. Grace hadn't hesitated in assuming the role as Lily's proxy mother, was revelling in it, in fact, her messages since Lily had been staying with the Jigginses sprinkled with smug titbits about how she was taking care of Lil with 'long talks' and 'home baking'. So why were the pair of them back here now, unannounced?

'DC Pemberton just called,' Grace said, breathless as they reached the house. 'Said she was on her way over and could we meet her here. Is that OK? Can we come in?'

'Yes, of course,' she replied, smiling at Lily.

Lily's piercing stare was a reminder of Matt's green eyes, and there was no smile in return. 'You OK, sweetheart?'

Lily said nothing, avoiding the question and any further eye contact as she stepped inside, Grace behind her. Nic was about to close the door when DC Pemberton arrived, her grey car then reversing into the space between the Volvo and the Evoque. The detective's expression was solemn as she too walked towards the house.

'Grace! Good! You're all here,' Pemberton said. 'Lily, you OK?'

Lily nodded to the detective.

'What's happening?' Grace asked. 'Is there news?'

'I've been up for eighteen hours,' Pemberton replied, rubbing at her left eye. 'I'd appreciate a very large coffee first if that's OK?'

They went through to the kitchen and Nic put the kettle on, the threatening letter then catching her eye. It was on the breakfast bar, where she'd left it for the detective to read, but thankfully she'd tucked it back in its envelope which was face down. It looked innocuous enough, just a white envelope, much like any other, but she didn't want Pemberton to remark on it in front of the others. Nic retrieved the envelope as surreptitiously as she could and pressed it into DC Pemberton's palm as Grace and Lily sat down at the table. Pemberton took it, glanced at it, then pushed it without comment into her trouser pocket, barely a glance exchanged. Grace hadn't noticed, too busy fussing over Lily, but Lily may have, her daughter's green eyes surveying them from across the room.

'Coffee for everyone?' she asked, grabbing the cafetiere. There were hardly any pods left.

Pemberton pulled out a chair and sat down with a sigh of relief, as if she'd been on her feet all day. 'Make mine strong and black, please, two sugars, and as I'm sure you're all desperate for an update,' she continued, mainly to Grace, who was sat beside Lily across the table and looked about to burst, 'let me just say that for now, there's nothing I can report; this is an ongoing investigation.'

Grace sighed loudly. 'You said you needed to talk to us! I assumed there was news?'

'I thought it would be easier to get you all together to follow up on this car of Lily's that you mentioned, Grace.'

Lily's head snapped round to her aunt. 'You did explain that I was sorry not to have said something before and why?'

'Of course,' Grace replied, avoiding Nic's stare. 'I told you, no one is angry with you.'

'Your message said it was a black Golf?' Pemberton said, consulting her black notepad and frowning. 'On a 2024 plate, is that right?'

'Yes,' Grace replied before Lily had the chance to.

'I'll need the full registration,' the detective told them. 'And any distinguishing features: decals, special wheel trim?'

'Think hard, Lily,' Grace said. 'A number? Letter? A dealership sticker?'

'I only saw it very quickly and I wasn't looking at the number plates,' Lily replied, her voice so small, Nic could only just hear as the kettle began to boil. 'There was this big bow...' Lily mimed the furls of the extravagant ribbon she'd found in the garage. 'It was still there when I showed Mum.'

Nic smiled. At least she'd called her Mum.

'You knew about the car?' Pemberton asked, turning round in her chair.

'No!' Nic replied, a spoon of ground coffee in her hand. 'I had no idea, not until Lily told me.'

'Right,' Pemberton said, standing up. 'I guess we'd better take another look in the garage.'

\* \* \*

The mid-afternoon air crackled with tension as the four of them went outside, Nic barefoot, Pemberton in her thick-soled white trainers, Grace in her clumpy Birkenstocks and Lily in flip-flops. But there was no jeopardy to this search; everyone except Grace had already seen that the garage was empty. Nic wondered what the point was, but maybe the detective was looking for something other than a missing car? Clues perhaps to its former presence.

She wasn't sure how she felt about that as they crossed the gravel, the stones digging in her feet again, heavy bunched keys in her hands. If Matt had walked back from the scene of the crash to steal the Golf and make a getaway, knowing that his faithful daughter would cover for him, then it was a calculated act, and callous for it, even by his standards.

She looked around for any sign of Matt and, in the process, dropped the keys. She was already behind the others, her progress slowed by lack of footwear. Grace looked back but made no move to help. Not that she wanted her to, but it was unusual for her excessively empathetic sister-in-law not to intervene. Nic snatched up the keys and ran ahead, then she slotted the right key in the lock first time. She'd been trying to think if she'd been in the garage between the supposed delivery of the Golf on Tuesday lunchtime and when they'd checked the garage on Friday night. She didn't think she had – she rarely went in there other than for the recycling which she stored at the back if the bin was full – but she still couldn't be sure.

The detective helped lift the heavy door she had unlocked. Then Lily ran in and pointed to the floor as the light came on, much as she had before, but with a dulled sense of outrage this time.

'It was there! It had a bow on top.' Lily retrieved the bedraggled pink ribbon cast aside in a corner and held it up. 'This was on top of it!'

'I don't understand,' Grace said, pacing the empty space. 'Matt surely wouldn't do something so... Not to Lily. He idolises her. It would be...'

'Cruel?' Nic suggested, arms folded as she watched from outside. 'You should tell everyone about finding your father washing blood from his hands on Tuesday lunchtime,' she told her daughter, noting how Grace's mouth fell open. 'Didn't Lily mention that, Grace? I'm guessing not by the look on your face!'

'He'd cut his hand clearing up broken glass in here!' Lily told the detective, who was also looking surprised. 'Before the car was delivered.'

'OK, everyone out!' Pemberton instructed. 'Grace? Out of here! Nic, where are you going? This is a potential crime scene!'

'Sorry, it's just...' she said, looking down at her footprints in the dust as she circled the garage. 'I just remembered... The bins go out Tuesday night for collection on Wednesday.'

'Is that relevant?' Pemberton asked as she checked round too, scanning every inch of the dusty floor before she shepherded Nic out.

'It's Matt's job,' Nic explained as they stood outside the open garage door. 'Putting the bins on the drive for collection day. I knew the blue bin wasn't that full, and there was a stack of packaging in the garage that I'd put in there ages ago.' She pointed to the flattened cardboard boxes from various deliveries which were stacked against the back wall. 'I offered to get the card to add in whilst he dragged the bin from round the side.' She pointed to the side gate. 'But he stopped me going in here.'

'He stopped you, how?' Pemberton asked.

'Said he'd seen a rat.' Grace stepped back from the garage, Lily doing the same. 'We do get a lot of rodent life out here,' Nic told the detective. 'We're bordered by fields, and Matt knows I hate them. But the card is still in there, he didn't move it, and I couldn't see any poison pellets put down either, and he said he'd done that too. Sorry, I hadn't connected those things before.'

Pemberton nodded and ducked back into the garage, looking around again before she returned to where they waited for her verdict. 'No sign of any poison or rats in there. No broken glass either.'

'That's because Dad cleared it up,' Lily said, stalking off back towards the house. 'I told you, he was covered in blood and dust!'

They all went inside. Nic and Grace and Lily to the kitchen, whilst Pemberton made numerous calls in the hallway, her phone still clamped to her ear when she eventually joined them at the kitchen table. Grace and Lily were back on the bench seat by the wall, Nic on the other side, the coffees she had made now going cold between them.

'So, Lily,' the detective said, downing a cold cup anyway. 'Tell me about this car of yours.'

'It was a birthday present,' Lily replied, glancing at Nic. 'From Dad.'

'And when did you first know about it?'

'Tuesday. Dad had taken time off work for the delivery.' Lily looked at Nic again, then Grace. 'What is it?'

'Your father was suspended,' Grace replied. 'He wasn't working for a couple of weeks before he went missing.'

Lily went to say something but for once seemed lost for words.

'Right,' said Pemberton, now writing stuff down, her empty mug pushed aside to make room for her notepad. 'So he was washing blood from his hands, because...?'

'Because he'd cut his hand picking up broken glass in the garage, as I said,' Lily replied. 'He was filthy, too, from sweeping up. He said there was a bag of soil or something, split open, and loads of dust?'

Grace grabbed Lily's hand. 'Explain to the detective about your dad calling you too, on Friday morning.'

'Yes, Dad called me Friday morning at 8.52,' Lily said, Grace squeezing her hand. 'He was driving at the time, I *think*. So maybe that was when he, I mean if he...'

'Stole your car?' Pemberton prompted.

Lily shook her head, a tear falling down her cheek. 'He rang to wish me a happy birthday and—'

Nic caught her daughter's eye, wondering what else Lily might say about what Matt had told her in that call, but she stopped talking and pulled her hand from Grace's.

'So no mention of where he was going?' Pemberton asked.

'Nope,' Lily said.

Nic smiled at her daughter, but Lily's gaze remained on her hands, now on the table. Grace looked like she might say something then, but Pemberton had picked up her phone, which hadn't rung, but vibrated on the table.

'Yes, Ry, sorry, hang on a sec...' Pemberton's voice trailed off as the detective got up and walked into the hall.

Grace shot her a look across the table. 'You must have noticed he'd cut himself? Lily said it was bleeding so much he'd had to dress the wound daily!'

'Yes, of course I noticed! He was changing the dressing all week, but he told me he cut it at work,' she replied. 'A nick from a scalpel.'

Lily looked up from her hands. 'I told you, that's what he said we should tell you.'

'But he couldn't have cut it at work; he wasn't there!' Grace pointed out.

'I only said what Matt told me,' Nic countered.

'So what are you both saying?' Grace asked.

'I think it's obvious,' Nic replied. 'Matt has lied to all of us.'

'No!' Lily said, staring at her across the table. 'He wouldn't.'

Nic's patience had worn thin now. 'Oh for goodness' sake, Lily, grow up!'

'OK, Ry,' Pemberton said, still talking on her phone as she came back in and interrupted the argument at the table. 'See what you can find without the registration details. Yeah, it will be the latest plate... Brand new black Golf. Oh, and there was a bow, baby pink?' Lily nodded as the detective looked at her. 'Ask around, might jog memories if the garage supplied the bow, and it was delivered here by tow truck. Thanks, Ry, oh and how's the —' Pemberton stopped talking and looked at the table again, then she turned around and walked out.

'So what does this all mean?' Grace asked, getting up and refilling the kettle.

'Hard to know,' Nic replied, following her over. If she hadn't been so beleaguered, she'd have commented on her sister-in-law's presumption in *her* kitchen, but she had no energy for another fight, or to make more coffees. She sat on a stool at the breakfast bar and sagged.

'There could still be a perfectly reasonable explanation,' Grace said as she rinsed mugs. 'And at least this proves he made it out of the crash and is alive.'

'Yes,' Nic replied, thinking of that threatening note. 'It does.'

'OK, my boss is on her way,' Pemberton announced, breathless as she came back. 'DS Stone,' she added, as if the name should mean something to them.

'Why is a DS coming?' Grace asked.

Nic had thought the same, turning to hear the answer.

'We just got the results on the blood samples from the BMW,' Pemberton replied. 'They're a good match for Dr, sorry, *Mr* Delaney's DNA,' Pemberton corrected, looking at Grace. 'But the samples also found another match.'

'Whose?' Grace said, asking the obvious question and before Nic had a chance to do the same.

'His former patient and the complainant,' Pemberton replied, a look of triumph in her brown eyes. 'Deena Jensen.'

'Deena's blood was in Matt's car?' Nic asked, finally finding her voice.

'Yes, in the BMW's boot, and traces on the steering wheel,' Pemberton replied. 'And there's also news on the search up at The Glasshouse. It's been a nightmare, to be honest,' she explained as she glanced at her phone. 'So much rock behind and underneath... And the gradient is...' Pemberton looked up. 'But after they brought in the cadaver dogs, things progressed and it looks like they've finally found something.'

'Found what?' Lily asked, speaking for the first time in a while and looking white as a sheet as she got up and walked unsteadily towards the detective. 'Tell me!'

## 26

MONDAY 10 JUNE 2024 – 5 P.M.

'It's actually good news when you think about it,' Grace suggested as she rinsed the last cup. 'I mean, she won't say what they've found, so it could be nothing.'

Pemberton had left the kitchen to take another call. Nic was still sitting on a stool, staring into space, and Lily was back at the table, looking as shell-shocked as Grace felt, despite her positivity.

'And Matt's out there,' Grace continued, still running the tap. 'Waiting to come home, when he's ready. Yes, definitely good news!'

'How can it be good news?' Nic asked, raising her palms in disbelief from her perch by the breakfast bar. 'Cadaver dogs – you know what that means, Grace? They're looking for and have possibly found remains of—'

'Yes, of course I do!' Grace replied, tilting her head towards Lily. Her niece was clearly close to tears, and Nic needed to moderate her comments accordingly. 'But we don't know yet that it's anything at all, could just be a dead fox or something. And if they can trace the Golf then maybe they can find Matt too and' – she lowered her voice – 'possibly that woman as well.'

She walked round to sit by her sobbing niece. 'It won't take your dad long to sort all this confusion, Lil.' She rubbed Lily's bent back.

Nic scowled, but Grace was only trying to keep up everyone's spirits, although sadly she got where Nic was coming from. It was getting harder to find the positives in this rapidly deteriorating situation.

'Don't try and pretend everything is fine, like I'm a child!' Lily said, startling her as she shrugged off her attempts at comfort. 'They're digging up the garden of Dad's psycho patient! They think he killed her, don't they? How could they think that?'

'No, of course not,' Grace said. 'I'm sure this will soon be cleared up, and your car, that's a breakthrough,' she persisted. 'If your father took it, that means he must have walked away from the accident in the woods, which means the blood in the BMW's boot was superficial, right?' Grace looked to Nic for some support, but Nic shook her head, non-committal at best. 'Maybe from when he went in the boot after the crash to get something out?' Grace suggested.

Lily looked receptive, nodding along.

'And I imagine this patient's blood, Deena's,' Grace continued, pre-empting what she imagined was Lily's next question as her niece looked at her expectantly, eyes filled with tears, 'hers was mixed with it because...'

'Because?' Nic prompted, spinning the stool round to face them.

'Because...' Grace had finally run out of steam, unable to explain the mixed blood samples in the boot. 'There will be an explanation.'

'Yes, there will,' Nic said, spinning back.

It was obvious Nic had given up on Matt, but Grace still tried to make it work in Matt's favour, hugging Lily to her side as she scrabbled for a theory. Had Matt and Deena been in the BMW together when it left the road? Both injured, maybe, and leaving blood trails when they grabbed their bags from the boot? They could well be hiding out somewhere, together! It felt possible, if far-fetched given the intensive search of the woods which had not found any trace of their escape, and no sightings since. Or, had Deena's blood been transferred into the BMW's boot by some other means Grace couldn't bear to think about – not now the ground had been broken near the Jensens' home, the search clearly finding something she could still only hope was a dead animal. And where did her conversation with Gary fit into all this? Had he helped Matt to get rid of... No, she couldn't think like that. No good would come of it.

'Maybe he went there, to Deena's home, I mean,' she suggested, looking again at Nic, who reluctantly turned round. 'To speak with her about the tribunal and found her in distress. He would have helped her,' she blustered, leaving Lily and returning to the cups she'd been stacking on the draining board and wiping them before she dried her hands on the same tea towel. 'I mean, that's his job, saving women's lives, and *very* Matt.'

She wasn't even sure anyone was listening any more. Nic was looking at her chipped nails and Lily was staring at her phone. It was a very difficult route to navigate to Matt's innocence, but she pressed on. 'Yes, he probably found Deena after she was attacked or hurt in her home and went to her aid... That must be it, surely?'

'Dad was so happy about giving me the car when he showed it to me,' Lily said, almost to herself. 'It was *her* who didn't want me to have it.' Lily stared at Nic. 'This is all her fault.'

'Are you suggesting I stole your car?' Nic asked, looking weary.

'OK, that's enough!' Grace told them both, waving the tea towel as if she were a boxing referee. 'Clearly, for reasons he is not here to give, your father felt compelled to take your car, Lily, but I'm sure he will bring it back undamaged on his return.'

Her intervention seemed to help, Lily nodding and sniffing, whilst Nic's head was then bowed to the counter, the widening bald patch on show. It looked awful and Nic was ashen when she briefly looked up again. She clearly hadn't slept in days. It was so sad to see her like that. Whatever had happened to Matt, and however much Nic lashed out in response, some compassion was required. 'You OK?' Grace asked, gently touching Nic's angular shoulder.

Nic jumped and lifted her head again. 'How can I be?'

Pemberton returned then and took in the scene. 'Why don't you take Lily back to yours now, Grace? I'll call you once there's news; these things can take ages. I'll stay with Nicole.'

Grace hadn't had a moment alone with the detective to talk about Gary's call, but it didn't seem like the time to engage her favourably in that conversation. DC Pemberton also looked exhausted and obviously had more pressing concerns than her mystery caller.

'Yes, of course, and thanks for updating us all,' Grace said, encouraging Lily away from her phone so they could leave.

Pemberton nodded, although she was back on a call so Grace wasn't certain she'd heard. And Nic barely gave them a glance, let alone a goodbye.

# 27

MONDAY 10 JUNE 2024 – 6 P.M.

Elan was waiting at the front door when they arrived home, her daughter's white face lit up by the early evening sunlight. Elan ran out and hugged Lily in that tight and unsettling way the cousins had recently developed with one another, but she side-stepped Grace's open arms. She pretended not to notice as the girls went inside, but it hurt, being rejected by your own flesh and blood. She felt for Nic too, in that regard at least.

Grace had never really thought about it much before, how excluding it must have been for Nic being the outsider in her family unit of three. Matt and Lily were always so close with one another, for obvious reasons, and it can't have helped that Grace had also tried to side-line her sister-in-law. Out of jealousy, she admitted to herself now as she went inside. Nic had undoubtedly stolen Matt's attention away from her, but as much as she'd resented that, she also knew Matt had loved his wife, and his daughter, so why had he upped and left them both? Her brother wasn't perfect, but he wasn't a bad man. That much she was certain of, and however hard it was, or would become, she still believed in him, even if Nic didn't. And as disappointing as it was to consider that Matt and Deena had unwisely gone off together in Lily's car, it was still her working theory. And better to think that than... Well, that was all there was to it. This was yet another unwise move by her often brilliant but impulsive, sometimes calculating, sometimes foolhardy, complex and wonderful big brother. The excavations up at The Glasshouse would prove to be the latest false move in an investigation which she had again lost faith in. Matt would return soon, of his own volition, once he'd had time to think about the consequences of running away, and it would be fine. Well, clearly not fine, there would be repercussions, but there would also be a resolution that would rinse him clean of the worst of the allegations.

The girls had already disappeared upstairs, and with no sign of Ed, she took a moment to herself, but her hands shook as she rinsed them in the downstairs bathroom, splashing her face with cold water. The thought of Matt turning the water in the cloakroom at Three Gables from clear to red sent a shiver through her. Or maybe it was just the cool water running over her hands? She splashed her face again; she was burning up. Bloody hormones!

'Hey!' Ed said, tapping her on the shoulder and making her jump. She'd thought he was upstairs with his trains, oblivious to their return and her trauma. 'Lily has told me the latest. Pretty tough on you.' He held out his arms. 'Hug it out?'

'Not now, Ed, I'm roasting,' she said, patting her face dry whilst Ed's arms dropped to his sides. 'I'm sorry, that was short of me. It's just been a very trying day. And there's something I need to tell you.' She dabbed at her face with the towel again. 'I should have told you this before, run it past you first in fact, before I... But Matt presented me with a, well, a very disturbing scenario... and now it looks as though he has definitely... I mean, we still don't know why... or if he will... but *if* he has run off intentionally...' She finally drew breath and looked her husband directly in the eye. 'I have a confession to make.'

Ed backed away, but they were both still in the confines of the tiny downstairs toilet.

'I gave Matt our savings!' she blurted out. 'Pretty much everything we had.'

She waited, but saw no surprise, no anger, not even the disappointment she'd expected.

'I was wondering when you were going to tell me,' Ed said at last, taking the damp towel from her grasp and slotting it back into the chrome ring.

'You knew?' she asked, shoulders sagging.

'I do check our accounts. Every few days. I saw it on Friday night, at the barbeque, on my banking app, but it didn't seem like the right time to add to your burden.'

'Oh god, Ed, I've been such an idiot! I'm so sorry!'

He shook his head and pulled her into the promised hug, clumsily kissing her cheek, her back pushed against the sink. 'You're *not* an idiot! You're better than your brother deserves, that's all.' He let her go and stepped outside, waiting for her to join him in the hallway.

She wiped her eyes and dried her hands again, then came out too. 'Thank you, and I'm hopeful we will get it back, of course, but if not I'll pay us back, bit by bit, take on more clients, whatever it takes.'

'Did you get a chance to return Nic's notebook whilst you were there?' Ed asked as they went into the kitchen.

'I meant to, I swear,' she said as he held up the kettle. 'No, thank you, I'm far too hot to drink tea.'

'You need to hand it back soon as you can,' Ed said, flicking on the kettle anyway. 'It's Nic's private notebook and clearly Lily stole it; Elan admitted as much.'

'Yes, I wanted to, of course, but there was so much going on, and the detective was there, of course.' Ed nodded, seemingly accepting of her genuine excuse. 'I'll go soon. I promise. Return it with an apology. She looks terrible, Ed. Her hair, she's pulling it out in clumps.'

'Poor Nic. You sure you don't want a cuppa?'

'No, I need to go over a few work things. Been neglecting my clients of late and I need to rearrange their appointments before I lose them to someone else.'

She went to her study after a quick squeeze of her hand from her placated husband. Ed thought he knew everything now, and he did, mostly. But it was an excuse about her clients. She closed the door and sat at her desk, opening up her laptop and clicking on a web page.

Grace had visited the General Medical Council website a few times in her capacity as a therapist, to check out doctors' credentials for client referrals, but she'd never typed in her brother's name before. Matt's list of qualifications filled her screen. His specialisms and long list of published papers were impressive, a familiar pride swelling in her chest, until she read down the long page. Deena Jensen's complaint was there, with no name of course, but the tribunal date was confirmed for the next day, although that obviously wouldn't now happen. She clicked on the link and read the details, the shock value of those words not diminished by their brevity.

The tribunal will look into the allegation that Mr Matthew Delaney was witnessed with Patient D in his consulting room, at The Trust hospital, by a member of staff, both parties engaged in inappropriate sexual behaviour.

As if that wasn't enough, she then spotted there was another link. To a previous complaint made almost nineteen years ago.

It seemed a colleague had reported some 'serious concerns' about Matt back then too, specifically the rationale and timing of a referral made by Matt in September 2005. Reading on, it stated that Dr Delaney, as he had been at the time, and the patient in question, Patient K, were seen together both before, during and after the patient's appointments with another consultant. The nature of Matt's personal and professional conduct had been called into question, although there had been what was deemed as 'insufficient evidence' to substantiate the claims of misconduct and it was dismissed as a clash of personalities between Matt and the consultant who'd raised the complaint. She vaguely recognised the colleague's name. A woman who had worked with Matt at The Trust, if memory served. A fellow gynae specialist.

*She's a nightmare, Gracie, impossible to work with; glad to see the back of her to be honest, and it means I can pick up her hours. Win, win.*

She closed her laptop and pushed back her chair, distancing herself from the information she had deliberately gone looking for and now wished she hadn't. It felt as though Matt had got away with something back in 2005. And it also felt uncomfortably like she was scraping at the top of a very large iceberg, the rest hidden beneath the murky waters of secrecy and cover ups. Two complaints were way too many.

What she was certain of was that Matt wouldn't have managed to fix things this time. Not without taking matters into his own hands, and in a more drastic way than engineering the discrediting of a 'nightmare' colleague.

She was no longer burning up; in fact, quite the reverse. She shivered as she looked behind her, to the closed door of her study. It had felt as if someone might have been watching her, but she was entirely alone.

## 28

As Nic had strongly suspected it might, Detective Sargent Stone's arrival at Three Gables half an hour or so after Grace and Lily had departed, had heralded another sea change in not only the investigation, but also the general tone of proceedings. As if the air temperature dropped as the senior officer clomped into the hallway in her sensible shoes and with her no-nonsense attitude. Stone was probably closer in age to Nic than Pemberton, but she felt even less kinship with the more mature detective.

'So, Nicole, I understand you've received a threatening note?' Stone asked. 'Can I see it, Amy?'

DC Pemberton passed the envelope over and they waited whilst Stone inspected it and then read aloud the contents, delivering the two short sentences in a monotone drawl. '"Don't pretend you don't know why I left. This is all your fault. Matt."' Stone then looked up, passing it back to Pemberton. 'Likely a prank, especially as it's printed. I mean, how would your husband have access to a printer if he's on the run?'

She'd wondered the same, but Matt was a calculating man, and a planner.

'Obviously, we will take it seriously,' Stone then said, adding, 'Bit late, Amy, but can you bag it for forensics?'

DC Pemberton found a plastic bag in her satchel, dropping the note and envelope inside and sealing it.

'He could have printed it out before he left,' Nic suggested to the two detectives.

'You mean he planned it?' Stone asked.

'I don't know, but that's my husband's work,' she said, pointing at the note, now inside the bag. 'I'm sure of it.'

'Why so sure?' Stone asked.

'The way it's worded feels like Matt. And he can be very calculated. I wouldn't put it past him to have planned the whole thing.'

'Any other notes, messages?' Stone asked, exchanging glances with Pemberton.

The message in the mirror was long gone, as was the trust he'd asked for, and she had held on to the postcard far too long to declare it now. She certainly didn't want to implicate herself further, or for her father to be subjected to a police search of his home on the basis of a picture postcard. Gerald was frail and asthmatic. At his age, the stress of it all could quite easily kill him. In fact, the more she thought about it, the more convinced she was Matt was much closer to home, waiting to make his move, whatever that might be. Watching her from the woods, and delivering threats. She needed the police to concentrate their efforts on finding Matt here, near home, and before he threatened her again. 'No, that's the first and only note,' she said.

'What do you think it means?' Stone asked as Pemberton walked outside to answer a call. '"Don't pretend you don't know why I left."'

'I imagine he's referencing the patient complaint; the

tribunal should have been happening tomorrow. That's all I can think of.'

'And how exactly is that your fault?' Stone pointed out.

'Well, clearly I don't know, but I've been trying to put myself in Matt's head and I guess he's claiming that he looked outside our marriage because I wasn't very receptive, maritally, after my hysterectomy last summer.'

Stone's eyes widened. 'I think I've heard every excuse for an affair in my time, but I have to say that ranks as one of the worst.'

'Yeah, it's not great,' she agreed.

'Anywhere we can sit and chat everything through?' Stone asked.

'We could go through to the sitting room?' she suggested.

Stone chose the armchair, whilst she took her favoured spot on the sofa, by the patio doors. The DS started talking, but she was craning to catch a glimpse of her trees. If she sat up, she could just about make them out through the whorled glass in the patio doors, but then she caught a flicker of movement out there, beyond the trees. She sat up straighter and looked again.

'Nicole?' Stone leaned forwards in the chair. 'Something wrong?'

'No, sorry, I thought I saw something.'

'Outside, you mean, someone there?'

'No, it's just me. I'm so jumpy. Can you repeat that?'

'Given we think Matt most likely drove away from here in your daughter's Golf after he crashed his BMW, but you also think he's hand-delivering notes, I wondered if you have any idea where your husband might be hiding out? We're two days behind, three in fact, on tracing this car. Be good to narrow the search. Any thoughts?'

Nic looked over to Pemberton, who was now hovering by the door and still on her phone. 'I have no idea where he might be, other than maybe nearby. And I called DC Pemberton many hours ago, so I don't think I'm entirely responsible for the delays.'

DS Stone looked over to DC Pemberton, Stone's seniority clearly there in the two detectives' dynamic. 'I was overseeing the search all day, boss,' Pemberton explained, lowering her phone. 'And in fairness, I got Ry straight on it once I knew about the Golf, and bless him, he's just discovered that Matt bought it from a dealership in town last Monday. Ry's sending over the paperwork to me now by email. It was a PCP agreement in your husband's name only, Nicole, apparently. No deposit.'

'I guess that makes sense,' Nic said, wondering at Matt's timing. He'd bought it on Monday, with the intention, presumably, of keeping the car a secret until the Friday when he'd planned to surprise them both, her and Lily, with the extravagant gift, a fait accompli, whilst making up reasons for her not to go in the garage in the days between; although his plans had changed, and he'd been forced to show Lily. 'I mean, given our finances are separate, I wouldn't have known,' she explained.

'Hello, yes, OK, where?' Stone said, getting up from the armchair, her phone to her ear now as she walked out. 'Hang on two ticks. I can't hear you! I'll go outside.'

It felt as though both detectives had one foot in Three Gables and another somewhere else. Back at the search of The Glasshouse, presumably. Pemberton took a seat beside her on the sofa, in the place where Matt usually sat. It was like a shit game of tag.

'So, this note?' Pemberton said, brandishing the plastic bag as she tucked her phone away in her satchel. 'You said it was waiting for you on the mat when you got home this morning?'

'Yes, around half-eleven.'

'Where had you been?' Pemberton asked as Stone's phone conversation cut across their exchange. The detective sergeant was outside now, but her deep voice carried in through the open front door and across the hallway, Stone now asking, 'Up behind the ornamental garden, you say? I said there was an odd smell...'

'Nicole?' Pemberton started waving the plastic bag in front of her face.

'Yes, sorry, I was out for an hour and half roughly, seeing my therapist, and it was waiting on the mat when I got home,' she replied, but she was more concerned by Stone's phone conversation right now; it sounded alarming. 'Sorry, what's happening in the search at the—'

'Ongoing,' Pemberton replied as Stone's voice receded. The DS must be walking further away from the house. 'And you believe Matt definitely is the author of this note?'

'Yes, I think so. Who else would want to threaten me?'

'We cannot discount the possibility of a hoax. There's been an appeal, so it's in the public domain and people are nasty. And...' Pemberton's brows knotted. 'I do agree with DS Stone; I'm not sure how this move fits in with taking the Golf. I'd have thought he'd be long gone after going to the trouble of walking back here to gain a car. Do you think it's possible your husband is being sheltered by a friend or family member? Your sister-in-law, perhaps?'

'Grace? No, she's frantic with worry.'

Nic's thoughts leapt back to her earlier theory that Matt was at her father's. It wasn't close enough by to chime with the note, but could Matt have gone there to hide out in the abandoned studio for those crucial first few days? No, her father had checked. 'I suppose it's possible he has been hiding somewhere close by, but nowhere springs to mind, and clearly wherever my husband may have been, he's now back, delivering threats to me, by hand.'

'Yes, any idea what he wants to achieve by this?' Pemberton brandished the note again, before shoving it back in her bag.

'No, not a clue.'

'OK, well we will investigate all options,' Pemberton said, glancing at the door, although there was no sign or sound of Stone. 'Would Matt have known you would be out this morning, a regular appointment?'

'No, I got a last-minute cancellation.'

'And Lily?'

'Yes, I messaged her my plans. As you know, she's been staying with Grace.'

The admission was difficult. A clarification of a situation which could easily be viewed positively, familial support, but which, the more she thought about it, only confirmed a rift that had been a long time coming and which Grace had capitalised on.

'Could Lily have told her father what you were doing this morning?'

'You think they might be in touch?'

Pemberton shrugged.

'Matt did call her on Friday morning, as you know, but she swears she hasn't heard from him since.'

Pemberton raised an eyebrow.

'I'm not aware of any communication since, although as you have probably noticed, things aren't that great between me and Lily.'

'Indeed, any particular reason for th—'

Stone came back in, offering a nod to her colleague which stopped Pemberton mid-question.

'The find, on the hill, behind The Glasshouse,' Stone began, then she paused, before sitting down heavily in the armchair facing them. 'Remains,' she clarified, as if she might have said *sock* or *tissue* or *book*. 'The cadaver dogs went straight to it and since the careful digging began an hour or so ago, we've uncovered a body which we strongly suspect to be that of Mrs Deena Hope Jensen.'

Nic fought for air as she swam in an abyss of horror, the detectives' faces receding down a long water-filled tunnel, her ears closing like gills as she sunk deeper and deeper. She was with the dogs digging down through the earth, filling her throat with soil so she couldn't breathe. Deena's eyes were uncovered first, then her torso, naked like the painting...Her skin dirty, hair matted. She could see it all as if she had claws in the earth herself. *Oh my god, Matt. You said you'd fixed things. Is this what you meant?*

'Do you understand what this means, Nicole?' Stone asked, leaning towards her from the armchair. 'Scott Jensen was out of the country. Mrs Jensen was at the house alone. And you've confirmed it was your husband on the CCTV visiting The Glasshouse on Tuesday morning at eleven. Then a couple of hours later, Lily finds him back here, washing blood from his hands, his clothing dirty and blood stained, which Lily said he told her was from the dirty garage floor and the cut sustained from clearing broken glass.' DS Stone leant back again. 'Which feels spurious at best, especially as he gave you an entirely different story. Matt wasn't at work; he was suspended,' Stone added. 'So the scalpel excuse is definitely a lie.'

'Yes,' she replied. 'It must be, I guess.'

'Right, so where were you on Tuesday, when the car was delivered?'

'Me? As I explained to your colleague' – she forced herself to look left, towards Pemberton's stern gaze – 'I was at Brackley, Lily's school. I am very involved, or rather was. If you need to check, you could talk with Amber Leatherby, head of Brackley

PTA. Many people saw me; I was there from nine until gone one.'

'I already checked,' Pemberton said, talking to Stone.

'Your husband knew you'd be out all of last Tuesday morning?' Stone asked, the detective's plain face still reflecting no hint of emotion.

'Yes, I'd told him my plans, but Lily came home earlier than expected, so I guess she surprised him.'

'Indeed. That much we *do* know,' Stone said.

'Do you know how Deena Jensen died?' Nic asked, her voice faltering.

'Multiple traumas, by the sounds of things,' Stone replied. 'We'll know more once the post-mortem is done, but if you have anything at all you want to tell us, now would be the time.'

'Such as?'

'Anything that might help us find your husband so we can talk to him? It would be better for Matt to come in now than to be found later. And better for you to tell us if you know where he is.'

All she managed was a small shake of her head, her fingers reaching into her hair. 'I don't know where he is, I swear.'

'OK, but I must insist,' Stone told her, 'that you have a family liaison officer here with you at all times. You said yourself' – she glanced at Pemberton – 'that you feel you are in danger, and we agree. Matt is clearly a desperate and dangerous man; he might come to you for help.'

Nic got up and walked unsteadily to the view of the garden. Her trees were out there and she needed them, their protection, not a stranger's. She needed to think. She needed to write in her notebook. To work out what all this meant and her next move. 'I don't want a stranger in my home; I've got good locks.'

Pemberton came and stood beside her, the detective's scent

familiar now. A mix of floral and almond oil and the toil of a long day. 'I know this is hard, but we have to ensure your safety. One of our officers will come and then keep you updated, act as liaison with us and the press, and they're trained to be as unobtrusive as possible.'

Nic tried to speak, but her throat was hard. All she could do was stare ahead, her trees swaying in the evening breeze. If she could just get out there, maybe she could work out what she should do, but if Matt was out there too, waiting...

'Amy,' DS Stone said, getting up then. 'Could you rustle up some tea? Two sugars for me, and three for Nicole.'

Pemberton left and Stone leant forward, patting the velvet sofa for her to sit down, as if they were going to have a nice chat. 'I'm sure this has all come as a huge shock, but I need to ask you a few questions. You up to that?'

She nodded and sat back down.

'Can you talk me through your movements last Tuesday morning?' Stone asked, taking out an identical-looking notebook to the one Pemberton used.

'I drove Lily to Brackley for her final exam, which started at nine, and we arranged to meet when she was finished, we'd said around one. I saw a few people, said some goodbyes myself, then I joined the outgoing meeting of the PTA, which dragged on, so Lily got a lift home with Will, her boyfriend, I think around midday. I've already told your colleague all this; she's clearly checked with Amber too, Will's mother. She said it checked out.'

'Yes, of course. Sorry, please indulge me. Anyone else you saw that morning?'

'Yes, the headmaster, David Kelm. He will vouch for me. I'm sorry, I don't understand why you're asking?'

'Sorry, bear with, it's just a bit of admin, to bring me up to speed,' Stone replied. 'And do you recall any conversations with your husband last week which stood out, or feel relevant now you know a little more? We're trying to piece together his movements, particularly last Tuesday.'

'You know he visited his sister's, first thing?'

'Yes, but he told you he was going into work?'

She nodded. 'Every day.'

'And you had no suspicion he was lying about that for almost two weeks?'

'No. He left in his work clothes, talked about the hospital a little when he got home; well, as much he ever does. I had no idea of the suspension.'

'You didn't try to call him at the hospital at all in the time you now know he was suspended?'

'No. He was always exceptionally busy, although it feels very odd, to be honest. The pretence of it, and that I have no idea what he was doing on those days.' She paused, considering that. 'We're a team, or so I'd thought.'

'A team,' Stone repeated, nodding. 'And to go back to the car he bought Lily. You say you had no idea about the Golf when Amy first asked you on Friday evening for details of other vehicles?'

'No, I thought I'd persuaded Matt out of what I considered to be an overindulgence. We were trying to make cutbacks.'

'I see, and yet you refused outright to sell the house to help with the finances; why was that?'

'As I said to DC Pemberton, I wasn't trying to be difficult; it's just Matt said we wouldn't need to sell and...' She drew a deep breath, now forced to explain something she'd hoped she wouldn't have to. 'Those trees out there...' She pointed them out as DS Stone followed her gaze. 'The three right at the back, by the wall.' Stone nodded. 'We planted one for each baby we lost before we adopted Lily. Two miscarriages, and a still birth. They are very precious to me.'

'I'm so sorry for your losses,' Stone said. 'But you could have taken the trees with you?'

'I think it's likely they'd have died, and of course, it was about more than the trees themselves. This place holds so many memories, but if I'd known the extent of the problem, I'd have been willing to help Matt in any way I could.'

'Even if you'd known about the affair and subsequent blackmail payments?' DS Stone asked. 'You'd have sold up, left your trees?'

Nic paused, unsure of her reply. 'Honestly? I don't know, but Matt didn't tell me the extent of the debt, let alone why. We've been married a very long time. I believed him when he assured me there would be no need to sell and that he would fix things.'

'How exactly was he going to *fix* things?' Stone asked, levelling the apparently simple but inciteful question.

'He said he'd speak to the patient concerned.'

'Your husband told you he would speak to Deena Jensen about the complaint?'

'No names – patient confidentially – and of course I said it wasn't a good idea, but yes, that's what he said he was going to do.'

'OK,' Pemberton announced, coming back in. There was no sign of the tea she'd been asked to make; it had clearly slipped her mind. 'Ry's checking for any local CCTV sightings for the Golf, but it's a long shot, unless we can narrow the search with a place Matt might be hiding?'

Nic shook her head, more fervently this time. She was cooperating with the police as much as she could, but she'd confirmed many times she hadn't seen the car. She hadn't even known it existed and had no idea where Matt was hiding out.

'The tea, Amy?' Stone reminded her.

DS Pemberton stuck a finger in the air and left the sitting room.

'You said those CCTV images of my husband at The Glasshouse gates were taken at eleven on Tuesday morning?'

'Yes,' Stone replied. 'Why do you ask?'

'Is there a chance there might be some later footage, maybe when he left, or someone else coming in, an intruder that Matt may have disturbed or who even followed him in?'

'The images Amy showed you are the last taken before the camera was smashed, and no other activity was captured before that, other than of Mrs Jensen herself.'

'Oh, I see.'

'I'm sorry. I know you want to defend him, but you're clutching at straws here.'

'Right, yes, I see,' she said, sinking back into the sofa.

'We know Deena left the house Monday evening and returned early hours of Tuesday,' Stone explained. 'She was a night owl, partying at a club in town, regular there, and the last contact with her husband was Tuesday morning, around nine. Although he tried to get hold of her continually after that until his return on Saturday. Her phone is missing too. Other than that, the cleaners came and went on the Thursday, and they didn't see her, or any sign of a break in, other than the smashed camera which they assumed was vandals, but sadly did not report in case they were blamed. I gather the Jensens were not the best of employers.'

Nic shook her head. 'I still can't believe it of Matt.'

'We think he was let in at the rear of the property by Deena. We've lifted his prints from the bedroom door.' Stone glanced up from her notes. 'And there was a rock, in fact there are plenty lying about up there; he could have used any one of them to smash the camera.'

'But none of that proves anything, does it?' she asked, sitting up straighter. 'You don't know how Deena died... and Scott told me Matt had visited often, so his prints would be there. Mine probably are too from when I went there on Sunday to talk to Scott myself.'

'Yes, but she was buried, Nicole, in a shallow grave. That would take a lot of strength, to drag her up the hill alone, and the only person who visited the house after she was last seen or heard of, was your six-foot two husband.' Stone sighed. 'Deena's blood was in the boot of his car, plus there is evidence Mrs Jensen was blackmailing your husband to the tune of a quarter of a million pounds. But let's see what we find up there; we've really just got started. Now, where's Amy? She's a good detective, but a lousy tea maker apparently.' Stone got up, stretching out her round shoulders and then her back.

'Before you go...' Nic said, stealing herself to share a confidence. 'The night before Matt disappeared...'

'Thursday night?' Stone said, looking down at her.

'Yes. Lily was away and I know it's not unusual for a married couple to be intimate' – Stone flicked up her bushy eyebrows – 'but it had been a while, sadly, a long while in fact... Sorry, is this is inappropriate? There *is* a reason I'm sharing this.'

The detective shook her head, as if nothing could shock or embarrass her. She must have seen every variation of humanity and inhumanity. 'Go on.'

'Matt was always passionate, but like I said, it had been a long while, and it felt... *different.*'

'Was he violent towards you?' Stone asked, sitting beside her.

'No! He was loving, like the old Matt. It felt like we'd reconnected, except...'

'What?' Stone asked, her interest clear.

'When he left the next morning, the last time I saw him...' She swallowed. 'He kissed me and told me he loved me, and he always would, and that whatever happened, I'd always been there for him and that I'd made him happy.' She looked into the mature detective's knowing eyes. 'How could I not have seen the signs? Why did I keep trusting him, even after—? I'm sorry, I've been such an idiot and I've got in the way of the search. I cannot believe I've been so blind!'

'You're not the first and I doubt you'll be the last to be taken in by a deceitful spouse,' Stone said. 'But you do need to be upfront with us from now on.'

'Yes, of course. I'm so sorry, I will be.'

'Let's have that tea, shall we?' Stone said, standing up. 'With lots of sugar. It's a good idea, when you've had a shock.' She waited for Nic to get up too, then said, 'Is there someone you can stay with for a few days? Your sister, Grace, is it?'

'Sister-in-law, and no, not really, we don't exactly... I mean, she's a good person but I'd prefer not to... I could go to my f—?' She caught herself just in time before the thought became a statement. If she did go to her father's, which suddenly felt very appealing, she'd prefer not to say, not yet at least.

'A friend?' Stone asked.

She struggled to think of anyone she could name as even an acquaintance. 'I could maybe ask Amber? But I'll need to check that's OK with her first.'

'Yes, of course, just let DC Pemberton know once you've decided. We will need to keep in touch.'

'Yes, of course.'

She wasn't sure why the idea of going to her father's was now so attractive. It was a long way, which was maybe part of the lure – and the detective might have refused on those grounds – but maybe it was more because she wanted to check the studio herself, just to be certain, and ideally before the police. The nagging doubt Matt might have gone there, to hide out for the crucial first few days, had resurfaced and taken hold as she'd talked to the detectives.

Yes, the more she thought about it, the more that salty sea air felt like a perfect escape. Just for a day or two, to order her thoughts and put some distance between her and Matt. She'd drive down tonight and notify Pemberton first thing of what she'd done. Once she'd seen for herself whether he'd been hiding out in Cornwall.

## 29

MONDAY 10 JUNE 2024 –10 P.M.

The uniformed police officer arrived at Three Gables' front door an hour after the detectives had left, summoning Nic from her preparations to get away herself. He seemed pleasant enough as she talked to him through the small gap in the front door, all the security chain allowed, but as she had already stated, more than once, she didn't want a stranger in the house.

'I have my orders,' the police officer explained, lines crinkling around his eyes as he smiled. He looked old enough to be retired. 'And I know what you ladies are like, not making a fuss, but it's no trouble, only vending machine coffee and a load of paperwork waiting for me back at the station; probably a drunk or two in the cells. Make me a cup of tea I can stand a spoon up in, and I'm happy. You won't even know I'm here!'

Her car was blocked in by his, which felt like a deliberate move, but maybe she was being paranoid.

'No, thank you, I'll be fine, honestly,' she replied, glancing past him to the distant woods, which had taken on an even more sinister character in the dark. 'I'm going to throw a few things in a bag, then I'm out of here, staying at a friend's.'

'Local is she, or he?'

'I said I'd message DC Pemberton the address, so I'll do that now, thank you.'

'Not leaving the country though, are you?' the officer asked, jamming a boot in the door as she went to close it.

'No, nothing like that,' she said, opening it the length of the chain again.

'Great stuff. Any concerns, call 999, Mrs Delaney. And do not answer the door to anyone before you leave.'

'I promise, and thanks again.'

She closed the door and watched through the glass panel as the marked car drove away. Maybe she should have asked him to check round before he left? But too late now.

She'd already bolted the back door but she checked it again, and all the window locks downstairs before she went up to the master suite and peeled away her sweaty clothes then stepped into the shower she'd been about to take before the door was knocked. The water pressure at her father's house was always abysmal and the only bathroom was damp and cold, and sadly not the cleanest, so it was good to feel the powerful jets of the ensuite's cooling rain shower once more before she left. But as she rinsed her hair of conditioner, the bald patch now worryingly large, she heard a thud outside the bathroom. It sounded like it came from the bedroom. She switched off the water and listened. All she could hear was the extractor fan and her own breaths. Maybe she'd imagined it? She grabbed a towel and wrapped it round her washed hair, wet footprints on the tiles as she pulled on her robe and eased open the locked bathroom door.

She walked through the dressing room and back into the bedroom, switching on lights as she went. The bedroom was empty, but the door was open. Hadn't she closed it before she undressed? Force of habit, even though Lily wasn't here.

She fastened her robe more tightly and crept out onto the empty landing, listening again before she ran downstairs. Each room was changed by the dark. She flicked on lights and called out, 'Matt? Is that you?'

Satisfied no one was in the house, the doors and windows checked, she poured herself a large glass of red wine, taking that and her notebook to the breakfast bar before unwinding the towel from her wet hair. The bald patch had felt horrendous when she'd shampooed her scalp, but she'd stopped pulling now, or would do soon. And although she'd planned to leave for her father's, pronto, she needed to calm down first. It was a long dark drive and her nerves were shot, although maybe the wine was unwise. She pushed the glass away and opened her notebook. It was three-quarters full already; so much had happened. Getting everything down was helpful, but the intended to-do list for the trip to Cornwall turned into something else as her thoughts cast further back. Way back. To another pivotal moment. One she still found incredibly painful to think about. For it was when she was forced to face up to the death of a dream. And not only her dream, but Matt's too.

\* \* \*

She'd been waiting to be discharged after the stillbirth of their son. It had been the most traumatic loss so far, but she still hadn't given up hope. She and Matt had talked about it and both agreed. She managed to fall pregnant three times. It would happen again, and next time, she would carry to full term.

Matt hadn't been there when the consultant made her rounds. Matt had briefly left to see his own patients. It often took hours to get the OK to go home. He'd be back as soon as he could and then he'd take her home to Three Gables. They'd even talked about planting the trees. It was a terrible time, but she kept hopeful.

'Most likely due to previous uterine abnormalities,' the consultant had told her when Nic had asked the question. 'Your notes are scant. It's a long time ago of course, but I'm guessing something happened when you were much younger, a nasty infection perhaps? The scans show a lot of scar tissue.'

'Yes, I had an infection when I was almost sixteen,' she'd replied. 'I was... It was a—'

The consultant had sat on the side of her bed and placed a hand on the blanket. 'You don't have to explain anything to me. And I'm so sorry for your recent loss. Stillbirth is a terrible thing to deal with, let alone the loss of a third baby, but you simply mustn't put yourself through another pregnancy. Do you understand? I have to insist that this be the end of the road. I'd strongly recommend you consider having a full hysterectomy.'

She'd refused, clinging to the chance of a miracle. But she didn't fall pregnant again. The consequences of a drunken night aged fifteen had rippled down the years to leave her scarred, inside and out. Life is endless in your teens, the future inconsequential. But the cost of her carelessness at such a tender age had proved unimaginable.

The wine glass tipped, red liquid seeping towards her notebook as she looked up from her account of that time. She could have sworn she'd seen movement outside again, in her peripheral vision. She slipped from the stool and ran to the patio doors. It was so dark out there, no streetlights, just the moon. She pressed her nose to the door but she couldn't see anything. Just the parasol creaking in the wind. Then she caught movement again, a figure beneath her trees. Or was it just shadows? She blinked and realised it was a swaying branch.

Her phone beeped loudly on the breakfast bar by the spilt wine. She righted the glass and wiped the phone dry with the sleeve of her robe. A message had arrived from DC Pemberton. The detective was requesting she supply a forwarding address. The family liaison officer she'd sent away earlier must have been in contact with Pemberton. It was getting late; time to get going.

She put her notebook back in her bag, the postcard tucked back inside it, and then she ran upstairs, past Lily's messy room and into hers. She pulled a leather holdall from the bottom of one of the mirrored wardrobes, then she remembered Matt's missing khaki rucksack and looked for it again, but it was definitely gone.

She took the holdall into the bedroom and pulled off the price tag before she started packing underwear from the drawers on her side of the bed. She'd bought the buttery soft overnight bag back in the January sales, in the hope she and Matt might manage a nice weekend away, maybe in London. She'd wanted to get tickets for *Hamilton*, but he hadn't seemed keen on going anywhere.

She threw in a waterproof jacket and some jeans, pulling clothes from hangers. The weather was so unpredictable by the coast, mostly clement at this time of year, but then without warning, it could turn ferocious. She packed a few more items of clothing, covering most eventualities, then got dressed in cropped leggings, t-shirt, hoodie and trainers. It was what she'd usually wear to the gym and it would be comfortable for the long drive. Then she went into the ensuite and began to drop toiletries into a washbag.

The smeared mirror looked back at her as she regarded her tired face. Was she truly running away from the man she'd loved for all these years? It felt ridiculous, but trust was such a tenuous thing, so easily broken and almost impossible to retrieve once compromised. She'd tried for so long to perpetuate the ideal of marriage she'd brought with her when she left home at just seventeen hoping for a fresh start. She was still a romantic at heart, despite everything, and ever hopeful of leaving the trauma behind, but Matt had let her down. Not only over the last weeks and months, but for many years before that too. He'd fathered a child with another woman. A betrayal too huge to truly forgive, or ever forget; however much they'd pretended that adopting Lily was the obvious solution to all their problems. It was never going to be perfect, not for her, not for anyone.

She grabbed her toothbrush and placed it in the washbag along with the last of her expensive moisturiser. There was just one more thing she needed to do, then she would be ready to leave.

The keepsake box was light but she used the plastic step she kept in the bottom of the wardrobe to reach it, lifting it from the top shelf next to the stack of filled notebooks. It had been some months since she'd felt the need to take it down, but she craved that connection to her lost babies now more than ever. She buried her face in the sleepsuit and inhaled a smell that now only existed in her memories but always pierced her heart. Then she looked at the scan photos. Three of them. It had been for nothing; pointless, all of it. And now Lily had read one, no two, she'd said, of her private notebooks. She reached up again and pulled all the filled notebooks down, the piles toppling, some hitting her as she stood on the plastic step, wondering which ones Lily had read and what they might have given away. It would be best to move them somewhere safer. Just in case. Especially as she was going away. But she couldn't bear to get rid of them; not yet.

She threw the keepsake box in the bin on her way to the car, almost changing her mind, but knowing it was meaningless now. Then she then tossed her leather bag into the boot before she turned back and took one last look at her home.

She'd loved Three Gables from the moment she'd persuaded Matt to drive them out, 'just for a look', after she'd spotted the auction notice in the local paper. The house had immediately captured her heart and would likely never hand it back. Much like Matt had when he'd strode into the rentals company where she'd worked, looking for a cheap place to live with his fellow medics, and also finding her.

'At least four kids,' he'd told her on their first date, as confident of that as himself. 'I want to fill the enormous house I'll own with tiny versions of me.'

\* \* \*

The heavy car's tyres kicked up clouds of dust behind her as she drove down the long dirt track, tapping the screen on the dash to access her phone contacts.

'Dad!' His immediate answer had surprised her; it was gone eleven. 'I thought you'd be asleep!'

'I couldn't settle.'

She checked her mirror as Three Gables grew smaller behind her, a pang of doubt in her chest, not only about leaving, but also that she'd thrown away the keepsake box, but since the police search nothing had felt sacred, although they hadn't disturbed her things as far as she knew. It was Matt's and Lily's stuff they'd concentrated on, for 'evidence'.

'Dad, I've just left mine, so I'll be at yours in about...' She tapped her dad's postcode into her satnav. 'Just under three hours, if that's OK?'

'You're coming here now?' her father said, his voice hoarse. 'And Lily?'

'No, just me. Lily is with Grace. That's OK, isn't it? I need to get away for a night or two.' She couldn't tell her elderly father about Deena's body being found, or Matt's threatening note, not over the phone.

'Of course, but wait until it gets light.'

'I don't mind driving in the dark; the roads will be much quieter now.' She'd reached the end of the track, the road pitch black other than the Evoque's headlamps, which illuminated the left turn she then made. 'Dad, is that alright? I've got my key, so no need to wait up.'

'Yes, sorry, of course, love. So you'll be here around two?'

'Yes, or just before.'

She was approaching the place where Matt's car had left the road, her headlights now angled into the wood as she followed the curve of the narrow road. Their beams arced through the dark spaces between the trees, and then, caught in the shadows and undergrowth, a pair of brightly lit eyes stared back at her. Her breath caught in her throat. The urge to let go of the wheel and allow the car's natural bias and the bend to pull her into the woods was a compulsion she had to fight until the very last moment. She snatched control back just in time and bumped back onto the tarmac road, the bend falling away behind her.

'Nicole? You still there? I said I'll wait up.'

'Yes, I'm here, Dad. Sorry, thought I saw... Must have been a deer.'

'Drive carefully, love, and don't rush; it's a long way in the dark. Love you.'

They so rarely said 'I love you'. It was implicit, as was the fact he'd do anything for her, but he had hesitated, hadn't he, before that, when she'd said she was coming? She ended the call and opened the driver's side window to keep herself awake as she headed south. She would feel better once she was there and she could check the studio for any signs of Matt that her elderly father may have missed.

## 30

TUESDAY 11 JUNE 2024 – 1.15 A.M.

A full moon hung above the rooftops of the Meadowfields estate as Grace looked out of the bedroom window. Ed snored in bed behind her, but she'd given up on sleep. She opened the door as quietly as she could and padded past the girls' silent room, feeling her way in the dark so as not to disturb anyone. They were top and tailing in Elan's single bed, but seemed to have settled.

She'd filled the kettle without thinking before she remembered she hadn't come down for tea. She unlocked the patio door and pushed her feet into an old pair of slip-ons she kept there for the garden and stepped out.

Her nightie billowed as she set off down the lawn, the lavender releasing its evocative fragrance into the night air as she brushed past on her way to the end, her phone lighting the way. There had been no news from Nic, or the detective, nothing since she'd left Three Gables with Lily the evening before. Which was good, wasn't it? If they'd found Deena's body, they'd have been in touch. Although she wasn't sure that was right. And as Nic had said, the use of cadaver dogs surely meant it was only a matter of time. But it could still be nothing. Surely Nic would have told her, if not? Maybe not, but DC Pemberton had promised to keep her in the loop.

She reached the water butt by Ed's shed and fished behind it for the Tupperware she kept there. Then she switched off the torch function and juggled her phone as she pulled open the tight lid to the plastic box and took out her cigarettes and lighter. The tobacco fizzed as she drew deep, a familiar feeling of light-headedness ensuing, as if she were floating away from her body. Then she exhaled smoke into the starry sky.

A vision of her brother washing blood from his hands made an unwelcome return as a bright-red tulip illuminated by the moonlight caught her attention. She'd brought the pots down here as the blooms were past their best, but one had sprung a new flower in the June heat. Was the blood on Matt's hands really from Deena? The woman he'd confessed to her only three days before his disappearance he'd tried but failed to 'shake off'? She dragged deep and contemplated her part in the sorry saga. She'd told her brother he had to end things, one way or another, but she hadn't meant for him to do anything drastic. And anyway, Matt wasn't capable of violence against women; he just wasn't. He saved lives. He didn't take them.

Her phone buzzed loudly in her hand, startling her so she dropped it in the grass. She picked it up and was surprised to see she wasn't the only night owl; a notification of a message from DC Pemberton was on her screen. Hands trembling, she clicked on the screen to open the message.

Thanks for info on your call from 'Gary', and
sorry for late reply. Have forwarded details to
colleague to trace number, but might take a
while, although I promise we are taking it
seriously. And just to update you, although I
expect you've heard from Nicole on this, we've
now unearthed a body up at The Glasshouse
which we strongly believe to be that of Deena
Jensen. More soon. DCP

A dog barked, a door slammed, but most of her neighbours
were likely in bed, as was her blended family. She sank into the
plastic chair by the water butt and tried her best to shut out the
rest of the world but her hands were trembling as she raised the
cigarette to her mouth again.

The reminders of Matt in his youth were coming thick and
fast.

'Is that true?' she'd asked her brother, watching him expertly
smoke one of their father's slim cigars at the end of their parents'
enormous garden. He was eighteen, a year older than her and yet
wise and worldly, or so it had seemed to Grace at the time.

He'd just shared his shonky but shocking medical knowledge
– pre-med-school – of how the arteries of heavy smokers clogged
with tar, like a blocked drain. And yet she didn't hesitate when
he'd then offered her a drag. She was already addicted by then,
Matt having got her started on 'ciggies' when she was thirteen.
She'd certainly never managed to give it up, despite her promises
to Ed that she hadn't smoked in years. In fact, her secret but long-
standing and passionate love affair with smoking had almost
been a deal breaker for Ed. His mother had died of emphysema
just before they met. He hated even the smell of it, so she'd
promised him, when they went on their first date, she'd been
about to give up anyway. And she'd lied to him about it ever since.

She crushed this latest cigarette under her slip-on and picked up the butt before flicking it into a bush. She then forced herself to walk back up to the house, but as she stepped into the kitchen Elan stopped her in her tracks. Her daughter was making some kind of smoothie in the dark, the blender then clattering ice so loudly she had to wait until the final burst had passed before she was able to speak.

'They look good,' she observed, switching on the light and watching as her wan-faced child turned, startled. 'I guess Lily is awake too, then?'

Elan added straws to the purple liquid before she picked up the filled smoothie glasses and tentatively walked towards the open kitchen door.

'You know, I was just remembering what it was like being with my brother when I was your age, and Lily reminds me so much of Matt. A bad influence too.' Grace forced a short laugh.

Elan dropped her eyes to the overfilled glasses and took a slurp through each straw.

'Not that I'm saying Lily is involving you in anything illicit, Elan, but there was that notebook of your aunt's, and you and Lily are always up there, together... Door closed, chattering away.'

Elan looked up the stairs longingly.

'I just want to ensure...' She suddenly felt extremely hot. 'I worry about you, sweetheart. Why is it you feel able to talk to everyone except—'

Elan left the kitchen and ran up the stairs, the purple liquid sloshing on the pale carpet in her daughter's haste to get away from her.

'OK, nice to catch up!' she called up after her, exasperation making her mean. 'Not like I'm going through hell here!'

\* \* \*

'I thought you were asleep?' Grace snapped, inexplicably angered by the fact Ed was sitting up in bed and reading his book as she went into their bedroom.

'Hard to sleep through the racket in this house,' he said, putting the weighty tome down on his bedside table. It was about the Battle of the Somme, and it had a sepia cover.

'I just had a message from DC Pemberton,' she told him, climbing in beside him. 'They found a body up at The Glasshouse, few hours ago. They think it's Deena Jensen.'

'Oh god, that's... awful,' Ed said, turning to face her, pillow to pillow. 'Just terrible. Does Nic know?'

'Yes, but clearly she saw no reason to inform me.'

'Police probably asked her not to tell anyone,' Ed said, as usual taking Nic's side. 'Send her a message, tell her we're here for her.'

'Are we?'

'Yes, we are; she must be worried sick. Should we tell Lily?'

They listened for the girls' voices through the thin wall but all seemed quiet again, so they settled on waiting until the morning.

'It could have been an intruder Deena disturbed?' she whispered after Ed had switched off his light.

'Yes, I was thinking that too,' Ed replied. 'It's a very nice property, tempting to a burglar who might have been watching the house when she was there alone.'

'Exactly!' she replied, feeling slightly more hopeful.

'But that still doesn't explain the blood in Matt's car.'

'Yes, I was thinking about that too,' she said, sitting up and switching her lamp on. 'If Matt went round to talk to Deena, after he borrowed the money from me...' She caught Ed's eye as he sat up too. 'From *us*, I mean, then he could have found her, after she'd been attacked by an intruder, and he would obviously have tried to save her. Which would explain the blood on his hands and in his car...' She noticed Ed's disbelieving expression in the low light of her bedside lamp, but she chose to ignore it. 'He must have panicked, knowing how it would look in view of the malicious complaint, and decided to run. It could have even been her jealous husband that killed her?'

'Wasn't he out of the country?' Ed asked, sitting up. 'And why was Matt there, anyway?'

'To persuade her to drop the lies about him, Ed! Please keep up! And no, not the husband then, you're right, but it could have been a burglar, or a drug dealer, or just some random madman? And don't discount Nic's part in all this!'

'What exactly are you suggesting, Gracie?' Ed asked.

'Nothing as such, but she knows something, don't you think?'

Ed rubbed his eyes. 'OK, there's a lot there to pull apart at this hour in the morning, but wasn't Matt the only person to be caught on CCTV going in or out other than Deena? And Nic was at Brackley, so I'm not sure what else there is to discuss.'

'Well, thanks! So you think my brother is a murderer?'

Ed shushed her, glancing at the wall between them and the girls. 'I'm not saying it was Matt, of course I'm not.'

'Good, because I know my brother isn't capable of taking a life. It would go against everything he's ever stood for.'

'But everything he ever stood for was on the line, Gracie. That's the point.'

'Oh, I give up!' she said, switching off her lamp and turning her back to him.

A soft snore soon came from Ed's side of the bed, but she was still going over their conversation in her head, and sadly coming up against the same issues as before. Every shred of evidence pointed to Matt being Deena's killer, but every fibre of her being knew her brother couldn't have murdered that poor woman. And she could not rest until she'd proved his innocence. Whatever it took, she would do it. Starting with an olive branch extended to Nic first thing in the morning. Unpalatable as that may be, she would clearly have to be the one to apologise if she were to keep the lines of communication open. Nic certainly wasn't going to, that much was clear.

## 31

It had been a much quicker drive to Cornwall than Nic was used to. One advantage of travelling through the dead of night with your foot to the pedal and no speed traps on the motorway, or at least none that she'd noticed.

She'd kept a close eye on her rear-view mirror though, looking out for police cars, and the black Golf, but once she was nearer to the sea, she began to relax. The final interminable section along the unlit and twisting coast roads always dragged the most, her tired eyes straining against lack of sleep for those last few miles, but then there it was, Chy an Mor: 'The House by the Sea'. The three-storey whitewashed upside-down house still clinging, somehow, to a promontory of rock overlooking the glorious bay far below. Not that you could see the beach in the dead of night, but she could hear the waves as she stepped out of the car, her limbs stiff and her eyes feeling gritty and sore.

Despite telling him not to wait up, her father was on the front step, the porch light shining down on his smattering of grey hair that now barely covered his balding pate. He waved, his back straight, although the stoop returned as he walked over to where she'd parked, an exaggerated slope beneath his threadbare cardigan which hung from bony shoulders like it was on one of those cheap metal hangers. His long socked feet were, of course, pushed into the same pair of tartan slippers he'd worn for years.

'Hey, Dad!' she called over. 'You go in. I'll just stretch my legs and breathe in some sea air.'

'Watch your step, love,' he said as she walked towards the gate at the side of the house. 'Path's getting worse by the day.'

'It's OK, I'll just take a quick peek at the sea. It's been a while.'

She'd successfully kept her fear of heights from her dad. What had happened in the studio was never discussed either. Nothing about that night was.

Ironically, she'd been a 'mountain goat' before that, at least according to her father, who'd often warned her to be careful of running along the narrow cliff path, much as she'd told Scott when he'd questioned her crippling vertigo.

She lifted the latch and slipped through the gate, closing it as quietly as she could. Few ramblers used this section of the path, although it was a public right of way, but the access was over their land and therefore it was mainly ignored as a route down to the sandy bay. And as her father had just warned, the path was crumbling badly in places, coastal erosion taking away edges that tumbled down the sheer cliff face to the sea below.

She tried not to think about that, but it was impossible as she was assaulted by a strong sea breeze, the briny smell taking her straight back to a time when she'd loved the cliffs, walking herself down to the quieter coves whilst her father tended his patients. It was a hundred-foot drop in places. But that hadn't been the real danger, not in the end. That had turned up unexpectedly, and on a beautiful night very much like this. The kind of benign darkness of summer you think will never wake up to the harsh light of morning. A night to take chances. To live a little. To be young and reckless and damn the consequences. A night that had irrevocably altered the course of the rest of her life. For so long, she'd thought the events that took place when she was fifteen would be the worst thing that could, or ever would, happen to her, but it seemed there was no limit on trauma and tragedy.

The sea shimmered under the moonlight as the clouds parted. The section of path that led to the rear of the house was easily discernible now, loose stones biting into the tracks of her trainers as she forced herself along, headed towards the second gate that gave access to the back garden. The white-washed side elevation of Chy an Mor loomed high above. Only another thirty paces or so and she'd be through and would able to walk down to where the studio was. But to her right, and only half a trainer's width away, the edge fell sheer to the waves that crashed in.

She counted down the final painful paces: twenty, fifteen, ten. She didn't dare turn her head to look out to sea, but the night she'd walked this path, just a few months before her sixteenth birthday, came back as clear as if it had been only days before. And although she tried everything not to think about it, she could do nothing but.

She'd fancied him for ages, the handsome sixth former with blond floppy hair who'd captained the rugby team and was going to be a policeman, like his dad. And because she was drunk on life and sun and heady on being a fifteen-year-old girl, she'd smiled as she walked past the group of lads drinking cheap cider on the beach. She been walking home, on her own as usual, but to her amazement, he'd run after her and asked her, shyly, from behind the blond fringe, if she'd like to join them.

She sat on the sand next to him and he'd slung a muscular rugby player's arm around her shoulders and placed a warm can of cider in her hand, his lips on hers to a chorus of catcalls. She should have known better than to dream of romance and flowers, but she didn't because she was too young to know that her life was about to implode that starry night.

The boy's father, the local policeman, turned up at some point and told them to put out the beach fire and go home. The lads bantered with him whilst she'd lolled drunkenly against the boy's shoulder. There may have been a wink offered to his son by the policeman with his notepad and dire warnings – to her, not them. It was all a bit of a haze by then; the vodka she'd mixed with the cider had made her sick. The boy held her hair and put a hand in her bra behind the rocks. It was now an hour past her curfew. Her father would soon be out looking for her. The boy said he'd walk her back along the cliff path to protect her from a fall, make sure she got home OK.

Fifty-four-year-old Nic rested a hand on the garden gate, gathering her breath before she went through, then securing it behind her with the heavy iron pin that slotted into a metal loop. The garden sloped away into the dark, the grass dry and scratchy as it brushed at her ankles, the far end obscured in deepest shadow, then out of the gloom came her mother's studio. The one place where Nic had felt closest to the woman who'd been missing from her life since she was a baby. This was where she ended up with that boy, although how she had got from the cliff path to inside the locked studio, she still couldn't remember.

Her father had half-killed the boy when he'd eventually found them. Nic had pleaded with her dad not to call the police, *begged* him not to report what had happened, knowing how it would play out in their small community. She would be even more alone. She was already an outsider at school with her missing mother and her father the GP who knew everyone's most intimate problems.

She'd sometimes wondered if her father had agreed to her request because he knew it would also be the end of his career. The boy's father, the village policeman, would have made sure of that. They were a thuggish family, but they knew everyone. She'd thought the boy was different with his shy manner and gorgeous blue eyes, but he'd held her down so tight, she'd feared she might die until her mild-mannered father had broken the door down and beaten the lanky scared-to-shit lad to a pulp. He'd then warned him not to tell anyone who'd broken his nose or he would report him for paedophilia as well as rape. The lad had promised and cried and then run off.

She had promised her father something too, that she'd go to the hospital the next day, get checked for all the terrible things he'd warned her she might have caught from unprotected sex with a lad like that. A bumpy bus ride away, on her own – her father had his own patients to see – she made a pretence but never went.

The burning inside had started almost immediately. She ignored it until it got so bad, she couldn't pee without crying. Her father drove her to A&E where he waited in the corridor. He'd trusted her once to go alone; he wouldn't do so again. She was asked to undress from the waist down and a man her father's age raised her feet in stirrups, telling her, 'Condoms, next time, young lady, if you want to have lots of lovely babies when you grow up, and take the antibiotics I'm going to prescribe.'

In fairness, the bruises on her inner thighs had faded by then, the blood that ran into her sanitary towel also abating. And anyway, the doctor was right; it had been careless of her. She had led the boy on, kissed him under the stars, pressed herself against him as the universe spun above her. This would be her punishment for being, as the lad and his friends shouted whenever she passed them at school afterwards, 'a slutty prick-tease'.

Her father hadn't said a word on the drive back from A&E, other than to ask what she'd been prescribed and make her promise to take the meds. He'd seen every kind of 'women's troubles' but she was still his baby. The daughter he'd raised alone and protected fiercely. But she would be fine if she took the antibiotics. No blame, of course. Her father loved her, understood it was his fault too; he would be a more attentive dad in future. She promised she'd take the prescribed tablets, but they made her sick, and anyway, she didn't ever want to be with a man again, let alone have babies. She'd been terrified for weeks she might be pregnant. It would a relief to be infertile.

She was a slut. A tease. She deserved to be punished, and boy, had she been punished! Especially since she'd met Matt. The man who wanted 'at least' four kids.

Connie had a different take. 'You were raped, Nicole. There is no fault on your part.'

* * *

She was almost at the studio door now. She paused in the long grass. Almost forty years and barely ten steps stood between her and the answers she craved about Matt. Had he been hiding out here as he'd suggested he might?

She reached for the door handle, turning it slowly, breath held, before she realised it wasn't going to be as easy as that. Her father had locked up the studio after the night she was attacked. The padlock, which was now rusted in the lock, barred her way.

She edged round to the window at the side, a nettle brushing her bare ankle beneath her cropped leggings, fire across the exposed skin. The windowpane was large but covered in green mould and sealed tight when she rattled it. She pressed her nose up to it and could just about make out her mother's paintings on the walls, and the door to the toilet which was slightly ajar. Then she spotted something else: a khaki-green rucksack on the floor by the moth-eaten armchair.

'What are you doing down there, Nicole?'

She spun round as her father walked towards her, his elongated features exaggerated by the shadows. The nettles stung her again as she clambered back to the studio's locked door, meeting her father there.

'Dad! You startled me.'

'I wondered where you were, thought I'd find you on the path.'

'Yes, sorry, I ended up here.'

'Right. Well there's a cup of tea made for you and going cold,' he said, turning and walking back towards the house.

'Dad, wait!' she called after him. 'Was Matt... I mean, I thought I saw, through the window... Is that his rucksack in the studio?'

Her father paused, as if he might answer, but then he kept walking.

# 32

TUESDAY 11 JUNE 2024 – 9 A.M.

Grace drove the brown Volvo down Three Gables' long track, the front windows wound down on account of the heat. Ed had kindly said he'd cycle to the office so she could use the car. He was being nice, but mainly he'd wanted her to return Nic's notebook without further delay. She'd agreed, but she was still annoyed with him from last night. He'd basically called Matt a murderer and she just wasn't having that. It was the fourth day since her brother had disappeared. She was hot, tired and heavy hearted. It hardly seemed fair that she should be the one extending the olive branch, but she'd made a decision to keep Nic on-side, and she would stick to that. Nic knew a lot more than she'd been letting on, Grace was sure of it, and the best way to find out what was to keep her as close as possible.

But Nic's car wasn't on the drive.

Grace knocked the front door, stepping back to look up at the master suite. The blind was pulled down, although the rest of the house was wide-eyed to greet the morning sun.

She called out a loud hello as she used her key. The last thing she wanted was to invade her sister-in-law's privacy, again. Not that she intended on confessing to reading the private notebook, not unless she had to. She would simply explain that she'd confiscated it from Lily. The alarm system starting beeping loudly as she went in. She tapped in Lily's date of birth on the pad by the door and called out again, just in case.

'Hello? Nic? *Matt?* Anyone home?'

The kitchen was a mess, dishwasher open and full of dirty plates, and a red wine stain slicked across the breakfast bar. She turned the key in the patio doors, the ones restored at great expense, or so Nic had always told her, and threw the bolt.

The garden didn't look as if it had been touched since the aborted party: the parasol was still unfurled over the patio table, and the bottle of champagne she'd helped to demolish now floated in water in the ice bucket. It was so unlike Nic to ignore any imperfections, but of course understandable, given the circumstances.

She went back inside and locked the patio door, then she found a cloth by the sink and wiped down the breakfast bar. She could leave the red notebook there. She took it from her shoulder bag and contemplated how that might look on Nic's return. The trouble was, it would implicate her in Lily's transgression. She popped it back in her bag and headed upstairs, to where Lily said Nic kept the notebooks. Hopefully, she'd be able to return it to its original hiding place. Maybe Nic hadn't even missed it?

Her nerves made her clumsy as they always did, a half-trip on the top tread propelling her face down onto the landing, but no one was around so she got up quickly and moved on, poking her head into the guest room first. Nic had turned it into a nursery as soon as they'd bought Three Gables, but it was now a very plain but tasteful guest bedroom where Nic's father occasionally stayed. Grace had been so jealous when Nic had shown off the exquisite nursery. Even though she had never wanted kids, it had felt like Nic had everything on a plate, as usual, whilst her burgeoning relationship with 'Steady Eddie', as Matt nicknamed him, felt like a compromise in every respect. That nursery sadly never saw a baby, the cot empty, the wallpaper steamed from the walls.

When Lily finally arrived, she was given the 'new nursery' down the hall, which was still her bedroom now. Lily's door was closed so she carried on, the master suite door facing her at the end of the long landing, and also closed. She opened it slowly and, although she knew it was unlikely anyone was home, she still called ahead, 'Hello, Nic? Are you there? Coming in!'

The ensuite, to the left, was a scene of devastation, at least by Nic's usual standards. Towels on the floor, a tidemark round the bath, the cupboard under the sink open and sprays and pots spilling out. The dressing room was just as disorganised, most of the mirrored doors open, even Matt's small section, and Nic's clothes on the floor. She kept going, and although the Evoque was gone and likely Nic with it, she still half-expected to find her sister-in-law spread-eagled across the huge bed, a pot of pills in one hand and a bottle of red wine in the other. She'd worried about Nic a lot over the years, and now more than ever, but thankfully the bed was messy but unoccupied, then a creak behind her on the landing made Grace jump. She spun round and ran back to the door. 'Hello?'

The long landing was empty. She doubled back, going into the dressing room, determined now to return the notebook and then leave. Three Gables was freaking her out.

The stack of filled red notebooks were stowed, according to Lily, on a high shelf at the top of the far-left mirrored wardrobe. There were indeed at least a dozen identical ones there, but all still wrapped in cellophane. She hesitated, then reached up and slotted the purloined one she'd confiscated from Lily beside the new ones, her height in her favour for once. There was a plastic step in the bottom that Nic must use to stand on and reach up. She would explain to Nic, if needed, that she'd acted on Lily's behalf, but she doubted it would ever come up. It was between Lily and Nic. Nothing to do with her. And she wasn't even the teensiest bit disappointed that the filled notebooks had been moved. No, she wouldn't have read them anyway. Her conscience would never have allowed it. Yes, it was definitely for the best that she would have to talk to Nic herself, as soon as she could. Find out in an honest and moral manner what she knew. She slammed the wardrobe doors shut and was about to leave when she remembered she'd promised to collect Lily's laptop whilst she was there.

It was charging on Lily's desk, the lid closed. Grace picked her way through the discarded clothes and shoes on the floor and opened the lid of the laptop to save anything Lily was working on. She tapped the trackpad and congratulated herself on her foresight, noting there was an unsaved document on the screen. She was unplugging the charger to take that too when the printer beside the laptop sprang to life, startling her as a document was spat out.

She picked up the expelled sheet from the printer, a few words of typeface spanning the otherwise blank page. She couldn't help but read the note. It was from her brother, after all. But why had it printed from Lily's laptop?

## 33

TUESDAY 11 JUNE 2024 – 9.15 A.M.

Nic's first thought on waking that Tuesday morning in her old childhood bedroom was for the rucksack she'd seen through the studio's grimy window. The same rucksack he used for documents when he travelled, but her father had insisted the key to the rusted padlock was long lost and that it therefore couldn't have been Matt's and she must have been mistaken. He'd promised to try to find the key in the morning.

Considering how agitated she'd been when she'd gone to bed, she also couldn't believe how well she had slept, and in a single bed. It was gone nine, so she'd had close to seven hours. The best night she'd had since Matt had left. She'd been exhausted of course, and the sea air invariably worked its magic, but given the circumstances, it still surprised her. In fact, she felt guilty about it.

She sat up and grabbed her phone, scrolling for any reports of Matt, but even the local news website back home seemed to have given up on the story. There were no messages from Lily either, just one from Grace asking where she was as she'd just been to Three Gables and found that she wasn't there. She was trying to work out how to reply when a loud knock at the front door jolted her from the creaky bed and to her door.

The bedrooms were on the ground floor, hers at the end of the hallway, her father's opposite. He came out and gave her look, as if to hold her there, then he went to open the front door, his stooped figure blocking her view of the visitor.

'Dr Wood,' a man's voice said. 'Is your daughter staying here? I've got my orders from up high to check if you've heard or seen from her since late last night.'

She edged along the hall to see better. The man was, as she'd feared, a uniformed police officer. It hadn't taken them long to find her, and she hadn't had a chance to check the studio properly yet. She gritted her teeth as she listened to the conversation, keeping back enough to still be concealed from view.

'Can't it wait?' her father asked. 'Nicole's exhausted. We were both awake until—'

'Ah, so she *is* staying here!' the officer replied, sounding pleased. 'Can you wake her up? I need to—'

'What is it, Dad?' she asked, walking towards them.

'It's fine,' her father said, turning to her. 'I'll deal with this.'

'Um, with respect, Dr Wood, you will not,' the police officer said.

He looked about her age, chin pulled in so hard it had doubled, his gaze falling somewhere south of where it should have been as she stood by her father at the door. Her nightdress was a thin lawn cotton. She might as well have been naked. She sheltered behind her father, who was looking shaky. 'Is this to do with my husband?'

'In a manner of speaking, Nicole,' the officer replied.

'Sorry, do I know you?' she asked, thrown by his familiar use of her first name. There was definitely something recognisable about him, but that wasn't her major concern right now and he didn't answer, just rocked on his boots. 'Why are you here?' she asked, stepping forward again, despite her exposure in the see-through nightie.

He stared again, unashamedly, then cleared his throat. 'A black Golf registered to your home address has been located close by,' he replied. 'I need you to accompany me to where it was found.'

'Oh my god, where? Is Matt OK?'

Her father looked shaken by the news too. She grabbed his arm, although she felt like she needed to be held up as much as he did.

'If you could get dressed now and come with me?' the police officer said, shifting from foot to foot. There were sweat patches on his shirt as he lifted his cap onto a pinking forehead, the smell of body odour acrid, even from a few paces away. 'I'll wait in the car, but be quick as you can. I don't have all day!'

'I'll go,' Gerald said as he began to close the door.

'No, it has to be Nicole,' the officer said before he turned and walked to his car, adding over his shoulder, 'And quickly!'

'It's OK, Dad, I want to go,' she said as she closed the door, firmly this time.

She hadn't thought about the Golf since she'd arrived late the previous night, the relief of putting miles between herself and that note diluting the sense of threat that had taken her so far from home. She'd been tired, could have easily missed him following her. Or maybe he had been here all along?

If she'd had time, she'd have run down to the studio again, but it was still locked, and the key missing, and a police officer was outside waiting for her. She couldn't risk it. So she heeded his brusque request and rushed to get dressed. Even her brief visit to the bathroom was hurried, but as she pulled on jeans, the questions circled round and round. Why wouldn't he tell her if

Matt was OK? Did silence equate to bad news? Her father's grave demeanour certainly indicated his feelings on the matter as she met him back in the hall, his shoes and jacket on.

'At least let me come with you, love.'

She zipped up the waterproof she'd brought in case of rain, and then replied, 'No, we don't know what's happened and you already look white as a sheet.'

'All the more reason to go together,' he said, but she shook her head and opened the door, stepping out into blaring sun.

The waterproof was clearly a poor choice for such hot weather, but she hadn't been concerned with what to wear, just to dress as quickly as possible. She was already sweating as she walked the few paces to the waiting police car. The officer was sitting behind the steering wheel, window down, an elbow hanging out.

'Oh, Dad!' she said, turning back to her father, who was watching from the door. 'Can you call Grace and Lily? Let them know I'm staying here and that Lily's Golf has been found.' Her father looked confused. 'I'll explain it all later. You've got Grace's number, in case of emergencies. I don't want to get into it with her myself, not now, but they should know.'

Her father nodded. 'Yes, OK.'

A car horn blared, making them both jump. She turned around in time to see the police officer shout, 'Literally don't have all day!'

'Dad, did you get all that?' she asked, ignoring the rude police officer.

'Yes, but I'm not sure I have Lily's number.'

She forced herself to be patient. 'Lily's staying with Grace; remember, I told you that last night when I called to say I was driving here? You've got Grace's landline number, I know you have, stored in your phone, OK?'

He nodded again.

'And don't get chatting to Grace about Matt; there are things I need to tell you first. Promise?'

Her father nodded and shuffled back into the house, glancing over again before he closed the door. He was looking worryingly frail. She wanted to go back, to keep an eye on him, and to go down to the studio. She'd smash the window if the key couldn't be found. She was certain that Matt's rucksack was inside last night, so he must have found a way in, and she would too. Although it had been dark when she'd peered through the dirty window, and she was exhausted from the drive. A loud blare of a car horn made her jump. It seemed she didn't have time for any of that, and she was desperate to get to the Golf and maybe Matt too. That had to be her priority now.

* * *

The police officer drove fast and the car smelt of his sweat and rancid food, all of which turned her stomach. She glanced across at him as the road widened and straightened, trying again to place him. His shirt collar cut into his flabby neck, his belt buckle straining. He'd taken off his sleeveless jacket but still only just fitted behind the steering wheel. The tattoos on his knuckles were the kind the boys self-inflicted on themselves in her youth.

'Did we go to the same school?' she asked.

He smiled. 'What do you reckon?'

She huffed. 'Do you understand the seriousness of the situation with my husband?'

He said nothing.

'My husband, Matt, had a car crash last Friday and has been missing ever since.'

'Not so good at driving then, is he?' he asked in his Cornish burr.

'What does that mean?' She glanced over, forcing herself to take a breath. 'There's a detective back home, DC Pemberton; I could call her? She will fill you in.' She took her phone from the pocket of her plastic jacket.

'No need,' he replied, putting on mirrored sunglasses as the car rounded the headland. 'She was the one who asked me to find you, but right now I am in charge of this matter, so less with the questions, Nicole, OK?'

'Could you at least tell me where the car was found?' she asked as the bay spread out in front of them. Pemberton's involvement was a shock, although maybe it shouldn't have been, and it was taking every ounce of her self-control not to lose her rag with him.

'Almost there,' he said as they drove inland, fields either side before the road looped back to the coast.

She looked out the passenger window, snatched sights of the sea to her left, blue and calm in the morning sun. It reminded her of the postcard, and the bus journey to school. She'd always felt sick then too, particularly those last few months. The dread of knowing that when she got there, the comments would begin.

'You were right,' the police officer said, making her jump. 'We were in the same year at Merryhill Comp.'

She stared ahead, her mouth filled with saliva. She swallowed. 'Did I know you?'

'Nah, but you knew my older brother,' he said, turning to deliver his line with a grin. 'Captain of the rugby team, and a handsome devil!'

She recoiled and pressed her cheek to the side window, her breaths short and sharp. She would never have placed him, the years had been less than kind, and clearly they hadn't been friends, but the mention of his brother and the details that placed her firmly back in the studio, that boy on top of her, holding her down, were enough to make her want to scream. If the car hadn't been travelling so fast, she'd have opened the door and bailed.

'It's been a long time,' he said, ignorant to her turmoil, or possibly not entirely ignorant but uncaring. 'Rich sends his regards, by the way.'

'He knows I'm with you?' She looked behind her, as if her rapist might be in the back seat, leering at her, a warm can of cider in his hand, blond floppy hair falling over his blue eyes. The devil incarnate. He'd been the stuff of nightmares for her whole adult life. His strength as he broke the lock and then held her down, so fierce her father had to kick his head in to make him stop, had never left her.

She gagged as she recalled the smell of the boy's body parts as he'd tugged them free of his jeans, how they'd been forced in her face, then inside her. The car was speeding too fast. She was hideously queasy now, her chest thumping, thoughts spiralling, breaths hard to catch as bile rose up.

'Easy tiger!' he replied, the smirk still there as he glanced over and grinned, or rather leered. 'I can see you thinking about him, but Rich is a family man these days, stationed in Manchester. I just sent him a quick text about you, but no fuckin' response as usual! Suits him there, bloody thug. You remember that night on the beach, don't you?' He looked at her again. 'Different times, eh?'

Had this man been there too? One of the gang plying her with cider and then vodka so his brother could—

'Mind you, he was so pissed that night...' He glanced across, smirking again. 'You were too! Rich claimed he'd been in a fight with a door when he got home!' He started chuckling to himself.

'More like fell off the cliff path, the piss-head! Bloody lucky he made it home in one—'

'Stop the car! Stop the car!' she shouted, trying to open the door, which wouldn't budge. 'I'm going to throw up!'

'Fuck!' he said, looking alarmed and pulling into a layby at the side of the coast road. 'We're here now anyway, but don't puke in my car!'

She rattled the door again and he leant over to release the door.

She half fell, half stumbled out, shedding her waterproof and running from the car towards the coast as she retched. There were police cars and rescue vehicles everywhere, officers shouting at her to stop as she zig-zagged between them towards the cliffs, wishing she could be sick and finding she couldn't. What she also couldn't do was stop, arms outstretched as she headed towards the cliff edge, officers grouped there, the steep gradient of the grassy expanse making her so fast, she thought she'd never stop, or want to.

'Oi! Stop!'

She dodged the nearest police officer's attempts to grab her and ignored the alarmed rescue team members in their green jackets who flashed past, her trainers fast in the grass, frantic calls to her to stop all ignored as she headed towards the drop.

She fell onto her knees with metres to spare before the ground fell away. People were running towards her then, from all directions, shouts and calls and concern as they realised she'd finally stopped.

'Hey, you OK?'

Someone was beside her, a female police officer, talking her back from the edge, but she had to see what was happening down there. She inched forward, despite the officer's impassioned pleas she stop. The cliff was eroded and crumbling away beneath her grasping fingers as she clawed at the crumbling sandy earth and looked over.

Fifty feet beneath her, maybe more, a rescue operation was underway, although surely no one could have survived that drop? She watched, flat on her tummy, the female officer's hand on her back as a black car was dragged by a tractor up the beach, water draining from the Golf like a giant colander.

# 34

The landline was ringing as Grace returned home from her visit to Three Gables. Ed had cycled to work and the girls seemed not to hear, music blaring upstairs. She ran to the phone on the hall table, for some reason thinking it might be Gary, although he didn't have the home number, just her mobile, and she hadn't heard from him since Sunday. Her attempts to call him had also gone unanswered. And nothing from the detective about tracing him either. It wasn't being treated as a priority, clearly.

'Hello?' she said, her bag falling from her shoulder. She placed it on the hall table. The typed sheet that had printed out from Lily's laptop, ostensibly from Matt, poking out. A reminder, as if she needed one, that she had questions for her niece. Urgent questions.

'Grace, is that you? It's Gerald, Nicole's father. Have I got the right number? Nicole asked me to call you.'

'Yes, hi, it's Grace. What's happened, Gerald? Is Nic with you?' Lily's laptop was still tucked under her arm, the cable trailing behind her across the hall. She placed it on the table too, turning round to see Lily, then Elan, appear on the stairs.

'I don't know if you know,' Gerald continued in his tremulous and slow baritone, his accent more public school than Cornish. 'Nicole arrived here in the early hours.' He sounded nervous.

'No, she didn't tell me,' she replied, ignoring Lily, who'd run down and was standing very close to her, mouthing questions, whilst Elan had stayed at the top of the stairs. 'Can I speak with her?'

'Anyway,' Gerald said, clearing his throat. He seemed not to have heard her question. 'A police officer turned up here a few minutes ago to collect Nicole. They've found Matt's car. Well, not his car, but another car, a Golf... Grace, can you hear me?'

'Yes, Lily's car,' she prompted, catching Lily's eye. 'Where was it found?'

'Have they found Dad too?' Lily asked, crowding her in the small hallway.

'No, just your car,' she told her, missing what Gerald next said as she switched the phone to speaker. 'Sorry, Gerald, Lily is here with me.' It was as much a warning as anything. 'Can you repeat that?'

'Hi, Grandpa, have they found Dad?'

'Lily, is that you, love? I don't know, I don't know.'

'OK, Gerald.' She wrinkled her brow at Lily. 'Take your time.'

'All I know is that Nicole has been taken to where the car is. I should probably get off the line in case she calls me. She said she'd let me know as soon as she knows more.'

'OK,' she said. 'Can you please call us back the moment you hear anything? This number is fine. We will be here, waiting.'

'Yes, of course. Bye, Lily. Bye, Grace.'

'It doesn't mean anything, not yet,' she said, her niece's grey-green eyes fixing on hers as she put the phone back on its base, the note poking out of her bag and catching Grace's eye. 'So let's not speculate,' she said, turning back to Lily. 'Not yet.'

'But if they've found my car near to Grandpa's house then that must be where Dad is too! We should go down there, now!'

'Maybe,' she replied, winding the cable around Lily's laptop and handing it over to her as she considered that option, which had of course occurred to her too. 'Let's see what the next few hours bring. I promised your grandpa we'd be here to answer his call.'

'Mum has her mobile, and if Dad is there, we need to be too! We can't hang around.'

'Yes, I agree, let's get down there soon, and in the meantime we need to have a chat about this!' Grace took the sheet from her bag and held it up, printed side facing Lily. 'Any thoughts?'

As soon as she saw Lily's face, and then the look Lily gave Elan, Grace knew she'd been right to suspect her niece's hand in this. 'Go upstairs, girls; I'll be up in a mo to talk to you both. Once I've gathered my thoughts.'

* * *

It was ten minutes before Grace was knocking lightly on Elan's closed door. She'd wanted to make Lily sweat, but there was no way Elan was more than an unwitting helper in a nasty little scheme to scare Nic with a faked threat.

She'd used the time to call Ed and tell him he needed to come home from work; they were going to Cornwall. She knocked again, music blaring, then she went in.

Lily was on her back on Elan's bed, feet up on the wall, scrolling on her phone. The room was a mess, the laptop Lily had been so desperate for her to collect abandoned beside her on the bed. Her niece didn't move when she came in, which struck Grace as rude, but she did at least tap her phone and the music coming from the speaker stopped. She'd thought the girls would be frantically getting their stories straight, but it seemed like they didn't care, either of them. Grace bristled. This was her house and Lily was a guest in it. It would do her niece well to remember that. Lily did at least sit up then, which was something, and Elan, who was at her desk, stopped typing on her ancient laptop and spun the chair round.

'Composing another threatening note, were you?' Grace asked her daughter, the words harsh and probably unfair. This was Lily's artifice; it had her meanness all over it. 'Talk to me!' she said, shoving the printed sheet under Lily's nose. 'I know this is your work; it came out of your printer!'

'What?' Lily asked, looking confused as she took it.

'Don't play the innocent with me!' she replied, snatching it back. 'This is your composition, isn't it?' Grace pointed at the offending laptop by Lily. 'I'm disappointed in you both, to be honest,' she said, folding the sheet over and blading the edge with her thumb nail as Elan looked at her, most definitely sheepish. 'Don't you think your mother has enough to worry about without you creating false threats?' she asked Lily. 'Thank goodness it was me that found it, not her!'

Lily's look of confusion had turned to contrition, finally. 'Um, I think she probably has seen it.'

'What?' Grace asked, looking at the sheet. 'You mean this isn't the only copy?'

'My printer wouldn't pair from here, so I got Will to print a copy which he dropped round yesterday morning.'

'Oh my god,' Grace said, looking from Lily to the folded sheet. 'I cannot believe I'm hearing this!'

'Please, Aunt Grace, don't involve Will,' Lily asked, not even trying to deny it, although the consequences seemed to finally be sinking in. 'He only wanted to help me out.'

'You want me to help you out?' She shook her head at her

niece. 'Can you imagine how your mother must have felt receiving this? No wonder she drove to Cornwall through the night! She must have been terrified.'

Grace unfolded the creased sheet and read the words with greater clarity now she'd confirmed they were the work of a spiteful teen.

Don't pretend you don't know why I left. This is all your fault.
Matt x

'And why do you assume this was all me?' Lily said, startling Grace. Lily then pointed at Elan and told her cousin, 'You said no one would ever know it was us!'

'Is this true?' Grace asked, turning round to her silent daughter.

But there was no reply from Elan, who dropped her gaze to her bare knees beneath the ubiquitous black shorts.

'So why do it?' she asked them both. 'To what end, other than vindictiveness?'

'Mum made Dad go away,' Lily replied, confirming Grace's initial suspicion of the rationale. 'Please don't tell Will's mum.' There was real fear in Lily's plea. 'He'll never speak to me again.'

'Is that all you care about?' Grace asked. 'Your boyfriend's opinion? Which by the way is worth nothing! And who devised the wording? It's clearly been thought through, although the kiss at the end hardly rings true for a threat! I assume that's how your dad would usually end his messages? Was there an envelope? Did you get Will to forge your father's handwriting on that?' Grace thought her imagination was running away with her, but Lily then explained the name on the envelope had been printed too. 'Oh good grief, this is just...' Grace held the note up. 'It frankly beggars belief!'

'I'm sorry, OK?' Lily replied, not looking particularly sorry at all.

'No, not OK. You have no idea why your father left, none of us do, not yet, and pointing fingers to scare people is...' She looked at Elan. 'It's sick, quite frankly.'

Grace walked out then turned around and came straight back. 'I'll have that back, on reflection,' she said, holding out her hand for the laptop, which Lily gave up without a fight, clearly realising she was in no position to argue. 'And the Wi-Fi is going off!'

Elan recoiled in her chair but said nothing. *Of course.*

'Oh, and...' Grace paused at the door to compose herself enough to deliver the bad news she'd almost forgotten to pass on, distracted temporarily by her rage about the note. 'I'm sorry to say that a body was found last night. It's Deena Jensen.' She looked at Lily. 'Your father's patient.'

Lily's face drained of all colour, and Elan's eyes stretched wider.

'Sorry, I didn't mean to blurt all that out,' Grace said, her anger draining away. The girls looked terrified, and they were only young. 'Look, let's try and all calm down and get ready to go to Cornwall, OK? I'm trusting you to make better choices from now on, though. Both of you. This is a horrific situation. We do not need to make it any worse, if that were even possible, which is why I must update the police about the true provenance of that note straight away.' Lily balked, but Grace held up her free hand. 'Think, Lily! If your mother shared it with DC Pemberton last night, the police need to know it was not from your father!'

Lily nodded. 'But can you explain it wasn't meant to...' Lily looked at Elan. 'It wasn't meant to scare her that much.'

* * *

Grace sat in her study and called Pemberton's mobile number over and over. It really was most frustrating. She could so rarely get hold of the woman. She reluctantly gave up and was leaving another voice note when the detective called back. Pemberton was in the car, by the sounds of things. Grace explained that the instigator and author of the threatening note was in fact Lily, but that it had been printed and delivered by Will Leatherby. The detective thanked her and confirmed there was no further news on the car, or Matt, then hung up.

Grace looked at her phone, dejected that yet again she was left waiting for news, and always the last to know anything. But Ed would be home from work soon, and then they could head down to Cornwall. She hadn't told the detective their plans. For once, she wanted to be on the front foot. Mind you, if Ed took much longer, she'd go without him!

Most likely her brother would be found in a state of distress after trying and failing to get away from his problems, so she needed to be there for him. But as she typed on her phone, googling for any news articles about cars abandoned or crashed recently in Cornwall, it was very hard to remain upbeat. The dearth of information was impossible to fill without finding more ways for this to end badly.

She ran back upstairs, shouting at the girls to hurry up and pack. 'The sooner we get down to Cornwall, the better!'

## 35

The police station Nic was taken to after she'd been coaxed from the cliff edge looked tiny in comparison to the modern headquarters where she'd met with DC Pemberton on Saturday. The cramped car park they swung into was tiny, and there, at the door, waiting for her, was a familiar face. It felt as if she'd been ambushed, but oddly she was pleased to see the detective.

'Nicole!' Detective Pemberton extended a hand. 'I'm sorry you've been on a bit of a tour. My instructions were to find you and bring you here so I could explain everything first-hand.'

Pemberton directed a pointed stare at the police officer who'd collected Nic from her father's and then taken her to the scene of the Golf's recovery. He nodded as if he had done nothing wrong, then he wandered inside, leaving a waft of body odour in his wake. Nic watched him go, every pace he took easing the tension of being in his company. She'd only got in his car again because she'd had no choice. Everyone else had returned to the recovery operation at the cliff's edge.

'Can you *please* tell me if Matt was in the Golf when it went over?' she asked, close to tears now. 'No one will tell me anything.'

'Of course. Come inside,' Pemberton replied, holding the entrance door for her.

She tried to go in, but her rapist's brother was in there, and she couldn't bear to see him again so soon.

'Can we talk in your car?' she asked, looking across to Pemberton's grey saloon.

'What's going on?' Pemberton asked, still holding the door. 'Is there something you need to share with me?'

Connie had advised her, more than once, that it remained her absolute right, at any time, to report the rape. It didn't matter that it had been almost four decades. It was a crime; more than one, in fact, as she'd also been underage.

She considered Pemberton's concerned youthful features and for the first time felt she might be able to start the process of seeking justice. This professional woman would be respectful, caring, and would listen without judgement. Then the same reason as always stopped her. *Guilt*. Not hers, but her father's. She'd assured him in the immediate aftermath of the attack that it wasn't his fault. He'd always done his best by her, whilst holding down a demanding job. He was a good father. Still was. She couldn't dredge all that up for him, especially as he was looking so frail.

'Nicole?' DC Pemberton asked again. 'What's wrong?'

'Sorry, just the shock of seeing Matt's car like that,' she replied, looking at the door her rapist's brother had just gone through.

'Yes, I can imagine,' Pemberton replied, shaking her head. 'Bloody incompetent local policing if you ask me,' she added, as Nic reluctantly followed her inside.

There was thankfully no sign of him in the reception area,

just a female desk sergeant who brought tea into the small interview room where they ended up, and then left them to it, closing the door after her.

'So,' Pemberton began. 'To go back a bit... A black Golf was spotted going over the cliffs at Money Cove around midnight last night. I assume you're familiar with that area? Not that far from your father's house, is it?'

She nodded. She knew every inch of the bay. Or used to.

'It's a favoured spot for late-night beach parties, apparently, and considering we found evidence of a fire, cans etc, it's a bloody miracle no one was hurt by that falling car.'

'Falling?'

'They're bolted to the floor,' Pemberton advised, pointing at the chair Nic was trying to push back from the table. 'Won't move, I'm afraid. You sure you're OK?'

She slid down in the bolted chair, one foot trailing behind the other, her body shaky and clumsy. 'Yes, I'm fine.'

'Let me explain what we *do* know about the car ending up on that beach,' Pemberton said, taking out her phone and placing it on the table. 'A 999 call came in, just after midnight. Sounds like a bunch of terrified kids from the recording, and they didn't stick around, just scarpered. You sure you're OK to continue?'

'Yes, please, I need to know.' She picked up her tea and sipped; it was disgusting, but it distracted her from the worry that her rapist's brother might be looking at her through the small piece of glass in the door, or maybe watching the interview via a camera, capturing her reactions and sending it to his computer where he'd no doubt smirk at her distress and maybe even share it with his brother.

'That incident on the beach was linked to my report of a stolen black Golf,' Pemberton continued. 'The car was partially submerged by the time first responders got there, and it was dark of course, but I've been advised both the passenger and driver-side doors were open when it was recovered from the water.'

Nic sat forward. 'So Matt got out?'

Pemberton raised a hand. 'It's still early days. Lots of work to be done by the search and recovery team.'

'Sorry, just trying to retain some hope; he's still my husband, whatever he's done.'

'Yes, of course, I understand. And on a related note, I just had a chat with Grace. It would seem the hand-delivered note you were convinced was written by Matt was actually a prank, as I suggested it might be.'

'No, that can't be right!' she said, sitting up. 'It was Matt's wording; I know it was!' Nic considered those words again, wondering then if she'd jumped to conclusions based on the other messages she'd received from Matt. Had she made connections that weren't really there? Then something else occurred to her. 'Are you saying Grace knows who sent it?'

'Yes, I'm sorry, it was Lily. And Elan, I think, reading between the lines, although Grace was very cagey about that, but it seems Will Leatherby was definitely the delivery guy. Any idea why Lily would do that?'

She swallowed the hurt and tried to process what this meant. 'Elan has always been a bit odd; she barely speaks, as I'm sure you've noticed. I could see her being vindictive, but my own daughter... I mean, we've had some issues of late. She's very angry with me...' She looked up and caught the detective's keen interest. 'As I said, someone to blame, but that note terrified me; that's why I came down here!'

'Do you want to press charges?' Pemberton asked, tapping her phone. There was a photo of three kids on it, all smiling faces.

'Against Lily? No, of course not! But you can throw the book at Will Leatherby for all I care!'

'I'll send Ry round to scare the shit out of him,' Pemberton said, smiling. 'I didn't get a great vibe off his mother either, Amber?'

'Brackley's biggest bitch, and that's saying something, but don't worry about the son. He's not worth police time.' She'd decided on reflection it would be best to limit further contact between the police and Amber. That woman already knew far too much about her private affairs.

'If you're sure?' Pemberton asked.

'Yes, quite sure.'

'Right, so to return to the situation with Lily's car—'

'It's definitely the same Golf? Lily didn't know the regis-tration.'

'Yes, same one, I got the plates from the dealership, remem-ber?' Pemberton lowered her gaze to meet hers and Nic nodded. 'And there was also a bag of clothing in the boot.'

'Matt's spare suit and shirt?'

'The contents are still being examined as we speak, but shirt, suit, much as you described to me, yes, and they look to be heavily bloodstained.' Pemberton leant back. 'So I will ask you again: is there anything you want to tell me? Like for instance why you're here in Cornwall, just as Lily's stolen car turns up?'

'It was your suggestion that I stay with someone!'

'Yes, but you gave me no indication you were coming here. In fact, you suggested you might stay with Amber Leatherby, who you clearly don't get on with.'

'Sorry, I just wanted to be on my own, and to get away from home.'

'Which feels like rather a coincidence given the car we now

think Matt drove here was pulled from the sea less than a mile away.'

'It *is* a coincidence, nothing more!'

'Did anyone else know you were headed to your father's?'

'Only Dad.'

'So you definitely haven't been in contact with your husband since last Friday?'

'No.'

'Or Lily? She didn't know Matt was headed here?'

'Not that she said but she's clearly not my biggest fan right now!'

'OK, I'll need to speak with your father as soon as possible.'

'But Matt hasn't been anywhere near his house; I checked.'

'And why would you do that?'

She looked down at her hands, wondering how on earth she could avoid explaining Matt's idea to hide in the studio for the first few days. She'd kept it a secret far too long to come clean now.

'Matt and my father have always been close,' she said, looking up. 'I thought maybe Dad had heard from him, but he hasn't, of course.'

Pemberton locked eyes with Nic. 'You never mentioned this, and now you are here.'

'Yes, to get away from that false threat.'

'I personally don't believe in coincidences. They're far too convenient.'

'But they happen,' Nic replied.

\* \* \*

There was no sign of her rapist's brother as they left the

interview room and walked back through the reception area, just the tea-making female police officer, who smiled.

Pemberton walked Nic to her grey saloon, chunky fobbed keys in the detective's many-ringed hand.

The return journey was taken at a much more comfortable speed. Pemberton was a competent and courteous driver, braking into the bends and accelerating out of them, then patiently driving behind a tractor for the final mile, whilst Nic's nerves were so frayed, her jaw ached from clenching.

Her folded waterproof was on her lap, returned to her when she'd been bundled back into the foul-smelling police officer's car at the cliff's edge. She looked at the yellow waxed jacket that had cost over three hundred pounds and wondered if she'd ever wear it again. Had she let herself down, and maybe others too, by not reporting her attacker? The man who'd raped her was a police officer too, apparently. Many women would have crossed his path, trusting him, as she once had, to get them home safely.

They were not far from her father's house now; if she wanted to say something, this was her moment.

'I spoke to Amber Leatherby again, about your alibi for last Tuesday morning...' Pemberton said, breaking into Nic's thoughts. 'The morning we believe Deena Jensen died.'

'I was at Brackley all morning, as I've told you.'

'Right, but I needed to get a better handle on the timeline, so I called her again.'

'Oh, right!' She tried not to show her concern, but it was hard not to worry that a detective investigating a murder was checking out her alibi, again.

'Amber definitely remembered seeing you at the outgoing PTA meeting,' Pemberton replied, glancing across as they drove the high-hedged lanes. 'Except she wasn't a hundred per cent certain, when pushed, that you were there the entire time.'

'Well I was!' Nic replied, yanking on the locked seatbelt and hating Amber fucking Leatherby even more, if that were possible.

'She said it was a packed PTA meeting, and she was too busy chairing to keep track of every attendee.'

'I was at Brackley from nine until one. Ask David, the head; I saw him too.'

'Right, David Kelm, isn't it?' Pemberton asked, slowing for the turn into Chy an Mor coming up soon. 'Interesting character... Anyway, he clearly recalls seeing you for coffee in his office. Around half-ten or so, he *thinks*. He's a big fan of yours, isn't he? Said you two go way back.'

'Sorry, I'm not sure where exactly you're going with this?'

'It's a complicated alibi in some ways. Multiple people saw you, but fluid timings. Jelly nailing, I call it.'

'Are you suggesting I'm lying about where I was?'

'Just trying to neaten everything up; that's my job.' Pemberton flashed her a smile, there and then gone. 'Did I tell you we think Deena might have fallen to her death? It's a big drop from the terrace, must be what, thirty or forty feet? Ah, is this the gate?'

Nic blinked hard and then warned Pemberton to slow for the tight entrance, narrow between two posts. It was a relief to see Chy an Mor at the end of the long drive. The white house was backlit by a brilliant blue sky and sparkling sunshine.

'Thanks for the lift,' she said, unstrapping her seatbelt and then pulling on the door handle. It held firm, but released as Pemberton pressed a switch on the driver's door. Nic got out and walked towards the house, but then she heard the detective's trainers crunching through the gravel behind her.

'I thought I explained,' Pemberton said as Nic looked over her shoulder. 'I have a few questions for your father.'

## 36

TUESDAY 11 JUNE 2024 – 11.30 A.M.

'Lovely spot,' Pemberton was saying as Nic climbed the stairs up to the first-floor sitting room, not easy whilst supporting a heavy tea tray in her hands.

Pemberton was looking out at the bay. Everyone did when they visited. It was a spectacular view.

'Ah, tea!' Pemberton announced, spotting her. 'I don't suppose you have—'

'No, sorry, only whole milk,' she replied, smiling at her father, who was standing beside the detective at the window. 'And that's on the turn.'

'Ah well, black as always,' Pemberton replied. 'I'm running on caffeine and sea air at the moment.'

Nic was trying to catch her father's eye to see if she'd missed much whilst she'd been in the basement kitchen. She hadn't wanted to leave them – he'd turned ashen when Pemberton had introduced herself at the door and explained she needed to ask him a few questions about his missing son-in-law – but her father had insisted he was fine and she should make tea for their visitor.

Pemberton moved the piles of newspapers so she could set the heavy tray on the table by the only chair, and her father then picked up the teapot to pour.

'It's OK, Dad, I'll do it,' she said, taking over. His hands were shaking so much, the tea was already all over the tray. He sank into the chair as Nic poured and challenged the smiling detective. 'I asked you not to quiz him before I got back!'

'I didn't,' Pemberton replied, returning to the view. 'We were talking about the topography of the bay, weren't we, Gerald? Money Cove must be, what, less than a mile from here?' the detective asked, then looked at her. 'Along the coastal path that runs down there, I mean?' Pemberton pointed to the narrow path along the cliff edge which began on Chy an Mor's property.

'Yes, but walking along there is not to be recommended,' she replied. 'Is it, Dad?' Her hands were shaking now too, as bad memories were stirred up by the detective's questions. 'It's very eroded in places.' She handed Pemberton a cup, the tea sloshing into the saucer. 'Sorry, I'll get you a tissue.'

'No worries,' Pemberton said, tipping the tea back into the cup and taking a sip. 'I'm guessing it would be an even more dangerous walk in the dark?'

Nic shook her head, not understanding the relevance, although more memories of her night-time walk home, with her attacker, were dredged up. 'Yes, it would be, very.'

'Can you see Money Cove from here?' Pemberton asked, looking out at the bay as she slurped her tea.

Nic handed her father his sweet milky tea, waiting until he had it in both hands before she looked too, although she knew the view all too well. 'It's a bit further round, beyond the next headland. You OK, Dad?'

Her father's hands were visibly trembling, his breaths laboured. She took his cup and saucer from him and placed them back on the tray before crouching beside his chair, a hand on his arm. 'Do you need anything?' Pemberton watched them, the detective also looking concerned. 'Your inhaler?' Nic suggested, scanning the room for it, but he shook his head, instead finding his handkerchief in his pocket and holding it to his brow. 'You sure? Where is it?'

'I'm fine, stop fussing!'

Startled, she straightened up. Her father never raised his voice to her. Not to anyone, or a hand, except that one time when he'd pummelled her attacker, blows raining down on the cowering boy.

'OK, sorry, but you don't look well. This is all too much for you.' She scowled at Pemberton. 'He needs to rest.'

'It's OK,' Gerald said, voice croaky. 'Let's help as best we can.'

'I'll keep it to the minimum,' Pemberton said, putting her empty cup back on the tray. 'Have you had any contact with your son-in-law since he went missing last Friday?'

He shook his head.

'No calls, nothing?'

'No.'

'And what time did your daughter call you yesterday to say she was on her way?' Pemberton asked, glancing at Nic.

'I guess it was around midnight?' he replied, looking at her too.

'Can you check the exact time, Nicole?' Pemberton said, pushing back a curl.

She took out her phone from her jeans pocket and stabbed at the screen. 'Eleven twenty-seven.'

'Thanks,' Pemberton said, finding her notepad and a pen from her satchel and noting it down. 'And the drive from here to Money Cove, along the coast road... Ten minutes, if that, at that time of night?'

'Yes, I guess so,' he replied, looking up at Nic again.

'I don't see what relevance any of this has?' Nic asked, although she could absolutely see what the detective was hinting at: that her father had sheltered Matt and then helped him to get away just prior to her arrival in the early hours. She wanted to ask him the same, but not in front of a detective investigating a potential murder.

'OK if I take a look around?' Pemberton asked, already headed down the stairs.

## 37

They walked through the house first, the three of them, from top to bottom, room by room. Her father was insistent he must come too, despite Nic's efforts to contain him to his chair in the sitting room, and Pemberton took the opportunity to continue questioning him regarding his recent communications with his son-in-law, which he again assured her were non-existent.

'You haven't maybe missed him, or he might have snuck in when you left the house?' Pemberton asked as they reached the basement kitchen.

'No, I only go out occasionally for supplies, and anyway, why would he come here? He never visited without my daughter.'

'Oh, I thought you said they were close?' Pemberton commented, looking at Nic down the messy galley kitchen.

Nic was stood beside the battered table. It was pushed up against the wall as there was nowhere else for it, a chair at each end. She'd eaten breakfast there, porridge, every morning before school, and often on her own; a latchkey kid. She leant against it, tempted to sink into a chair. 'Yes, they were close, in their way,' she replied. 'Both doctors, isn't that right, Dad? You two always talked shop.'

'Did you think we were close?' her father asked. 'I wouldn't have said that.'

'No, maybe not close, but you got on well,' she said, wishing he'd take the hint and stop talking, which he did, nodding instead.

'OK, so that's the house done, I guess?' Pemberton asked, poking her head into the pantry where cleaning stuff was kept. 'So I just need to see any sheds, garages, outhouses?'

Nic tried not to look at her father, but even so, the detective must have noticed the quick exchange of glances between them and the hesitation as her father eventually replied, 'There's the studio, but it's been locked up for many years. I don't think I have a key to the padlock, either. We never go in there.'

'Where do you keep your spare keys?' Pemberton asked, opening a drawer.

And as luck would have it, or not in this case, there it was, with all the other keys her father had accumulated over his long life; a tiny padlock key. And although he expressed doubt it was the right one when Pemberton plucked it from amongst the other large and ornate keys that opened and locked Chy an Mor's old-fashioned doors, the detective suggested maybe they should try it anyway.

'I'll take it, Dad,' she told him, palming the small key and heading out the door that led to the back garden. 'Your eyesight is getting worse every time I see you, and your memory!'

Nic had no idea what, if anything, her sharp-as-a-tack father was up to, but if he had been sheltering Matt for some reason and lying to her about it, and now the police, she wanted to be the first one to find out. Although with DC Pemberton hot on her heels, there wouldn't be any time to retrieve the rucksack before Pemberton saw it, if it was still there. What on earth had her father been thinking?

She took long strides down the sloped and overgrown garden, sweating as she rushed ahead.

'Nicole?' Pemberton called after her. 'I think your father needs our help.'

'You OK, Dad?' she called back, noting he'd stopped to mop his brow. She was about to carry on when she caught Pemberton's disapproving look. He did look as though he was really struggling. 'Dad, you go back!' she shouted, but then he looked like he was about to collapse and she was forced to retrace her steps.

She offered her arm, supporting her father for the rest of the way down to the studio, Pemberton following close behind. He'd been most insistent he must come, and refused all her suggestions he go back. She longed to ask him what he knew, but even in a whisper, the detective would hear, so she settled for sideways glances, her father giving nothing away.

The rusty lock released easily as Nic slotted in the found key and turned it, the padlock falling to the long grass.

'Shall we?' Pemberton asked as they stood at the unlocked but still closed door, Nic's heart thrumming and breaths harder with each draw in and out.

She'd wanted to be the first inside, worried for her father's involvement and angry with him for lying to her if he had been hiding Matt. If the rucksack was still there, she'd planned to hide it, if there was time. The trouble was, now it came to it, she found she couldn't go in. She squeezed her fists, digging her nails in her palms as she tried to build up the courage to pull on the handle and open the studio door. She hadn't set foot in there since that night almost forty years before.

'Nicole, what's wrong?' Pemberton asked.

When she didn't answer, the detective lost patience and pulled open the unlocked door, forcing her to step aside.

Nic closed her eyes, pushing away the memory of being on that dusty floor, cradled in her father's arms and half-naked after the boy who'd raped her had limped away. Her father's voice had been ferocious as he'd shouted after him that if he ever came near his daughter again, he'd kill him. She squeezed her eyes tighter against the memory, but it wasn't only the past she could smell in the trapped air that had released when Pemberton flung open the door. She turned to her father, but as she went to speak, the detective went in.

'Smells of cigarettes in here,' Pemberton said, looking at her from the shadows. Then to Gerald, 'You a smoker, Dr Wood?'

She couldn't read her father's expression. He looked greyed with tiredness but then he stood a little taller, shoulders back, voice clear as he stepped forward and replied, 'Well, when you get to my age, you have to have the occasional vice. I do like a cigar or two.'

'Oh, I thought you were asthmatic?' Pemberton replied, looking doubtful. 'And didn't you say the studio was locked up and you didn't know where the key was?'

Gerald tapped the side of his head. 'Must be losing it in my old age.'

Pemberton looked unconvinced, then went further inside.

Nic tried to catch her father's eye, but he turned away. She tapped him on the arm, her back turned on the studio as she mouthed to him, 'What's going on?'

He gave no reply, other than a dismissive shake of his head, then Pemberton looked out the door again. 'Smells like bleach in here too. You going to take a look, Nicole? I'd appreciate your thoughts.'

She was desperate to check inside the studio, especially now she'd smelt the familiar and distinctive tang of Matt's Cuban cigars, but she still couldn't force herself to make that move.

'It's OK,' her father said. 'Let's go in together.'

Pemberton looked at Gerald, then at her. 'Am I missing something here?'

'I was...' But she couldn't say it.

'My wife left when Nicole was a baby,' Gerald explained. 'This studio was Sylvie's art studio. It holds some painful memories of that abandonment, for us both.'

Nic smiled at her father. He'd saved her, yet again. Then he took her hand and said, 'Come on. I promise it's fine. Nothing in there to worry about.'

He went in first, forced to drop her hand as he stooped for the low door. She stepped in next, cobwebs making her jump as they tugged at her hair.

There was only one bulb, either not switched or not working, and the window was so dirty, it barely let in any light. It had always been sparsely decorated, but she'd forgotten how small it was. A chair, a workbench, a rug, and in the corner, an easel and a box of dried-up paints. The seascapes on the wall her mother had painted in the short time before she left them were of wild seas and grey skies. And in the tiny bathroom, a strong smell of bleach hit her as she went in. The smell of stale cigar smoke also pervaded the studio, but she was more concerned where the khaki rucksack was. It had been beside the motheaten chair opposite the grimy window, but it wasn't there now. Or immediately obvious anywhere else as she paced the shadowy room, circling her watchful father and the detective whilst she 'casually' looked for it.

Pemberton gave her a long meaningful stare. 'Thoughts?'

So many, but what could she say without incriminating her

father? It seemed glaringly obvious that Matt had been here, and unless her father hadn't known, which felt unlikely, then he was covering for Matt. That betrayal almost made her speak the questions that burned inside her, but all she said was, 'Well, Matt's clearly not here now, is he?'

Pemberton frowned, looking at Gerald. 'No, it seems not. But was he?'

They stepped into the bright sunshine. Nic was relieved to be breathing in the sea-scented air, but questions hung on the faint breeze.

'Think carefully, Dr Wood, before you reply,' Pemberton said, pulling cobwebs from her curls. 'Your son-in-law is our prime suspect in the murder of Deena Jensen. You know about her unexplained death and the background to that?'

Nic shook her head at the detective. 'We haven't had time to talk. I was going to tell you, Dad. Sadly, a patient of Matt's has been found dead.'

'We suspect foul play,' Pemberton explained. 'She and Dr Delaney had been engaged in an affair for some months.'

The detective paused for a reaction which Gerald did not reward her with. All he said was, 'I told you, I haven't seen him.'

'He was cheating on your daughter, so why cover for him?'

Nic looked at her father and he looked back, deep sorrow in his eyes. 'Is this true, Nicole?'

She nodded, noting the fear that sparked in her father's eyes. She felt it too, deep in her heart.

Pemberton pointed to the open studio door. 'Are you certain, Gerald? No contact at any time in the days since he went missing last Friday? Nicole told me she asked you to check down here; did you see anything suspicious? I know your son-in-law smoked cigars regularly. Come on Gerald, tell the truth now!'

His gaze fell on Nic, then it slipped, a hand to the air as he reached out to her. She caught his wrist and supported him, although he was surprisingly heavy. Pemberton then rushed to help, taking his other arm.

'We need to get him back up to the house,' Nic said, the rattle in his chest disturbingly loud. 'I told you he wasn't up to your questions!'

# 38

TUESDAY 11 JUNE 2024 – 12.30 P.M.

'Where on earth have you been all this time?' Grace asked her husband as he walked through the front door that hot Tuesday afternoon. 'I called you hours ago!'

'I do have a job to do, Gracie! I left as soon as I could, and it's a long cycle.' Ed pulled the bicycle clips from his chinos.

'Well, we're all packed and ready to go,' she said, glancing up the stairs. 'The girls are waiting in Elan's room, so if you just throw anything you need in the bag on our bed, we can finally leave.'

'Can I just catch my breath, love?' he asked, pecking her on the cheek. 'And a brew would be nice; I'm parched!'

'Fine,' she said, wiping away his sweat from her cheek. 'But you can take it in a travel cup. The traffic will be a nightmare down to the coast on a hot June day like this.'

'Have you told Gerald we're coming?' Ed asked as he followed her into the kitchen.

She lifted the kettle and waggled it to check there was water inside, then flicked it on. 'No, I haven't heard from him since he called to say Nic was carted away by a policeman.'

'She wasn't carted anywhere!' Ed said, raising a brow. 'And please tell me you've messaged her to say we're coming,' he added, looking less than impressed.

'Matt's my brother,' she said, bending down to the corner cupboard to look for the travel cup. She retrieved it and straightened up. 'And Nic didn't tell me she was going to Cornwall, so why should I?'

'Two wrongs don't make a right,' Ed suggested. 'And presumably we will also be asking to stay the night?'

'I need to be there, Ed. No one tells me anything. For all I know Matt could be—'

'OK, OK,' he said, relenting as he rubbed her back 'But you owe Nic the courtesy of—'

'Oh, for goodness' sake, Ed! We are way beyond that!' she said, dropping a teabag into the travel cup. 'You're telling me she didn't know anything about Lily's car? Or that Matt had driven it to within a mile of her father's house?'

'Quite possibly, no, she didn't.'

She poured boiling water. 'She's lying to us, Ed! And I need to get down there and find out for myself exactly what's happening because— Oh, hi, Lily!'

Ed turned around too, both of them caught out by Lily's silent arrival at the kitchen door. 'Elan asked me to check when we're leaving. Hi, Uncle Ed.'

'Now!' Grace said. 'We're leaving right now!'

* * *

It was so hot in the Volvo, Grace thought she might self-combust as they drove out of the estate. There was already so much sweat trickling down her spine, only five minutes into a long journey, spontaneous death would probably be a sweet mercy. The girls whispered in the back, Grace trying to catch her daughter's words and unable to. She was simultaneously amazed that Elan was holding a conversation and incandescent that she wasn't party to it. Even when she found a packet of Werther's Original in her bag and offered them round, Elan said not a word of thanks. But her daughter did do one thing: she smiled at her, and that was the first time she could recall her doing so in months. They'd parked the argument about the threatening note, other, greater concerns taking precedence. She hadn't even told Ed. He'd only make a bigger deal of it.

The motorway was horrendously busy, as she'd feared it might be, and she held Ed accountable for their slow progress, although she knew it was unreasonable of her. At this rate, the journey would take the rest of the day, and although she had her mobile, and checked it regularly, there were no updates on the car recovery, or the search for Matt. Gerald would ring the home phone, but she'd wanted to be there, in Cornwall, when they found him. Matt would be alive and well, of course. He had driven down there in Lily's car and then simply abandoned it. She could not think otherwise, although her brain kept trying to take her there. She switched on her mindfulness app and when she couldn't concentrate on that, she turned on the car radio, but Lily complained about the choice of station, and Lily's alternative was unbearable, so they crawled along in near silence.

They arrived at Chy an Mor at five, after an interminable journey. The traffic down to the coast had been monumental, as she'd warned Ed it would be. Lily got out and ran to the door, knocking loudly. Grace followed, both of them waiting there when Nic eventually answered.

'Any news on Matt?' Grace asked, glancing at Lily, who was clearly hanging on the answer to that question as much as she was. The journey had taken four hours, ample opportunity to message ahead, or call, but in the end, they'd collectively decided whatever news there was, better to hear it in person.

'No, I'm waiting to hear more,' Nic said as she dropped the bucket she'd been holding and reached out to her daughter with rubber-gloved hands.

Lily stepped back from the offered hug.

'What are you all doing here?' Nic asked.

'Isn't that obvious?' Lily asked as she pushed past to go inside.

'It was a sudden impulse to be close to where Matt is,' Grace explained. 'I'm sure you can understand that?'

It was more of a statement than a question and one she expected Nic to challenge, but her sister-in-law was more concerned with what Lily was doing.

'Leave Grandpa,' Nic called after her daughter, who was tapping on a closed door at the end of the hallway. 'He's resting, he's not been well.'

Lily ignored her mother, instead opening the door and going inside the bedroom.

'And you've brought Ed and Elan,' Nic said, peeling the gloves from her hands as she looked past Grace to the Volvo.

Ed was getting the bags from the boot. He waved, but Elan, who'd now got out of the car was staring over at them, at Nic in particular, in fact.

'I have spoken with both the girls about that awful note,' Grace explained, turning back to catch Nic's frosty stare. Grace then dropped her voice to a whisper as she added, 'Ed doesn't know. He thinks Elan is his little girl who can do no wrong. Fathers and daughters, eh? Although Lily was, I believe—'

'As I understand it, Elan was the main instigator,' Nic replied, cutting across her.

'That's just not true!' Grace replied, biting back. 'But both the girls are very aware that sending that note was extremely unwise.'

'A little more than unwise. I was terrified; the tone was very threatening. That's why I had to get away.'

'And I hope you understand why I had to come here too. Can I come in?'

There was a long pause before Nic said, 'I suppose you'd better now you're here.'

Grace stepped into the relative cool of the hallway, a long wood-panelled room that smelt of damp. Ed ambled in behind her, the girls' heavy bags dropped just inside the door.

'What's this about a note?' Ed asked.

'I'll tell you later,' Grace said, shaking her head at him as she noticed his gaze fall on the back of Nic's head.

The patches of exposed scalp had grown in size and number and Nic seemed to have given up trying to conceal them; an impossible task in fairness, unless she'd worn a hat. Ed wasn't known for his ability to pick up on subtle hints. Her husband shook his head in confusion and she frowned back, then he went back to the car.

'I've messaged DC Pemberton, several times,' she told Nic, who was staring at the closed door Lily had gone through. 'I guess she's busy coordinating the search. Must be difficult at a distance. Do you think she'll come down?'

'She's already here,' Nic said, turning round. 'In Cornwall. Fowey, in fact.'

'Oh! Since when?' Fowey was just across the bay, and was the nearest town.

'Where do you want these?' Ed asked, bringing in more bags. 'Sorry for just turning up like this, Nic!'

'Take your pick!' Nic told him, opening the two doors closest to the front door, one on either side. 'It's all a bit of a mess. Dad just can't cope these days. He's not well enough. That's why I was trying to clean up a bit.'

Whilst Ed and Elan were depositing the bags of clothes and shoes into the two spare bedrooms, Grace and Nic went up the steep winding staircase of the upside-down house to the first-floor sitting room.

Grace had never been to Gerald's home by the sea, but she'd imagined it would be much larger from the descriptions she'd heard and the photos she'd seen over the years, mainly from Matt, who hated going there, and Lily, who loved it. It was a tall house, over four storeys including a basement, but narrow, with small rooms and low ceilings.

One of the spare bedrooms had been so full of Gerald's books, it was impossible to see the bed on the other side. That would be for the girls, regardless of where Ed put their bag, but the other room wasn't much better, and it smelt horribly damp. Nic's efforts at cleaning up which they'd interrupted had not made much, if any, difference, at least as far as she could tell. Especially in the sunny sitting room, where the brightness illuminated the thick layers of dust. It looked like an antique shop, piled with books and papers and with only one chair, which was set in front of the huge picture window that framed a glorious view of the bay.

'So you said DC Pemberton is in Cornwall?' she asked, walking to the window.

'Yes, I met with her after I was driven out to where the car was found.' Nic stood behind the empty armchair, her hand to the back of it, partially covering a greasy stain where Gerald's head must usually rest.

'And yet you saw no need to tell me any of this?' Grace said, turning from the view.

'Sorry, my father hasn't been well.'

'Yes, and I'm sorry to hear that but I didn't know for hours, or about Deena's body being found.'

'Right, yes, sorry. It's been hard to cope.'

'I understand, but I'd like you to tell me everything now. Leave nothing out. I'm fed up of being the last to know.'

\* \* \*

Ed joined her in the sitting once he'd triple-checked the car was locked, although they were miles from anywhere, and who'd want to steal the Volvo anyway? Nic had gone down to make tea, so Grace updated him on what she knew, although it was still frustratingly little. Just that the Golf had been recovered from a place nearby called Money Cove, and no sign of Matt in it, and possibly even more worryingly, bloodstained clothes were found in the boot.

'What kind of clothes? Matt's?' Ed asked, picking up a photo from the dresser at the far end of the cluttered sitting room.

'Yes, I think so,' she replied, taking the frame as he passed it over, dust transferred to her fingertips as she wiped the glass. 'This place is a health hazard!'

The photo was of Gerald with a young Nicole. Nic looked about ten, and Gerald was very handsome, with a full head of dark hair and a moustache. They were seated side by side in raincoats at the back of a ferry boat. They'd passed the ferry as Ed drove them round the bay on the way here. It was only a short run across the water from one side of the bay to the other, but Lily had told them how much fun it was when she came down to stay; even dogs went on the small boat to Fowey.

'Nic's still covering something up,' she whispered, eyeing the top of the stairs for Nic's return with the tea. 'Seriously, Ed, she claims she has no idea why Lily's car ended up so close to her father's.'

'Do we know where this cove is?' Ed asked, looking out at the bay. 'Those cliffs must be, what, a hundred foot high in places?'

Grace covered her mouth and stifled a sob. 'He's dead, isn't he?'

'Come on, Gracie,' Ed chivvied, hooking an arm awkwardly around her shoulders. 'Keep the faith. We don't know anything yet. He might not have even been in the car when it went over.'

'Are the girls OK?' she asked, extracting herself from his embrace.

'They're fine; I gave them the carrier bag with crisps and cans of Coke in, hope that's OK?'

'Yes, of course. Apparently, Gerald has been feeling unwell all afternoon, ever since DC Pemberton left, and considering his age, that is one thing I *do* believe.'

Ed turned from the view. 'The police were questioning Gerald?'

'Nic said the detective was asking him if he'd seen Matt, but Gerald wasn't up to it; the stress brought on his asthma.'

Ed shook his head, contemplating another dusty photo and holding it up for her to see. It was of Gerald with Lily, taken on the beach. Lily was maybe five or six, in a red swimsuit, gap-toothed as she grinned. 'Poor old chap,' Ed said, putting the photo back down. 'I guess they're just doting i's and crossing t's.'

Grace frowned. She did not share her husband's generous view of the old man's involvement. He'd always seemed nice when she met him, but age did not excuse everything. 'I think there's a lot more to it than—'

She stopped talking. Nic had appeared at the top of the stairs, a tray in her hands. Ed rushed over and took it from her, looking around then for somewhere to put it down.

'Must have been such a great place to grow up,' Ed said as Nic helped him set the tray down on the table next to Gerald's chair. 'I mean, that view!'

'Isolated though,' Grace added as Nic started to pour the tea. 'You must worry about your father here, all alone, no one close by.'

'Especially in winter,' Ed said, missing the point as usual.

Grace had been edging towards the fact she believed, possibly like the detective from what she'd gathered, that Gerald knew more than he had been letting on about Matt's disappearance. She wanted to ask him directly if he'd been sheltering Matt, but as he wasn't available, she would nudge Nic instead. And she was getting fed up of being polite about it.

'Doesn't it seem odd to you, Nic?' she began, ignoring Ed's frown. 'That Lily's car was found so close to here?' She walked to the window, wondering if the bay where the car ended up was visible from here. 'Bit of a coincidence?'

'Yes, it is odd,' Nic replied, adding milk to a cup. 'But Dad hadn't seen Matt; I'd checked with him straight away, just in case.'

Grace caught Ed's eye as Nic handed him his tea.

'Are the police still searching the area for Matt?' Ed asked, taking a biscuit from the plate Nic held out.

'Yes, I believe so. There was mention of a helicopter, to scour the coastline.'

Grace swung round from the view. She couldn't say it, but surely everyone was thinking the same? That if a helicopter was being used, the supposition was Matt had been in the car when it went over and been washed out to sea, or dashed on the rocks.

Ed began crunching down on a custard cream.

'Sorry, not much food in,' Nic said as Ed helped himself to another. 'These are Dad's favourite. Actually, I should go check on him.' Nic poured another cup and added a biscuit to the saucer then disappeared down the stairs.

'She knows something!' Grace said, looking down the spiral stairs to make sure Nic was definitely gone. Something she should have done before speaking, on reflection. Although she didn't much care.

'She's worried, Gracie, we all are,' Ed replied, crunching the second custard cream. 'Her father's sick, her husband's missing...' he added, spraying crumbs onto the threadbare rug. 'She doesn't need you asking things we're all thinking but don't want to say. We just need to stay calm and hopeful.' Ed shoved in the last of the biscuit.

'Stay calm!' she hissed, trying to keep the volume if not the anger from her voice. 'How am I supposed to stay calm?'

'I know,' he said, chewing. 'It's hard. Although, it *is* a bloody coincidence about the car turning up here, I agree with you on that.'

'Exactly!' she said, pouring her own tea as Nic hadn't offered her a cup. Or a biscuit, although she didn't like the look of them. They were covered in a similar dust to the one that cloaked every surface of the sunny room.

'And what's all this about a threatening note?' Ed asked, his words mashed up with chewed biscuit.

## 39

'Where's Lily?' Nic asked as she went into the semi-darkness of her father's bedroom and handed him a cup of tea, a crumbly biscuit in the saucer.

He was sitting up in bed fully clothed and looking a bit better than when she'd last checked, but his pallor was still grey.

'Oh, she didn't stay long,' her father said, managing a weak smile. 'Lured away by the promise of snacks!'

She nodded and sat beside him on the bed. 'Grace is asking a lot of questions. You up to answering some for me so we can make a plan?'

Her father nodded, but then he started coughing again. She took the cup and set it on his bedside chest, handing him his inhaler instead. She waited as he hacked into his handkerchief. It was so frustrating, but she forced herself to be patient, yet again, hoping the inhaler would help as he finally used it.

Ever since she'd persuaded DC Pemberton to leave on the grounds her father must rest, she'd been desperate to ask about his involvement in Matt's disappearance, but he'd been in a deep sleep when she'd returned from seeing the concerned detective

out. She'd wanted to shake him awake, the relief that he was resting, and breathing, mixed with anger and frustration. It was her
right to demand an explanation of what was surely a huge
betrayal. Her father had repeatedly lied to her. Matt had clearly
been in the studio, smoking his damn cigars. But even she
couldn't be that callous, so she'd slipped out and left him to rest,
just for a little while.

She'd used the time her father slept to carry out a rushed
inspection and clean-up of the studio. Pemberton was likely also
using the hiatus in questioning to organise an official search, and
however mad she was with her father, however many questions
fought for space in her crammed brain, she wanted to save him
from the serious consequences of his misguided actions. Getting
in the way of a police investigation was definitely an arrestable
offence – she had been warned of the same herself – and even
the threat of that would likely kill him. So she'd dusted and
wiped away any marks on the few sticks of furniture in the
studio, looking for clues to Matt's former presence. She'd even
mopped the floor, pushing down her fear of being in there as she
obliterated any evidence of Matt's stay, but there was not a
dropped cigar stub or a stray dark hair caught in her damp cloth
by the time she was done. Which led her to the conclusion her
father must have also cleaned up; and he'd definitely put bleach
down the toilet. She couldn't wait to get out of there and back to
her father, but as she'd come back into the house with her mop
and bucket, Grace was knocking at the door, and now time really
was running out.

'Dad?' She glanced at the closed bedroom door. 'Was Matt
here the whole time, in the studio?'

The hollow wheeze in his chest was horribly loud in the
quiet room. His curtains were unlined and a dull orange, like the
bedspread, lending an eerie glow to his features as the late after-

noon sun came through. They'd been the same fabric as long as she could remember. He opened his eyes and looked at her, then he nodded.

'He *was* here?' she asked, amazed at the confirmation. She'd suspected it, of course, but it was still shocking.

Gerald nodded again, more firmly this time.

'Oh my god, Dad! Where he is now? Is he OK? What did he tell you had happened?'

'You know what he told me!'

Nic sat back and met her father's penetrating stare. 'What does that mean?'

Gerald fumbled for his inhaler and she found it on the bed and passed it to him again. He brought the mouthpiece to his pale lips and took several puffs, some colour returning. 'Just, give me a minute, love.'

'We don't have a minute! The detective will be back with more questions and we have a houseful now.' She paused, drawing breath herself. 'Look, I'm on your side here. I've cleaned up the studio as best as I can, but I saw Matt's rucksack in there yesterday, you know I did, and he sent me a postcard of the bay that arrived on Saturday, so I guessed he was here, but you convinced me he wasn't so you have to tell me the truth now. What's been going—'

She stopped talking and placed a finger to her lips. Grace was upstairs in the sitting room with Ed, but the girls were just down the hallway. She looked at her father, then she got up and went to the door and opened it, looking left and right. No one was in the hallway, and she could hear Grace talking upstairs, although she could have sworn she'd heard footsteps. The bathroom was next door, and the door was closed, but she could hear that the toilet had recently been flushed, the cistern refilling as she checked inside, but there was no one in there now. She went back into the bedroom and closed the door then sat beside her father. 'It's fine, must have been one of the girls using the bathroom.'

'I'm so sorry,' he said, his voice raspy. 'I should have told you straight away.'

'Look, forget that for now, we don't have time for apologies. Just tell me what happened. When did he arrive, and how was he?'

'Friday night it was, around nine, I think, I'm not exactly sure. No, must have been a bit later; it was getting dark.'

She nodded, thinking about the first call she'd made to her father, the one he hadn't answered, and how he'd sworn to her Matt wasn't here. Maybe he wasn't at that point; she'd certainly believed him.

'I noticed a light in the garden, so I went down. Matt had it on his phone, you know?'

Nic nodded. 'The torch function.'

'He was trying to break into the studio,' her father explained. 'Smashing a stone against the lock.'

'Oh my god. How was he?'

'Bit bashed about from crashing his car. Said it had been worse than he'd planned it; he hit a tree. Had a nasty bump on his head. And a cut to his hand, but he'd dressed that and it looked infected, so I think maybe that was older. He said he'd come in Lily's car, parked it on the drive, but round the side under the willow that's needed trimming for years, in case anyone came looking. He begged me to help him.'

'So you protected him and lied to me?'

'Well yes, but he said if I could just let him rest in the studio, he'd explain everything. And he was already saying things about that woman's death, terrible things.'

'What things?'

'All kinds of stuff. He had a concussion, I assumed he was, you know... hallucinating. He said he could see her, but she was dead. I found the key and let him in, then I gave him a sedative, to calm him down, and I... I locked him in.'

'You sedated him and then imprisoned him?'

'I was scared. He was ranting about blood and stones, and all sorts. I thought, maybe if I kept him down there, let the concussion pass, talked to him later, he'd change his story.'

'His story?' she asked as her father coughed. 'What story?'

She glanced at the door. This was taking too long. Grace would come down soon, or Lily would tap and come in, but there was no way she could leave it here, unfinished.

'He admitted he'd done some terrible things,' he continued, clearing his throat. 'He said he'd betrayed you and his profession. He knew he'd hurt you, and Lily, and he would never forgive himself, but he said he'd had to get away, for all your sakes. He asked me to help him to start over, move on to a new life. For all your sakes.'

'So you did?' She threw a hand in the air. 'You lied to me for days, Dad! And then you helped him escape!'

Gerald coughed hard. 'I did what I did to protect you, and Lily, of course!'

'From what?' she asked. 'The man we loved, and who clearly still loved us?'

'The man who cheated on you, with his patient, and not for the first time!'

'What?'

'You think I don't notice things? Lily is a hundred per cent his, and don't tell me I'm wrong!'

She got up and went to the curtains, pulling one back to see out as he coughed. The bedroom looked towards the sea. She couldn't see the water from here, just the edge of the cliff path, but the sun would be dappling the waves, and a helicopter was hovering over the bay, way in the distance. Pemberton had said she was hoping to get one in the air a few hours before dark, to search the coves and cliffs for Matt.

Gerald still coughed. She turned back, regarding her sick father as he looked at her. He was a very old man, pitiable, but something nasty curdled inside her as she saw his rheumy eyes filling with tears. 'So where is he now?'

'I don't know.'

'When did he leave?' she asked, wondering how much time had already been lost.

'Last night,' he replied, wiping his eyes with a handkerchief. 'Just after you called to say you were coming here.'

'So you warned him I was driving down, and he took off again?'

'Matt was still sedated; I had to drive.'

Her father hadn't driven in years, not since she'd insisted on taking the keys off him and selling his car when he'd had a near-miss on the coast road. He'd been on the wrong side coming round a bend. He could have died.

'Why would you do that?' she asked, incredulous. 'Why continue to help him run away from me?'

'Because of the threat he posed,' her father said, voice steely. 'You know what I mean! I couldn't let him go, could I?'

An insidious dread that had been building since he'd first admitted to her that Matt had been here then began to take shape into something even darker in her knotted stomach. 'I have no idea what you mean.'

Her father didn't reply; instead, he folded in on himself. Then he began weeping. Uncontrollably. She wanted to comfort him, but she was scared of what he'd done, and why, and she was scared of what Matt had done too. And she was angry. So angry, it frightened her. She sat beside him again. 'OK, tell me what happened after you drove the Golf to Money Cove. Did you leave him there, or take him someplace else?'

She waited as he wiped his eyes and blew his nose, pushing the handkerchief into each of his large nostrils. His wrist was so thin, she was sure she'd be able to get her small hand right around it if she wanted to.

'I told him to get ready to get out the car when we were close to the edge, then I let the handbrake off and we both opened the doors and jumped.'

'My god, Dad! There were kids on the beach below; you could have killed someone! You could have killed yourselves!'

Her father wiped away more tears. 'I didn't know the kids were there until we heard the shouts and screams come up. I was terrified someone would have been hurt, but I checked and they were a distance away.'

'I can't believe any of this. What were you thinking?'

He looked away, cleared his throat and wiped his eyes again, then he looked her in the eye as he spoke slowly and with purpose. 'I couldn't allow Matt to walk away from me into the night. I just couldn't. He would always be a threat to you, always. You know it's true.'

She looked away then, towards the door. She could hear footfall again, people moving around the house, but if she stopped her father talking now, she might never know the end of this sorry tale. Her heart thrashed as she asked, 'If Matt was running away to a new life, what threat was he to me?'

He fixed her with his watery eyes. 'That he might tell the truth one day.'

She met his gaze then she reached out and grabbed his wrist. She'd been right; her grip went right round. She squeezed tight and leaned in. 'Tell me what happened to Matt after the car went over the cliff.'

Her father drew back in alarm and she let go. 'We walked back here, along the cliff path.'

'It's a mile, Dad! In the dark. My god, one of you could have...' She got up, shaking her head as she went back to the window, and the implications of what he'd told her began to sink in.

The helicopter was now overhead, circling blades whirring loudly. She waited, precious seconds until it moved on, then she forced herself to look back at her father and say, 'Are you telling me Matt lost his footing and fell?'

'I wish he had, that was my hope, but we were almost home and he was still there, behind me.' He shook his head. 'God forgive me, but whatever I did, I did it for you.'

'You pushed him over, deliberately, to his death, didn't you?' she asked, scarcely believing the question, let alone the answer as it came.

'Yes, I did.'

The door flew open and then someone was on the bed, raining blows down on him, her father cowering as Nic watched, helpless.

'You killed him!' Grace screamed as Ed pulled his wife away. 'You killed Matt! You monster! You pushed him over! You bastard! You killed my brother!'

## 40

Grace watched from the sitting room window as the helicopter circled the length of the bay, back and forth. Then she heard a siren, close by, lights flashing round the front of the house. Was it a second ambulance arriving, or the first one finally leaving? She was wondering again if she cared whether Gerald lived or died when Ed came running up the stairs.

'Grace.' He tapped her on the shoulder. 'Gerald is hanging in there, just. They've taken him away in the ambulance, at last, and Nic has gone with him.'

'I hope he dies and rots in hell,' she said, shrugging off Ed's unwanted hand.

'You don't mean that,' Ed said.

'Don't I?' she said, turning round. 'You heard what he did! He pushed Matt off those cliffs! He killed my brother!'

'We should call the police now,' Ed said, pointing at the red helicopter as it came back. 'Tell them what we know; it might help narrow the search.'

'Yes, you're right,' she said as she took out her phone. 'That

324                AMANDA REYNOLDS

bastard needs to pay for what he's done.' Then she sobbed into
her husband's shoulder as it all came back to her again. 'I can't
believe it, Ed. I just can't believe it.'

She'd heard Nic's raised voice downstairs, maybe an hour ago
now, competing with the helicopter that had caught her eye as it
circled the far side of the bay, and although Ed had tried to
dissuade her, she'd gone down to Gerald's door and listened to a
conversation she could still barely believe she'd overheard. A
confession that had rocked her world so hard she'd barely
known what she was doing. Ed had dragged her pummelling
fists from Gerald's chest, but she'd still wanted to kill the old
man. Even when the girls came out to see what the commotion
was, it was all she could do to stop herself back from throttling
elderly, sick, kindly Gerald, retired GP and Lily's grandpa. The
man who had deliberately pushed Matt off the cliff path, and
surely to his death? Although, maybe there was still a tiny shred
of hope that he'd somehow survived the fall and made his
escape.

Ed shoved his mobile in her face as she watched the red helicopter disappear into the evening sun.

'Take it! 999.'

'Which emergency service do you need?' the operator
repeated as she held Ed's phone to her ear.

'Um, police, I think,' she replied, startled then as heavy
knocks at the front door came up through the house.

Ed looked at her and she shooed him away. He took the hint
and ran down the stairs. The girls couldn't be relied on to
answer; Lily had been hysterical when Elan took her into their
bedroom to try and calm her down.

'I think my brother fell from a cliff path near here; he's being
looked for,' Grace explained to the operator. 'But I need to let
you know exactly where, so you can rescue him.'

* * *

'It was a delivery,' Ed said, handing her a package as he came back up. 'They work long hours these days, those Amazon guys. You reported what we know to the police?'

She nodded, swapping his phone for the padded envelope which she turned over, but there was nothing written on it. 'Who is this for?'

'He said it was for "the doc",' Ed explained. 'Bit of a thuggish-looking chap— Gracie, where you going?'

She hurtled down the spiral stairs so fast, she fell the last few, picking herself up to run at the front door and fling it open.

A Mercedes car was already driving away. She ran after it, shouting and waving. 'Gary, wait, it's me, Grace!'

The helicopter's down draft whipped dust or maybe sand in her eyes as it flew over the house again. It was right above her now, blinding her. When she looked again, the car had disappeared out the gates, taking one post with it, the splintered remains left in its wake. She hadn't even had time to note the number plate.

The helicopter hovered, deafening now. Ed came out and the girls joined them as they looked up, Lily's face tear-stained and Ed's voice raised as he pointed at the package still her hand and asked, 'What is it?'

She ripped into the padded envelope and saw that a passport was inside. She took it out and flicked to the photo and held it up to Ed, who stared at it in disbelief. Lily grabbed the passport from him and looked at the photo too. It was the same one Matt had shown her when he'd last updated his real passport, complaining to her he looked old. He didn't, not at all. Definitely not old enough to...

She covered her mouth to stifle a sob.

Ed led them back inside, but the helicopter was still loud as he asked, 'Who is Rufus Hamilton anyway?'

She shook her head and then looked at Lily, who'd started crying again, presumably as she realised the implication of that falsified passport. He had been planning on leaving her; all of them, in fact.

'Does that name mean anything to you, Lil?' Ed asked gently.

'No,' Lily said, mournful.

Then Grace remembered. Rufus had been the name they'd given to their dog. The one they'd never been allowed by their parents, so she and Matt invented a faithful shaggy but imaginary companion instead. He'd been one of the abiding and happiest memories of her childhood, and the thought of that finished her off, her sobs so loud they eclipsed Lily's as Ed drew them both into his open arms.

* * *

They went up to the sitting room to wait for news, the four of them. Elan and Grace squashed into the only chair, watching the helicopter as it hovered so close to the house it was at times intoxicating, despite the fear of what it might find. The closeness of her daughter would have also been more of a comfort, if it weren't for the circumstances. She traced a finger on Elan's tattoos, finally seeing the beauty in them. She loved her family; they were everything to her. It broke her heart to see Lily at the window, her niece's shoulders shaking as she tried not to cry and failed.

'So he was clearly intent on running away,' Ed said, looking at the fake passport again and stating the obvious.

Lily turned from the window and took the passport from Ed,

studying her father's photo for the millionth time, as if looking at it would bring him back to her, then she wiped her face and said, 'I hope he has. Got away, I mean. I think he will have, but he will still come back for me, one day. He promised.'

'There is every chance he has got away,' Grace said, although as she looked out at the cliffs, Elan pressed to her side in Gerald's chair, it felt increasing unlikely. How could anyone have survived a fall from such a great height? It had been over twenty hours now, so even if he had somehow sustained only broken bones, the chances of him being found fit and well felt slim to none. But maybe Matt was down there with shattered dreams and cracked bones and nothing worse. She made a silent prayer and hugged her daughter.

The helicopter was hovering over the cliff edge just a few hundred feet away now. The beauty of the red rescue copter against the sunset was breath-taking.

She got up and pressed her face to the window in time to see a man in a bright-orange jacket and helmet was being winched down towards the cliff edge, then further down and out of view. She craned to see more, aware that Ed had come to stand beside her, Lily the other side, their hands slipping into hers. And Elan had stood on the chair, a hand on her father's shoulder to steady herself. The four of them watched as the seconds and minutes ticked by, then the winch was coming back up and the man in the orange jacket was no longer attached to it.

Grace squinted to see against the sun, dazzling now, and the winch was at least a hundred meters away, maybe more, but she could make out enough to recognise there was a stretcher attached to the winch where the rescue worker had been. A stretcher that contained a person. Her heart leapt, but as the stretcher spun on its twine, she saw the prone figure was covered from head to toe. The body bag twisted beneath the circling blades, then it was taken into the waiting helicopter by outstretched hands.

'No!' Grace said, turning to Ed. 'No!'

'We don't know it's him,' Ed said.

But they all knew. They just knew.

# 41

TUESDAY 11 JUNE 2024 – 8.30 P.M.

It must have been almost an hour now, maybe more since her father had been taken away for 'assessment'. Time expanded and became meaningless in hospital. Nic had arrived with hm by ambulance, the blue lights flashing their way along the coastal road as he lay there, strapped in and being worked on until his pulse was stronger, his breathing regulated.

She'd been taken to a waiting room for family members after the initial checks in A&E, her father whisked away for further tests. There had been talk of a heart attack, maybe a stroke; they'd know more soon. The waiting room wasn't a patch on The Delaney Family Room, but it was all hers, for now. She paced and drank her crappy coffee from the vending machine that she'd kicked when it stole her money on the first attempt. She needn't have bothered. She threw the cup into the overflowing bin and coffee splashed onto her trainers.

It was incomprehensible to think Matt was dead. Pushed over the cliff edge so close to Chy an Mor that she was afraid she might have seen his crumpled, decomposing body from the sitting-room window and mistaken it for the patina of the rocks or a speck of colour that could have been a lost beach towel. Although his body hadn't been found as yet, not that she knew of, so maybe Matt wasn't dead? He was a survivor, her husband. That much was established.

And even more incomprehensible was that her father had lied to her, sheltering Matt for days, only to push him off the cliff path last night in the name of supposedly protecting her. She'd pressed him on that again as they'd waited to be seen by the on-call consultant in the curtained bay in A&E, mayhem all around.

'Why would you do that to Matt? I still don't understand.'

Beeps and shouts and groans and screams were coming from all directions as she leaned in to catch his rasping reply.

'He was talking about a new life, starting over, in another country, new passport, new documents to practice medicine when he got there. He was going to get away with it, Nicole.'

'So why not let him?'

'You know why,' her father had said. 'You know full well, and you should thank me! Because I have saved you!'

The door to the waiting room opened and a nurse came in, hauling her back from that moment with her father an hour ago to the worry of his present condition.

'It's not about your dad,' the fresh-faced male nurse said, pressing a reassuring hand to her arm. 'He's still being assessed, but there's a DC Pemberton here to see you; she says it's urgent.'

Pemberton was the last person she wanted to see, but the nurse said the detective had been most insistent, so would it be OK to allow her to come in? Nic looked to the glass panel in the door and saw the familiar curls. Then Pemberton raised a hand, but no smile, and her heart sank even further.

Pemberton came in as the nurse went out. They sat in two uncomfortable plastic padded chairs, looking at one another. 'I know this is a terrible time,' Pemberton said. 'But I have news of the search for Matt I should pass on.'

'They've found him?' she asked, wiping away the tears that would not stop. Why was she crying for a man who'd cheated on her, more than once, and then planned on abandoning her for a new life? But she'd loved him far too long not to mourn his loss.

'Yes, we have found him, and I'm afraid it's bad news.'

She nodded, feeling strangely calm. 'Where?'

'Quite close to your father's house. On the cliffs below the coastal path. I asked for air-sea recue to start around Money Cove and the search was then narrowed down after a call from your sister-in-law. It's OK,' Pemberton said as Nic went to speak. 'I understand your father is extremely unwell; I won't be asking to speak with him until he's up to it.'

'You're certain it's Matt's...? His... his body?'

'Yes, he was still carrying ID, and some cash. No sign of his laptop, but in cases like these there are often loose ends... My best guess is, and Stone agrees, that he dumped all devices after he made that call to Lily and the anonymous tip-off too.'

'That was Matt?'

'Yes, phone records have now verified the call was from his number.'

'Wow, he planned it all. Well... nearly all.'

'Can I call anyone, ask them to sit with you?'

'No, there's no one,' she said, her tissue so sodden, she used her flattened hand instead. 'But can you make sure Lily is updated? And tell her I love her and that I know she doesn't want me right now, but...' She stopped explaining. 'Just say that, when she's told the news. She loved her father so much.'

'Of course, I will deliver the update myself.'

The nurse was back, tapping at the door, then coming in. 'I'm so sorry to interrupt, but the doctor would like to speak with you urgently, Mrs Delaney. It's about your father.'

## 42

TUESDAY 11 JUNE 2024 – 9 P.M.

No one had moved from the sitting room window. Not the girls, not Ed, and definitely not Grace. They were waiting for news of the search, hope clinging to them despite the body bag which had been winched to the helicopter that had then flown off into the dazzling sun. The sitting room only had one chair, and it was getting dark outside, so Ed suggested they went down to the kitchen. It was a good idea, except Grace wasn't sure she could move.

'Come on, Gracie,' Ed said. 'Take my hand.'

The girls took the two chairs at the tiny kitchen table, whilst Ed made tea.

'Bloody tea, always tea,' she muttered under her breath as she scoured the fridge for food and checked her phone, again. No calls, from anyone.

'Pass the milk,' Ed said.

She passed him up the dregs of a curdled single pint and closed the fridge door. How could she want to eat at a time like this? But she was hungry, and empty.

She searched the damp cupboards and found nothing except custard creams, packets and packets of them. She checked the dates, all past, and opened one, chucking the packet on the table without taking one. Then she went into the pantry to see if there was anything else she could fashion into a meal. That's when she noticed something unusual right at the back, behind the cleaning stuff. She pulled it out and held it up.

'That's Dad's!' Lily said as Grace returned with a khaki rucksack.

'Yes, that was my first thought too,' she said, searching frantically through the pockets, but every one of them was empty.

'What are you looking for?' Lily asked.

The thing was, despite everything that she'd heard through Gerald's door, or perhaps because of it, now more than ever she was certain that Matt didn't kill Deena. She knew her brother, and he didn't have it in him. Yes, he was a cheat, a liar, a chancer, a coward with his plans to run away, but that did not make him a killer. And Gerald hadn't said he was. He just said Matt was a continuing threat to Nic. Which also didn't make sense if Matt was running away. How could he be a threat from the other side of the world, unless Matt knew who really killed Deena?

'Ed?' she said, giving him one of her pleading looks.

'Yes?' he said, looking confused. 'What is it?'

'Sorry, I think I might be sick; can you come with me?'

She dropped the rucksack and ran from the room, hoping Ed would follow, which he did, up the stairs and into the only bathroom, along the hallway and next to Gerald's room. She pulled Ed inside the dank room with its mildewed shower curtain across a stained bath and locked the door.

'I'm not going to be sick!' she said as he went to hold back her curly hair.

She closed the toilet lid and sat down on it. 'I need to talk to you about Nic. I don't think Matt was the one who killed Deena.'

Ed shook his head. 'I think you need to accept now, that—'

'Shush!' she said, getting up and pulling him towards her. 'We should have quizzed her more,' she whispered. 'Something isn't right. Think about it, Ed! Gerald didn't say he pushed Matt because he'd confessed to killing Deena. He said he'd done it to protect her.'

'Yes, because Matt was a dangerous man, a threat to Nic *and* Lily.'

'But Matt was running away; he was no threat. Not from the other side of the world; I heard Nic say the same herself!' She took the passport out of her tunic pocket and held it up. 'The only threat was if Matt knew something he could pass on, a key piece of information about the real killer. Something that person would always fear and a loving father would want to eliminate. That's what Gerald said, I heard him, that he did it for her, in case Matt decided to tell the truth one day, and Gerald also said that Nic knew why he'd pushed Matt over.'

Ed shook his head and backed away. 'I was thinking you meant in terms of her not wanting to lose the house and therefore covering for Matt... An insurance scam. This is something else entirely.'

'But it makes perfect sense. Nic kills Deena because, you know, Matt was cheating on her, and Deena was also the complainant, so Matt stands to lose his career, and Nic the house, and he knows he looks guilty as hell, so he thinks his only chance is to run away, but it goes wrong and he ends up here, at the mercy of his father-in-law, whilst he's waiting for this to turn up.' She brandished the passport again.

'But he had bloodstained clothes in his car.'

'Yes, I know, because he was there when it happened, but he didn't do it, I know he didn't!'

Her phone rang in her other tunic pocket. She pulled it out and looked at it, then handed it to Ed. The call was from DC Pemberton.

## 43

TUESDAY 11 JUNE 2024 – 9.30 P.M.

DC Pemberton was waiting for Nic when she came back to the waiting room. She thought she'd have long gone, but there she was, holding on to Nic's bag which she'd mistakenly left behind after the nurse had come to fetch her to say her father had taken a turn for the worse. There were now three other people in the room besides the detective: a couple who were holding hands as if their own lives depended on it, and a cleaner with a trolley of mops and brushes. They all looked up as she came in, but she ignored them and took her bag as the detective held it out to her. 'Thanks, you didn't have to wait.'

'My sincerest condolences,' Pemberton said.

'Oh, you heard?' she asked, slinging her bag across her dirty top and running her hands into her hair. It must be looking shameful.

'Yes, the nurse came back to let me know. How are you doing?'

'Numb.'

'Of course. Are you leaving now? I'll walk you out.'

They walked the long corridors following exit signs that

never seemed to end, and eventually, Pemberton asked what had happened.

'Well, it seems as if it was peaceful,' she replied, feeling stone-hearted to it all. 'They think a stroke, maybe heart attack. Trauma, I suppose. He was almost ninety. It's all been too much for him.'

'I'm so sorry.'

She wasn't sure if the detective was apologising generally, or for her part in it, as she'd hassled him with too many questions. It was probably a meaningless statement, one the police said many times in their line of work. Nic couldn't think straight, anyway. She had learned in one evening that her husband and father were both dead. It would be too much for anyone to process in such a small space of time, but she had a feeling her heart had hardened long before.

'Can I offer you a lift back to Chy an Mor?' Pemberton said as they at last found their way outside.

It was raining, heavy droplets of water splashing from the roof of the hospital's entrance porch onto their heads. The dripping c-shaped ends of the detective's curls brushed the shoulders of Pemberton's raincoat as she belted it. Nic hugged her thin hoodie to her chest and looked for a taxi, or a bus, but it seemed she had little choice but to accept the only lift available.

'Thank you, that's very kind.'

\* \* \*

'It must be an extremely difficult time for you, especially given the circumstances of Matt's death,' the detective said as she drove the dark narrow roads back to Chy an Mor.

Nic looked across.

'Do you know why your father acted as he did?' the detective asked. 'That's a dramatic step, to say the least.'

'My father was caught up in a misguided attempt to protect me,' she replied. 'Matt threatened him and he rightly thought he was dangerous. Much as you had said to me yourself.'

'I see,' Pemberton replied, sounding less than satisfied. 'Oh, and just to say it could be a couple of weeks before Matt's body can be released for a funeral, so if you wanted to go home in the meantime...?'

'I'll need to make the arrangements for my father's funeral first.'

'Of course, yes, just thought I'd mention...' Pemberton glanced over. 'I know it's not exactly the best time, so we could talk tomorrow if you'd prefer, but there are a couple more details I'd like to discuss, when you're up to it?'

She briefly met the detective's eyes before Pemberton's attention flicked back to the road. 'What details?'

'Regarding a sighting of your husband; near here, in fact.' They were driving through the village now, down in the bay. Nic hadn't even noticed the slight detour until she sat up straighter.

'I thought he went straight to Dad's?'

'No, he apparently bought toiletries, food, water on Friday afternoon, in the local post office.' Pemberton pointed to the closed shop in the harbour.

'I don't see how this matters now, though,' she said, slumping back in her seat. 'We know my father was sheltering him, for reasons none of us will now fully understand, me included.'

'Yes, just one odd thing though,' Pemberton said as she turned the car back along the coastal road. 'Matt also bought a postcard and a stamp in the shop. A view of the bay, the owner recalls, as not so many postcards are sold these days. The same view as you can see from the sitting room at Chy an Mor. Was that sent to you?'

Nic glanced down, her bag within easy reach at her feet. The postcard was inside, tucked between the pages of her latest notebook. She'd ripped off the cellophane but had barely written a word since she'd arrived in Cornwall, which was a relief as the detective had been nursing her bag, but then another, possibly even more alarming thought occurred. Had the detective looked inside and seen that postcard? Surely that was unethical? 'I don't think I've been sent a postcard in years,' she replied.

'Well, Matt clearly intended to send a card to someone. If I could find a travelling bag, rucksack or suitcase, it may still be in there?' Pemberton looked over as Nic shrugged. 'I see. Like the disappearing rat traps in the garage. You never saw it!'

'No, and you can't blame me for my husband's lies.'

'No, of course not.' Pemberton shook her head, the detective's damp hair spraying Nic's face with a fine mist. 'Just one final thing.'

'What's that?' she asked, losing patience now. Didn't she have enough to cope with, without this interrogation? But they'd be at Chy an Mor soon and she could leave this woman's car, and hopefully never see her again.

'You parked in the layby at the top of the hill when you visited Scott Jensen at The Glasshouse on Sunday morning?'

'Yes, what of it?'

'I parked there too, during the search, and I hung around a bit afterwards, met a few regulars up there: dogwalkers, ramblers.'

'Really?' Nic adjusted her seatbelt. It was cutting into her and she felt travel sick. She needed to escape; she felt breathless and hot, held captive. 'Why was that?'

'I wanted to ask if anyone had spotted Matt's car, specifically on the day Deena died.'

'And had they?'

'Yes, there was a nice lady, blue van, lots of dogs; she gave me a positive sighting of Matt's BMW last Tuesday morning, at eleven, and the thing is...' Pemberton chanced a quick look across before the dark twisty road required her full attention again. 'This dogwalker also said there was a white car parked next to it, and she recalls a well-dressed lady getting out and walking up the hill.'

'There are lots of cars that park there,' she said, glad of the shelter of the darkness to cover her reaction. 'Could have been anyone. Did she get the registration?'

'No, she didn't, sadly, but she remembered that it was a white Evoque.'

'There are loads of those too.'

'Of course, but she told me she remembers it particularly, because she saw it again when she banged her door into it on Sunday morning.'

'That was my first ever visit! She's clearly mixed up.'

'Right, so you deny being there on the Tuesday before?'

'Yes! You have my movements; it all checks out. I was at Brackley, nine until two, as I have said many times.'

'She said you refused her offer to exchange insurance details, despite your car being damaged. So I was wondering if that was because you didn't want her to place your car there the previous Tuesday as well, and then have your details to pass on to our appeal line?'

'Well, that's just not—'

'Because I think you would have had enough time to leave Brackley on Tuesday morning after your coffee with the headmaster and follow Matt up to The Glasshouse for a meeting he'd pre-arranged with Deena Jensen, that you'd somehow found out about, and then after whatever happened to Deena, however she died, you could still, in theory, be back at Brackley before that interminable PTA meeting finished and create your rather leaky but nevertheless somewhat convincing alibi.'

'That's ridiculous!'

'Is it?'

Pemberton slowed for the turning into Chy an Mor. The house was lit up as they pulled in, narrowly avoiding a gate post that had been ripped from the ground.

'What's been going on here?' Pemberton asked, slowing down to park.

'No idea,' Nic replied, looking up at the house. There were lights on at every window.

She couldn't wait to get out, but she wasn't looking forward to facing Lily and Grace and the others. She released the passenger door handle, but it was locked. 'Can you let me out?' she demanded, rattling the door. 'I need to see my daughter.'

'It was you who smashed the camera, not Matt, wasn't it?' Pemberton stated, as if it were fact, not a question. 'You're petite but not stupid, clearly, and you go to the gym, you have the strength. Then you followed him in through the bedroom door, maybe only a minute or so behind. Then you killed Deena with the same rock you smashed the camera with.'

'This is crazy!' Nic rattled the locked door again. 'Matt smashed that camera.'

'The film runs on for at least a minute before the feed cuts; plenty of time for you to have followed him and smashed the camera; you're small, and like I say, clever.'

'No! I wasn't there! Matt smashed the camera before *he* killed Deena and then he tried to run away, because he was scared and guilty and a fucking coward!'

'So why would your father shelter him?'

'I told you, because he was scared to death of Matt! Matt was a desperate and violent man, you said so yourself. Now please let me out!'

The door released and she stumbled out and then up the drive. It was only then, as the detective turned her car around and drove away – the relief of escape overwhelming at first – that she realised the Jigginses' Volvo was no longer there.

## 44

TUESDAY 11 JUNE 2024 – 10.30 P.M.

It was much cooler in the car than it had been on the way down. The lateness of the hour had chilled the outside air so Grace felt a little calmer too as Ed drove them further and further away from Chy an Mor and into the night.

The motorway that had been so busy just a few hours earlier was clear of traffic as they joined it. And the girls seemed fine now, seated in the back, side-by-side, and energised by their shared mission and hastily devised plan. Ed pressed his foot to the pedal, just a little, advising they would be at Three Gables in an hour and forty minutes, give or take. Then hopefully in and out before anyone knew it and with, Grace hoped, the evidence they needed. She was amazed Ed had agreed to it all, but relieved to have him on board. And also astounded she could feel quite so fine given what had just happened. She knew of course that her pain and grief for Matt was waiting to pounce, and maybe some guilt about Gerald too after a call from DC Pemberton had broken more bad news, but first she needed to do this, for her brother.

'OK?' she asked the girls, turning round. Lily looked

tearstained in the headlamps that zoomed by, but Elan's expression reflected her own determination. 'You sure about this, sweethearts?'

'We're doing this for Dad,' Lily replied. 'We can't back out now.'

'Yes, yes, you're right,' she replied, ashamed she'd voiced her doubts, but still mindful of involving the girls in what was potentially a risky move.

'Yes, we need to do this,' Elan said, smiling at her. 'For me as well as Uncle Matt.'

It was still shocking to her when Elan spoke, although her daughter had talked at length after she and Ed emerged from the bathroom to see their daughter stood there, on her own, waiting to tell them everything.

'Do you need the bathroom?' Ed had asked, standing aside.

'No, thanks, Dad, but I need to say that I agree with Mum,' Elan had replied, looking directly at her. 'Aunt Nicole killed Deena Jensen. No doubt about it in my mind. We just need to find a way to prove it.'

Grace hadn't known if she was more shocked by Elan speaking to her, or what she'd just said, but then Ed began shushing them as Lily came up from the kitchen too. But Grace needed answers. 'Go on, Elan. Tell us what you think.'

'I don't *think*; I *heard* them,' Elan explained.

'Who?' Ed asked.

'Gerald and Aunt Nicole, when I went to the bathroom earlier; you remember, Lily?' Elan said, turning to her cousin, who looked dazed. 'You were talking to Will on your phone and the signal was bad, and Mum and Dad were upstairs, so I went for a wee and that's when I heard them, talking loudly, just the other side of the wall.'

'What did you hear them say?' Grace asked.

'She already knew Uncle Matt was here, in Cornwall. She'd had a postcard from him; it arrived on Saturday.'

'What?' Lily said. 'Why didn't she say, or come down here sooner?'

'Because, sadly, Lily,' Ed explained, 'your grandpa lied to her about your father being here, although I'm sure he did it with the best of intentions.'

'And she asked what Uncle Matt had said about what had happened,' Elan went on. 'You know, what he'd told Gerald about why he'd run away, and he said... "You know what he told me, Nicole.".'

'Oh my god,' Grace said, exchanging glances with Ed. 'It *was* her!'

'You think Mum killed Deena?' Lily asked, voice small.

'No one is suggesting that,' Ed replied.

'I think we are,' Grace added.

Things had been tense between Lily and her since Grace had lashed out at Gerald, and the conversation outside the bathroom hadn't helped much, but it was important, vital in fact, that they get to the truth.

'She is really mean, Lil,' Elan had said then, taking Lily's hand. 'I told you what she said to me last summer.'

'What did she say?' Ed asked.

'How I'm really weird, and how I should... maybe try harder with my appearance and stuff. It started about a year ago, the comments, and it's got much worse. She can be pretty cruel.'

'She said all that?' Ed had asked, a rhetorical question, his voice filled with unfamiliar anger. 'And to think I've always defended her!'

Elan shrugged, although she'd looked close to tears. Lily had given her a big hug then.

'Why didn't you tell me?' Grace asked, resurfacing from her

thoughts about Nic to tune in to a new worry. 'I could have helped you work through it, I am a trained...' She never finished the sentence, realising she'd answered her own question.

'I knew you'd try and help,' Elan replied, confirming what she'd thought. 'And I just couldn't face therapy sessions with my own mum. Sorry.'

'OK, that's enough for me!' Ed then announced. 'How do we go about proving this theory of Nicole being complicit in murder?'

Grace could have hugged him, but it made her so sad to think of Elan suffering in silence. The hurt was clearly too raw for Elan to immediately share Nic's wicked comments that had continued for almost a year, during which her daughter had withdrawn into near silence. A way to take back some control from her bully. They'd packed up everything in a frenzy after that, keen to get away before Nic's return from the hospital. A vital head start. Although with Ed driving, they could easily lose that.

'Can you go a bit faster?' she asked, and he cranked the Volvo from seventy to seventy-five miles an hour, which was pretty much the car's and Ed's top speed.

## 45

WEDNESDAY 12 JUNE 2024 – 12.27 A.M.

It was another two hours before they arrived. Ed's renewed caution after a possible flash from a speed camera had made the second half of the journey unnecessarily slow. But Three Gables was dark and looked empty, thank god. And no sign of any cars on the drive, except theirs.

Grace took out her keys and unlocked the perennially impressive front door whilst Ed helped the girls exit the jammed back doors of the Volvo, then she tapped in the alarm code as the girls joined her. If Nic came back unexpectedly, they'd agreed they would say they were collecting more of Lily's things. Ed would wait in the car: their slow but steady getaway driver.

Lily was first up the stairs, eager to get to where the stack of red notebooks was kept, even though Grace had already warned her they'd been moved. The plan was to comb the many filled notebooks for any references to the day of Deena's death. If Nic was involved, she'd have written it down, that's what Lily said. But as Grace had told her niece, explaining how she'd tried to return one and only found a stack of unused ones, the notebooks could well have been destroyed.

They split up, hunting high and low. In old handbags, a suit-case, anywhere Nic might have hidden her scribblings. Even the kitchen bin was turned out on the floor by a frantic Lily, who called her mum anything but 'Mum', many of the names so unpleasant, Grace still felt she must censor their use, despite her hatred of the woman.

Grace then went outside to check the dustbins.

Ed opened the car door as she passed and asked if she needed his help, but she told him to stay put; he was their look out. She went through the side gate and down the path, then threw the wheelie bins on their sides and searched the contents in the moonlight, picking up card and empty tins and bottles and flinging them back into the righted bins, but still no sign of the red notebooks. She kicked at an empty juice carton in frustration and wiped her sticky hands down her tunic, then shook her head to Ed as she passed him again on her way back inside.

She was wondering where to look next when Lily came hurtling down the stairs and told her they'd forgotten Matt's study. 'She was in there,' Lily said, running ahead and opening the door. 'I saw her, at Dad's desk, scribbling like a crazy psycho bitch!'

Matt's desk was locked and there was no sign of a key. She and Elan were still hunting for it as Lily prised open the drawer with a letter opener and a hotchpotch of identical red notebooks was revealed within. They couldn't believe it! There must have been at least twenty in there. They took a few each and scanned the pages, fast, and although Grace remained unsure about the morality of reading Nic's private thoughts, her desire for justice for Matt easily overcame that.

'Bloody stupid to-do lists!' Lily commented, throwing one notebook away and taking another from the stack beside her on the desk. She was sitting in Matt's chair, long legs splayed in denim shorts. 'It has to be here. *Fuck!*' Lily looked up. 'She was raped?'

'What?' Grace asked, taking the notebook and scanning the horrific account.

Elan flicked through them too, commenting on the trees, the babies. It was all so sad. They were losing their way, and there were more filled pages than they could have guessed at.

'It's in here!' Elan said, thumb stuck in the middle of a red notebook ten minutes later, hand shaking as she held it up. 'All of it, the whole thing. *Shit*, I can't believe it!'

'Let me see!' Grace replied, dropping the one she was reading – an account of when she and Nic had first met and how she'd immediately taken a dislike to Grace.

Grace leant over Elan's shoulder and tried to read the small writing. 'I was starting to think she wouldn't have implicated herself in it at all.'

'No, you don't understand,' Elan said, holding it closer to Grace. 'She says she killed her! She says it all, look, here!'

They both looked at Lily then, her green eyes threatening tears, but then she smiled. 'I knew Dad didn't do it.'

They collected up the notebooks and headed towards the front door. They'd decided it was best to take them all, not just the important one, and the plan was to drive straight to the police HQ building across town at first light, where they would hand them straight over to DC Pemberton, if she was back there by then. If not, anyone would do. The sooner the better.

Grace opened the door, juggling her share of notebooks, but Ed stopped them dead. He was out of the car and pointing behind him, as if they wouldn't have already noticed that Nic's white Evoque was parked in the drive. Grace gasped and almost dropped her haul, but there was no sign of Nic inside the car.

'I told her what was going on,' Ed said. 'Asked her to come in, talk to us, but she headed round the side. You wait here, Gracie, and I'll go talk to her.'

'No!' she said, handing him all but one of the notebooks. 'Let me go.'

'No way!' Elan said. 'She's dangerous, Mum.'

'I'll be fine, sweetheart.' Grace tossed a look to Ed and then gave him her phone, balancing it on the notebooks he now held but looked about to drop. 'Call DC Pemberton, her number is in there and tell her everything, and if she doesn't pick up then call 999, but let me do this. I need to, for my brother.'

## 46

WEDNESDAY 12 JUNE 2024 – 1.15 A.M.

Nic watched from beneath her beloved trees as Grace came in through the side gate. Her sister-in-law had triggered the security lights on the patio. The repetition of Grace's previous means of entrance on the night of the barbeque was another annoying liberty taken, but there was also relief. Like a long-awaited but dreaded diagnosis, or confirmation of a suspected affair, the freedom of knowing she no longer had to fear the worst, because it was happening, was strangely liberating. And at least she was home.

DC Pemberton had been suspicious too, so Nic had suspected one or other of those two women would work it out eventually, and when she saw Grace was clutching one of her precious red notebooks, Nic knew there was no point denying anything. The pen was mightier than the sword, the evidence in Grace's hands. Again, a relief. Like when her father had told her he'd killed Matt, and for a few short hours, she thought she might actually get away with murder. Not that you ever 'get away' with anything as terrible as that, but she had hoped she might be able to stay here, with her trees. For a while longer, at least.

'How are you?' Grace asked, joining her on the bumpy ground beneath the cherry tree. 'I didn't expect you back home quite so soon; don't you have stuff to sort out for your father's funeral?'

Nic pressed her back into the nubbly bark. Her feet were bare as she'd kicked off her trainers. This was no time for small talk. Instead, she looked up, drinking in these final moments with her trees. It was dark, cold, and the moon had slipped behind a cloud, but she imagined bright sunshine soon, the boughs above beginning to bend under the weight of their cargo of fruit. She'd known the second she saw the Volvo was gone from Chy an Mor's drive that she was on borrowed time. Grace, maybe Lily too, had overheard something, and with not a word why they'd all gone, she'd guessed where they were headed. She could have got in her car and driven away, absconded just as Matt had tried to, but it was far too late to run. She'd seen where that got you. And she wasn't ready to die. Not for a long time yet. So she'd come home.

'Do you understand what I've read in here?' Grace asked, brandishing the notebook in the gloom. The security lights had gone off again.

'Well, I have a number of them, but I could take a wild guess which one that is!'

She hadn't realised how angry Grace was until she looked at her then, and for a second, fear rose inside her at the thought Grace might attack her, as she had her father, the hatred as naked and fierce as it had been a few hours before when Ed had to pull his strong and tall wife away. Grace was so much bigger than her; she could easily kill her. Was that why she'd come round the back of the house alone, to confront her? She edged away from Grace, just a little.

'How did you know Matt was going to The Glasshouse the day Deena died?' Grace asked, her tone cold but measured.

'Because I'm not a fool, even though you and Matt always seemed to think I was. I've learned the hard way to pay attention, check messages, listen in on calls. Deena was so much his type. I knew he'd fuck up, and he did.'

'You followed him there, the day she died?'

She nodded. 'He was never going to end it, not on his own. We both knew that!'

'So you ended it for him?'

'They were having sex! Out there on the terrace! Deena's legs spread as Matt pushed inside her, grunting, ecstatic. How was I supposed to react?'

Grace turned away, no stomach for the truth of her precious brother's infidelity and sexual appetite, but she forced herself to look back and say to her, 'You pushed Deena over the terrace! You killed her, not Matt! Admit it; it's all here!' Grace held the notebook an inch from her face. 'You are Deena's killer.'

'I don't remember exactly what I wrote,' she replied.

But she remembered it all too clearly, sadly. How she'd followed Matt into the house through the open bedroom door. How she'd heard them, out on the terrace, opening champagne, and how they'd been fucking when she found them. Deena hadn't seen her until the last moment, maybe not at all, and Matt had his mind on other things. He didn't see his wife run at them, a blur of rage and fury condensed into just one small shove. That's all it took. Matt had tried to hold on to Deena, cutting his hand in the process as her long nails ripped his grasping palm. They'd been locked together to the last, but he wasn't able to save her.

Vertigo had slammed into Nic so hard as she looked over to

see Deena's broken body, she'd thought for a second she might tumble after her. Then Matt was shaking her, telling her to leave; he'd fix it. 'Just go! You're fucking hysterical. Get out of here. I said I'll fix this!'

'Matt must have tried to help Deena, I know he would have!' Grace said now, her hands shaking as she held the closed notebook and stared at it.

'Oh yes, of course, good old Matt,' she replied. 'The trusted doctor and every woman's saviour! Covered in her blood when he finally admitted defeat and dug a grave. He said he'd disposed of the body at work, and I believed him! So trusting!'

'So he took the blame to cover for you?' Grace asked.

'I don't think it was quite so gallant as that,' she replied. 'He was a coward who tried to run away and he got caught.'

Matt wouldn't talk to her in the days after it happened; he shut down, completely. Wouldn't discuss the affair, or the tribunal, or the events at The Glasshouse. He withdrew, told her to leave him alone, he needed to think, shutting himself in his study. Then they'd had sex the night before Lily's party and although she didn't think their relationship was as easily fixed as that, she'd believed that they were a team again, and they would pull together. That's what she'd held on to. Even after he ran away. But he wanted a new life, without her, and a way to rebuild his career, which was, in his own words, his whole world.

'You should have confessed to save Matt!' Grace screamed in her face. 'You said you still loved him. That's what love is!'

'He just did too many bad things, Grace,' she replied, feeling much calmer for having settled that much in her own mind. 'And once trust is lost, what did he expect? Everyone has their limit.'

They both looked towards the house then. There were no lights on, but the side gate had opened and the scrape of wood over stones had caught their attention. She squinted to see who was there, for a second thinking it was someone else. Her husband, returned at last. Then the security lights came on as DC Pemberton walked towards them.

# EPILOGUE

Nic hated this time of the day. The sound of doors closing for the night. The endless shouts and knocks and even screams. She was lucky in that she had a cell to herself, but that was for a specific reason, one she preferred not to think about but understood fully. They looked through the door once an hour to check she hadn't taken the easy route out. But she wouldn't do that. She had too much to do. Too many wrongs to right, or rather 'write'. Starting with another list.

She'd asked for one of her specific red notebooks when she'd been transferred to this unit and her request was denied. So she'd had to make do with the lined sheets of paper and blunt pencil she'd been given by the counsellor. She didn't like Izzy as much as she had Connie, but Izzy also ascribed to the 'getting your feelings onto paper' form of therapy and that suited Nic just fine.

The lists comprised mainly things to tell Lily in case she forgot. Her daughter hadn't visited, and had ignored every request from Nic for her to do so, but one day she would come. And in the meantime, there was something she, her mother, could save her from. A thankless task. The lights had been turned off, but Nic could see well enough to write, and tonight the one thing she had never written down, let alone talked about with any of her many therapists, would hopefully come tumbling onto the page as if it were yesterday. A gift to her daughter. The gift of knowing what had happened to her birth mother.

It had taken Nic an hour that day in early December 2006 to settle six-month-old baby Lily for her afternoon nap. She could have cried when Lil was then disturbed minutes later by heavy knocks at the front door. Her daughter's green eyes popping wide open in fright, and for a second, she'd wanted to shake her, hard, but she didn't, of course. She loved her.

Nic wasn't even dressed, hadn't brushed her teeth at three in the afternoon after, at best, two hours' sleep the night before. If it was the overly friendly postman, she would not be held responsible for her actions.

She wound the tinkling mobile over Lily's cot and slipped out the new nursery, cursing whoever it was who'd bothered them on a drizzly December afternoon only a few weeks before Christmas.

The new front door stuck again as she fought to open it. She made a mental note to get the carpenter back, and then finally wrenched it open to see a most unwelcome visitor, and behind them a taxi, engine still running.

'I've come back for my baby,' Katie Creel, Lily's birth mother, said, pushing her way in. 'Where is she?'

'My god, Katie! I thought you were on the other side of the world... What do you mean you've come back for her?'

But of course, it was perfectly clear what Katie meant.

'It was a mistake leaving her behind, a *huge* mistake,' Katie said, heading for the stairs. 'I can hear her. Is she up here? I don't have long; I'm booked on the next flight home.'

She had to think quickly, and she did. 'Go on up, last door on the left.'

The taxi driver asked for a hundred pounds to abandon his fare to the airport, all the cash Nic had in her purse, but she paid it over willingly as his radio belted out Mariah's 'All I Want For Christmas'. All she wanted was to get Katie away from her perfect home before Matt got back from the hospital, but she needed time to come up with a plan first. She couldn't lose Lily. The baby was the only thing stopping Matt from throwing in the towel on their ailing, sexless marriage, and despite everything, she loved Lily too, with all her heart.

Lily was burbling happily in Katie's toned tennis-player's arms by the time Nic got back upstairs, the taxi now gone.

'She looks like me, don't you think?' Katie asked, youthful exuberance radiating from the nineteen-year-old. 'I was adopted too, then fostered when the adoption didn't work out. I can't do that to Margot. I'm her family.'

'Her name is Lily. Lily Sylvie Delaney.'

Katie smiled. 'I don't know about that, but you can come visit Margot if you like. And Matt can, of course.'

'Put Lily down,' she told her, barring the way out of the nursery by stepping into Katie's path.

The piles of Christmas presents she'd already wrapped toppled across the carpeted floor as they scuffled. There was no way she would be able to persuade Matt that a couple of long-haul visits a year were adequate replacement for having his daughter with him full-time, but Katie was younger, fitter, stronger; even holding a baby, she easily overpowered her.

'I know what you've been through, but she's *my* baby and I have a plane to catch,' Katie said as she pushed past then ran down the stairs and opened the stiff door, Lily still pressed to her chest.

'I let the taxi go,' Nic told her, following her outside into the freezing day.

'You psycho bitch! Why would you do that?' Lily was thrashing in Katie's arms as she turned back. 'Fine, I'll just have to walk until I can hitch a ride!'

Nic ran after them, cold air catching in her throat. 'I'm sorry. I panicked, but you can't walk, and you won't thumb a lift out here. It's too remote. I'll drive you myself. Please, let me at least do that. Lily... I mean Margot will freeze to death. It's almost dark. Think of your daughter, please. I promise, I won't try anything. This arrangement hasn't worked out for me either, to be honest.'

They went back inside, Nic dragging Katie's suitcase that the taxi driver had unceremoniously dumped on the drive. Nic hauled the heavy case upstairs then placed in neatly folded rompers and the soft lemon cot blanket, then the plush giraffe Matt had come home with a few months back, tiny socks and mittens and vests tucked in between Katie's cropped tops. Katie bounced and cooed a contented Lily on her hip, smiling when Nic zipped the case closed. 'Thanks, I really appreciate you being so cool, but I really do need to leave now.'

Katie carried a by then wriggling Lily to the car. The 'family' car Matt had bought Nic when Lily had arrived six months before. It hadn't been the motherhood experience Nic had dreamt of, but neither was she about to give it up without a fight. Lily might not be hers, but she was the closest she was ever going to get, and that baby was the price she paid to keep Matt. A sticking plaster keeping their marriage together, and one she could not risk ripping off.

She strapped Lily into her car seat in the back, because Katie couldn't work out how to do it, then she climbed into the driver's seat and said, 'Sorry, Katie. I left the front door open; would you mind? I'll keep the heater running. For Lily... Sorry, Margot.'

Katie looked doubtful. 'You're not going to do a runner, are you?'

'For god's sake! Trust me, will you? I said this suits me too.'

Katie frowned but she walked towards the house as instructed. She was a rangy thing. Muscular. Absolutely no way Nic could take her on in a fight and expect to win. Katie closed the tight-fitting front door without much effort at all, then she jogged back towards the car.

That was the moment Nic released the handbrake, foot to the pedal as she smiled at Katie and ploughed straight into her, pinning her against the metal garage doors. As Nic reversed the car, Katie's body slid to the ground, then she drove at her again, tyres bumping over those long bones.

\* \* \*

'It's only a garage door!' Matt had said, looking unimpressed when he'd returned that evening, dog-tired from another long day at the hospital, to hear his wife's confession of a freak accident that had ruined their garage door, and the new car. 'The important thing is no one was hurt, Nic.'

Matt was bouncing Lily on his hip as Nic stirred a risotto, if memory served, whilst she explained how one minute she'd been checking on Lily in her car seat, then the next she was zooming towards the garage. She was just so sleep deprived, that was the trouble. She'd only been popping to the supermarket, but she must have mixed up the car's pedals.

'I'm sorry,' he'd said. 'I should do more to help, and I will. A new start, for both of us, yes?'

'Yes, sounds good,' she'd said.

Mostly, she was able to put what had happened with Katie to the back of her mind, although Christmas was always a reminder. The presents, the festive tunes, especially Mariah Carey. And sometimes, she'd come round the bend just before the turning into Three Gables track and see Katie in the woods, looking out from the exact spot where she'd buried her. Those dark eyes watching her, full of reproach, grey, just like the tiny flecks amongst the green in Lily's. As if the daughter was sometimes the mother, Lily a constant reminder of what she'd done.

No one had ever come looking for Katie. The adopted and fostered child who'd gone travelling and then disappeared. No one ever walked that way through the woods either, except sometimes Nic, Lily strapped to her, or later hand in hand. She'd trudge through the leaves and mulch just to make sure the plastic wrapping she'd used in the car hadn't unearthed. And in the end, she'd mostly reconciled herself to what had happened. A necessary act to preserve something much more important than a teen who slept with married men. She did it for them: her perfect family. And no one had ever found out.

'That's what you do to protect the ones you love,' she told Lily as she finished writing, although it was just the darkness she spoke to. And she wasn't sure she'd tell Lily what she'd done to her birth mother, after all. There were some secrets far too large to share. Far too big to forgive. After all, everyone has their limit.

# ACKNOWLEDGEMENTS

This is my sixth published book! Hard to imagine, but true. I have loved every single one of them, but *Her Husband's Lie* is an idea that has been with me for many years, so seeing it finally in readers' hands is very special. Every book goes on a journey, but this has been a long one, with many skilled hands involved beside mine.

Thanks firstly to my editor, Emily Yau. With her insight and keen eye for pace, style and story, she has infinitely improved *Her Husband's Lie*, and to the whole team at Boldwood, including my copy editor and proof reader, cover design, publicity and marketing, production, audio, and the visionary Amanda Ridout; thank you all for loving this book too.

Special thanks go my agent, Hannah Todd, who with Georgia McVeigh and Madeleine Milburn helped me in the early stages of this story and provided invaluable editorial critique and support. Hannah is my constant ally and I adore her mix of optimism and industry expertise. She is so talented and I'm very lucky to have her.

To my fellow authors and friends, Kate Riordan, Hayley Hoskins, the Ladykillers and all my colleagues and writers at The Novelry who are never more than a message away with support and understanding, I appreciate each and every one of you.

And the brilliant booksellers and festival organisers who have supported all my books, especially Will at Cleeve Books, and my fellow crime writer, Jackie Kabler, my 'partner in crime' at many events, and Jane Bailey, friend and fellow author and fantastic events chair.

Also, all the wonderful readers and reviewers who champion my books through social media and come to events and signings. It's so humbling to know you love reading my words.

And my family and friends. Especially Chris, Beth, Dan and George. Always there, always needed. And of course, Scout, my companion when I'm suffering from writer's insomnia. And my parents who press books into friends' hands constantly, thank you!

And lastly my beautiful friend Caroline, to whom this is dedicated. We laughed and talked about this story and so many other things, but there was never enough time and now I cannot think about you without wishing you were here, and my heart aches. You were kind, beautiful and I miss you more than any of my stupidly inadequate words can say. Amanda X

# ABOUT THE AUTHOR

**Amanda Reynolds** is the bestselling psychological suspense author whose debut novel, *Close To Me*, was adapted as a major six-part TV series for Channel 4 in 2021. Her books have been translated into multiple languages. Amanda lives near Cheltenham.

Sign up to Amanda Reynolds' mailing list here for news, competitions and updates on future books.

Visit Amanda's website: https://www.amandareynold sauthor.com

Follow Amanda on social media

X x.com/amandareynoldsj

(O) instagram.com/ajreynolds2

f facebook.com/amandareynoldsauthor

## ALSO BY AMANDA REYNOLDS

The Assistant

The Wife's Secret

Her Husband's Lie

# THE
## *Murder*
# LIST

**THE MURDER LIST IS A NEWSLETTER DEDICATED TO ALL THINGS CRIME AND THRILLER FICTION!**

**SIGN UP TO MAKE SURE YOU'RE ON OUR HIT LIST FOR GRIPPING PAGE-TURNERS AND HEARTSTOPPING READS.**

## SIGN UP TO OUR NEWSLETTER

BIT.LY/THEMURDERLISTNEWS

# Boldw**oo**d

Boldwood Books is an award-winning fiction publishing company seeking out the best stories from around the world.

**Find out more at www.boldwoodbooks.com**

Join our reader community for brilliant books, competitions and offers!

Follow us
@BoldwoodBooks
@TheBoldBookClub

**Sign up to our weekly deals newsletter**

https://bit.ly/BoldwoodBNewsletter

Printed in Great Britain
by Amazon

45987676R00208